THE GHOST TREE

A *Betty Church* MYSTERY

M.R.C. KASASIAN

First published in the UK by Head of Zeus in 2020
This paperback edition first published in 2021 by Head of Zeus

9 7 5 3 1 2 4 6 8

A catalogue record for this book is available from the British Library.

ISBN (PB): 9781788546454
ISBN (E): 9781788546423

Typeset by Divaddict Publishing Solutions Ltd

Printed and bound in Great Britain by
CPI Group (UK) Ltd, Croydon CR0 4YY

Head of Zeus Ltd
First Floor East
5–8 Hardwick Street
London EC1R 4RG
WWW.HEADOFZEUS.COM

Also by M.R.C. Kasasian

THE GOWER STREET DETECTIVE

The Mangle Street Murders

The Curse of the House of Foskett

Death Descends on Saturn Villa

The Secrets of Gaslight Lane

Dark Dawn Over Steep House

BETTY CHURCH MYSTERIES

Betty Church and the Suffolk Vampire

The Room of the Dead

THE GHOST TREE

M.R.C. KASASIAN was raised in Lancashire. He has had careers as varied as a factory hand, wine waiter, veterinary assistant, fairground worker and dentist. He is also the author of the much-loved Gower Street Detective series, five books featuring personal detective Sidney Grice and his ward March Middleton. He lives with his wife, in Suffolk in the summer and in Malta in the winter.

For Tiggy,

with all my heart

PART 1 – 1914

1

MOLLUSCS AND THE LADY

18th July

When he arrived for his appointment, Mr Lorris had a crinkled mouth, folded flabbily like the lips of a mussel. By the time my father had extracted his patient's stumps, tossed them in a kidney dish and crammed in two blocks of vulcanite decked with porcelain, Mr Lorris looked like an exhausted horse.

'I can't speath proper,' he whinnied as I burst into the surgery.

'Properly,' my father corrected him.

'Etterly is missing,' I cried.

'Missing what?' my father asked.

He didn't mind me coming in, even though I was a minor. I often helped, cutting up squares from a fat roll of gauze to staunch bleeding, fetching things for him or rinsing forceps under the tap to be ready for the next extractions. Today, my mother, bored with nursing, was reading a copy of *The Lady* that a previous patient had forgotten in her nitrous-oxide-addled hurry to leave. My mother would already have done her duty, holding Mr Lorris down while he clawed semi-consciously at my father's wrist, because – and dentists never tell you this – it is very difficult to gas someone completely to sleep without killing them.

Mr Lorris was straining to pull his lips together, but they were not designed to stretch that far.

'Mithing wha'?' he asked, in case I hadn't understood.

'Missing whom?' my mother asked, in case I hadn't understood and because she thought it sounded more grammatical.

'She has gone missing,' I explained, because they had all misunderstood.

'Ah,' my father commented unhelpfully.

My mother flicked through the social announcements.

'I see the Honourable Peregrine Botherleigh is to be interred in Titchfold,' she announced.

My father perked up. 'Does it say when?'

'Oh,' my mother sighed. 'It was yesterday.'

My father huffed. I don't think they knew the gentleman in question, but they did love a good funeral and a chance to mix with what they saw as their equals.

'Mithing?' Mr Lorris enquired, proving that at least this poorly educated knife grinder could stick to the topic. 'Fwom where?'

His lower set shot into his lap, bouncing miraculously unscathed onto the lino.

'The King's—' I began, interrupted by an ominous snapping noise when my father stepped backwards. 'Oak,' I ended, and my father glared.

'Well, pick it up,' he ordered angrily, leaving me in no doubt that it was my fault for having distracted him.

I recovered the two halves and rinsed them under the tap.

'The Ghost Tree?' Mr Lorris sprayed bloodily.

'It won't glue,' my father asserted. 'You'll have to pay for another.'

'Oh.' His patient grinned lopsidedly. 'Dint you worry 'bout tha'. I can speak more better without it.'

'That's a matter of opinion,' my father piffed.

'Why do they call it the Ghost Tree?' I asked Mr Lorris, offering him the two halves uncertainly.

'Because terble things do happen there,' he told me, wiping

his chin until the side of his face and the back of his hand looked like he had had a terrible accident with his grinding wheel.

'Stuff and nonsense,' my mother protested, tossing her copy of *The Lady* aside angrily. 'Women will *not* be wearing blue this summer.'

2

THE DAYS OF STRAW AND THE MONKEY'S EYE

We could not have known it at the time, but this would be remembered as *The Golden Age*, days of peace and security before the world hurled itself into a frenzy of slaughter. It was a time of long summer afternoons, of tea on the terrace and croquet on the lawn – a time when our navy patrolled the oceans and the globe was liberally painted in British Empire red. In France they called it *La Belle Époque*. In Sackwater, because the months of sunshine with no rain had turned every lawn and meadow into dry pale yellow stalks, we called it, less romantically, *The Summer of Straw*.

When I was thirteen, Etterly Utter was my best friend. She was born two years before me – quite a difference for playmates, especially as I was still at boarding school and Etterly had been working in her father's jeweller's shop since she was twelve, but I always preferred to be with older girls and Etterly was young for her age. The *Sackwater and District Gazette* was to label her – unfairly, I thought – as *simple*, but there was nothing simple about the way she came to their attention.

The sunshine was disastrous for local farmers. Ponds evaporated and streams became dry beds. Sheep – the source of Suffolk's ancient wealth and power – had sparse natural grazing and the harvest of beets, the main local crop, was the worst in living memory. Yet still the sun blazed. Even the nights, usually cool if not cold on the East Coast, were suffocatingly hot.

The drought was not all bad, though. In the heat people

flocked to the coast, the women in their wide-brimmed, out-of-fashion-everywhere-else picture hats, the men in their boaters, many paddling, the young and the brave plunging into the North Sea, which the summer had warmed from icy to painfully cold. Anglethorpe, north of the River Angle estuary, was filled to capacity and the overspill oozed south into Sackwater. Even the huge Grand Hotel, built by a local consortium overly blessed with money and cursed with too much optimism, was booked up for most of the season.

The beach was packed with visitors jostling for ice creams, donkey rides and cockle stalls, roaring with laughter at Mr Punch beating his baby unconscious, packing the Lyons Corner House, queueing for creaky music-hall shows in the Pier Pavilion, already slightly dilapidated after its Victorian heyday.

When not by the sea, my friends and I liked to play in The Soundings, a large square in the Georgian part of town. There was not much there – roughly cropped grass bordered by iron benches and a low hedge and conker trees, a great source of entertainment in the autumn. At one end stood the King's Oak, huge, leafless and hollow, with an inverted V opening through which we could enter. When we were younger, the tree became a castle or ship or hospital or shop, whatever we decided it should be. The more nimble of us could scramble up through the middle and emerge from the hole at the top, the braver of us sliding out to straddle one of the few remaining branches. Now we were older it was more a place to stow our coats and bags.

The day before Etterly went missing was Rowdina Grael's birthday and she had been given a rounders bat. Rowdina was very sporty. She was captain of the netball team and came second in the East of England Girls' Cross-Country run. There were only six of us that day but we were getting along nicely using our cardigans as bases and marking out the bowler's square with twigs, avoiding any of the many molehills that had been erupting through the grass lately.

Major Burgandy sat on his usual bench. He was there most days and rarely paid attention to us.

Mrs Cooksey, the solicitor's wife from number twelve, came out to watch. She was one of the younger residents – prettier and more fashionably dressed than most of the others – and had not lost her sense of fun, applauding every bowl, hit, run and catch. She used to play for Surrey before she moved, she told us, and she showed Rowdina a better way to grip the bat before going off to fetch something.

We restarted the game and were getting along quite nicely until the boys turned up. *Boys bring trouble*, Etterly's mother used to recite, and we both used to laugh about that. *I hope so*, Etterly whispered once, but neither of us could have known how prophetic her mother's warnings would turn out to be on that fateful day of July 1914.

3
THE SMACK AND THE SEA SCOUTS

Nobody was overly concerned at first. Etterly was a trustworthy girl but a bit of a daydreamer. At school, she was always getting into trouble for not paying attention, and she had lost her first job, in Hobson's Dairy, for flushing away a full vat of milk when she was supposed to be cleaning the empty vat next to it. That was why her father had taken her on, though he had no real need of assistance. As far as I know, he worked conscientiously, but Kendal's the Jewellers had a big shop on High Road East and it was there, rather than Mr Utter's dingy premises above Mac the Bookmakers on Slip Street, that people tended to buy their clocks and watches, only taking them to Mr Utter for repairs.

Perhaps, Mrs Utter suggested, Etterly had wandered off to Folger's Estate Farm, where Delilah, the carthorse, had had her first foal. Maybe Etterly had gone to play tennis and forgotten to tell me. That didn't seem likely to me.

Mr Utter – short, and delicately built, with an unusually large head and a not very successful moustache, peppery to match his centre-parted hair – came into the hall, grumbling about his own lunch being ruined, and took his jacket off a hook.

'Not too big for a smack,' he muttered, though, strict as they were, he had never raised a hand to his daughter in her life. 'As if Mrs Utter int got enough on with her sister bein' taken sick.'

Wherever Etterly got her looks, I thought uncharitably, it was not from her parents. Etterly was tall and slim, with thick black hair that I was always envious of. Probably her most striking feature was her eyes – big and flashing green, and she was already learning how to flutter her lashes. Etterly's behaviour was not especially mature but her figure often made people take her for a good two years older than the sixteen she was approaching.

Mr Utter had a prominent brow and bow legs, both symptoms of rickets – all too common in his and my generation – and he swayed side to side as he marched off to fetch her. Where he was going to he did not say, but Etterly, I remembered, liked to potter in the back room of his shop, making cheap costume jewellery from scraps. She had given me a ring once, made from a slice of copper pipe that she had bevelled and engraved with my name. I loved her gift, but neither my parents nor my school approved of children wearing such things.

'People will think you're engaged,' my father had objected.

Really? At twelve? And I wore it on my little finger.

'Who would have her?' my mother had countered, and she patted my arm as if she had been sticking up for me.

I went to the Sea Scouts' hut. I couldn't tell her parents but Etterly and I liked to stroll past there, hoping the boys would chat to us. It was all quite innocent but Etterly had taken rather a fancy to Gary Garner, who had close-cropped blond hair and looked very smart in his uniform. As luck would have it, Gary was there, but he had not seen Etterly since she had gone by with me two weeks earlier.

'Give her my regards,' he said with a flicker in his eyes that I would have to wait a while to find familiar. I was still a girl, but my friend was blossoming into a young woman and boys are never slow to notice such things.

I went to Sammy's Sweets but Mr Sterne hadn't seen her either. I was hoping he would give me an aniseed ball, which he often did, but he seemed preoccupied. It did not occur to me that his German accent, which we found rather amusing, might cause him problems with the tensions between our countries. I was vaguely aware that an archduke and his wife had been assassinated but Sarajevo was no more real to me than Ruritania in the adventure stories.

I made my way along the promenade. It was busy with day trippers who didn't have the sense to go to Anglethorpe or any of the many other nicer Suffolk resorts. Etterly and I loved to stand there on a windy day, holding the railings, feeling the spray of the tossing ocean in our faces and imagining we were on a ship to exotic places. I had no money to go onto the pier today but the plump man in the kiosk at the entrance might remember her passing through his turnstile in the last couple of hours.

'I'm looking for a friend,' I told him, and he leaned forward to scrutinise me.

'Bit young for me,' he said. 'But thanks for the offer.'

It took me a moment to realise what he meant.

'No, I mean a friend of mine might have come through. She's fifteen and quite tall for her age. She's wearing a blue dress with a white collar and has black hair tied back in a blue ribbon. Oh, and she has freckles.'

Etterly would not have liked me mentioning that last bit. She hated her complexion and said it looked like somebody had spat chocolate at her. Most people thought she was very pretty. Why else would she have been picked for carnival queen the previous year?

The man puffed out. He had something that looked like chicken soup all down his red jacket.

'Lot of *trippies* goo on the pier. That's what it's for, gooin' on.'

A *trippy* was a day tripper and usually meant in a derogatory way.

'We see her,' a woman's voice declared, and I spun round to

see an elderly couple standing hand in hand in the queue behind me. 'She goo into the Leopold Hotel about ten minute ago.'

'Was she by herself?' I asked in surprise.

'Oh yes,' the man assured me.

My relief turned instantly to alarm. The Leopold was not a suitable place for any lady, let alone a young one, and especially not by herself.

'Are you sure?' I checked.

'Course we are,' he insisted.

'Only,' his wife continued, 'she dint have freckles. We commented how clear her skin is.'

'And her hair is ginger,' the husband recalled. 'But it's definitely her.'

I should have taken warning then. I should have realised I was heading for a life of misinformation. Whether stupid or deceitful, the majority of witnesses were no more reliable than the shelf my father – rather than pay a man – had put up in the pantry with some of my mother's best crockery on it.

4

MANNERS AND THE SHADOW OF A MAN

18th July

I recognised three of the boys as being from the fourth form of St Joseph's Grammar School, which made them about fifteen – older than all of us, except Etterly. Georgie Orchard and I used to chat to them sometimes and they were usually polite and pleasant. Today, though, they had come equipped for cricket and were more than a bit miffed to find us occupying what they regarded as their pitch.

'Sorry, girls.' Godfrey Skillern tipped the peak of his Sackwater Cricket Club cap. 'We have to practise, and the SCC ground is being used by the seniors.'

'We are just as entitled to be here as you,' Etterly protested.

'And we were here first,' Georgie pointed out.

'Then you can leave first,' Lloyd Hog told us. I knew him from previous encounters, and I didn't like him. He had a taste for practical jokes, which were usually nasty and never funny. *Hog* was an apt name for Lloyd, who had a broad upturned snout and squinty pink eyes, leading us to cruelly, if unimaginatively, christen him *Piggy* behind his back.

'We will leave when we are good and ready,' Etterly insisted. She was a working girl and not afraid of schoolboys.

'You can't hog the ground all day,' Godfrey asserted, unaware until we giggled of his unintentional pun, and Lloyd glared at him.

Godfrey was tall and good-looking, with brown hair falling

over his pale-blue eyes. He was nice as a rule and had told me when another boy – probably Lloyd Hog – had pinned a note on my back saying *I smell like a farmyard.*

'But we have only just started,' I reasoned with him.

'Then you can just stop,' Hog chipped in.

'You can't make us,' Rowdina Grael said – unwisely, because a boy I didn't know and didn't feel I wanted to, gangly with a long hooked nose and spotty skin, grabbed hold of her bat.

'Steady on, Jarvis,' Godfrey Skillern said uneasily, but he did nothing to intervene and Rowdina kept a tight grip on the handle.

Both sides were in a position now where they couldn't back down without losing face.

At that point, Bridget Yollender stepped between them. Yolly worked on her father's farm and rarely got time off to join us, but the hot, dry weather had brought some of their activities to a halt.

'Want to fight me for it?' Yolly challenged.

Jarvis paused and looked at her. Yolly was a hefty girl and she was more than capable of dealing with the average boy, having to cope with the unwanted and unsubtle attentions of the local clodhoppers. It wasn't likely that the boy could outfight her and to be beaten by a girl would be almost as shameful as beating one.

Jarvis shrugged, trying to make out he didn't really care, and let go.

'You won't be able to play if we stand in the way,' said good old Piggy.

'Nor will you,' I pointed out.

It was Etterly who broke the deadlock.

'Why dint you join us?' she suggested, and I heard one of them snigger, 'Dint? What did they teach her at school?'

'They taught her better manners than you ever learned,' I retorted.

'Yes, shut up,' Godfrey Skillern snapped. 'The lady was making a civil invitation.'

'Lady?' Hog mocked, but everyone ignored him.

'To play rounders?' one of the boys asked incredulously. 'It's a girls' game.'

There was a general murmur of agreement at this remark and the way he said *girls'* left us in no doubt that this was a shameful thing to be. We were about to return to our game when Georgie said, 'Of course it's a girls' game. It requires more skill. We don't need a dirty great paddle to hit a ball with.'

'Oh, forget it,' Etterly jibed. 'They're just frightened they'll lose.'

'Frightened?' Jarvis asked incredulously. 'We don't want to embarrass you.'

'But we shan't be the least bit embarrassed to beat you,' Georgie assured them. Even at that age, she knew how to pull boys' strings. It came from having a much older brother, who she absolutely adored when she wasn't plotting ways to murder him.

'What do you say, you chaps?' Godfrey turned to his friends. 'The sooner we lick them, the sooner we get on with our cricket.'

'Count me out,' Piggy said, and thrust his hands in his pockets.

'Good,' I said with feeling. 'Then we have two teams of six – unless the rest of you are too scared as well?'

'Scared?' Jarvis echoed, more incredulous than ever.

'You have missed your vocation,' I told him. 'You should have been a parrot.'

It occurred to me too late that Jarvis might think I was mocking his big nose, but everybody laughed and even he smiled at my remark so I decided he might not be quite so bad as I had thought.

'Oh God,' Etterly whispered and I glanced at her in surprise. All of a sudden she had turned pale and looked lost.

'Are you all right?' I worried.

'What?' Her eyes flicked about. 'Oh yes. I've just got a headache.'

'Are you all right to play?'

'I said I was,' Etterly snapped uncharacteristically.

'Do you want some of your lemonade?'

'Stop fussing,' she said sharply, and I retired, wounded.

Mrs Cooksey came over, leaving her handbag on the bench, and I hoped she was not going to stop us.

'You'll need an umpire,' she told us, and nobody needed to ask who that would be.

'So how do you play?' Godfrey asked. 'I've seen my sisters at it but never paid attention.'

'The batter stands there.' Mrs Cooksey pointed to the first base. 'The bowler must stand in that square – no running up. You bowl underarm and the ball can't go lower than the batter's knee or higher than her head.'

We gathered round and, even though I knew the rules, I was so intent on listening to her and sneaking looks at Etterly that I paid little attention to Douglas Carpenter standing shyly on the pavement outside the hedge. Douglas had been fostered by the Hornbys, a wealthy couple who lived on the prestigious Mount Chase Avenue. Some people envied him for this, forgetting what he must have been through when he lost his parents. We sometimes called him Dougy, which Etterly turned into *Doggy*. She was always mangling names, amusing some people and annoying others, but this one stuck because it seemed particularly apt. Douglas hero-worshipped Godfrey and followed him everywhere. He called *hello* with a lopsided boyish smile that was one of the more appealing things about him, and I returned his greeting. I hardly noticed the figure of a man standing in the shadow of a horse chestnut in a far corner.

5

THE AROMA OF HIPPOPOTAMUSES

18th July

I went back to Bath Road and the way Mrs Utter's face fell from hopeful anticipation to dismay when she saw who it was told me immediately that Etterly had not been found.

'Mr Utter is gone to make a report at the police station,' she told me, craning out to look up and down the road. 'You best goo home.'

And so I did. It was almost teatime, but my parents were still in the surgery – Sammy's Sweets gave my father a lot of work in what we came to think of as those prosperous days – but my news about Etterly couldn't wait, which was why I burst in with my announcement.

My maternal grandmother had come to stay while her husband was off on a failed bid to attract Walter de la Mare to his struggling publishing company. She was the only family member to acknowledge that I was upset.

'Come and sleep in my room,' she urged.

I didn't really want to, but I knew she was trying to comfort me, so I did. Granny was a kind old lady but she snored like a hippo and smelt like I imagined one would. I suffered a restless hour but after she sat bolt upright screaming *Push the entrails in*, before flopping into a peaceful sleep, I gave up and crept back to my own room.

There wasn't much light from the sliver of a moon when I sat by my window. The church clock was striking midnight, a time for ghosts and witches I had been told, so when I thought I heard crunching on the gravel, I hid behind my curtains. By the time I had plucked up courage to peep out again, I thought I saw a shadowy figure creeping towards the front gate. I drew back. Was this the man I had seen in The Soundings? Had he come to get me? The possibility that it might have been Etterly coming to me for help, as we had often discussed, made me force myself to look again, but there are few things more deceptive than shadows and whatever I might have seen had disappeared.

6

BATTENBERG AND THE BLOODHOUND

Mrs Cooksey was still explaining the rules of the game. She had a lovely profile, I thought, and her auburn hair flowed back in the breeze. I was always jealous of women with darker hair than mine until I found they were all jealous of me being blonde.

'If she hits the ball she must run, but she can run when she misses if she wants to. You have to try and get right round to score a rounder, but you can get half if you get to the third base. You get her out by catching the ball that she hits or the base she's running to or her before she gets to it. You must stay touching the base or you can be got out. If—'

'Sounds simple enough,' Jarvis broke in. 'I'm sure we'll pick the rest up as we go along.'

'Very well.' Mrs Cooksey shrugged. 'Only don't complain if you are out for a Battenberg.'

I looked at her quizzically and was just about to ask when she gave me a wink.

'Stick your wickets in the ground, boys,' she ordered. 'They will make much better bases.'

We cleared away the cardigans we had been using and placed them in the hollow of the oak, along with a bottle of lemonade that Etterly's mother had made.

'Who goes first?' Godfrey asked.

'You toss for it,' Mrs Cooksey said, and I saw Etterly's eyes widen a fraction as Godfrey delved into his pocket and selected a penny from a handful of cash. He must have had at least five shillings in his hand – a tidy sum for all of us but a week's wages for Etterly.

'Call,' Mrs Cooksey instructed as Godfrey spun his coin high.

'Heads,' Rowdina said. There was no dispute that she should be captain. Apart from owning the bat, she was far and away our best player.

The penny landed and Mrs Cooksey peered over.

'Heads it is,' she announced.

Rowdina went first. If anyone could show the boys how rounders was played, it was her. A quiet boy called Dicky Joiner took the ball. I had seen him sometimes driving his mother and sisters to St Luke's Church in a pony and trap, but I didn't really know him. He was a big boy with ruffled sandy hair and the ball was almost lost in his huge fist. He bounced the ball a couple of times experimentally, like a tennis player about to serve, drew his arm back and threw. I had never seen an underarm throw travel so fast. We usually gave each other a gentle toss but this ball flew straight at Rowdina. If I had been on the receiving end it would probably have struck me hard on the chest, but our captain whipped her bat down, bringing it up in an arc and cracking against the ball, sending it soaring into the air through the branches of a conker tree with Godfrey running backwards hopelessly because it was obvious he could never get there in time.

Rowdina was off. She tapped the first base wicket with her bat before the ball had even hit the ground and still she raced on. The second base post went flying as she struck it on her way round, and then the third, and she was racing to the last base to five excited cries of encouragement when we heard a shout of *howzat*? And all the boys cheering.

'Not a term we use in rounders,' Mrs Cooksey remarked, 'but it was a good catch and the batter is out.'

And in confirmation of her verdict Godfrey held the ball triumphantly aloft.

'How?' I asked, baffled. We had all been so busy watching Rowdina that we weren't paying attention to Godfrey's efforts.

'It bounced off the tree trunk and straight into his hands,' Mrs Cooksey explained. It was obvious she was not happy with her own decision, but she had to at least try to be impartial.

This was a disaster. With our captain and best player out for no score, we had all but lost our own game to boys who had never even played it before. We would never be allowed to live that down.

'Sorry,' Rowdina muttered, handing the bat to Nelly Havard, who really didn't look like she wanted it. I didn't know Nelly very well because she had only come to Sackwater after Easter, when I was away boarding at Roedene Abbey, and she was not a girl to push herself forward.

Nelly went to her square with the air of Marie Antoinette approaching the guillotine and her bat quivered as she pulled it back behind her head. Dicky Joiner assessed his next victim. He didn't need a bloodhound to sense the fear oozing from her and, from his determined expression, she could expect no mercy. They wanted us all out quickly so they could get on with their precious cricket. The fielders closed in.

Without warning, Dicky let loose. Nelly squawked and swung wildly and the ball caught the edge of her bat, bouncing erratically over the grass.

'Get it,' Godfrey yelled as it flew past Crossfield to roll between Major Burgandy's feet and stop under his bench.

'Run,' we shouted at Nelly, who stood surveying her effort in astonishment.

Crossfield dashed over and knelt before the major.

'Excuse me, sir.'

Crossfield tried to reach between Major Burgandy's ankles but the old man kept staring straight ahead, smiling lightly, presumably lost in one of his happier memories.

'Run, Nelly, run,' we screeched, and she was off, tapping the bases as she went, first, second, third and home. Nelly, to everyone's surprise, especially her own, had scored a rounder and we had a game on.

Nelly returned to her square, sweating and panting more than the heat and her efforts had warranted but at least less timorously this time. She gritted her teeth and Dicky let fly.

'Too high,' Mrs Cooksey called. 'No ball.'

The man was still there in the shadows, I noticed. It was probably nothing. Plenty of adults walked past and often stopped to rest in the shade, but I nearly said something to Mrs Cooksey – only she was busy telling Dicky to accept her decision or be sent off with a penalty rounder to the girls.

Douglas Carpenter had moved too but I didn't pay much attention to him. He was not part of our game and never really one of the boys.

'Beware lonely people,' Sidney Grice, the famous personal detective, had once warned me, but he gave me so much advice that I couldn't possibly live by all of it.

7

THIN FYNN AND THE OUTRAGE

The police were questioning all the children who had been at The Soundings that day. Rowdina Grael had already been interviewed by Constable Fairey and all the girls were hoping we would get him too. Fairey was tall, with features that Michelangelo would have been proud to have sculpted, but – even more importantly – Constable Fairey was kind. He had helped Simon Laflin, the chemist's son, retrieve his kite from the sea, and if there was a kitten up a tree, Fairey was your man.

When I answered the door the next day, though, it was to Sergeant Fynn. I had seen the sergeant on the promenade and did not like him. He was forever ticking children off for throwing pebbles, even when they were doing no harm, and had stopped me walking on a wooden breakwater though there was no law against doing that. Etterly had renamed Fynn *Thin*, though *Skinny* might have been more accurate. How he passed his medical examination when he joined the force still puzzles me. His chest was caved in like he had had a serious traffic accident and bones stuck out under his sallow skin in surprising places, so that his face reminded me of a sack of hedge cuttings.

'Where are your mummy and daddy, little girl?' he asked, with the sort of smile you might be able to force out of a man at gunpoint.

This was enough to get my back up before he had even entered the house, but I resisted the urge to tell him I did not have a *mummy* or a *daddy* and that I was most certainly not a *little girl* and simply said 'Yes' – which, I realised, didn't actually answer the question, but the sergeant seemed to think it did.

'Tell them I am here,' he ordered, stepping onto the coconut mat uninvited and looking about like he was thinking of purchasing the property. Fynn sniffed the nitrous-oxide-antiseptic-stale-blood aroma that pervaded much of the ground floor of Felicity House. 'Dentists,' he commented. 'I hate 'em.'

He didn't look like he had seen one recently. His dentures were chipped and dirty – quite an achievement, since it's difficult to stain glazed porcelain that badly.

'Really?' I enquired politely, because this was a very unusual thing indeed to say. Most people simply adored clutching the arms of a leather chair while my father treadled away, cord running over spinning wheels, drill rattling to set a steel bur grinding their teeth, filling their nostrils with the dust of decayed enamel and smoke of burned dentine.

My mother came out of what served as a waiting room by day and our sitting room out of dental surgery hours. She had on a long loose green dress, with a long ribbon tied in a bow at the waist. I think she had read in *My Weekly* that this was the fashion, but it made her look like a badly wrapped and unwanted present.

'Inspector Fynn,' she greeted our visitor and he preened.

'Sergeant,' he corrected her modestly.

'I am Mrs Church. Do come through.' She motioned him into the room, and I followed. 'I do not know if you have met my husband.'

'I have not had that *pleasure*,' Fynn smirked, weighing down the last word with heavy sarcasm and underlining it with a laugh that sounded like a cat coughing up hairballs because, of course, my father would be the first to sympathise with our caller's opinion of the dental profession.

My mother smiled starchily, torn between politeness to our

guest and loyalty to her husband, but my father regarded him stonily.

'Until now,' Fynn added uneasily and unconvincingly.

'Do take a seat.' My mother pointed to an upright wooden one in the bay, but our visitor settled into an armchair by the fire, never made up until there was a lacy frost inside the windowpane.

My parents settled in the other two armchairs and, rather than sit ten feet away across the room, I remained standing.

'Utterly Etter,' Sergeant Fynn began, and my parents listened politely though they must have known it was wrong. I wondered how he would react if I called him *Fynngent Sar* but didn't have the nerve to try it. 'Is gone and disappeared.'

'Goodness,' my mother exclaimed like this was news to us all.

'And we have reasons to believe that your daughter' – the policeman's hand shot out accusingly – 'Elizabeth...' This was going too far. I had never been *Elizabeth*, not even on my birth certificate. I waited for my parents to correct him, but they nodded along as he continued, his hand falling onto the arm cover of his chair, 'may have been one of the last, or indeed *the* last, to see her.'

It didn't occur to me at the time that at least he didn't add alive. I was only aware that all eyes were on me and I was not sure if I was expected to say anything.

'I...' I began, but the hand rose again, this time in a halt sign.

'You goo speak when I do ask a question,' he commanded.

Surely my parents would not let him talk to me like that. *How dare you barge in here presuming to correct our daughter's manners, you ignorant... ignoramus*, my mother would berate him, but instead she murmured, 'I have been trying to teach her that for years.'

'I've given up,' my father said, rubbing his knees as if he had barked them. It would have been nice to have seen him do something energic enough to have such a mishap.

'Right then,' Fynn proceeded briskly, 'no shally-shillying, girl. Where is Utterly Utterly?'

'Etterly Utter,' I corrected him timidly.

'Stop playing for time,' Sergeant Fynn barked. 'You know she has run off to be the parador of some filthy lecturer. Who is he and where have they gone?'

This was a new suggestion and I wasn't entirely clear what Fynn meant. I only knew it sounded disgusting and Etterly was not that kind of a girl.

'Tell the officer,' my mother urged urgently, but at last my father decided to speak up.

'This is outrageous,' he fumed in a tone he normally reserved for David Lloyd George, the chancellor of the exchequer. 'You have been in our house for ten minutes and nobody has offered you a cup of tea.'

8

THE SIDELINE AND THE PITY

Nelly faced the bowler again and, forgetting the rules, Dicky Joiner bowled a bouncer – another no ball and a half-rounder penalty to us. Nelly just got the tip of her bat to the third ball and sent it off at such an odd angle again that Godfrey, so confident at the beginning of the game, fumbled his catch and Nelly, suddenly finding herself the star of the game, made it to the second base to give us the whole rounder, her second and two more than we would have bet on.

You would have thought we had won the game from our cheers and, from the disconsolate look on Godfrey and Dicky's faces, you would have thought the boys had lost it.

The man was still there, I noticed, and it looked like he was watching us. I started towards Mrs Cooksey.

'Stop trying to break up the game,' Piggy shouted from the sideline.

'You're next,' Rowdina told me, and I went to fetch the bat from Nelly, who touched the wicket with her hand to stay in contact as the rules demanded.

As I stood ready in the square, I saw Godfrey go over and speak quietly to Dicky, who nodded and smirked.

'Now who's wasting time?' Georgie demanded.

'Play on,' Mrs Cooksey instructed.

Dicky changed his posture to stand almost side-on to me. He screwed himself up and twisted back, sending the ball in a curve.

I presume it was meant to swing in at me, but it went wide and well clear of any fielders. I took a breath and ran.

'Go,' I yelled to Nelly, who was still on second base.

'But you didn't hit it,' she reminded me in bewilderment.

'You don't have to,' I panted, coming up to her just in time to see the base wicket go flying.

'Howzat!' came annoyingly from all around.

'Out,' Mrs Cooksey confirmed, 'and you must go to the next base,' she told Nelly.

'Oh, but...' Nelly realised there was no point in arguing – a pity she hadn't realised that earlier, I thought bitterly as she set off, but Timothy Prince was tapping her base with the ball before Nelly had gone a yard.

I didn't say anything, but my expression must have said it for me.

'Well, I scored two and you didn't get any,' Nelly said tartly as I handed the bat to Yolly.

'Only because...' I began, but what was the point? 'Well done,' I said as nicely as I could, which wasn't very nicely at all.

'Bad luck,' Georgie consoled me, and whispered 'silly cat' in my ear.

She went to line up behind Etterly and she didn't have long to wait. Yolly stood alert as the bowler hurled straight at her.

'Good luck,' Nelly shouted so suddenly that Yolly glanced up as she swung and miss-hit the ball straight into Jarvis's cupped hands.

'Not as easy as it looks, is it?' Nelly, suddenly the seasoned player, sympathised, and Georgie scowled.

'Like to go for a walk, Nelly?' she asked. 'There's a nice one towards the cliffs. Just keep going when you get there.'

Etterly was next but she looked even worse now. Her face was white and glistening, but she avoided my eye and so I didn't ask.

It was an easier ball, I thought, but Etterly stepped outside the square before she had hit it.

'Out,' Mrs Cooksey called, and Etterly thrust the bat into Georgie's hand without a word. It wasn't like her to be so unsporting or downright rude, I reflected as she strode towards the King's Oak. Was it my imagination afterwards or did I see a shadow from behind that tree?

'Hard luck, Etterly,' Douglas Carpenter commiserated as she passed, but Etterly didn't give him a second glance.

Douglas looked hurt, as he often did. He was a tubby boy and something of an outsider – not because of his weight but because of his swank. He was always boasting about his rich foster-parents. Mrs Hornby had met Queen Mary. Douglas was going to be an architect like Mr Hornby. They lived in an enormous house with three bathrooms, tennis courts, two live-in maids and a full-time gardener. Etterly and I always felt sorry for Douglas, though. No amount of money could compensate for the loss of his parents.

9

CONSPIRACIES AND THE ASYLUM

My mother rang the bell.

'You may have to wait a while for your tea,' she told our visitor. 'Our servant is doing something to lamb chops.'

'Cooking them, I hope.' Sergeant Fynn grinned, then, not finding anyone sharing his hilarity, leaned sullenly towards me.

'Now, girl,' he said. 'Where is Etterly Etterly and with who goo she elope with?' He tensed, like he was preparing to spring at me. 'Tell the truth, Lizzy,' he urged, and my mother mumbled something that sounded like *That'll be the day*. If so, her remark was not entirely unjustified. Like all children, I told fibs to try to get out of trouble, but I was hardly a compulsive liar – nothing like as bad as both my parents, with my father telling people dozens of times a day *This won't hurt* and my mother claiming that her hair was naturally black. Also, I never said *honestly* if something wasn't true, which is more than you could say about either of them.

'I...' I began.

'Tell him the truth, Bettyboo,' my father urged, never at a loss for the most embarrassing time to trot out his pet name for me.

'I...' I began.

There was something in the way Fynn was looking at me that made me uncomfortable.

'The *truth*,' my father emphasised, in case I thought I was being asked to fabricate a web of deceit.

'I...' I began.

'The truth never hurt anyone,' my mother philosophised absurdly.

It would hurt her if my father told her what she really looked like in that long purple dress she had had made up by Miss Tillingford, and it had hurt me even more when I came clean about who had dented the banister rail while tea-tray sledging down the stairs.

'I...' I began, confused now at not being interrupted. 'I don't know.'

Fynn watched closely as I straightened my skirt.

'Tell the Major,' my mother prompted me, and I saw Fynn's eyes swivel away from me as he tried to work out if that was better or worse than the inspectorship she had already bestowed upon him.

My father was working his lips as he often did before he spoke, so, rather than face another string of exhortations, I burst out with, 'I don't know where Etterly is...'

'Utterly,' Fynn corrected me, but I ignored him.

'She hasn't got a man friend and I don't believe she has run away.'

'Are you serious expecting us to believe that she goo be eaten by that tree?' Fynn demanded, his upper teeth suddenly elongating as his denture dropped.

It was the first time I had heard that theory and it seemed so childish and bizarre coming from a grown man in uniform that I burst out laughing. I expect I was a little hysterical by then, with my friend missing and me being harangued by three adults.

My mother folded her arms under her bosoms and shifted them side to side.

'See what we have to put up with,' she declared. 'Small wonder we had to send her away.'

'To school,' my father explained, in case the sergeant thought she meant on holiday to one of those foreign places where Fynn never goo, or to the lunatic asylum I was beginning to realise I already lived in.

I think I actually gasped at this revelation. Up until then I had been led to believe that my parents were making great sacrifices to give me the best start in life, not that I was so unpleasant that I had to be banished.

Fynn put a thumb in his mouth and I thought he was going to suck it, but he was pushing his upper set back into place. 'That's what they all do say,' he told my parents. 'They dint know where she is at or with who she is with.' He sagged in his seat, exhausted by the effort of constructing such a perfect sentence. 'Know what it do sound like to me?'

The truth, I imagined him saying.

'No,' my mother said.

'What?' my father asked, and Fynn nodded wisely in that way only the unwise do.

'A conspiracy,' he said dramatically. 'This girl do know somethin' and I goo find out what that somethin' is if it kill her.'

'A little harsh,' my father observed mildly, and he folded his arms to mirror my mother as they both sat back to watch.

10

A PORTUGUESE GRANDMOTHER AND THE STONE BOTTLE

Georgie was on next. She was a good tennis player and runner but, as she admitted to me, she had hardly ever played rounders. Godfrey took over the bowling. It was obvious when we met that he had a bit of a thing for Georgie, and what boy wouldn't? Georgie was tall but in an elegant rather than the awkward lanky way that most girls go through. She had thick wavy black hair and a profile like Ellen Terry, who Etterly and I had on cigarette cards. Also, Georgie had a golden tan from her Portuguese grandmother, something very exotic in a town where people from the adjacent county of Norfolk were regarded as foreigners.

From his first throw it was obvious that Godfrey was not going to give Georgie any quarter. If she hadn't shied away, the ball would have smashed into her face and I was impressed how cleanly Jarvis took it in one outstretched hand.

'Howzat?' he yelled.

'No ball,' Mrs Cooksey declared, 'too high.'

'But it only went over her head because she ducked,' Godfrey reasoned, and our umpire hesitated.

'That's debatable,' she conceded. 'You can have an extra throw.'

Godfrey ruminated for a moment before deciding he would be better accepting the decision, and Georgie had hardly raised her bat in readiness when the ball shot out again, and only a fraction lower, but this time my friend was ready for it and sent it looping off to the far end of the grass, lodging in the privet hedge. Two boys ran for it, but Georgie was already being congratulated on the home base before they had retrieved the ball.

From then on, things deteriorated. Georgie was run out having nearly completed another rounder, and we did not make another score before we were all out. When we were on friendly terms again, I would ask Godfrey how they bowled so fast underarm. It wouldn't be something he had ever done playing cricket.

Rowdina organised the fielders, pushing us back further than usual on the assumption that the boys were big hitters.

'Where's Etterly?' she asked.

'She went into the tree,' I told her, 'to have a drink, I think.'

'She's been gone a long time.'

'I'll go and get her.'

The King's Oak was about fifteen yards away and even though the entrance faced me it was difficult to see inside, with the sun in my eyes, until I got close up.

'Etterly,' I called, but there was no reply.

Repeating my call, I went right up and poked my head into the tree. Our clothes were still there in fairly neat piles and the lemonade was still within easy reach. I called again.

'Get a move on,' Rowdina shouted.

'She's not here.'

Could she really have stormed off in a sulk for being got out so easily? Normally she wouldn't have cared.

Piggy Hog marched over. 'Hurry up, Church.'

'It's nothing to do with you,' I told him crossly. 'You're not even playing.'

I peered down St Bartholomew's Road, which led south-west towards the sea. A lady was struggling with pushing a pram and trying to control an excitable collie on a lead, but there was no sign of my friend.

'Run away, has she?' Piggy mocked, flapping his arms like wings and making chicken noises.

'You are much more convincing as a farmyard animal than a boy,' I told him.

Rowdina came up and several others were starting to head my way.

'What's happening?' she asked.

'I can't find her.'

'Marching off to the tree in a temper, last time I saw her,' a chubby boy said, though how he could see through those thick, greasy lenses beat me.

I crossed to the opposite side to look up the road. Some little girls were playing with a hoop but there was nobody else in sight. Major Burgandy had gone but I had not noticed him leaving, and there was no sign of Douglas Carpenter either. Perhaps he had taken umbrage at Etterly's slight, or had he gone in pursuit of her? He liked following Godfrey. Maybe he thought he'd tail her for a change.

Mrs Cooksey gave up any pretence of umpiring a game and brought the others over.

'Etterly had a headache,' I told her, 'but it's not like her to go off without saying anything, and she wouldn't leave the lemonade.' It was in a stone bottle with a bung on a wire hinge and her mother would want that back.

'Is her cardigan still there?' she asked, and I went into the tree to look through the piles. Etterly's cardigan was blue and had a slightly darker darn under the left armpit.

'Yes. This is hers.'

'I don't suppose she left a note?'

'Not that I can see.'

'Did anybody see her go?' Mrs Cooksey asked.

Georgie, Yolly, Nelly and Crossfield thought they had seen her enter the tree, but nobody had seen her emerge.

Mrs Cooksey sent everyone out in pairs up the roads leading off The Soundings with instructions to return in two minutes. Most of them were away longer but nobody came across her.

'I asked two ladies who were waiting for a bus on Heath Drive,' Godfrey told us, 'but they hadn't seen any girls come along in the last twenty minutes.'

'She might have got worse and gone home,' I suggested. 'And the Utters have their main meal at lunchtime.'

'Oh, good heavens,' Mrs Cooksey cried. 'I have a plum pie baking.' She turned to me. 'Can you check at Etterly's home and let me know what happens? I'm at number twelve.'

I went to Etterly's house. She was sure to be there. I had almost convinced myself of that when her mother – tiny and prematurely grey – answered my knock. She had a blue apron scrunched in her hand, presumably having just remembered to take it off before she opened the door.

'Tell Etterly her lunch is going cold,' she said, and I only wished – then and for the rest of my life – that I could.

Mrs Cooksey looked worried when I called on her.

'I suppose if Etterly's parents know, it's up to them to decide what to do.'

'Mr Utter says he will find her,' I said.

'I hope so.'

'How was your pie?' I was a bit worried about my friend, but I was even more cross. She had let us down by her behaviour and made us look bad sports in front of the boys. Besides, I was hungry and hoping she would offer me a slice.

'Charcoaled,' she told me.

This was not going to be my day.

11

CUPS, CHOPS AND CONFESSIONS

Pooky, our maid, brought tea and while she was plonking it on top of the ragged magazines on the low table, I dragged a chair across to sit in front of them all – I hadn't realised it was going to be such a prolonged interrogation – and was about to thank her when I saw that there were only three cups. Presumably I was old enough to be accused of deceit and conspiracy but not to have a hot beverage. When I was a mother, I vowed, I would be nice to my daughters. I planned then to have at least three – and no boys – but my career put a stop to that idea. It's one of the few things I ever regretted about putting on a uniform.

My mother poured, getting very little tea in the saucers and only a bit more of the milk.

'The drink that cheers but does not abbreviate,' Sergeant Fynn quoted only slightly inaccurately, slurping with great satisfaction at his erudition and beverage.

When I was little and first heard about the cup that cheers, I used to put my ear to my mug and try to hear it, until I accidently poured my father's coffee into my hair and gave up.

'Now then.' Fynn balanced his cup and saucer on his right knee, steadying it with one hand. 'Betsy.' I felt myself twitch. Only Etterly ever called me that. Was the sergeant hinting that he knew something? I could only hope somebody did. 'You and I goo get off on the wrong foot.' Fynn did the same forced grin he had given me when he arrived. 'So what you say we start again?'

I was unfamiliar then with the nice-policeman-nasty-policeman routine and I have rarely seen it performed by one man, but Sergeant Fynn, I realise now, was making a stab at it.

'Yes, please,' I said, wondering briefly if I had to go and readmit him.

'That's better,' my mother cooed fondly, but at our visitor, not me.

'How well do you know Utterly?' Fynn enquired as nicely as he could.

I should have said *Well enough to get her name right*, but I only said *Quite well, thank you* – which, I realised later, sounded like he was enquiring about my health.

'Good girl.' Fynn patted his left thigh like he was summoning me to fetch a stick. 'So do she goo tell you her secrets?'

'Yes, I suppose so,' I replied warily, hoping the newcomer was not expecting me to break any confidences.

Fynn showed his lower denture. 'And what is those secrets?'

Clearly my hopes had been in vain and I had learned enough by now to realise that any hesitation would be regarded as suspicious. My mind whizzed through what I should or should not reveal. Etterly had stolen a shilling from her father's till once but had put it back a guilt-ridden hour or so later. I could tell him that, but he would label her as a thief, whereas it had just been a silly impulse.

'She smokes cigarettes sometimes,' I told him, but omitted to add that she often shared them with me.

'That int a crime,' Fynn said dismissively.

I didn't say it was and you didn't ask for one.

'No,' I agreed, 'but her parents don't like her to do it.'

'Has lots of argues with them, do she?'

'Not really,' I said.

They had had a big one last Easter, sending Etterly to her room with no supper for saying *oh Lord* when she spilled her glass of water. *They say I goo takin' his name in vain*, she had told me. *You could have been talking about Little Lord Fauntleroy*, I had suggested, and Etterly had laughed. *I remember tha' nex' time.*

'So sometime they goo row?' Fynn pressed.

I watched in fascination as he let go of his saucer.

'Well, occasionally,' I granted him, but didn't tell him that I had far more disagreements with my parents than Etterly ever did with hers.

'You know what girls are like,' my father chipped in.

'No,' Fynn replied flatly, without taking his pale brown eyes off me. 'What do they goo row over, Lizzy?'

I racked my brain. Mr and Mrs Utter would be better placed to answer that question.

'Staying out too long,' I said. Etterly's parents would get annoyed if she was late for a meal, but I had never heard of any who didn't.

'With boys?' Fynn sprang on my declaration like he was the one chasing sticks now.

'Sometimes,' I admitted.

'Which boys?' the sergeant asked.

'Well, Godfrey Skillern sometimes,' I said wretchedly. I had never had myself down as a police informant, snitching on my friends, but I knew my parents would approve of him. His parents were well-to-do and Mr Skillern was rumoured to be master of the local masonic lodge, which my father hoped to be invited to join. 'And Gary Garner. Dicky Joiner once in a while.'

'*Richard* Joiner,' my mother corrected, though I didn't think she had ever met him.

'And what do you do with these boys?' Fynn asked.

'Usually we just walk and talk.'

'Walk,' my father repeated in disgust, like I had said *romp in the sandhills*.

'Talk about what?' my mother demanded. She had a perpetual fear that I would reveal a family secret to *outsiders*, as she called anyone who wasn't a blood relative or Pooky. I only wished she would give me a scandal worth divulging.

'Nothing, really,' I said, which seemed to satisfy them all.

'And what' – the sergeant folded his hands behind his head as if he were basking on the beach, the cup wobbling unnoticed, by everyone except me, on his knee – 'games do you play?' He laid more than enough emphasis on his words for me to know I was suspected of something obscene.

'We sometimes skim stones on the sea,' I told him, briefly forgetting that was a prohibited activity under Fynn's Law. 'Or hide-and-seek.'

We had to be really bored before we did that. It was a very juvenile activity for our mature years.

'So where do you hide?' Fynn asked.

'It varies,' I said, but the silence that met my answer told me it was not sufficient. 'In various places.'

'Various places,' Fynn repeated thoughtfully. 'And what do the boys do when they find you?'

'They say *found you*,' I told him.

Fynn licked his lips. 'And do they ever tickle you?'

My father spoke up for me at last. 'My daughter is not that kind of girl. She is not in the least bit ticklish.' I was, actually, but my father's idea of tickling was to dig his fingers in as if he were trying to remove my pancreas.

'Do they touch you?' Fynn continued.

'No,' I said, because I had a pretty good idea of what he was getting at.

'Where don't they touch you?' Fynn persisted.

Was that supposed to be some kind of trick question, whereby I would be fooled into naming every part of me except the bits boys did touch? Or was the sergeant just stupid? The second option seemed more likely.

'Anywhere,' I said.

'So, Elizabeth,' Fynn began again, but he was interrupted by a crash – the teacup and saucer, having discovered gravity, had slid off his knee and smashed in the hearth.

'Ohhhh,' my mother howled in anguish. This was one of the last pieces of Spode Imari-pattern porcelain that she still had after my father's attempt at shelf building.

'Oh my goodness,' the sergeant cried, and he leaned sideways to inspect his trousers. 'Don't worry,' he reassured her. 'No harm done.'

All three of them, I realised, were looking at me.

'I'll go and get a dustpan,' I said, and slid into the hall.

Pooky had a tray of chops on an asbestos mat and was pricking them in little darting movements with a fork.

'The policeman has broken a cup,' I told her.

'Never a policeman when you need one,' she muttered, sticking the meat back in the oven. 'Always a policeman when you don't.'

For a moment, I had an almost overpowering urge to run away. I could hardly bear that horrible man and my horrible parents any more, and I realised I was glad they had sent me to boarding school. I put my hand on the back-door handle and only then did it hit me – despite all my daydreams with Etterly, I didn't have a clue where I could run away to, and she was the only person likely to have helped me.

12

BLACKFLY, THE BIANCHI BOYS, SNOWBALLS AND THE WEASEL

Sergeant Fynn primped his moustache. It was one of the few impressive things about him – so much so that it didn't seem to belong on his face, the heavy bristles sweeping out as if he were playing Kitchener in the Sackwater Amateur Dramatic and Musical Entertainment Stage Society, aptly referred to by some as SAD-MESS.

'If you are hiding something,' he told me sternly, 'I do warn you it is a highly serious offence.' He tried to outstare me, but looked away first. 'A prisonable offence,' he added dramatically if ungrammatically. 'Do anybody goo watch you...' and I was about to tell him about the man in the shadows when he ended with, 'as a rule.'

'Well, there is a man,' I began reluctantly, and all three of them jumped like I had said *and he's here now with a machine gun.*

Fynn paused to push up his denture again. 'What man?' he demanded. 'Is it one of those black Spaniards?'

The men he must have been thinking of were actually Italian – Giovanni Bianchi's family, who ran the Napoli Restaurant in Germaine Street – and they were golden tanned, which was dark by Sackwater standards but hardly put them in the league of the blackface minstrels who performed every summer in the Pier Pavilion.

'No,' I said firmly. Lorenzo and Marco, his sons, were four

or five years older than me and, unlike their British peers, the Bianchi boys knew how to treat a girl with respect, if only – I realised as I grew up – to give them a better chance of treating her with disrespect in the future.

'We don't need foreign muck in Sackwater,' Fynn muttered, and I was not sure if he meant the Bianchis or their food, which was mainly fish and chips or pork chops and roast potatoes followed by delicious home-made ice cream. You would never persuade a Suffolk man to eat spaghetti. 'Coom on, girl, who is it then?'

'Major Burgandy,' I said reluctantly.

'I might of knew.' Fynn clicked his fingers like he was trying to get something sticky off them. 'Goo stark raving mad in tha' war, he do.'

It was difficult to imagine a less maniacal man than the major. He moved slowly, limping and leaning heavily on a stick, and when he spoke, which was rarely, his voice was quiet and his manners gentle.

Lots of men were badly affected by their experiences in the Transvaal and I only found out years later that the major had been captured by the Boers and suffered horribly in retaliation for his countrymen's shameful conduct. 'He's nice,' I said.

'What does he get up to?' Fynn demanded.

'Nothing really,' I said. 'He just sits on a bench.'

'A bench,' my parents breathed, shaken to the core.

Sergeant Fynn was not so easily rattled though. He had his notebook out and was licking his pencil.

'So...' He sprayed saliva over torn magazines on the central table between us but, mercifully, I was just out of range. 'This Burgandy – watch you, do he?'

'Well, sort of,' I said. It was just that we were in his line of vision, I thought, but I didn't really know how to say it.

'Sort of *what*?' Fynn pounced on the word like a weasel on a fledgling.

'Well, not really,' I tried to explain.

'What?' Fynn half-rose and leaned towards me. 'Speak up, girl.'

'She always mumbles,' complained my mother, who was constantly telling me I was too loud.

'One girl' – he flicked back through his notebook – 'Georgina Orchard' – he had managed to get Georgie's name right, even though she hated being called that – 'she do say Burgandy gave you sweets before the Utterly girl goo missin'.'

The sergeant slapped his notebook shut, as if he had just proved the major guilty of something terrible.

'Last Christmas,' I remembered. 'He brought us all a box of—'

'A box,' my mother cried, because it was obvious that I had finished speaking and there was nothing more horrible to give to innocent children.

I had thought this would make things better for the major but, for some reason, it made them worse.

'Did he, by Jove?' Sergeant Fynn exclaimed in what was an oddly upper-class expression for a Suffolk *boy*. I doubt he even knew he was referring to the king of the gods. 'What kind of box?'

'Turkish delight,' I said.

'Turks,' Fynn said in disgust. 'They aren't even half English.' He turned to my mother. 'The more I investigate this case, the more I'm sure certain there's a foreigner involved.'

My mother shuddered. 'I had no idea she was consorting with such people.'

'*Consorting*?' the sergeant repeated in alarm and wrote the word down. 'Is Burgandy there the day Utterly Etter goo missin'?'

He nodded firmly to make sure I knew that the answer had to be *yes*.

'I think so.' I cast my mind back. 'But he wasn't there when we noticed that Etterly had disappeared,' I added hastily, because I knew the major would never harm any of us and that information would put him in the clear.

'I bet he wasn't.' Fynn rubbed his hands like someone trying get warm after throwing snowballs.

I shifted in my seat uncomfortably. The trouble was I didn't know exactly when Etterly left and I didn't really notice the comings and goings of Major Burgandy. He had no part in our games.

I never got to mention the figure in the shadows, but doubtless he was a foreigner too.

13

THE NIGHT VISITOR

Etterly Utter came to our house. This would have been unusual in normal circumstances. My mother rarely allowed any of my friends into the house. During surgery hours they would make too much noise, she forecast, and unsettle my father's patients, who, as far as I could tell, were hardly settled in the first place. Out of hours they would disturb his rest, and he had a great deal of that. Besides which we lived in Cormorant Road, with its grand Victorian detached villas, whereas Etterly lived in Bath Road, which had terraced houses and was therefore nasty and common.

In light of recent events, this was very surprising. Etterly had disappeared four days ago and had not been reliably sighted since. Also, this was the middle of the night. Who had let my friend in and allowed her to come up to my bedroom? She was wearing a long white nightdress that gave her a ghostly appearance. It glowed in the moonlight shining through my window. Even her raven hair sparkled.

'Etterly!' I whispered, anxious not to alert my parents or Pooky, at least one of whom must have been awake.

'Betsy,' she said softly.

I sat up and saw that Etterly had bare feet and that they were whiter than her gown.

'Where have you been?' I asked, and great sadness came over my friend.

'I've been awaitin' on you,' she said, 'but you dint coom.'

Etterly came noiselessly towards me, not even her nightdress rustling.

'But I didn't know where you were,' I protested.

'Oh, Betsy,' Etterly sighed, her breath misty because the room had turned icy. 'I never left.' My friend started to shimmer. 'Take heed, Betsy,' she warned, her voice getting fainter. 'Dint trust him.'

And even though she never gave me his name, I knew who Etterly meant.

I realised, even before she melted away, that this was not really my friend, but no matter how hard I tried to tell myself that it was just a dream, her voice and appearance had been too real – and how could I explain the chill in the air on that warm May night?

I jumped out of bed and rushed to the side window. The street lights were out but there was a clear sky with a bright enough moon for me to see the road was deserted. I ran to the back window, pressing my face to the glass to peer into the garden. Was there something behind the old apple tree? The shadow of that man? I watched for a long time, hardly daring to breathe. A fox strolled across the moonlit unmown lawn and a bat swooped down from the eaves. Later, a hedgehog snuffled along the base of the ragged privet hedge. But there was no sign of Etterly and something told me, with a deep, desperate, heart-breaking certainty, that I would never see my dear friend again.

14

THE IMAGE OF ETTERLY AND THE HALF-FORMED CLAY

In its Edwardian heyday, the town had two police stations – Sackwater Central, where I was to be posted later, and Sackwater Coastal, which closed after being damaged in the storms of 1929. Even in the heady days of 1914, though, there were not many police officers in the town, and they were probably more than were needed on a regular basis. While some more successful resorts suffered from waves of crime, Sackwater barely had a ripple until Etterly Utter disappeared, and even then nobody was sure that an offence had been committed.

Could Etterly have had an accident? Had she gone swimming and been washed out to sea? The Anglethorpe lifeboat was launched and patrolled the coastline as far down as Felixstowe and local fishermen were asked to keep their eyes open.

The biggest search in Suffolk since the 1896 mass breakout from Fleiton Asylum for the Furiously and Criminally Insane was launched.

Men – and every officer in Suffolk was a man until I spoiled things – were drafted from surrounding stations spreading as far down as the hub of Suffolk, Ipswich. Door-to-door enquiries sent constables in every direction but eventually led nowhere.

The Utters did not have a camera and had not had a professional photograph of Etterly taken since she was ten – and she had grown a lot since then – but Etterly's picture had featured on the front page of the *Sackwater and District Gazette* when she was May Queen the previous year. Mr Gregson, the editor, reprinted my friend's image with an appeal and the promise of fifty pounds' reward raised from local businesses by Mr Filby, the mayor. Etterly looked very pretty in her long gown and floral crown, but her happiness seemed incongruous in what was now an alarming time.

The townsfolk set up search parties, with churches and societies organising volunteers. There was genuine concern for Etterly and sympathy for her parents and many people gave up a great deal of their free time to help. To give my parents credit, they did their best. They attended meetings and joined a hunt through the sand dunes and pine woods and my father put up a framed copy of Etterly's photograph in his waiting room. He had a great many patients in those days, when he had no real competition and was less grumpy and clumsy and had better eyesight. I was not allowed to join in any of these activities, though. Apparently I was old enough to lose a friend but not old enough to help look for her.

It was ten days before we had any real news. My father told me. His face, always like a half-formed clay model in shape, even resembled it in colour now. He sat me down and held both my hands, so I knew it must be serious.

'I'm afraid I have some bad news… very bad indeed,' my father began, his brown eyes strangely lustreless. He had a strong grip – years of wielding forceps and restraining patients had given him that – and I don't know whether it was him crushing my fingers or my dread of what he was going to say that brought tears to my eyes. 'I'm afraid,' he repeated, 'they have found a body…' He paused and, at first, I thought that was all he intended to tell me. He smacked his lips, almost as if he were enjoying a tasty snack, but I have since seen countless people do it when they are upset. 'It was that of a girl on the shingle spit of Orford Ness, five miles south of Aldeburgh.'

I think I gasped. I tried to pull away but he had a tight, painful hold of me, and it was quite a relief when he let go and I could let the blood flow back into my fingers and put them to my mouth.

'Well, now you know,' my father said. He stood up and, to my surprise, walked from the room, clearly feeling that his duty of informing me did not extend to consoling me afterwards.

Even in my shock I felt resentment at this and annoyance at the way he had so painfully given me the news, followed by exasperation with how my father was shutting the door very slowly and quietly, as if he were afraid of waking me up. If only, I thought through my misery, that could be possible.

15

DEBORAH AND THE POTTING SHED

The sun was setting when I went for a walk a couple of days after my father had told me the news.

Many parents would not have liked their daughters to be out that late but, so long as I appeared for meals, mine didn't seem to bother. It was not that they were liberal – far from it – it was just that they didn't care. There was more concern and a great many more tears when Deborah, my father's canary, disappeared than when I missed going to Georgie's birthday party because I accidentally locked myself in the potting shed.

I was not sure why I went to The Soundings. It had come to hold a terrible fascination for me since Etterly had disappeared. After all the games we had played there it was eerily quiet. An owl hooted somewhere close by in case I didn't find the place spooky enough.

There was an odd rustling coming from the King's Oak as I approached from behind and then a low moan, followed by a woman saying, 'I'm getting very strong vibrations.'

Then another woman asked tremulously, 'Is there anybody there?'

To begin with I thought they had heard me, but the first said, 'I can see her aura.'

I crept to the back of the tree.

The second said, 'Perhaps we should not disturb her, especially since she was murdered.'

'Is that you, Etterly?' the first called. 'Show yourself, dear.'

This was going too far. I had just been told that my friend was dead, probably drowned, and here those silly women were playing games with her. Did they really think we wouldn't have noticed if she had been killed inside the tree?

I crept closer and wailed as spectrally as I could.

Both of them squealed.

'It's her,' the first woman yelped.

'What in heaven's name?' the second gasped.

'Get out of my tree,' I whispered as loudly as I could.

'Crikey, it *is* her,' the first shrieked, and I hurried away as quickly and as quietly as I could.

Later, I felt guilty about pretending to be my friend, but when I thought about it, Etterly would have loved the joke and I was sad we couldn't share it.

16

THE INSTABILITY OF HOPE AND STOVEBURY PRISON

I didn't see Mr Utter for quite some time but I heard from Rowdina, who had glimpsed him getting the milk off his doorstep, that he had aged ten years and gone white overnight since the police drove him to Orford.

It was Pooky who was delegated to tell me. Perhaps it went against the grain for my parents to give me good news, or maybe my father didn't want another embarrassing emotional scene.

I was helping to scrub saucepans after dinner. Pooky hated the job but I didn't really mind, probably because it was a novelty for me. I never felt any desire to do it for a living.

'You missed a bit,' Pooky complained, pointing to the undersurface of a copper pot and plunging it back into the sink before I could disagree. 'It wasn't her.'

'What wasn't?' I puzzled, and Pooky put her skeletal hands on her bony hips and rolled her eyes to indicate that if there was a more stupid girl in East Anglia, Pooky – despite an exhaustive search – had not discovered her.

'The body wasn't,' she tutted, because she couldn't possibly have been talking about anything else.

'Etterly?' I tried to clarify.

'No,' our maid sighed. 'That's what I'm trying to tell you. It wasn't Etterly Utter.'

'Are you sure?' I gasped, and Pooky held up her arms like she was worshipping the sun.

'It's not for me to be sure,' she asserted, letting her arms fall one at a time in a semaphore kind of way. 'It's for Mr Utter and if he was certain, you can hardly expect me to disagree.'

'So Etterly might still be alive,' I cried, throwing the scrubbing brush back and splashing us both with dirty water.

'She might be,' Pooky agreed, wiping herself crossly with a wet tea towel. 'There again, she might be dead somewhere else.'

Was that the only reason she had raised my hopes – to have the pleasure of capsizing them?

'Yes, but she might be alive,' I tried again.

'I have already said as much,' Pooky reminded me sharply. 'But even if she is – and that doesn't seem likely – some fearful fate may have befallen her. She could be locked in a pantry being forced to scrub dirty pots for a pittance with less time off than she'd get in Stovebury Gaol.'

The prison had closed in Stovebury when I was five, but people still spoke as if it were a going concern.

She would make a better job of it than you, with less complaining, I thought, but only said, 'Do you know whose body they found then?'

'A young woman,' Pooky said.

'Do they know her name?' I asked, and Pooky folded her arms – a complicated process that took a few goes before she was sufficiently satisfied with the result to speak again.

'Miss Betty,' she said patiently, 'you have mistaken me for someone grand and important that the police confide in.' She unfolded her arms with some difficulty. 'The only thing people ever tell me is' – and here Pooky went into a passable imitation of my mother – 'Do this, Pooky. Do that, Pooky. Hurry up, Pooky... Fetch this, Pooky. Fetch that, Pooky.'

She was still chunnering as I left the room and I could hear her from the end of the corridor. 'That's right, leave me to do the rest of the pots.'

Another time I might have stayed to help, even though it was her job, but my mind was spinning. I had given up Etterly for dead and now, I felt sure, she was alive. If only I was older and had fulfilled my ambition of being a policewoman, I would be able to conduct a proper search for my friend, and I made a vow there and then that I would trace Etterly come what may. I never dreamed it would take so long or in what circumstances I would find her.

17

DELILAH AND THE HARRISONS

Folger's Estate Farm used to be a favourite haunt for Etterly and me in those long summer days. We would often go together or with friends to look at the animals and visit the Harrisons, who lived there and worked at the forge and stables or helped on the land. They were always welcoming, and it was innocent fun, we thought, but none of us could have foreseen the tragic consequences of our visits.

Delilah was almost exactly the same age as me, having been born two days earlier, but we were very different creatures, for Delilah was a Suffolk Punch. Even people used to working around horses cannot help but be awed by this breed. Punches are massively built and can be up to six foot at what I foolishly called the *shoulders* until Harkles told me amusedly it was the *withers*. With their heads up, they tower over any man, and when I was thirteen and trying to put away my childish things, Delilah was a mature mare who had just foaled for the third time.

We used to love watching her being harnessed to pull the heavy iron plough steadily up and down the fields, her muscles bunching powerfully under her skin, bright chestnut with a long white mane and short socks.

'She goo all day, tha' one, and never a mither,' Harkles would tell me as he patted her fondly.

Harkles, the youngest son, had thick wavy black hair, over his collar at the back, wore a red polka-dotted handkerchief tied loosely around his neck, and, at seventeen, he had the beginnings of a beard and moustache, which rather suited him. Like the rest of the family, he had startlingly green eyes. Emeralds did not glitter so brightly in the sunshine as the irises of the Harrisons.

I liked Harkles. Everybody did. Apart from being handsome, he always had time for a chat and let us help brush Delilah down at the end of the day. He was unfailingly cheerful and welcoming, though we must often have interfered with his work on the farm. Perhaps he was glad of the diversion and a bit of female company that wasn't his twin sister, Darklis.

Their mother had left them for a man in Great Yarmouth, Harkles confided in Etterly and me. Darklis often threatened to join them. Darklis was tired of living with men who expected her to take over their mother's duties, she complained, and for some reason she resented her father, who seemed a jolly, good-hearted man to me.

All of the Harrisons were short – Morphus, the father, was no taller than me. He worked the forge and, rather than the hulking giant we imagine smiths to be, he was a compact, wiry man. Morphus wore a thick, heavy belt with iron hoops that he would tuck hammers and tongs through while he was working and a leather apron with nothing above, so that his upper body and face were scarred by showers of sparks. It fascinated us to watch him work, hammering a glowing iron bar over the pointed end of his anvil into a horseshoe shape, punching the holes into it, plunging the red-hot metal into a bucket of water. And, when he knew a horse to be placid, Morphus would let us hold its bridle while he cleaned the hooves.

Bosko, at eighteen, was the tallest and most muscular of the brothers. I did not care for him at all. I'm sorry to say Bosko was ugly. His upper lip was twisted into what looked like a sneer the whole time and the bridge of his nose was so severely flattened the air whistled through it when he closed his mouth.

His left eye was clouded and he was almost blind in it. None of that was his fault – he had been trampled by a stallion when he was a baby, Harkles told us, and nearly died – but Bosko's manner was ugly too. He was surly and abrupt and never looked directly at anyone.

'He's a good sort really,' Harkles assured us. 'Perhap just a spot weensy.'

But I was not convinced. I knew plenty of people who were shy – or *weensy*, as locals called them – but they didn't behave like that.

The oldest son was Shadrach, who was amicable enough, but we rarely saw him. The estate had acquired a tractor and he was one of the few people who could drive it, so he was more often working in the fields than with the stables or forge.

Etterly, Georgie and I went to see Delilah and her new filly, Brandy, in their stable one June morning. Godfrey Skillern was already there with his very much younger brother, Lenny, who had run off to inspect the geese. Douglas Carpenter was there too, trotting around after his hero, Godfrey, but keeping well back because he was frightened of the horses.

Godfrey was talking to Darklis. She had the same tanned complexion as the rest of her family, and the same black hair – hers flowing back freely over her shoulders. Etterly was pretty but Darklis was beautiful. She had high cheekbones, a long slender nose and full, deep-red lips. She had matured into a young woman since we first met her, her slim figure filling out in a way that fascinated Godfrey. I wondered if Etterly had noticed how closely he paid attention to Darklis in the way he usually did to her and, if so, whether Etterly minded. Darklis, I suspected, was all too aware of her own charms.

Etterly made a great fuss of Delilah, telling her how clever she was, patting and stroking her and giving her a chunk of carrot pinched from Mrs Utter's kitchen. Brandy lay on her straw bed, her legs so flimsy it was hard to believe they could support her.

'It looks like she's wearing a garter.' I pointed to a brown ring around her back right white stocking.

'Hello, Brandy.' Etterly stepped forward and the filly rose to nuzzle her mother. At that instant, Delilah reared, her docility transformed instantly into a furious bray, her huge iron-shod front feet rising, thrashing in the air. Etterly fell back, crouching against the wall, her hands over her head, paralysed by shock.

'No, Delilah,' I yelled uselessly, but there was nothing I could do. You cannot control two thousand pounds of enraged animal. Delilah came down, one of her hooves crashing into the hay rack just above where Etterly had tumbled, smashing the wood into splinters, and she was lifting her feet high for another attack when Bosko vaulted over the side rail of the stall, grasped Etterly's hair and dragged her out under the rail just as both hooves came hammering onto it.

'You're hurting me,' Etterly complained tearfully and Bosko let her slump, curled up sobbing on the straw-strewn brick floor.

'You ruddy idiot,' he shouted, letting her hair go. 'You dint never goo 'tween a mare and her foal. She near kill you.'

Everyone came running into the stable. Godfrey, sensibly, stood clear. Harkles put a hand to Delilah's flank but her blood was up and she twisted her neck, slavering, teeth bared to try to bite him, and he whipped his arm away.

'She'll hurt her baby,' Georgie cried as Darklis pushed her way through.

The mare stamped frenziedly and clattered round to face the latest intruder, but the moment she saw Darklis, Delilah stood still. She was breathing heavily but her head stopped tossing and she made no objection when Darklis reached out for her neck, stroking down in long slow sweeps. Darklis wiped the froth around Delilah's mouth with a handful of hay and lowered her forehead to rest on the horse's, softly singing something I could not understand.

Etterly stood up.

'Are they all right?' she asked.

'They'll be right as sunshine when we leave them alowun,' Darklis reassured her, and we trooped outside.

'She only goo protecting her young 'un,' Bosko explained to Etterly.

'I'm sorry,' she told him. 'It was stupid of me. I know better than ge' 'tween a cow and calf so I should of thought. It's just, she always seem so… gentle.'

'She is tha',' he agreed, and started slightly as Etterly took his hand.

'That was very brave on you,' she said. 'You save my life.'

'I was just there,' he mumbled, and he tried to take his hand away but Etterly leaned forwards and brushed the mop of hair that had fallen forward over his eyes.

'Thank you,' she whispered.

'Best be back to work,' Bosko muttered, head down as he made his way towards the paddock.

I went afterwards with Godfrey to look at the other horses. Limelight was corralled by himself, having become too 'tentive towards the mares, we were told by Morphus, and I had the impression that Limelight's attentiveness might be of a sort that young ladies shouldn't hear about.

Limelight had been a racehorse once and was, I believe, a good runner, but jockeys didn't like him. He was too keen to be off, so riders had to battle to keep him behind the starting line, and he was easily distracted by noises from the crowd. Usually, horses with his record would have been destroyed rather than kept at unnecessary expense, but Limelight had been a pet project of Rodney's – Squire Folger's son – before Rodney was killed in a motorcycle crash, and so the horse was kept.

Most people, given a choice, kept clear of Limelight. He was a bad-tempered horse who, unlike Delilah, bit and kicked without reason. Morphus had come off worse in an argument with Limelight himself.

'I tell him he goo need a new shoe,' Morphus related over his lunchtime jug of beer, 'and he tell me he dint.' Morphus grinned minus several front teeth. 'He plant his old shoe in my mouth to show how good it is.'

'I bet I could ride him,' Godfrey boasted, and Morphus frowned.

'You keep well clear,' he warned, but the ex-racehorse held a fascination for Godfrey that I never really understood.

'He just needs the proper handling,' he explained to me on another occasion as Limelight ambled over.

I stood well back, but Godfrey fed him a clump of fresh grass torn out of the meadow and patted him confidently.

'Many a professional jockey tried,' I reminded Godfrey, and he shrugged.

'Yes, but they were just interested in winning races,' he said.

Godfrey was a good rider. He had been out with the hounds when he was my age and Sir Hugo Capricorn, the master, would never have tolerated anyone who couldn't keep up with the hunt.

'I don't think the Squire would let you,' I warned, but Godfrey's face glowed at the idea.

'Bet you can go like the wind,' he told the horse, and, as if agreeing with him, Limelight tossed his head.

18

PC48 AND THE TERBLE SCRATCHET

Etterly had been missing for six days when Pooky sent me on an errand. She had run out of sugar and was up to her elbows in a bowl of flour. I was quite happy to go for her and took tuppence from the petty cash that she kept hidden in an old Peek Freans Pat-A-Cake biscuit tin.

'Now, don't you go buying cakes and chocolates from that,' Pooky warned, as if I would be getting pounds of change.

I didn't like the cleverly named Grocer's Shop in Bailiffs Way but it was closest and Pooky needed the sugar quickly, she told me, if the entire meal was not going to be a calamitous catastrophe. Pooky used bigger words than my parents and usually more correctly than my mother. It didn't occur to me to wonder why our maid didn't speak broad Suffolk like every other domestic servant I had met.

The clapper had been missing from the bell in the Grocer's Shop for as long as I could remember, so there was no merry tinkle when I entered, but it was such a small shop, with the counter facing the door, that you would have to be in eternal rest not to notice a customer coming in.

'Those spirit goo take her,' I heard Mrs Hurren, who worked there three days a week, tell a customer. 'She's never truly of this world. I only—' She stopped dead, flicking her eyes in my direction.

'Tha' girl she goo friend with,' the customer responded, oblivious of the full stop Mrs Hurren had come to and the warning wiggles of the shop assistant's eyebrows, 'she's a strange one too. Dint be surprised if she goo next. Always hangin' 'bou' that tree she is.'

There was some truth in that last remark – I had taken to visiting the King's Oak most days. I refused to call it the *Ghost Tree*. Whatever had happened to Etterly, she had not been eaten by a lump of wood or abducted by goblins. It wasn't that I expected to find my friend there. I was trying to rekindle my memory of that day, but becoming less and less certain of what I had seen and what I imagined in retrospect. The shadowy man haunted me now. He had become a sinister figure in my dreams, once dripping blood from the carving knife in his hand, and I wished I had told somebody about him now. Perhaps if I had alerted Mrs Cooksey at the time, a tragedy might have been prevented. I had not liked or trusted Sergeant Fynn enough to confide my fears in him, but I had tried that morning with my parents.

'I think I saw a shadow,' I had begun tentatively over breakfast the day after Fynn's visit.

'That's nothing to boast about,' my mother had rebuked me.

'No, I meant...' But my parents were rarely interested in what I meant unless they wanted me to explain why I had committed some tiny infringement of their rules, in which case Dr Crippen was never so thoroughly cross-examined.

'We all see shadows all the time,' my father had explained ploddingly. 'They are caused by an opaque object blocking the passage of light.'

'See.' My mother had pointed to the windowsill. 'There is a shadow and' – her arm swung about until she found a satisfactory example behind the teapot – 'there is another.'

I gave up and went to the kitchen, where Pooky gave me a spoon to lick and an errand to do.

As I ambled home with the sugar, I passed two men in flat

caps standing by a pillar box on one corner of The Soundings. They glanced towards me.

'Hear a terble scratchet round middlenight yisdee, I do,' said the older one, who might have been the father. 'Wailin' and scritchin' it is. Sound like two cat fightin'.'

'Must be the ghost on tha' girl, I do believe.' The one who might have been the son shuddered. 'They do say she haunt the place where she is took.'

Even at my tender age, I thought the cat explanation more likely. Several people in the area let them out at night.

'Need a parson to exercise it, it do.' The older one nodded wisely, and they strolled on.

Obviously they could not have known about my connection to Etterly, but was that really the sort of conversation adults should be having in front of a child?

Neglectful of my mission, I took a detour to the King's Oak. Was that the major limping away down Frost Road? A figure drifted by a window in number twelve but I could not tell if it was Mrs Cooksey, who, some locals whispered, had been negligent or complicit in Etterly's disappearance.

I put my bag of sugar on a bench, went to the tree and pressed my cheek against it. Obviously Etterly wasn't there and I knew I couldn't communicate with her, but somehow it made me feel closer to my friend. The bark was rough and warm and if a tree could possibly have a personality, I would say this one was benevolent.

Oh Etterly, I whispered, *wherever can you be?*

It was then I heard a scratching. At first I thought it might be a bird, but then I heard a cough. I skirted the tree, keeping a good ten feet away to give myself a head start if there was any trouble. It was difficult to see into the darkness of the hollow, but I definitely heard another cough and took a couple of steps closer.

'Hello,' I called then, feeling a little foolish in case it was a dog. 'Is there anybody there?' This getting no response, I added, a bit more boldly, 'In the tree, I mean.'

There was a third cough and a dark silhouette appeared in the opening. It bobbed down and stepped out, instantly taking the form of a young police constable holding his upturned helmet like Oliver Twist asking for more.

'Oh, marnin', miss,' he greeted me cheerily, patting the shoulders and sleeves of his jacket one hand at a time. 'Dust get in my gizzard, it do.' He coughed again to demonstrate.

'Good morning,' I replied, and he came towards me.

'Lookin' for clues,' he told me, ''bout the girl.'

'Etterly Utter?' I asked, though it was unlikely to be anyone else.

'Tha's the one.' He was a tall man, lean, with a fresh complexion and a deep dimple in his chin. 'You happen to know her?'

'She's a friend of mine,' I replied, and he raised his eyebrows.

'And wha's your name?' He had a way of asking that didn't make me feel I was in the dock.

'Betty Church.'

I didn't have the temerity to ask what he was called, but I could see on his epaulette that he was number forty-eight.

'Well, Betty,' PC48 said chattily, 'dint suppose you have an idea where she might be?'

If Fynn had asked questions in such a civil manner, he might have got better answers. I didn't deliberately conceal anything from the sergeant, but he didn't exactly encourage me to open up.

'No,' I said. 'I was over there' – I pointed – 'when she disappeared, and I saw her walking towards here, but she was probably about where I am now when I stopped looking.'

'You goo play rounders with the boys, I do believe.' The constable put his helmet back on, strap on chin but never under it, as per regulations, to stop an officer being strangled, I was to find out years later. 'Who won?'

'We abandoned the game when we noticed Etterly had gone,' I told him. 'But we were holding our own.'

The constable grinned. 'Bet the boys are glad to get out of a thrashin'.'

'Possibly,' I agreed.

'Play tennis with my little sister,' he chattered on. 'Dint tell anyone but she win every time. So you dint see Etterly goo in?'

'Nobody did.'

The constable unbuttoned his top left jacket pocket. 'Some folk say the tree goo swallow her.'

'I don't think trees do that,' I replied.

The constable listened gravely. 'Never coom 'cross one myself like tha'. Make me think twice 'bout a picnic in the pine woods if I do.'

'And I don't believe a woodland spirit took her,' I continued.

'Dint seem likely neither,' he agreed. 'What goo you think then?'

'I think she was kidnapped,' I said, and stopped in shock.

That was the first time I had ever put my fear into words. I didn't much believe in fate, but I had tempted it – and was it possible that expressing my fears could somehow have made them happen?

19

PECK AND THE MANIAC

It took me a moment to recover from my thoughts. Pooky had made suggestions about what happened to Etterly, but I rarely took her bizarre speculations seriously. She had been convinced a missing meat tenderiser had been stolen by a maniac who would use it to batter down our bedroom doors – though they were never locked – and smash our heads like walnuts, before she remembered that she had thrown it at a squirrel she thought was trying to steal her particulars off the washing line. Now, however, it struck me that there might be a grain of truth in Pooky's ideas about Etterly being kept prisoner somewhere. Most of the other theories I had heard were tosh, including Nelly Havard's assertion that Etterly had buried herself to hide for a joke but suffocated, and all the people trampling into the hollow had beat the earth hard again.

'Kidnap int common these parts,' the policeman assured me. 'Most young'uns what goo missin' have run away and come back home when they're hungry.'

'She would never have gone without telling me,' I insisted, fighting back the tears.

'Mayhap,' the constable conceded. 'Must be unsettlin' for you, losin' a friend and not knowin'.'

'It is.' I nodded miserably. 'Do you think you will find her?'

'If she's to be found, we will,' the constable assured me. 'If she int, we dint,' he concluded less reassuringly.

'Did you find anything in there?' I asked, without any hope. I and most of the others had had a good look inside at the time and several members of the public had looked in out of curiosity, some even posing for photographs beside the oak or in the entrance.

'Mayhap yes, mayhap no,' the constable said, and I was starting to go off him. He was doing the usual adult trick of speaking in meaningless riddles, but then he saved himself by adding, 'Int sure.' He brought his notebook out of his top pocket. 'I find some marks inside – lot on scratchin's with penknives – that sort on thing.'

I listened, puzzled. Lots of people carved their initials in bark. I doubt there was a tree in The Soundings that didn't have at least a dozen love hearts cut into them with the dates underneath. Etterly and I had been fascinated to find one that read 1832.

'Some on those markin's int'rest me,' the constable continued. 'Names and such.' He flicked open his notebook. 'M love D frinstance. Tha' look recent.' It took me a second to realise frinstance wasn't D's surname. 'M love D,' he repeated, but I greeted the announcement blankly.

No doubt I could have come up with many names, male and female, for each initial, but it would have been uninformed guesswork.

'G and H,' he tried, with no more success.

'Sorry,' I said.

'Lots of hearts,' he informed me. 'Some with arrows and some withou'. Some other drawin's not so nice.' He grimaced.

'There are more carvings on the outside,' I pointed out.

PC48 turned a page. 'More interested on the inside.'

'I carved a BC once,' I confessed.

'Seen tha' one.' He turned two pages on and gave it a tick. 'Some whole names too. Edward love Edwina… No? … Ferris love Edwina too. Must be a pop'lar girl.'

'There's a Ferris Jones who works at the dairy.' I remembered him because I had helped my father to gas him.

'Perhap I goo have a word with him,' the constable said

unenthusiastically. 'Sometime things you think lead nowhere solve a case. Most time,' he added mournfully, 'they dint.'

I was to spend many a year finding out how true that statement was.

The constable shut his book and put it away.

'There was something else,' I blurted out, because he seemed about to go.

'Goo on,' he said intently.

'I saw a man watching us,' I said. 'At least, I think I did.'

'When?'

'During the rounders game.'

'Where do you see him?' the constable asked with a tilt of his head, and I pointed to the far corner.

'Over there, beside the horse chestnut.'

The constable shaded his eyes.

'Do you get a good view?'

'No,' I said.

'Bit dark under those branches,' he confirmed. 'What do he do?'

'Nothing really,' I said, feeling quite silly now. 'He just stood there for a long time, and when Etterly went back towards the tree, I think I might have glimpsed him again.'

'Anyone else see him?'

'I don't think so.'

It struck me then that, if I hadn't mentioned it, it was no more likely that anyone else would.

The constable wrinkled his forehead, his helmet lifting a fraction with the movement.

'Do you tell anybody about this?'

I swallowed. 'No,' I confessed at last, before bursting out with, 'I tried to tell my parents but they weren't listening.'

'What 'bout the police? Who question you?'

'Sergeant Fynn,' I said, and he pulled a sour face.

'Dint s'pose you find him easy to talk to.'

'No,' I agreed. 'He was...'

'Horrid,' the constable filled the gap. 'Lucky he dint clap you in irons,' he said wryly. 'He love a n'arrest, he do. Can you describe the man?'

'Not really,' I said stupidly.

'But he is a man?'

'Yes, I think so. He was more a shadow.'

'Tall? Short? Skinny or fat?' he probed gently.

'About average, I should say,' I did say. 'Sorry, I...'

'No, that's very helpful,' PC48 assured me with a wink, 'for I never coom 'cross a n'average man so he should be easy to spot.' He buttoned his top pocket. 'Ever see him afore or a'ter?'

'No. I don't think so.'

'Let me know if you do, or if you think on anythin' else. My name is Constable Peck and I'm at Sackwater Central Police Station, the one on Tenniel Road.'

I knew all too well where that was. An irate elderly copper had dragged me in once for trying to steal his helmet when I had only been trying it on.

'I will,' I promised, and Constable Peck tipped his peak in salute.

'Good day, miss. Have a care.'

I had lots of cares, but at least one of them had been relieved. I had told a figure of authority what little I knew and I felt certain he had taken me seriously. I had wanted to be a policeman since I was tiny and Constable Peck had just reminded me why.

'Spent all the money on aniseed balls, did you?' Pooky demanded when I returned home.

'Oh my goodness,' I cried. 'I left it in The Soundings.'

Pooky leaned back against the draining board.

'Well, you had better run straight back and fetch it,' she commanded, 'or that's a shilling you owe me.'

'But I only took tuppence,' I protested, and Pooky folded her arms carefully.

'Oh, Miss Betty.' She gazed at me wearily. 'Don't add deceitfulness and thievery to the list of your vices. It is quite long enough already.'

20

CHANGING THE GAS AND NOT CHANGING FLOWERS

One night, three weeks after Etterly disappeared, Godfrey Skillern went missing. I found out first thing in the morning when his older brother, Gordon, rang our front door bell. Godfrey had been hit in the mouth with a cricket ball a few days earlier, which made his upper lip split and swell and loosened some teeth a bit. Was it possible he had come to see my father?

Nobody had turned up yet, I assured him.

'I didn't think it likely,' Gordon admitted. He was virtually a man now at eighteen, with a deep voice and a nicked upper lip from shaving. 'I mean no disrespect, but he hates dentists and he would have got our mother to make an appointment. We are just trying everywhere we can think of.'

His bed, Gordon said, had not been slept in. I remembered Aunty M telling me of Mr G's scorn when that assertion was made. 'Can nobody other than a maid straighten sheets or plump up a pillow?' he had demanded.

'How can you tell? I asked.

'Because Lenny made him an apple pie bed,' Gordon explained, 'and the sheet was still doubled over so he couldn't have got into it.'

'It's not like Godfrey to wander off without saying anything,' I mused, and realised I had said the same about Etterly.

'It's not,' Gordon agreed grimly.

He was pale and apprehensive.

'Have you tried Dicky Joiner's house?' I asked.

'My mother and Mrs Green, our neighbour, are calling on all the people we can think of,' he told me.

'He wouldn't have gone fishing, would he?' I suggested, but Gordon shook his head.

'His rods are still in the shed.'

My parents appeared, my father from his surgery where he was changing the gas and air cylinders, my mother from the waiting room where she was titivating some not-quite-dead flowers in a vase. They would last another day or two yet, she had insisted as a few more petals floated down.

'How did he get out?' my father asked, proving that he must have been listening in.

'We have an iron fire escape at the back of the house,' Gordon replied, clearly fretting to get back on his way. 'Godfrey sometimes uses it to get into the garden rather than walk over the hall floor when it's been washed.'

'Fire escapes.' My father sucked his teeth. 'Staircases for burglars, if you ask me.'

Clearly Gordon hadn't asked and didn't want to stand chatting about it.

'Well, I am sorry to have disturbed you,' he said, stepping off the front step.

'I know where he'll be,' my mother called, and Gordon perked up expectantly. 'He will have gone for a moonlight walk in the sand dunes and fallen asleep.'

Gordon's face fell.

'I hope so, Mrs Church,' he said politely. 'Well, thank you, all.'

'Give your father my regards and tell him he's due for a check-up,' my father called out. 'And your sister.'

Gordon rubbed his brow distractedly.

'But I don't have a sister, Mr Church.'

'Your mother only had boys,' my mother realised. 'How very fortunate she was.'

Gordon took a few steps backwards along the gravelled drive. He was grey with anxiety.

'Where are you going?' I asked.

'The Soundings,' he told me, hurrying off, and I rushed after him.

'Where are you going?' my parents chorused.

'The Soundings,' I told them.

'Have you done your teeth?' my mother called.

That was one of the few things she ever worried about when it came to me and strangely, given his profession, one of the many things my father didn't.

'You've forgotten your coat,' my father yelled, far louder than would have been necessary if I was already a hundred yards away.

No I haven't, I thought, but pretended not to hear.

21

GOBNAIT AND THE RUNNING BOARD

I caught up with Gordon.

'Godfrey's developed a sort of preoccupation with that tree,' he told me, walking so quickly that I had to break my step to keep up. It didn't seem to occur to him to ask why I was coming, which was just as well because I didn't really know. 'He's half convinced that Etterly or her ghost is somehow trapped inside it.'

This was news to me. Godfrey had never mentioned the subject since Etterly disappeared but then, I supposed, he probably hadn't wanted to upset me.

'You think he might have come out to investigate?' I asked, a bit breathless, and Gordon sighed.

'I'm running out of ideas,' he admitted.

It was a warm day and I was glad I had ignored my father's warning.

'He's probably gone home already,' I tried to reassure him, something I would find myself doing on a professional basis for many years to come.

'Perhaps,' Gordon conceded, and his voice sounded strained when he added, 'I hope so.'

He strode and I trotted, both in silence for a while. The milkman was heading back to the dairy with an almost empty cart and Gordon called out to him.

'I don't suppose you've seen a boy, fifteen, looks a bit like me but blond hair?'

The milkman pulled his plodding horse to a halt and pushed his peaked cap back.

'Dint notice anyone.' He looked like he had too many fingers on his left hand but I wasn't close enough to count them.

'His name is Godfrey,' Gordon told him. 'Godfrey Skillern.'

'I dint ask folk's names as I go by.'

'I just meant, if you should see anyone like that, you could ask his name and tell him to go home,' Gordon explained.

'I could,' the milkman agreed.

'There's five shillings for you if you do,' Gordon promised, and the milkman pricked up his ears.

'I goo back the long way,' he decided. He flicked his reins, clicked his tongue twice and was off. 'Just a mo',' he called after us. 'How do I know where to goo for my money?'

'Godfrey will tell you,' Gordon promised, and the milkman set off again around the corner with us trailing not very far behind. He was hardly out of our sight when we heard him shout, 'Hold on there, boy. Do you be – oh botheration, what's your name? – Jeffrey Skillington?'

We broke into a trot. The Soundings looked deserted except for the milkman still sitting on his cart, his horse lowering its head to nibble a little clump of weeds growing out of the gutter.

'Dint go back in there,' the milkman warned. 'Folks tha' do dint never coom back.'

'Have you seen him?' Gordon gasped, more from anxiety than lack of fitness, I would think.

'First I dint, then I do.' The milkman half stood on his running board to get a better view. 'Now I dint again.'

'Where?' I asked as the milkman slumped back onto his wooden bench.

'He coom out tha' Ghost Tree.' He pointed like a picture I had seen of the young Bonaparte urging his troops into battle, except that Napoleon was astride a rearing charger rather than sitting on a tattered blanket behind an exhausted nag. 'Then,' the milkman continued, 'he do get pulled back in again.'

'Pulled?' I queried, but Gordon was off, shouting over his shoulder, 'Wait there, Betty.' But I was already in pursuit, shouting over my shoulder, 'Wait, please. We may need help.'

Gordon was nearly there, with me twenty or thirty feet behind, when he fell. He had been so intent on his destination that he had not paid any attention to the molehills between him and it, and stumbled, twisting his ankle.

'Botheration,' he cursed, struggling to his feet as I rushed past. 'Come back, Betty.'

My parents and teachers often accused me of not listening and Pooky was forever haranguing me about it. This was not the time I intended to prove them all wrong. I raced to the tree, swerving around it to stop, panting, a few feet in front of the entrance. There *was* somebody inside the King's Oak.

'Hello,' I called, and thought I heard a faint grunt. 'Is that you, Godfrey?'

Gordon caught up, dipping sideways with a painful limp.

'There's somebody in there,' I told him.

'Godfrey?' Gordon stepped forwards and the figure came towards us in a crouching shuffle through the inverted V hole. It took me a moment to recognise Godfrey, even though I had been hoping to see him. He looked like a tramp in his tattered, dirty clothes. The usually glowing face was blanched. His golden hair was blackened and he had mud on the top of his head.

'Godfrey!' Gordon cried in concern, and tumbled towards him. Godfrey staggered and they both fell to their knees. Gordon took his brother by the shoulders. 'What happened to you?'

Godfrey struggled to speak but only a moan came out of his oddly curling lips.

'Have you had an accident?' I asked, and Godfrey pulled his lips apart in a tortured grimace.

'Ahh-aah-aye.'

I think he was trying to say *I* but it came out as a sob.

'What's happening?' Gordon asked me – rather bizarrely, I thought afterwards, but the person who behaves normally in such circumstances must be very abnormal indeed.

I hurried to Godfrey's side. The mud on his head was oozing brown over his face. I went to wipe it away. My fingers sank in and Godfrey screamed, his hands going up to grab mine. In that instant, I realised what was happening – but it took me much longer to believe it.

22

CONFUSION, DISTRACTION AND CONCERN

I reeled back in shock, my fingers crushed in Godfrey's grasp.

Gordon still had his brother by the shoulders, looking at him in utter confusion.

'Godfrey?' was all he could manage, then, 'What is it?'

But Godfrey was beyond hearing. He only knew the unrelieved pain as he clawed at my hands, driving my fingers in deeper, and I realised then that what I had thought was mud was thick clotted blood and that the back of his skull was a crater.

'Are you hurt?' Gordon asked confusedly.

Godfrey whipped his head from side to side, trying to fling off the pain.

'Pull his hands away,' I told Gordon, who regarded me distractedly. 'He'll hurt himself. Pull them away,' I shouted, and he got the message, but even then the two of us had to use all our strength to wrench Godfrey off me and all the time he was howling and shaking.

'My head,' he said clearly.

'You'll be all right,' I told him. 'We'll get you to hospital.'

I turned, hoping the milkman was still there because the tree was blocking my view, and shouted, 'We need help. He's hurt. Fetch a doctor.' I thought I heard a grumbling, so I added insistently, 'Now.'

Godfrey stared at his hands and then at me. 'Now?' he asked, like it was a foreign word.

'You'll be all right, Godfrey,' Gordon assured him. 'We've sent for a doctor.'

'Where am I?'

'The Soundings, near the King's Oak,' I told him.

'The Ghost Tree,' he said, and I was not sure if it was a question or a statement. He twisted to look back at it and then he smiled contentedly. 'I saw her,' he said.

'Who, Godfrey?' Gordon asked. 'Who did you see?'

'Her,' Godfrey told him with great satisfaction, but he seemed to be struggling with his thoughts. 'She's all right, isn't she?' he asked in alarm.

'She's fine,' I said, no more sure than Gordon who his brother meant.

Did he think he had seen Etterly? Had she come to him as she had come to me in my bedroom?

Godfrey went limp and we were just laying him back a bit when he sat bolt upright.

'It hurts.'

He punched himself on the right temple, pulling back to swing his clenched fist again.

'Stop him,' I cried, and managed to get a grip on Godfrey's sleeve.

Gordon snatched at his brother's arms but could only deflect the blow so that Godfrey struck himself on the nose.

'What the—' Godfrey glanced at his brother and then at me. 'He hit me,' he said accusingly.

'No,' Gordon protested. 'It was an accident.'

Godfrey's eyes flicked side to side and he cleared his throat noisily.

'So hard,' he gasped, and toppled backwards. 'I tried,' he said clearly.

Godfrey's mutilated head fell into my lap, spraying my dress with fresh blood as I struggled not to overbalance and drop him on the ground.

I think I cried out and Godfrey looked at me in concern, but his gaze soon drifted. He panted a few times, gave a little whimper and went limp.

23

THE AUTO CARRIER SOCIABLE AND THE ENEMY

Gordon stared down at his brother in stunned horror.

'Is he…?' Gordon managed to say at last.

I heard footsteps and glanced up to see the milkman approach.

'Oh my good godmother,' he gasped. 'Dint know you is goon kill him.'

'He's still breathing.' I pointed to the bubbles in the blood around Godfrey's nostrils.

'Oh, thank the Lord,' Gordon whispered, and pulled himself together. 'We must get him to hospital.'

'My horse int no good,' the milkman told us. 'She's slow 'nuff at the start on her round, let alowun the end.'

Gordon tried to stand and winced. 'My ankle,' he remembered.

'I'll go,' I said. 'In the meantime,' I said to the milkman, 'you can knock on doors and see if anyone can help – a doctor or a nurse.'

'Righto.'

I didn't wait to watch the milkman trudge away but set off. I was good at running when I was young and still had both arms. At thirteen I could beat many girls two or more years older than me, and that day I had more than a competitive spirit to spur me on. I leaped over the hedge, hardly looking as I crossed the – fortunately – traffic-free road. Up the street I pelted. An elderly man had stopped to light his pipe and it flashed through my mind to approach him, but it would take too long to explain and he would be too slow on his stick to assist.

I turned off, pumping my arms hard, head down. A little cream motor vehicle approached – an Auto Carrier Sociable, I think, with its third wheel at the back. The driver was a middle-aged man giving a young woman a ride. I waved both arms frantically and the passenger waved back.

'Hey,' I shouted, but I doubt they even heard me above the roar of the engine for I was already out of breath. 'Stop.'

The driver honked his horn in greeting and they sped away.

I filled my lungs with air and carried on.

'What's your hurry?' an indignant nanny shrieked as I rounded the corner, nearly colliding with her pram, but I had no time to explain.

'So-sorry,' I managed.

'You want to learn some bloody manners,' she yelled in my wake.

I stumbled on a loose paving stone but managed to keep on my feet, fleetingly grabbing at a telegraph pole to steady myself before I crossed into and over the next road, tripping on a high kerb and flying across the pavement, skinning my hands and barking my knees as I tried to stop myself skidding.

'Ouch,' I said tamely and battled on.

The Royal Albert Sackwater Infirmary was set back off the main road, up a short flight of stairs. What genius thought it a good idea to make it difficult for the sick and infirm to enter a hospital? Admittedly there were side and back entrances, but I had no time to go to either. I would probably have hardly noticed them usually, but now they represented a minor obstacle course as I struggled up, launching myself through the door and sending it crashing into the wall behind me.

The receptionist, a nurse who seemed old enough to require nursing herself, looked up sharply, but her expression changed instantly from disapproval to concern. She jumped up out of her chair, grasping a large hand bell – the sort the nuns used to summon us in when breaktime was over – and swung it vigorously while shouting, 'Doctor, come here, please.'

The nurse plonked the bell back down and hurried round the desk.

'I…' I managed.

'Don't try to speak,' she instructed.

'I…' I tried desperately to catch my breath. 'I…' I said a third, and increasingly useless, time.

'Sit down, dear,' the nurse said, guiding me backwards towards a chair, but I needed to stand to try to get some oxygen into my lungs.

'No, I…' I protested, but her kindness and the power of her muscles were too much for me.

'What is it, dear? Have you been run over?'

'Not me,' I gasped.

A young man came in, slipping his arms into a long white coat. He hardly looked old enough to have left school.

'What is it, Nurse Hockwill?' he asked cheerily. 'Have we got a fire?' He caught sight of me and his grin evaporated. 'Oh my goodness. What happened to you?'

'She's been run over,' the nurse explained, then, with a little creative flair, added, 'by a speeding motor bicycle.'

'Oh my ears and whiskers,' the doctor quoted oddly from *Alice's Adventures in Wonderland*, but I suppose he couldn't have used any of the expletives he would have learned in his student days.

At least their chatter literally gave me a little breathing space.

'It's not me,' I managed, and the doctor patted me kindly.

'But it must be you,' he philosophised. 'You can't be anybody else.'

'No,' I panted. 'It's not me who's hurt.'

The nurse tilted her head sadly and the doctor tilted his sympathetically.

'She is probably concussed,' he diagnosed. 'We need to get her wound cleaned and X-ray her skull.' He turned back to me and asked slowly, 'Are… you… in annny… pain, little girl?'

I was actually, from my fall, but we had no time for such distractions. I took some more deep breaths.

'The doctor was asking, where does it hurt?' the nurse explained loudly.

'It's my friend…' I said.

'No-no,' the doctor interrupted. 'Pain is the enemy and must be defeated.'

'My friend is very seriously injured,' I blurted out, and inhaled a couple more times. 'Most of this blood is his.'

The doctor looked dubious, pulled a not-very-white handkerchief from his trouser pocket, spat on it and wiped my forehead.

'By George, she's right,' he agreed. 'Where is he?'

'In The Soundings,' I said. 'Please come quickly. I think he might…'

With the very thought of what I was going to say, I burst into tears.

'Wait there.' The doctor rushed back into the room he had emerged from. I heard some clattering and he was back, black leather Gladstone bag in his grasp. 'Send an ambulance, Nurse Hockwill,' he ordered, 'and try to get hold of Dr Samson.' He hurtled across the lobby – and I tried to follow, but the nurse took hold of my arm – through the still-open door, almost tumbling down the steps in his rush before snatching at the railings and skidding to a halt on the front drive and swinging round to look back up at us.

'Where exactly is The Soundings?' he asked sheepishly.

24

NURSE HOCKWILL AND THE SPOON

Nurse Hockwill was a local woman – I had seen her occasionally in her civvies cycling along High Road West – and she gave the young doctor concise instructions.

'Now,' she said to me, 'tell me exactly what happened.'

She sat on the edge of a bench and tried to take my hand, but I evaded her grasp.

'I'm sorry. I must go,' I told her, and shot off.

I trotted rather than ran on the way back. The doctor came into view, coat flapping at the end of the street, twirling on his heels, clearly lost.

'Turn left,' I called and he set off to the right.

'The other way,' I yelled, and he turned around.

I doubt he was there more than twenty seconds before me, but he was already crouching and grasping Godfrey's wrist when I arrived. Godfrey lay flat on his back, Gordon kneeling ashen beside him.

'Buck up, old chap,' Gordon was urging. 'Buck up.'

The doctor bent low, his ear to Godfrey's nose.

'Got a mirror?' he asked, but it was a good few years before I was to carry one of those routinely.

'No, I—'

'Spoon?' he suggested even more hopelessly.

'No. Sorry. I can try one of the houses.'

The doctor shook his head and straightened up. Godfrey was waxen. His mouth gaped but the fresh, clotting or clotted blood was not disturbed by a breath through it or his nostrils. He stared dully. The doctor put a thumb on one eyelid and a first finger on the other and slid them down with practised skill.

'I'm so sorry,' he said to me, and he looked genuinely upset as Gordon stared, stupefied. 'What was his name?'

That was the first time I had heard Godfrey spoken of in the past tense and I was never to hear him spoken of in any other way again.

The milkman was leaning against the tree, smoking a cigarette with a tragic look on his face.

'Dint s'pose I get tha' reward now,' he mourned, flicking his ash into my face.

25

THE TRIBUTE AND THE HUNT

We found out a little of what had happened through our parents – mine being the least and Georgie's the most informative – but our main source of information was the newspapers. The *Suffolk Courier* and the *East Anglian Chronicle* wrote about the accident. The *Sackwater and District Gazette* did a two-page tribute to Godfrey Skillern, with a portrait photograph of him in his Sackwater Cricket Club Juniors' Captain's outfit on the front cover. His headmaster said what a tragic loss it was and what great promise had been destroyed.

Godfrey, we were informed, had gone to Folger's Estate Farm on the evening before he died. He had told his family he was going to his room to read before having an early night but he sneaked out by the fire escape. Nobody paid much attention when he turned up. We were always hanging about there, Godfrey more than most because he had the dual attractions of the horse and Darklis, and I was not sure which had drawn him more strongly. Darklis was not there that day. She had had another row with her father and gone off, as she had threatened, to stay with her mother in Great Yarmouth.

Morphus was mending an iron gate but he paused for a brief chat. His sons, he told Godfrey, were digging in new posts for a broken fence on Old Billy's Meadow.

Godfrey went to the tack room, helped himself to what he needed, took it to the paddock and saddled up Limelight. Morphus saw Godfrey ride off and shouted, but was too late to stop him.

Morphus thought about following but Godfrey was heading across country away from the roads and it would take too long to get another horse ready. Besides, they had nothing that could match Limelight. Morphus watched him go and made a resolution to give Godfrey a tongue lashing and ban him from the estate when he returned.

'Young fool,' he said afterwards. 'Sort of thin' I did do at his age.'

It was over an hour before Limelight returned, wild-eyed, with saddle askew. The boys were still out working so Morphus wiped the horse down. Limelight seemed more agitated than usual but then he had had to find his own way home. It was only when Morphus was picking the hooves clean that he saw what looked like blood on a front hoof.

Morphus sent a boy to fetch his sons. He was more angry than concerned. Godfrey was disrupting his work at the forge and his sons' work on the farm. Squire Folger would not be best pleased when he found out. Harkles and Bosko took two hacking horses and set off across the fields. Shadrach, the only one who could drive, went down the lanes on his motorbike. They took hunting horns to notify each other when they found Godfrey. They never used them.

Morphus didn't notify the authorities.

'Lock me up soon as look at me,' he reportedly told Fynn when the sergeant arrived to investigate the accident, and his claims were not unjustified. The Harrisons came from Romany stock and were the first generation to stop travelling. As far as I could tell, they were a decent family working hard to earn an honest living, but to many people – the police, I am ashamed to admit, included – they were filthy gypsies and habitual criminals.

We stopped going to the farm after that. Somehow, it didn't seem right.

*

They put padlocked wooden doors over the opening to the King's Oak around that time. I was told it was to protect other children, but I would find out years later that the women I had come across were by no means unique. Residents of The Soundings were always getting their sleep disturbed by people holding seances. The only thing that puzzled me was why they didn't just board it up permanently. For what reason would anybody need to gain entrance to the tree?

'Why, to look for people who shouldn't be in there,' Pooky explained patiently but confusingly. 'Haven't you finished peeling those potatoes yet?'

My parents went to the funeral, though they hardly knew Godfrey, but I was kept at home because, as my mother explained, it would be a sad occasion. They didn't mind making me sad normally, I pondered.

Georgie and Rowdina went, as did most of the boys.

'It was awful,' Georgie told me tearfully.

'It was lovely,' my mother gushed, like I had missed a great treat. 'And the flowers! Oh, you have never seen the like.'

'Coffin a bit ostentatious,' my father carped, then instantly brightened. 'Nice slice of Victoria sponge, though.'

As I listened to them, I wondered if it had occurred to my parents that I had recently lost two friends.

There must be something I could do, I fretted, to help find one of them.

26

SHERLOCK AND THE POLECAT

Interest in Etterly faded. It wasn't that people didn't care, just that they didn't know what else to do. It rose a little when somebody rushed out a pamphlet called *The Sackwater Ghost Tree*, listing other people, mainly children, who had entered the King's Oak never to be seen again. All of these other people turned out to be fictional, however – except for Rowdina Grael, who was very much alive and not missing – and the flurry of sightseers wandering around The Soundings dwindled.

Understandably, the death of Godfrey Skillern shocked people more. Here was an undoubtable tragedy that they could give their attention to, rather than a hotchpotch of speculation and superstition. I even heard rumours that Etterly had not been in The Soundings that day and we had all made it up to help her escape from a forced marriage to an elderly millionaire in Anglethorpe. Strangely, nobody seemed to know his name.

The day Godfrey died, I stopped going to the tree. There was nothing there now but horrible memories.

It was Pooky who first gave me the idea and I can't imagine why I didn't think of it before.

'What we need,' she informed me as she watched me scrub the scullery step, 'is Mr Sherlock Holmes.'

'I don't think he's real,' I puffed.

It was hard work getting the stain out from where Pooky had dropped a jar of beetroot.

'Not real?' Pooky laughed hollowly and she obviously liked that sound because she did it again. 'Not real? Why, he's in magazines and books and newspapers. He's even been in a moving picture show *and* my friend saw him in London walking down the street plain as I can see you not putting enough effort into that job.'

I scrubbed harder and faster.

'You should write him a letter,' she urged. 'One Hundred and Twenty Five, Gower Street.'

And then it hit me. Pooky had the right address. It was just that she had chosen the wrong man.

'Thank you, Pooky,' I said. 'I shall do that right away.'

I dropped the brush into the bucket and jumped up.

'No hurry,' Pooky assured me in something of a hurry herself. 'You can finish here first.'

'I need to catch the post,' I told her.

'Fine thing,' I heard her grumble as I went into the hall, 'when a maid has to clear up her own mess.' She raised her voice to an unattractive whine. 'Treat a skivvy like a skivvy, why don't you?' followed me up the stairs.

I wrote a letter – not to Mr Sherlock Holmes but to my godmother, March Middleton, known affectionately by me as Aunty M. Miss Middleton was the godchild of Sidney Grice, whose real-life adventures from 125 Gower Street were so extraordinary that more people believed in his fictional Baker Street counterpart than in the flesh-and-blood man himself.

Aunty M had gone to London as a young woman and advanced from being a resented witness and chronicler of Mr G's investigations to a valued – though he would never have admitted it – assistant. She had even worked on a number of cases by herself or, sometimes, with her friend Harriet Fitzpatrick. Aunty M's professional services were especially sought after by female clients who had heard of how her guardian had raised misogyny to new heights.

'Your choice of personal detective depends on whether you want sympathy or a solution,' Sidney Grice told one young lady having already remarked that she reminded him of a polecat.

Inexplicably – to Mr G at any rate – Aunty M told me with a chuckle, the client decided to engage her.

I got out my stationery set. Uncle Thaddeus had given it to me for Christmas when I was nine, mainly, I suspected, so that I could write and thank him for it and that was about the only use I had for his gift. I did write twenty-eight invitations to my tenth birthday party but my father, who I had to go to for stamps, 'forgot' to post them. It wouldn't have been such a grave crime if he had told me and not let me spend tearful weeks wondering why nobody had replied. It was the biggest argument I ever had with Etterly and the closest I came to falling out with Georgie.

Dear Aunty M, I began. *I trust you are well.*

I screwed up my first attempt and wrote *Dear Aunty M, I hope you are well.*

This too ended up in the bin.

I absent-mindedly sucked my nib and had to go to wash my lips, leaving the door ajar when I returned to my dressing table that served as a desk.

The gong went downstairs.

'Grub's up,' Pooky bellowed because she knew it embarrassed my mother, who had seven ladies from the Sackwater Christian Union of Mothers – otherwise known as SCUM – round for what she called a *Hwisst* drive.

I pretended not to hear. It was cold mutton with yesterday's mashed potatoes and soggy cauliflower.

Dear Aunty M, I began again.

'Come and get it,' Pooky hollered, banging the gong like it

was a fire alarm. There was a low conversation. 'Yes, I know you said not to call you today but I forgot, being so busy cleaning up from Miss Betty dropping a jar.'

I knew there was no point in running down and protesting. Pooky, who was guilty, was better at protesting innocence than I, who wasn't.

I need your help, I wrote.

I was hoping March Middleton would give me some advice. I knew she was always busy but she was a kind lady and I felt sure she wouldn't mind me asking.

27

THE GOAT AND THE UNICORN

I was helping Pooky and my mother rehang some washed net curtains in the waiting room – by which I mean I was putting them up while my mother gave useful advice like *Be careful* and *Watch what you're doing*. The wires hooked high on the tall sash window frames and I had to stand on tiptoe on a wooden chair that Pooky was holding for me, though it didn't require any steadying. Pooky would have done it all herself, she had explained, only she had no head for heights – and that from the woman who had taken me to the fair and made me stand and wait while she ran up the helter-skelter and whizzed down, squealing, with her skirt flying enough up her legs for the local clodhoppers to stand at the bottom whistling and cheering each of the twenty times she did it.

I had just managed – by stretching my left arm further than nature had constructed it – to hook one end of one curtain when the doorbell went.

My mother put her hands on her hips – something she was always telling me was *common* – and I realised they were both looking at me.

'Well, go on then,' Pooky said, forgetting her place.

'Well, I can't go,' my mother said without giving a reason and forgetting that the maid was forgetting her place.

'And I'm holding the chair,' Pooky reminded me.

I began to scramble down but tripped on the loose end of

netting, falling heavily on the floor and banging my head on a table on the way down.

'Oh my goodness,' my mother cried, 'you could have ripped it.'

'Stop acting the goat,' Pooky scolded.

'Oh for heaven's sake, do I have to do everything myself?' My mother marched off, leaving the door wide open.

Even in my semi-stunned state – the pain would come later – that seemed a bit rich. The only time my mother ever lifted a finger was to hook the handle of teacup.

'Don't be ridiculous. She never has telegrams,' we heard her say as I staggered to my feet. 'Give that here and go away. My maid will give you sixpence next time you come.'

He would have a long wait, I thought. On average, we got about one every two years.

'A telegram?' Pooky cried. 'Oh, I knew he would send for me.' She ripped off her starched white hat and flung it in the hearth. 'Well, good riddance and bad luck to the lot of you, you festering poxballs.' Pooky performed a little jig and she had her apron untied, over her head and crumpled before my mother returned, sidestepping the outstretched hand of our maid with a grace I imagined Barry Bennetts, the only rugby player whose name I knew, would have been happy with, and passed the folded message to me.

A telegram? I sat down. Telegrams meant somebody had died, though who it could be that I would be notified in preference to my parents, I didn't have time to contemplate.

'What have you been up to?' my mother demanded.

TRAIN ARRIVES NOON, I read silently, *MM*.

'It's Aunty M,' I said.

'Don't be ridiculous,' my mother told me. Almost everyone was ridiculous in her eyes except the one truly ridiculous person she saw every day in the mirror. *'It's aren't E M*? What's that supposed to mean?'

'It's the way young people talk,' Pooky misinformed her.

'March Middleton,' I explained. 'She is coming here.'

'The policewoman?' Pooky hissed. 'She can't prove anything.'

'Oh, Father,' my mother gasped, 'I told you your sins would find you out.'

'What?' I rubbed my knee with one hand, clutching the paper in my other.

'Just a little joke,' my mother tinkled. 'Here? Let me see.' She snatched the telegram from me then brayed in relief. 'You silly goose. She has just written to tell you when a train arrives. She is not coming here at all.'

'But why?' I asked, genuinely baffled.

'Oh, you know what they're like in London.' My mother waved the paper over her head like she was trying to place a bet.

I didn't actually, but I still felt fairly sure I was right.

'Anyway, MM could be somebody else,' Pooky theorised, picking up her hat and glaring at me. 'Mr Mayne, for instance.' And seeing our blank looks, she explained, 'Ernie Mayne, the fat man who sings "Fried Fruit Fritters".'

'Anyway,' my mother pointed out, 'it doesn't say what day.'

'And it can't be today because it's after twelve already,' Pooky reasoned.

'What's going on?' My father came into the room, hair shifted strangely sideways by his nap. 'I heard a crash.'

'Oh, that was just Betty showing off,' my mother explained.

'Mr Show-Off went to town,' my father quoted, but I never found out what for, or even what happened to the gentleman in question.

'Miss Betty' – Pooky rubbed a smudge into her hat – 'has received a telegram.'

'Has Philly died?' my father asked hopefully. We all liked Aunt Philly, but my father liked the idea of her money even more.

'March Middleton is coming to town,' I got in before my mother could witter on about trains again.

My father paled.

'What have you told her?' he asked me hoarsely.

'Just that Etterly is missing and I wanted help to find her,' I said.

'So you didn't mention—' he began.

'Tra la laaaa. Trally lally lally la,' my mother sang loudly and actually quite tunefully, for her.

My father had mouthed something, but I couldn't catch or lip-read it.

'I was just—' he began again as Pooky tied her scrunched-up apron on in a bow.

'Tra la laaaa,' my mother sang again, and then, as if my father was the only one who could possibly catch her words, 'Traddeley remember Triddely what dee we said. Tra la la.'

It was then, thank goodness, that the doorbell rang.

28

SWEAT, BLOOD AND SALIVA

Pooky, rather bedraggled, went to the door.

'My card,' a man's voice said, and I recognised it immediately. Had March Middleton sent her guardian in her place?

'If you are selling something—' Pooky began.

'Read it, girl,' Sidney Grice commanded, and I rushed into the hall just in time to catch sight of Pooky smirking – a revolting spectacle – because it was a long time since anyone had called her that. 'And do not attempt to occlude my ingress.'

Our visitor brandished his cane like that Spartan warrior who guarded the pass at Thermopylae.

'Uncle G,' I greeted him, and he took my hand gravely.

Sidney Grice was a small man, slightly built, his long lashes and bow lips giving him an almost effeminate appearance. He had a dimpled chin and although he was in his early seventies by then, his hair was still thick and black. Later I wondered if he dyed it. He was certainly vain enough to.

'You are indebted to me, young lady,' he said, his voice soft but not soothing.

'Indeed I am. This—' I began.

'For the postage and penalty I was obliged to disburse to receive your unfranked missive.'

'But…' I turned to Pooky. I hadn't wanted my parents to see the letter, so she had agreed to buy a stamp and post it for me.

'I needed a cream cake,' she told me.

'Why are you a maid?' Sidney Grice demanded.

'What?' she blustered. 'I don't—'

'You have a grade sixteen accent on the Grice Phonological Revised Social Scale,' he told her, 'which the uninitiated might reasonably describe as middle middle-class, and though you have lived in the better environs of Mayfair,' Sidney Grice continued, 'you were raised in Cheltenham, above rather than below stairs.'

'I fell on hard times,' Pooky admitted.

'Little wonder you despise your parvenu employers,' the great detective sympathised. 'It is rare that I find anything in common with an unkempt serving wench,' he said, thereby offending every adult present, though I did not mind in the least.

'Good afternoon, Mr G,' my mother greeted him. Her knees buckled and I thought she was going to collapse, but from the way she pinched her dress at the sides, I realised she was trying to do a curtsy.

'Mr Grice,' he corrected her. 'Miss Middleton is permitted to address me in such a familiar fashion because she has occasionally proved not useless to me and I have extended that permission to your daughter because I dislike her less than every other infant I have had the misfortune to encounter.'

'Oh,' my mother said, and would have said more had he not ploughed on, 'I suspect you were wishing me a good afternoon rather than informing me that it is one. It is not and I shall not be having one.'

'Oh,' my mother managed again.

'Welcome to my home, Mr Grice.' My father stuck out his hand but Sidney Grice glanced at it in disgust.

'Kindly make more valiant endeavours to practise manual hygiene before you thrust that part of your anatomy at me again,' he instructed. 'The combined stenches of saliva, sweat, blood, an assortment of chemicals, which I shall only enumerate if you implore me to...' The great detective paused but, finding no such request was forthcoming, continued, 'four different, though all unpleasant, types of combusted tobacco, bodily sweat and another fluid to which I shall not ascribe a title within the auditory range of your alleged daughter and impoverished ungainly maid.'

I noticed that he was not concerned about my mother's sensitivities.

Sidney Grice looked my father up and down. My father cleared his throat. The detective ambled clockwise around him, cane over his shoulder, returning with a sigh, and all that time my father stood as erect as his portliness allowed, eyes front like a guardsman being inspected by his monarch.

'Your great secret,' Mr G told him, 'is safe with me.'

From the way my father gasped, he must have been holding his breath.

'Thank you,' he said earnestly.

'By which' – Mr G resumed his stroll in an anticlockwise direction – 'I mean I shall ensure that the knowledge of it never dies.'

My father gulped, but Sidney Grice had become engrossed in my mother, something very few men, in my experience, had ever managed to do.

'What a splendid specimen you are,' he said, and she simpered. 'Of mediocrity,' he concluded.

'Has Aunty M not come?' I asked, and Uncle G swished his cane like he was clearing his way through a nettle patch.

'Miss Middleton has not *not* come to Sackwater,' he told me. 'She is delayed in purchasing supplies of cigarrrretes.' He rolled his Rs like Harry Lauder Roaming in the Gloaming.

'And gin,' March Middleton said, stepping in through the open door.

29

THE DEATH OF AREANUS AND THE ALIAS TREE

I rushed over and March Middleton opened her arms.

'Aunty M,' I cried happily as she gave me a big hug.

At the age of thirteen I was almost the same height as my godmother and she must have noticed the same for she held me by the shoulders, her face wreathed in smiles, and said, 'Betty, darling, how you have grown. Quite the young lady now.'

'Still a mere girl,' Sidney Grice muttered.

'Do not mind him,' Aunty M told me. 'He is sulking because I made him come.'

'Nobody makes me go anywhere,' he sniffed. 'I came because I am bored and, much as I detest anywhere that is not London and a great many places that are, at least this is not' – his voice sank dramatically – 'the north-west.'

'But what is wrong with that?' I asked, and he wrinkled his nose.

'Nothing good has ever come from there,' he assured me.

'I came from the north-west,' Aunty M remarked mildly.

'Nothing,' he repeated drily, and set about tapping the wall with the handle of his cane, his ear pressed against the flowery wallpaper.

March Middleton shook hands with both my parents, though I couldn't help noticing that she wiped her fingers discreetly on a powder-blue handkerchief after greeting my father. I suppose I had always thought that was how he smelled. Most of the ground floor of our house did as well.

'I am sorry we have come—'

'So am I,' Mr G concurred.

'At such short notice,' she continued, 'but we are on an important case' – she ignored her godfather's indignant *We?* and finished – 'and have our passages booked on a ship this evening.'

'This is indeed an honour,' my father grovelled, like an ancient retainer being introduced to his monarch.

'Be quiet,' Uncle G snapped, rapping so hard in one spot that I saw a number of dents appear. He stopped and raised his pince-nez on the string around his neck with as much straining and grunting as if he were raising an anchor. 'Ah.' He clipped his pince-nez onto his long slender nose. 'So…' He produced a magnifying glass as if from thin air and peered through it at a mark on the stem of a rose. 'This is where she was killed,' he announced, spinning around to face us all.

'Whom?' my mother quavered, because she thought whom was more correct, however it was used, in formal circumstances.

'Areanus Diadematus,' Sidney Grice proclaimed.

'I don't think I know her,' my father said in confusion. 'Was she a patient?'

'It is an orb weaver – a kind of spider,' March Middleton explained.

'But hwhy is it important?' my mother asked, with her posh extra h.

Sidney Grice stepped over to examine her through his glass.

'It is almost as plain as the nose on your face,' the detective told her, tossing the magnifier into the air, where it appeared to hang for an unnaturally long time before disappearing. He had once promised to teach me that trick just as soon as I told him how it was done, which was the closest I ever knew to him making a joke. 'But' – he whipped off his pince-nez – 'you are wasting my time.' He pointed his cane in my direction. 'I wish to scrutinise the so-called King's Oak alias the Ghost Tree and you, Miss Church, are the very person to accompany me there.' He jabbed the cane towards March Middleton. 'You may come too, if you promise not to misbehave, for I am fearful that the saline-polluted air may encourage your penchant for frivolity.'

'I am unlikely to have an opportunity to do anything too dreadful,' Aunty M chuckled.

'Come, youngest and least obnoxious Church,' Mr G urged and, whipping his card back out of Pooky's grasp, he marched out of the door, stopping so suddenly on the gravel driveway with me at his heels that I ran straight into his back. 'Dear me,' he said as I cringed in expectation of a rebuke. 'It might be safer for us both if you walked by my side.'

We made our way to the pavement.

'Wait for me,' Aunty M called. 'I had to tidy myself up.'

'If only she would,' Uncle G murmured. 'I have fifteen words of advice for you and they are these,' he said confidentially. 'Do not let Miss Middleton distress you. Her bark is much worse than her bite.'

'She seems very kind to me,' I told him as we waited for a funeral procession to pass by.

'That is only,' he assured me, 'because she is.'

And then, to my astonishment, Sidney Grice took hold of my hand.

30

KING CHARLES AND THE VERMIN

It took a great deal longer than usual to get to The Soundings. We had to stop several times for Sidney Grice to scoop samples of dirt from the gutter or pluck leaves from a privet hedge, all of which he placed in tiny test tubes sealed with corks, labelled in his own secret shorthand and placed into his bulging shoulder bag.

We stopped at the end of Tennis Court Road, where a middle-aged man was spraying his roses.

'Lady Mary Fitzwilliam,' Uncle G told me. 'Do not fritter your hours in seeking pleasant perfumes from hybrid tea roses for they have none worth pursuing.'

I sort of knew that, but I liked to listen to him telling me things.

Mr G flicked open a penknife, selected a flower and, watched by the owner in disbelief, sliced it off.

'Oy,' he shouted. 'What's your game?'

'I shall not attempt to respond to that interrogation, since I play no games of any category, but shall counter your enquiry with one of my own,' Sidney Grice told him grandly. 'Do you know who I am?'

'No,' the man admitted, clearly under the impression that he should.

'Good,' Mr G said. 'Then you will find it more difficult to track me down and secure a prosecution… unless you intend to physically detain me, and you would not enjoy that.'

'What?' The man gaped incredulously.

'I believe I spoke clearly and at sufficient volume.' Sidney

Grice slipped the rose into his buttonhole. 'And that, even in the un-rugged wilds of East Anglia, a rudimentary form of the English language is attempted and, in some measure, understood.'

Aunty M opened her handbag, rooted about, and produced a packet of Parma Violets.

'Would you care for those?' She offered the man the whole pack. 'They will sweeten your breath.'

'Why, thank you very much, ma'am.' The man bowed. 'My missus will be well pleasured.'

We crossed Pelican Road, Uncle G taking hold of my hand again.

'Mr Grice and I have been following the case in the newspapers,' Aunty M told me, ignoring her guardian's mutterings about the vermin of Fleet Street, 'and I sent to both Sackwater Police Stations for further information but we had a case in Ostend and only got back to Gower Street last night.'

'And you came straight here,' I marvelled.

'I am still unclear as to how you intend to reimburse me,' Sidney Grice told me.

'I shall pay your fee,' Aunty M said, and Mr G's grip tightened.

'You most certainly shall not,' he insisted. 'I am still struggling to recover from the first and last time you did that.'

I had heard something about the Mangle Street Murders but it was a few years before I was able to read all the gruesome details. Many believed that Sidney Grice had sent an innocent man to the gallows. It had, Aunty M confided, almost destroyed her godfather's career.

'I am sorry, Uncle G,' I said, 'but you are hurting my hand.'

Sidney Grice let go and bent to peer at my fingers.

'It is I who should be sorry' – he straightened up – 'but I so very rarely am.'

We came to The Soundings.

'How did it get its name?' Aunty M asked.

'I don't know,' I told her. 'I never thought about it.'

'Asinine girl,' Mr G whispered in a way that sounded almost affectionate. 'One should always think about everything.'

'Is that possible?' I queried.

'I shall think about that,' he promised.

'It might be because sailors call measured depths of water "soundings",' Aunty M suggested.

'Nobody, other than yourself, is interested in your ill-educated speculations,' Mr G told her. 'Now, Miss Betty Greene Vardiman Black Church' – I hated my father for naming me after the man who had classified dental cavities – 'am I to take it that' – Sidney Grice produced a pair of binoculars, though we were only thirty feet away – 'this is the angiosperm, *Quercus robur*, in which I am expected to take an interest?'

'No,' Aunty M replied. 'It is a double-decker bus.'

I laughed and Mr G winced. 'I fear your godmother is mistaking stupidity for wit. Exactly how old – give or take fourteen weeks – is it?'

'I don't know,' I admitted. 'King Charles—'

'Though his very life and kingdom were imperilled' – Sidney Grice waved his cane like a demented conductor – 'His fecund Majesty was never so desperate as to be obliged to visit Sackwater. In that he had an incalculable advantage over me.'

I was not sure if I was expected to respond to that but soon found out I wasn't, because Mr G set off as if a starting gun had been fired. He had an odd run, his shortened right leg making him dip sideways as if he were falling over, but he could still get up quite a speed.

'Let him go,' Aunty M said as she strolled in his wake. 'He is never happier than when he has the scent of something.'

'Do you think he will find anything?' I asked.

We went through a gap in the hedge.

'He always finds something.' March Middleton rolled her eyes. 'He has a fortified warehouse full of things he has found,' she told me despairingly. 'If there are any clues, Betty, be sure Mr G will discover them, but all the evidence may have been destroyed by now.'

I looked at the oak as we got nearer. What had once been our den now stood gaunt and menacing before us.

Sidney Grice was walking around the tree, watching it carefully like a wrestler looking for the best way to grapple with his opponent.

'Who,' he demanded as we approached, 'constructed and fitted that?' He rapped at the door with his cane.

Was he expecting a footman to open it for him? Unsurprisingly, nobody did.

'I think it was done because—'

Mr G stopped me with an upheld hand. His fingers were long and slender and I had not noticed before that his little finger was the same length as his ring finger.

'Do not worsen my poor opinion of you, Miss Church, by pretending to imagine that you are answering my question.'

'I think Mr Beddingfield, the carpenter, made it,' I said. 'At least, I heard talk that he was going to.'

'Beddingfield with two Ds?' he asked.

'I think so.'

'That is' – Sidney Grice twirled his stick like a drum major – 'the best way to spell it. One D would be parsimonious; three would be extravagant. You may now tell me why.'

For a second I thought he wanted me to explain the spelling.

'Because people were worried that somebody else might go in and not come out again,' I told him.

Mr G brought a cigarette case out of his bag and flipped it

open. I had seen his collection of picks before and he had even given me a lesson in using them, but, to my relief, he did not expect me to put my training to use. He crouched and selected a series of what looked like hooked toothpicks, sliding them into the top lock and giving each a little twist. I understand a great many things,' he informed me, though I knew that already, 'but I fail to comprehend why Pepper and Sons, the manufacturers, are allowed to market these inelegant ornaments as security devices.' He tapped the casing twice with a fingerplate, as he liked to call it, and the lock fell open.

'Where did you play your game of rounders?' March asked me.

'Does she ever stop chattering?' Sidney Grice groaned.

He had probably spoken hundreds more words than his ward, but I did not think it my place to point that out.

'Yes,' I answered him a little nervously.

'Indeed she does,' he agreed amiably.

'Over there,' I replied to my godmother. 'We put the base in front of that gap in the hedge.'

'When I was your age, many girls were not allowed to play vigorous sports at school,' she told me. 'It was thought jumping around would harm a lady's... internal organs.'

'Did you never play games?' I asked.

'Oh, all the time' — she smiled — 'but then I never went to school.'

I found myself walking arm in arm with my godmother towards the site of our pitch.

'But how did you learn?' I asked in amazement, because she was the cleverest woman I had ever met.

'My father knew a great many things and loved telling me about them,' Aunty M told me. 'And also there was an extensive library in The Grange, our home in Parbold, and I have always loved to read.'

'It was about here.' I stopped.

March Middleton surveyed the square.

'You said in your letter that you saw a shadowy man,' she remembered.

'Behind that tree,' I said, 'then later near the oak tree.'

'Was it as sunny as this?'

'Yes, and about this time,' I told her.

'And where were you?'

'On first base, over there.

'I wonder if I could ask you to stand where he was,' Aunty M proposed, and I went to the spot.

'Can you see me?' she called, shading her eyes.

'Clearly,' I answered.

'Shall we go and see what Mr Grice is up to?'

I joined her and we walked back.

'I could only make you out in silhouette,' she told me, 'but I could tell you were a girl, so it makes sense that you knew it was a man.'

'Thank you,' I said gratefully. 'I was beginning to think I couldn't have.'

We stopped to watch a squirrel tightrope-walking along a telephone wire.

'The first time I came to East Anglia was almost my last,' Aunty M said sorrowfully. 'But that was near Ely and a long time ago.'

Sidney Grice was standing a few yards back from the tree, staring up through his binoculars. His cane projected from a knothole.

'She did not climb out at the top,' he announced, 'nor did anybody else. That lichen has not been disturbed for at least nine weeks. I have not entered the cavity yet because I want you to tell me how the interior has changed since the last time you saw Miss Utter gain ingress.'

I peered into the hollow.

'A lot of people have been in since then,' I warned. 'Some of them dug the earth up because there was a rumour that Etterly was buried here or there was a secret trapdoor to a tunnel.'

'Anything else, dear?' Aunty M encouraged me.

'We left all our cardigans inside and Etterly had brought a bottle of lemonade.'

'What sort?' Mr G asked.

'Home-made,' I told him.

'Good.' He clapped his hands. 'The commercial products are an affront to the gustatory organs of humanity.'

'I think that's about it,' I said. 'A policeman found some names and initials carved inside and wrote them down.'

'What an enterprising fellow,' Mr G said approvingly. 'In nine minutes' time you will give me his name and serial number and any other details that I see fit to extract from you.'

'He…' I began, but he stopped me with a finger to his lips.

'In your juvenile enthusiasm you have commenced your report eight minutes and fifty-three seconds prematurely.' Sidney Grice bent at the knees, leaned backwards and limbo-walked through the hole. 'But I am preparing to commence to consider forgiving you,' he called from inside, his voice strangely eerie, as if the oak really did deserve to be known as the Ghost Tree.

31

THE SINISTER MIRROR AND DIMENSIONALLY STABLE PUTTY

A weird buzzing noise came out of the King's Oak.

'He is humming,' Aunty M responded to my puzzled looks. Mr G's musical efforts seemed to consist of two notes at varying speeds. 'A composition of his own,' she explained.

'I thought he hated music,' I said.

'Oh, he does,' she confirmed. 'He wrote this piece to illustrate to me how annoying it can be and, heaven knows, he has achieved that purpose. He hummed it all the way here. Luckily, we had the carriage to ourselves – well, after the first stop,' she giggled.

Despite being in her mid-fifties, there was still something skittish about my godmother and I suspect it was her reaction to living under the same roof as a man who professed to despise any pleasure that did not serve a practical purpose.

'I am delighted to note,' Mr G announced, appearing suddenly through the hole like a woodland creature with his pince-nez clipped to his nose, 'that all the evidence – with the exception of approximately seven hundred and forty-four dehydrated blood droplets, twenty-four plasma smears, eighty-four human hairs and one hundred and twenty-four carvings, some of which the fine constable, if I am to give credence to your evidence, detected and made copies of, though I do not trust him sufficiently as not to make my own exquisite replicas – has been removed or destroyed.'

Sidney Grice waved his notebook triumphantly while I reconstructed his declaration to try to make some sense of it. March Middleton shrugged to show that she could not enlighten me.

Does he never take a breath? I marvelled.

'Why are you pleased that the evidence has gone, Uncle G?' I asked.

'That was the one thousand, three hundred and twenty-sixth most intelligent question I have heard in the last fourteen years,' he told me. 'Miss Middleton would do well to try to emulate you.' Mr G turned back to the tree. 'And kindly tell your alleged godmother to stop projecting her oral musculature in my direction. I would direct her myself, but she rarely heeds my instructions.'

Aunty M retracted her tongue.

'How—?' I began.

'I have an ingenious device, which directs images to my retina, attached to the outer perimeter on my pince-nez,' he explained, whipping it off to show me two tiny mirrors on the right-hand frame.

'Why do you have one on both sides?' I asked, because his right eye was made of glass.

And please don't tell me what number that question is, I prayed, and was then slightly insulted that he didn't think it merited such an honour.

'I have fourteen reasons for the dexter positioning of a reflectorrr,' he purred, 'but I shall only reveal two of them for the time being. First, so that I can use it to scrutinise the view behind me whilst holding the pince-nez in a seemingly casual manner with my elegant digits. Second, to balance the weight of the sinister mirror.' Sidney Grice bent his knees as if he were sitting on an invisible bench. 'I have written a fascinating monograph on the dating of arboreal carvings. To simplify the thrust of my research, it is possible to calculate their age with a margin of error in the region of eight and one quarter per centum by, amongst other factors, observing the degree of discolouration of mechanically exposed wood instigated, amongst yet other factors, by dehydration and oxidation of the lignin therein.' He straightened up. 'And the one to which I wish you to give your attention presently would appear to have been created shortly prior to the so-called Miss Etterly Utter's putative departure.' Mr G opened his notebook very carefully, as if he expected something to jump out at him. 'The carving, which I have reproduced here on a scale of one and seven-eighteenths to one and four-nineteenths, attracted my attention more than its fellows for, amongst other reasons, it is not recorded in Dr Palimbo P. Polimba's *Encyclopaedia of Unskilled Engravings*.' He lowered the book, reluctantly it seemed. 'Do you have any constructive remarks to make about that?'

Mr G jabbed the page with his thumb, but he was still holding it so high that I had to stand on tiptoe to get a peek before he whipped it away.

'Yes,' I replied.

'That is the most interesting syllable you have given utterance to since I arrived in this filthy para-marine territory,' Mr G told me approvingly. 'What do you wish to tell me about it?'

'I don't know what the sign means,' I said, 'but I have seen it before.'

'Can you remember where, dear?' March Middleton asked.

'Of course she can,' her godfather insisted. 'Not all females are as hare-brained as you.'

'Nor all men as bigoted and rude,' she observed with surprisingly little malice.

'In Mr Utter's shop,' I remembered. 'It was on a scrap of paper behind the counter. I saw it when I went to see if Etterly could come out.'

'And could she?' Sidney Grice demanded.

It seemed an irrelevant question at the time, but I wished afterwards that I had given it more consideration. Mr Utter was usually easy-going about giving his daughter time off. After all, he hadn't really needed her in the first place, but that day he made me feel distinctly unwelcome.

'Thank the Lord somebody do come to get her out from under my feet,' he had joked with me previously, but today I had seen an uncharacteristically grim man.

'Dint pay her to goo out playin' all day,' he had told me gruffly.

Etterly had been on the brink of tears, not indignant as she would be normally, at the restriction.

'I'm sorry,' I had muttered, and I was. I hadn't meant to cause trouble between them.

Mr Utter had been totting up some figures on a brown paper bag. This in itself was unusual because Etterly usually did that, being better at sums than her father. Perhaps they were receipts and he was anxious about the slackness of his business. I wasn't trying to read what he had written but I couldn't help but notice the symbol in the bottom right-hand corner.

'No,' I told Mr G. 'Her father wouldn't let her.'

'Dear me,' Mr G sighed, and he looked genuinely put out but immediately recovered. 'And what do you infer from your observation?' he questioned me, pointing his cane at the sky in a schoolmasterly way.

'Well, he might have drawn it himself or just picked up a bag that Etterly had been drawing on,' I began.

'Those are two of the nineteen most likely explanations,' Mr G told me encouragingly. 'Whilst you and Miss Middleton were taking the air—'

'We were examining the scene,' Aunty M corrected him, but her words went unheeded.

'—I was gainfully employed.' He put a finger to his right eye, but I suspect this was more from force of habit than to prevent it from falling out. His glass eyes fitted much more accurately since his goddaughter had started supervising their construction and fitting. 'In making an impression—'

'He never fails to do that,' Aunty M whispered, and was rewarded with a click of the tongue.

'—of the carvings in Grice Patent Pending Fairly Rapidly Setting and Exceptionally Accurate and Dimensionally Stable Putty,' he continued.

'Catchy name,' she commented.

'Do not feel obliged to smirk at Miss Middleton's forays into the world of sarcasm,' Mr G told me, though I had smiled quite spontaneously. He brought out a flat metal box, rather like one I had for my watercolour paints and brushes, and hinged back the lid to reveal it was almost exactly like my set, except that the sections for the tablets were bigger and filled with what looked like clay rectangles with various shapes raised from their surfaces. 'Have you brought a magnifying glass with you?'

'I am afraid I haven't got one,' I confessed.

'Why on earth would she?' Aunty M asked.

'Why on earth would she not,' he retorted, letting go of his cane, which stayed standing unsupported but upright. 'There is little to fear in your omission,' he reassured me. 'Fortunately for you, I have come equipped with my second favourite loupe, which I am lending to you...' Mr G opened his hand to reveal a jewellers' eyeglass nestling magically in his palm. 'Now,' he declared.

I took the glass uncertainly and wedged the carved ivory cylinder between my eyebrow and cheek.

'Examine it carefully.' A giant blurred finger jabbed the air just above a block in the outline of a heart and I bent over it. 'Note the profile,' Mr G instructed. 'To make matters simpler for your feeble feminine cerebrum, I shall elucidate. The incision in the wood is broad at the surface, tapering to a point at the base, as even you, an ignorant and ill-educated East Anglian progeny, can observe after I have drawn your attention to the matter.'

'Yes, I see.' I agreed with the statement, though not with the way he had expressed it.

'Whereas this one' – his finger darted to the one we had already discussed – 'has...'

He paused, awaiting my response.

'A flat base,' I said.

'Concisely and not too inaccurately summarised.' Mr G snapped the lid shut so fast that he almost nipped my retreating fingers. 'Now give me a plausible interpretation of your findings.'

'The carving with a thin base was cut with a knife but the flatter one was cut with something blunter,' I stumbled, and Mr G blinked slowly, his right eye not quite closing.

'*Exempli gratia*?' he asked, and I had reluctantly learned enough Latin at school to know that meant e.g.

'A small screwdriver, such as one a watchmaker might use,' Aunty M said, slightly to my annoyance because I was about to suggest a blunt knife, then to my relief for the same reason.

Sidney Grice glared.

'How is your goddaughter to become a policewoman whom you will not be embarrassed by and ashamed of if you persist in coaching her with your wild but freakishly accurate guesses?'

My heart soared. Sidney Grice, the greatest detective in the British Empire and therefore – in his estimation – the world, had said that I could be a policewoman.

'I shall never be embarrassed by Betty, though I often am by you,' March Middleton retorted, 'and as to being ashamed, you need not think I have forgotten the Affington Affair.'

'I was not to know that she had not eaten him,' Mr G flared.

'Etterly used little screwdrivers to help repair watches in her father's shop,' I realised, and they broke off their squabble to look at me.

'Ah!' Sidney Grice barked, and fell to the ground as if he had been shot.

32

ARMADILLIDIUM CHURCH AND THE WORM CHARMER

Sidney Grice lay face down on the dry patchy grass. I had read about this sort of thing in *Armstrong of the Amazon*, where leopard-skin-clad tribesmen blew poisoned darts from high in the trees, causing Armstrong's canoe-paddling tribesmen to clutch their necks and fall into the water and a bloody frenzy of piranhas.

'Uncle G,' I cried, and was about to kneel beside him when March Middleton caught my arm.

'It is all right, darling,' she told me. 'He is just showing off.'

The great detective was snuffling at the soil, his fingers raking through it like a truffle hunter in search of his prize. He stopped and took a tiny pinch of soil between his right thumb and little finger, his left hand going behind him like he had been put into an armlock by Crusher Kent, who used to set up a ring on the promenade, challenging passers-by to fight him, while he wore a blindfold, for a shilling entrance fee and a ten-guinea prize.

Mr G slipped a hand into his satchel and brought out an envelope to drop his find inside, licked the flap and sealed it. He shuffled backwards like a confused crab, taking more samples and saving them as he went, handing his envelope up to his goddaughter with instructions to label each one with a number, beginning at forty-eight.

'Stand clear,' he warned, and leaped straight onto his feet.

'What have you found?' I asked.

'A new species of *Armadillidium*,' he declared.

'Woodlouse,' Aunty M explained.

'Which I would like to name *Armadillidium Church* after you.' He brushed some earth off his waistcoat, but left a great deal untouched.

'Why, thank you.' I glowed at the honour. Nothing had been named after me before and probably never would be again.

'But I prefer to name it *Armadillidium Grice* after myself,' he told me. 'Also, nine particles of ferric oxide and six osseous slivers.'

I did not realise at the time that he meant *rust and bone splinters*. I was too busy feeling miffed at having my honour snatched away.

'Godfrey Skillern.' Sidney Grice said the name so suddenly that I shrank back. 'Tell me,' he commanded.

'Do not upset her,' Aunty M warned.

'If Miss Church is discomposed, it is by events and uncertainty.' He tapped a bare patch of earth with his cane lightly, many times, a bit like Etterly and I had once watched a worm charmer failing to charm any worms to the surface.

'I saw him die here,' I said, and Mr G clicked his tongue.

'I have read a great deal on the subject and was given to understand that you set off on an admirable, though ultimately purposeless, mission to summon medical assistance,' he told me, 'and was informed that Master Skillern expired whilst you were on your quest. Was I misinformed?'

'No, I... He was dead when I came back,' I said, fighting back the tears.

'Then why,' Sidney Grice demanded, 'did you attempt to mislead me by claiming to witness his demise?'

'I...'

Aunty M put an arm around my shoulder.

'You are confusing Betty,' she protested. 'Can you not see she is distressed?'

Mr G clipped his pince-nez back on.

'She does appear to be disquieted,' he conceded.

I choked unhappily.

'In which case,' Mr G resumed, 'I shall postpone voicing the observation that Miss Church herself could have been implicated in causing or accelerating the demise of young Godfrey Skillern.'

'You have gone too far,' March Middleton raged.

'Too far for what?' he asked, perplexed.

'For Betty,' she said furiously.

'Are you sure?' he asked with something approaching consternation.

'Of course I am sure,' March Middleton railed at her guardian furiously.

I blew my nose.

'I bow to your judgement in such matters,' Uncle G said gravely. 'For you have a greater empathy than I with immature female histrionics.'

Aunty M was right that Sidney Grice had gone too far, but now he had gone beyond even that. I have never been a cry-baby and I knew how the great detective despised any sign of weakness, but I couldn't help myself. I burst into tears.

'Let her go,' Mr G told his goddaughter, though I had not yet gone anywhere. 'I have accumulated all the evidence she requires and she is of little use to me in such a hysterical condition.' This was too much. I rushed towards the hedge. 'Come, Miss Middleton,' Sidney Grice urged unheedingly. 'We must board that ferry if we are to have any expectations of apprehending the so-called *Parasite of Palma*.'

'I am sorry, Betty,' March Middleton called after me.

'So you should be,' Mr G assured her. 'You know how it upsets people to hear me criticised.'

I heard nothing more from or about Aunty M or Mr G until three weeks later, when Pooky took mournful delight in drawing my attention to a newspaper headline PARASITE OF PALMA APPREHENDED, MARCH MIDDLETON GRIEVOUSLY INJURED.

'Looks like she isn't immortal after all,' she gloated, though I did not believe Aunty M had ever claimed to be.

It was some time before I realised that Pooky bore March Middleton a grudge for sending that telegram, but it was hardly my godmother's fault that Pooky had been expecting a summons from somebody else.

I wrote at once to express my concern and enquire about my godmother's health, but received no reply. It was obvious, though, from a blurry photograph in the *Daily Mail* several months later with the caption MARCH MIDDLETON CORNERS FIEND OF FENCHURCH ON ROOFTOP, that she was still very much alive.

It would be twenty-six years, however, before we discussed Etterly Utter again.

PART 2 – 1940

1

DUNKIRK, HURRICANES AND THE THIRD FEAR

It was a lovely day on the Angle Estuary. The sun shone and there was only the lightest of breezes. A mistle thrush was collecting moss from a post on the landing stage to line her nest. Our hens pecked contentedly at the scraps I had given them and our rabbits nibbled in the nettle patch, unconcerned by my approach. All seemed right with the world, but very little was.

However much the BBC tried to present the situation, the British and French armies had not so much retreated from the Germans as fled in disarray and now, only eighty miles from where I stood, the bulk of our men were trapped at Dunkirk with the Royal Navy – the greatest force ever to patrol the oceans – apparently unable to help them.

Captain Carmelo Sultana heaved his bulging canvas kitbag up onto the deck of *Cressida* – the landlocked boat he had built for his home on Brindle Bar.

'Madonna it is half hot,' he complained.

'Can't be as bad as home,' I commented.

'This' – he swept an arm from the direction of the Angle Estuary behind us to Treacle Hill rising in front – 'is home.' The captain was very proud of his British citizenship and he had more than justified it in the last war. 'In Malta it would be nothing,' he conceded, 'but there I would not be dressed like Scott of the Antarctic.'

Despite the heat, Carmelo had his duffel coat on. It was too bulky to pack and he would need it when he got to Ramsgate on the Kent coast, where most of the boats were expected to dock.

'Come back safely,' I fussed, and Captain nodded.

'I fear three things above all others,' he told me. 'The sea, the military might of Germany.' He stopped.

'And the third?' I prompted.

'You.' He grinned. 'So you can be sure I shall obey.' He shouldered his bag and leaned towards me. 'Goodbye, Qalbi.'

I kissed his cheek, a prickly experience because Carmelo had not had a shave for the last few days. A growth of stubble – or, better still, a beard – protects your skin from the salt spray, he had told me.

'I shall have to take your word for that,' I had assured him.

The captain straightened his old naval cap, his pigtail swinging behind it. He had not had a haircut since I had met him – only five years, I realised in surprise, because it felt like we had known each other all my life.

'Just don't do anything reckless,' I said – a useless instruction when we both knew he, and hundreds like him, were taking terrible risks and he was not a man to try to avoid them.

'It has to be done,' he said simply.

The sea was nothing like deep enough at Dunkirk for the warships to get within a mile of the shore, the captain had explained, which was why he was going to help an old shipmate sail his shallow-draught boat across the Channel.

I watched Carmelo clamber into *Genevieve* and remembered how I had nearly been swept out to sea in that old rowing boat one night. He pulled strongly across the narrow stretch of water to Shingle Bay, jumped heavily out and beached his craft. There was a rope tied to a cleat at the stern so that I could pull her back again.

The captain strode steadily, despite his load and the sun beating down.

'Don't die,' I whispered and, as if he had heard me, Carmelo turned and gave a final wave.

It was not often that I was by myself on *Cressida*. It doesn't worry me to be alone, but I get bored quickly with nobody to talk to. Even Jimmy wasn't there to annoy me. Carmelo's great-nephew was stationed nearby at Hadling Heath Aerodrome and, from the wiggle of the wings of his Hurricane in greeting as he passed overhead, was in and out on sorties many times a day. He was unlikely to be sent to France, he had told us. His squadron and many others were being kept in reserve for the invasion that must soon be launched now that Hitler had the Russians on his side and most of Europe in his clutches. We had lost the best of our army and much of its equipment already and it didn't seem likely that a fleet of fishing and pleasure boats could rescue many men, especially with the blue skies providing perfect conditions for the Luftwaffe to strafe them.

If truth be told, I should not have been back on duty for months yet. I had still not fully recovered from being too close to a stray bomb earlier in the year and then being held prisoner with no food or drink for two days – but I had had enough of my own company and was ready to impose it on somebody else – the East Suffolk Constabulary might not appreciate it, but I did not intend to give them any choice.

2

STARFISH AND THE LISTENERS

I sowed a line of Gallaher's and rolled a cigarette, inordinately proud, as always, of my ability to do it one-handed, sparked my Zippo Windproof and lit up, leaning over the rail like a passenger on a cruise to enjoy my first smoke of the day. Tobacco was not rationed yet but stocks were already running low, so I eked out my supply, trying to smoke less and making my roll-ups thinner. Many people had started nipping their cigarettes, keeping the unsmoked half for later, but I refused to be reduced to smoking dog-ends. It was one step away from picking them up off the street.

I went downstairs – or *below*, as the captain insisted I should call it – to my cabin. My left forearm floated like a prize salmon in an anatomical specimen jar filled with formalin. I had lost it while I was still a sergeant in Bloomsbury and that would have ended my career if it was not for March Middleton's influence and my shameless blackmailing of a commanding officer. Its steel-framed replacement hung on a hook on the wall at the foot of my bunk.

When I had taken off my nightclothes I padded my stump with cotton squares and slotted it into the cup, passing the leather straps around my chest and buckling them up before I put on my uniform and surveyed myself in the mirror. Since war had been declared, policewomen's skirts had risen, I was happy to note, to a height that was almost modern, but we were never so fashionable as the Women's Royal Naval Service – *Up with the lark, to bed with a Wren*, as many a sailor liked to quote optimistically.

I pinned up my blonde hair. There was a bit too much of it to tuck easily into a helmet, but it hid my right ear, the top of which was missing since Dodo had accidently shot it off. Besides that, my friend Toby Gregson, the editor, reporter, photographer and columnist of the *Sackwater and District Gazette*, told me it looked better long and I saw no reason to disagree with him.

The false arm was heavy and rubbing already but I had promised my godmother that I would persist with it and I was determined to keep my word. Spiders, starfish and salamanders have the ability to regrow limbs, I had read, so why couldn't we? I never thought I would have reason to be envious of a lizard.

I was still getting tinnitus and occasional blinding headaches from a stray German bomb that had exploded uncomfortably close by and my sense of balance was not as good as it used to be, and so I walked rather than cycled to work. Once I had climbed through Treacle Woods, the view from Fury Hill never failed to gladden my heart. The river below meandered through the flat fields. It saddened me, though, to see the hedgerows being torn up for more efficient food production; the ancient patchwork landscape was starting to resemble photographs I had seen of the prairies. Sackwater lay ahead and, beyond the town, the sea – never blue like in storybooks, but at least a cheerful shade of grey.

Sackwater Central Police Station was deserted when I arrived. The reception area rarely bustled unless there was a pot of tea on offer, but it had been very quiet since the Grinder-Snipe twins had left.

'Dohhh but Mam!' Algy had wailed when it was announced they were being transferred across the estuary. Anglethorpe was short of constables, while we had a surfeit of them.

'Who shall loook afteh…' Sandy began helplessly.

'Uz?' His brother completed the question and I tried to explain that, as policemen, they were supposed to be the ones looking after other people.

'Oh, but weh can't do…'

'That.'

I had seen policemen cry before – even the toughest coppers had been moved to tears by the fate of Dindy Hackson – but I had never witnessed any man in uniform wailing and sobbing the way they did when I broke the news. I liked the Grinder-Snipes as people, but as police officers they were an embarrassment on a good day and they had very few of those. I couldn't help feeling sorry for them as they clutched each other in a panicked embrace, but at least, I tried to console them, I had been able to make sure they were sent to the same posting.

'Good riddance,' Inspector Sharkey, known unaffectionately as 'the Shark' or 'Old Scrapie', had smirked as they stumbled out of the front door like innocents being evicted on a stormy night. The Shark was not known for his sympathetic nature. He had gloated quite openly when Constable Rivers, trying to get extended leave for his bad back, was aghast to find that the medical board took his complaint seriously enough to force him into retirement.

I looked about. The umber lino was cracking where the two rolls met in a ridge and a piece had broken away, leaving a passable map of Australia on the glue-caked floorboards below. The spiked bit of Queensland was chipped off, but nobody would miss that. The blackout screens had been taken down so, assuming they had been put up the night before, somebody must have been in before me.

'Hello,' I called, my voice ringing unanswered down the empty corridors leading on my left to the offices and my right to the cells.

I dumped my gas mask onto the high front ledge of the desk. There was a scurrying and a dark shape shot up onto the lower back ledge. I jumped and yelped 'What the—', before realising that it was a cat – a big, ragged black one with crumpled whiskers.

'What are you doing here?' Why do we do that – talk to the animals when we know we'll never get an answer, unless you're Dr Dolittle? I could have done with him when the only witness to the strangulation of Siphal Slange was his goldfish.

The cat stalked towards me over a pile of unfilled charge sheets. I reached out my good hand to give it a stroke and it burst into a hissing ball of spikes, claws raking the air an eighth of an inch from my fingers.

'Ftit bokkard,' I swore, putting Captain Sultana's lessons in Maltese expletives to good use, but, short of taking the fire axe from where it hung on the wall, I knew this was not a battle I was going to win.

Sergeant 'Brigsy' Briggs often dozed slumped, corpse-like, behind the desk, but his chair was unoccupied when I peered over, keeping well out of range of my new friend.

'Anybody here?' I shouted, feeling like the man in that poem who knocked on the moonlit door. Even the cat showed no interest in my yell and ambled off to curl up at the far end of the desk, but keeping one eye on me in case I tried to be nice to it again.

The ashtray had a dottle of tar-soaked pipe tobacco and ash. Beside it was a half-drunk tea and when I touched the mug, it was stone cold. It was not like Brigsy to leave a beverage unfinished. I went around and ripped off the duty roster – a scruffy scrap of paper pinned to the noticeboard. Brigsy should have been there. Sharkey was on duty, as were Constables Box and Bank-Anthony and Woman Police Constable 'Dodo' Chivers. The constables should be on patrol. I liked being out and about, but Sharkey thought it beneath his dignity to pound the beat and commandeered our Wolseley Wasp official car at the slightest excuse.

I lifted the register and opened it. Apart from two big cases we had had since I arrived back in Sackwater, the rest were drunk and disorderlies or drunk in charge of a motor vehicle or drunk in charge of a minor. There wasn't much to do here except get drunk, and even those cases were in decline with rises in the prices of beer and spirits and many of our more or less able-bodied men being summoned into the forces.

The back door closed and heavy footsteps approached.

'Don't you fret, my lovely,' Brigsy's gruff tones called. 'I do got your breakfast.'

'That's very kind,' I replied as he came into the room carrying a paper parcel. 'But I will thank you to be less familiar while we are on duty.'

It was unfair to tease the sergeant, I knew. If ever there was an officer less likely to philander, I had yet to meet him. Brigsy had been acutely embarrassed when Dodo told him how she had slipped in the bath.

'Ladies oughtn't to discuss their abolutions in company,' he had told her, to be greeted with her recital of my mantra that WPCs are police officers and not ladies. 'Still int right,' he had muttered.

Brigsy froze.

'I...' he managed, before the front door swung open and a scruffy boy entered, an equally scruffy mongrel trotting merrily alongside, its tawny frowzled fur coordinating nicely with its master's bedraggled hair.

'No animals in here,' Brigsy snapped without a tinge of irony.

'I needs speak to a copper,' the boy announced, clearly of the impression that the ban didn't apply to his companion.

He wore a stained seaweed-green pullover gone at the elbows and black shorts that must have been cut down from a man's trousers, so baggy were they around his skinny legs and bunched up around his waist with a belt of rope. His grey socks sagged over his scraped, broken-laced shoes.

'I am a police inspector,' I told him, and the boy wrinkled his nose.

'Are you as good as a man then?'

'Better,' I assured him, ignoring my sergeant's grunt of protest.

'If there's a reward, do Gripper get it or me?'

He was about twelve, I estimated, and to judge by the tidemarks on his neck and wrists, he had not wasted much time in those dozen years bathing.

'Maybe you could share it,' I suggested. 'But what's it for?'

'Reportin' a crime,' the boy asserted, and his dog sneezed like it was sniggering, but the boy's tone was deadly serious.

'What crime?' I asked wearily.

If this was about the little girl who threw a pebble and hit Inspector Sharkey on the ear, I already knew who did that and held her in high esteem.

'Murder,' the boy declared dramatically, and I would have questioned him further there and then had it not been for an unearthly, ear-splitting scream. It came from close by but neither I nor Brigsy nor the boy had made it.

'Oh Lord no!' Sergeant Briggs jumped backwards in undisguised horror. He stooped briefly and stiffly and let out a little cry of his own, and when he straightened again the hand he put to his face was dripping with blood.

3

THE GATHERING OF BONES

Brigsy held up his lacerated hand.

Yet who would have thought the old man to have had so much blood in him? I remembered learning from *Macbeth.*

'Stand on Roger's tail,' he explained. 'Got claws like a lion, she do.'

Roger? She? I would worry about that later, if at all, I decided.

'What—' I began, but my sergeant had something more important to say.

'If this is a joke,' Sergeant Briggs growled, placing his smouldering pipe in the ashtray and tilting in an almost mechanised way over the desk, 'I give you fair warnin', boy, women int got no sense of humour.'

'I know tha',' the boy agreed wisely. 'My mam—'

'What murder?' I broke in, partly because I had to find out, even when I knew there was going to be a stupid answer, and partly because I wasn't interested in what didn't amuse the boy's mother, but mainly because I objected to being talked over by a lower-ranking officer and a grubby child.

'You suppose to be the detective,' the boy insisted. 'Tha's for you to work out.'

He had sticking-out ears that were simply begging to be clipped.

Supposed? I pounced on the word. If he was messing me about, I would prove Brigsy right by demonstrating exactly how humourless I could be.

The boy plonked his cap on the desktop and I was about to sweep it away when he said, 'An' there goo the evidence.'

'A cap?' I huffed. 'You found a cap and that proves murder?'

'I int sure it does, madam,' Brigsy corrected me.

'Open it up,' the boy urged, and I nearly told him to do it himself, but his voice had an earnestness that was difficult to dismiss.

There was a lump inside and the cap did not look very savoury. I took hold of the peak gingerly with my thumb and forefinger. If this was a ferret and the boy was hoping I would scream, he was going to be disappointed, but if it bit me I would give him a day in a cell to think about the folly of playing pranks on a police officer.

Steeling myself not to jump, I unfolded the cap, and nestling in that threadbare greasy lining was part of a lower jawbone. It was too big to be a rabbit and too small to be a sheep. There were two molars and a premolar and the socket of another premolar in front of them and I had seen enough teeth in kidney dishes in my father's surgery to recognise them as human.

'Well, I'll be blowed,' Brigsy muttered.

Another thing he would be, I reflected, was half killed by Mrs B. He had dyed his shirt cuff an unattractive and possibly permanent shade of yellowy brown from the antiseptic mixed with blood dribbling down his arm.

I looked at the bone. It was dark and obviously old. The condyle – the bit that hinges into the base of the skull – was missing and its thin neck was stained on the fractured surface, but the front part of the jaw was white inside, like it had been snapped recently.

'He do be gnawin' on it,' the boy explained, 'but last time he eat a bone he choke so I ge' it off him.' He held out his right hand, lifting his dog off its front paws, and I saw the little finger was bandaged in a soiled and bloodied rag. 'Bit me, he do.'

This was obviously a dangerous time to have a pet, I reflected, with a glance at Brigsy's equally gory handkerchief.

'Where did he get it from?' I asked, and the boy scratched his armpit.

'Priory Lane. Gripper goo off in Cain's Pit and back he coom with tha'.'

My heart sank. Cain's Pit was a disused flint quarry overgrown with brambles, nettles and thorny bushes. If the boy could not pinpoint exactly where his dog had found the jawbone, a small army would have trouble searching the area and our small army was currently pinned down in France.

'Tha's a big old spot,' Brigsy commented. 'Where do he goo in?'

'By the milestone,' the boy said, then added cheekily, 'the one with miles on it.'

Brigsy shot him a warning glance but it missed its target by yards.

'An' where he coom out?' he asked sternly.

'Same place,' the boy said, 'only backward.'

We were supposed to be removing or burying all our road signs in anticipation of the invasion, but that one must have escaped attention so far.

'What were you doing there?' I asked, and the boy sniffed noisily.

'Gooin' to school.'

'Which school?'

'Sackwater Primary Dump.' The boy informed me.

'Best place for rubbish,' Brigsy told him.

'So why int you there then?' the boy retorted, and Brigsy bristled warningly.

'You little—'

'What's your name?' I asked. They could bicker to their hearts' content as far as I was concerned, but I had a feeling my sergeant would come off the worse from it. 'And I want your real one.'

I was not in the mood for any pranks. The boy's eyes flicked to the left.

'Humphrey,' he mumbled, 'Humphrey Smith. People call me Hump but I dint like it.' I knew there and then that he was telling the truth. Adults will often call themselves Smith, especially when they are signing hotel registers, but children have much better imaginations. No boy, though, would give himself a first name that cried out to be ridiculed. I once cuffed a youth for claiming to be Baron Alfonse de Lyon, only to find out from an outraged French ambassador that he really was.

4

GOLDEN TEETH AND RELICS

Sharkey emerged from his lair and cruised over to the desk.

'Been playing in the graveyard?' he asked, a little too casually to be convincing. If there was a case in the offing, my colleague would want it. There was little glory to be had in his present investigation of reported criminal damage to a cucumber frame.

'This boy's dog found it in Cain's Pit,' I told him.

'And what were you doing there?' Sharkey asked sharply. 'Poaching rabbits?'

Humphrey puffed out his chest indignantly. 'Just taking Gripper for a run,' he protested – quite convincingly, before he ruined his case by adding, 'Int my fault if he catch somethin' sometimes.'

''Tis your fault if you take it home,' the Shark reminded him, and he picked up the jawbone, lifting it to the light like a diner checking the clarity of his wine.

Please don't let him find anything I've missed, I prayed silently but without confidence. If God works part-time, I wish he would tell me what his hours are because he rarely answers my calls.

'Did he dig it up?' Old Scrapie demanded, and I wished I had had the sense to ask that.

'Don't know,' the boy replied. 'He's rootin' about inside and coom out with it in his mouth.'

'I don't think it could have been buried,' I reasoned, anxious to make some contribution to my own enquiry. 'Look at the cavity in that tooth. There's no soil in it.'

'Maybe he cleaned it up,' Sharkey suggested.

'He dint look like a boy who cleans things,' Brigsy pointed out reasonably, in defence of my claim, and Humphrey bridled in outrage.

'You sayin' I'm dirty?' he demanded. 'I have a bath…' He scratched his scalp vigorously, no doubt disturbing the abundant wildlife that inhabited it. 'Sometime,' he concluded. 'Anyway, I do give it a rinse.'

My heart sank. First, he might have washed off an important clue but, more annoyingly, he had proved my colleague right.

'Why?' I asked.

'Think it might have a gold tooth,' Humphrey told me. 'My pal take a couple on his grandad's what fell out and Mr Kendal give him a thruppeny bit for they.'

Mr Kendal, the jeweller who Mr Utter couldn't compete with, was a cheating miser, I thought. I knew from helping with my father's accounts that the precious metal in a dental crown was worth far more than a penny halfpenny.

'And do it?' Brigsy asked. 'Have any gold,' he clarified, fixing the boy with a stern stare. 'Be sure I goo find out if you've been sellin' any.'

'I int,' Humphrey protested. 'There's just mud.' He had another scratch. 'And dog spit.'

Inspector Sharkey tossed the jawbone back so carelessly I was surprised it didn't break.

'Careful,' I protested.

'Of what?' he scoffed. 'Some ancient relic?'

'How can you know that?' I challenged.

'Priory Lane,' he said flatly. 'What d'you think used to be there?'

This was most annoying. He was speaking to me in the same way that I spoke to my juniors.

'As I do recall there's a priory round there once,' Brigsy did recall, and I cursed silently. 'But the farmers and gamekeeper take the stone for houses and barns and walls.' I hadn't realised the sergeant was such an erudite local historian. 'They do say you can still hear the bell for prayers on a stormy night.'

'They didn't ring the bells at night,' I pointed out weakly.

'That's it then,' Sharkey concluded triumphantly. 'Look how yellowed it is. A bone won't go like that in a few weeks. It'll be the remains of some medieval monk. Dig the neighbouring field up and you'll find a hundred of them buried there.'

'What about my reward?' the boy grumbled, and Sharkey looked him up and down.

'Why aren't you in school?' he demanded.

'It's Satdee,' the boy objected, not very convincingly for someone who had assured me he was on his way there.

'Friday,' Sharkey told him firmly, and the boy threw out his hands.

'Well, knock me down,' he exclaimed. 'I'd've swore.'

And with that he scarpered – or would have if I hadn't grabbed his collar before he reached the door.

'Not so fast,' I insisted as he wriggled in my grip. 'You can't hand in body parts and just disappear. I have to make a report and, as our sole witness, you are going to give us an official statement.'

'For no reward?' he objected. 'You're jokin'.'

'You have a choice,' I told him. 'I can take you to school now and report you for truancy or I can take you later and say you were helping the police.'

The boy cogitated, but not for long.

'Later sound best to me,' he decided, to nobody's surprise.

5

THE NAMING OF TOES AND CONTINENTAL DRIFT

Teddy Moulton bustled away between two rows of shelves. There were countless books in his shop but it never ceased to impress me how he knew where any of them were. Nothing seemed arranged by subject or in order of writer or title. Teddy hauled his towering set of steps back towards me, not an easy task since one of the wheels had rusted up after a water-mains burst in 1937 and Teddy had not got around to oiling it.

'Excuse me,' he puffed, dragging the steps over my foot and down the next aisle.

'Damn,' I grunted involuntarily.

'Language,' Teddy corrected me. He had banned customers for much milder expletives than that.

'I only said Dan,' I improvised, wishing I could take off my shoe to relieve the throbbing, but police officers do not strip in front of members of the public – unless they are about to save them from drowning, and the longer I worked in Sackwater, the fewer people I would feel inclined to rescue.

'Why?' Teddy interrogated me.

He had missed a bit shaving his upper lip and, judging by the length, he had missed it several days in a row.

'It's what I call my big toe,' I told him, with a fresh insight into why suspects get themselves tangled up in their own lies.

'I see,' Teddy murmured in a way that showed he didn't,

parking his steps and scrambling up them with an agility that might prove useful one day. In his spare time – and he had a lot of that – Teddy was an ARP warden. This was not too onerous a position yet, since we had only had one bomb so far, but he had not proved very useful in rescuing me from that. 'So what do you call the other toes?'

That tuft on his lip was really annoying me and I itched to snip it off.

'They don't have names,' I replied. 'That would be silly.'

Teddy hmmmed dubiously and tapped his bulbous knuckles along three rows of leather and cardboard spines like he was checking for a secret passageway.

'Now, where are you? Dickens, Enid Blyton, Ruskin, Hemingway, Mrs Beaton. Ah, here we are, Matterson.' He trotted down and back to me with a disappointingly small, thin volume. I couldn't imagine there would be much information in that. '*Matterson's Longer History of Sackwater and District from Magna Carta to Modern Times.*'

Longer? The book looked shorter than its title, but Teddy was leafing through it with great satisfaction.

'Aha!' he cried. 'Found it.'

'The site of the priory?' I tried to peer over his shoulder but Teddy was like a boy in a school exam determined that nobody else could copy his answer. He hunched over the book, his left hand blocking my line of sight from the side.

'An account of the destruction of the first pier,' he said, sliding his tortoiseshell specs up his nose with the tip of his right thumb before running a hooked bony finger over the lines. 'Apparently the builders didn't drive the piles deep enough into the seabed.'

'Yes, but does it say anything about the priory?' I asked impatiently.

'Of course not,' Teddy replied crossly. 'The whole chapter is about the pier.'

'In another chapter,' I urged, and Teddy tutted. 'Patience is a virtue,' he quoted piously.

'Helping the police with their enquiries is a civic duty,' I quoted tetchily, 'and you can read the book to your heart's content when I have gone.'

'Why the urgency?' Teddy demanded. 'There hasn't been a monk there since…' He leafed through a few more pages with his thumb. 'Fifteeeeen…' He bent even lower, waggling his head side to side until he seemed to be turning the pages with the hooked tip of his long nose. 'Thirteee…' He turned the page with infuriating slowness. Continents drifted more rapidly than Teddy when he was engrossed in a book. 'Nine,' he concluded triumphantly.

'Yes, but where exactly was the priory?'

'Why, Priory Lane, of course,' Teddy told me, as if I was almost as stupid as he was making me feel, 'but it has since been demolished and the materials used by farmers and gamekeepers for their houses and drystone walls.'

'And barns,' I chipped in, thanks to Brigsy's erudition.

'One barn,' Teddy conceded.

'So was there ever a graveyard anywhere near Cain's Pit?' I asked.

'Ummm.' Teddy twiddled a strand of his floppy brown hair. 'Do you mean graveyard or cemetery?'

'Is there a difference?'

'I am not sure.' He slid his specs halfway down his nose. 'Shall we look it up?'

'No,' I said firmly. 'Was there any kind of burial site in that area?'

'When?'

'Ever.'

'No. Never.' Teddy clicked his tongue.

'So where were the monks interred?'

'Why, Tringford, of course,' Teddy told me, as if no monk could possibly have been entombed anywhere else in the world.

'Not Sackwater?'

'Not Sackwater,' he confirmed. 'Tring-ford,' he repeated firmly, 'which, as I am moderately confident you know, Inspector, is not Sackwater.'

I wondered briefly if it was an offence to be a pompous know-it-all and decided, regretfully, that it wasn't.

'I wonder why,' I mused.

'I am sure you do,' Teddy agreed, but showed no inclination to enlighten me. 'If that was all you wanted to know, you should have said.'

'I was going to.'

Teddy slapped the book shut, no doubt slaughtering whole populations of dust mites in the act and propelling vast numbers of them up my nostrils.

'It is an offence to waste an air-raid precautions warden's time,' he told me officiously.

I blew my nose, but it didn't help. They were already setting up home in my sinuses.

'Only if he is in uniform and on duty and after a verbal warning in front of two independent witnesses,' I bluffed.

Teddy was not the only one who could talk tosh, I reflected, and wondered, as I stepped outside, why I was so proud of that.

6

SPILSBURY AND THE VICAR OF TITCHFOLD

Usually I would have consulted Tubby Gretham. He was our local GP but also jumped at any chance to perform post-mortems. *I much prefer my patients dead*, he would tell me. *They don't whinge or go into labour at three in the morning.*

To be fair to Tubby, one of his greatest joys was delivering babies when the midwife was unavailable or wanted help with a difficult case, but even the most dedicated of us need our sleep and Tubby needed more than most. He was a heavily built and heavily bearded man, like a grizzly bear in appearance, and sharing its fondness for hibernating. Though he was often gruff, I had never found him intimidating, even when I was a child.

But Tubby, unfortunately for my purposes, had gone to Ramsgate ahead of Carmelo. If men were being rescued from battle, he reasoned, they would need medical help and he'd had plenty of experience of dealing with wounded soldiers in the last war.

I rang March Middleton. If anyone had access to an expert opinion, it was her.

'I would steer clear of Bernard Spilsbury,' she advised. 'He has become a victim of his own brilliance and come to regard his hunches as infallible doctrine. The frightening thing is that judges and juries almost invariably share his opinion.' I knew my godmother had tried to get a retrial for Jack Hewitt, the fifteen-year-old convicted, on the strength of Spilsbury's testimony, of the murder of Sarah Blake at Gallowstree Common. 'And Keith Simpson is occupied in Devon.' She ran through the names of half a dozen other less-famous pathologists who were either busy or, in her view, unreliable. 'Why not get your father to take a look?' she suggested at last.

'My father?' I queried in surprise. I had thought Aunty M's opinion of him was no better than my own.

'He gave me some good advice in the Tewksbury Triplets case,' she told me.

'My father?' I repeated incredulously. 'Harold Church?'

'You have more than one father?' she chuckled. 'Yes, him. I am not sure he is the kindest of dentists, but he knows his teeth.'

'Blimey,' I muttered.

Was March Middleton going senile? She didn't sound it and I had little to lose by following her advice.

'What on earth is it now?' my mother greeted me, as if I were constantly pestering them for food or money or to do my laundry.

'I am here on official business,' I told her stiffly.

'Dodo is not at home,' she told me, apparently auditioning for the role of footman, and made as if to shut me out.

'I know that,' I said, because it was me who had sent Constable Dodo Chivers with Bantony to investigate reports of a vicar behaving suspiciously on Titchfold High Street. 'I wish to see my father.'

My mother gripped the edge of the door and put a foot behind it, as I had seen her do when patients turned up at inconvenient hours just because they were haemorrhaging from botched extractions. I considered my options. In my time I had gained entry past many a hardened thug, but I could hardly shoulder-charge my own mother out of the way.

'If it's about the wireless,' she said, 'he is going to pay that just as soon as he remembers.'

Oh good grief. I knew money was tight, but surely they could afford the ten shillings for a licence.

'It's about…' I paused to impress her as to the seriousness of my visit, 'a possible murder.'

My mother braced herself.

'He was with me all night,' she declared, her fingers blanching as she clutched the woodwork.

'Which night?' I asked automatically, but without any real interest. My father was far too boring to commit a homicide.

'Every night,' she insisted.

'Good,' I said, 'then he will welcome the opportunity to give the police the benefit of his expert opinion.'

My mother wavered.

'Expert?' She chewed the word, rolled it around her mouth and swallowed, like it was a rare truffle and she actually liked them.

'Opinion,' I confirmed. 'Based upon his extensive clinical experience.'

My mother hesitated. The idea of her husband being anything other than an incompetent was appealing, if implausible.

'You had better come in,' she decided at last.

7

ZINC PHOSPHATE AND THE ART OF LOVE

My father put on his glasses. For years he had pretended he didn't need any, but he was finally persuaded that he did after he introduced himself to my mother, his wife for forty-one years, and she accused him of trying to seduce her.

He picked up the jaw, turning it side to side like he was hoping to find the manufacturer's name printed on it.

'Well, it is definitely human,' he decided at last.

I had been hoping for a bit more than that.

'Can you tell me anything else?'

My father sucked in noisily, like a plumber wondering how much he can bump up his bill.

'There isn't much to go on.'

I think *I* could have told *him* that.

'Anything at all?'

My father blew out slowly, like he was trying to cool his dinner – not something he had had to do very often since Pooky had left and my mother had taken over the so-called cooking.

'Wellll.' He stretched the word so far that it almost snapped. 'I am at a severe disadvantage not having the ascending ramus and condylar head.' Even I knew they were the bits that stuck up at the back of the jaw and slotted into the head. 'But I would say it is female.' He picked up a dental probe and pointed with the handle. 'Judging by the delicate construction of the oblique line.' He ran the handle along a ridge. 'Where, as you are aware, the depressor labii inferioris and depressor anguli oris muscles attach.'

'Of course,' I murmured, though he could have said *the obli-dobli-quantisorus muscles* and I would have pretended to have known.

'Though it could be a slightly built youth.'

'Can you make a guess as to the age?' I asked.

'No,' my father said flatly, and I was just about to thank him and go when he added, 'but I can make an educated calculation. Sixteen.'

'Sixteen,' I repeated stupidly, because I was so unused to him making an informed judgement it took me by surprise.

'Or thereabouts.' He prodded the back tooth. 'Lower permanent second molars usually erupt at about twelve and the wisdom teeth at about eighteen, though they vary enormously. I had a woman who got pain under her upper denture that turned out to be a wisdom tooth breaking through when she was fifty-eight. This lower second molar is fully erupted but there is not even a bump in the bone where the wisdom tooth should start showing itself.'

'So why not twelve?' I asked, and my father gave me one of those superior smiles that grown-ups give small children when they ask about Father Christmas.

'Because this tooth has not just erupted. It has been in the mouth long enough for the cusp tips to show signs of attrition.'

'Can you tell how old it is?' I asked, and my father gave me another look, the one that let me know I was a moron when I couldn't prove Pythagoras's theorem, even though he couldn't either.

'Sixteen,' he said, in that really patient voice that only really impatient people use.

'No.' I tried to explain myself better. 'I mean, how long ago the person died.'

'What?' my father asked scornfully. 'You think I can take its core temperature to estimate the time of death?'

'No.' I was feeling more the stupid child with every word that either of us uttered. 'It's just that Inspector Sharkey thought it might be medieval.'

My father made that sort of sniggery snuffle Sister Millicent used to give when I tried to parse Ovid's 'The Art Of Love' – an odd choice of study material for a convent school, you might reasonably think – in its original Latin.

'Silver amalgam may have been in use for a decade or two before Greene Vardiman Black published his improved formula in 1895, but certainly not much longer than that,' he told me, as if I should have known that and as if it were relevant.

'But there are no fillings in those teeth,' I objected.

'Precisely,' my father agreed annoyingly, before deigning to explain. 'But why is that second premolar discoloured at the cervical buccal margin?'

This was quite a disturbing experience. It wasn't often I heard my father talking rationally. I peered at the tooth more closely. True, there was a hole near where the gum would have been and it was blackened, but I was so used to seeing rotting teeth that I had not thought anything of it.

One should always think something of everything, I remembered Sidney Grice advising me, but it still seemed an impossible rule to follow.

'Decay,' I suggested, and my father snorted contemptuously.

'Clearly there was decay,' he conceded, 'but it has been removed and the tooth restored with dental amalgam. See' – he indicated with the tip of his probe – 'that dark line? It is caused by mercury leakage from a poor mix with the silver.'

'Ah, yes,' I said wisely, and my father began to pick at the base of the cavity.

I was not sure he should be interfering with evidence but, since he was the only one to have reached any useful conclusions so far, I left him to it.

'There you are,' he said triumphantly, scraping a dark yellow powder onto the table. 'Zinc phosphate cement. I don't know the exact date of introduction, but it hasn't been used for more than a hundred years.'

'Sorry, do you mean nobody has used it for a hundred years or nobody used it before a hundred years ago?'

'Before,' he huffed.

'Can you tell me anything else?' I asked, slightly in awe of this new, knowledgeable father.

'Yes,' he said. 'You need a haircut.'

8

THE TRAGEDY OF JERICHO ALLEY AND THE GREATER NEEDS OF MEN

Apart from eating and sleeping, I was spending most of my time at the station that May. It wasn't my workload, but *Cressida* was a lonely place without the captain's fatherly presence or Jimmy calling in. I still spent the nights there, not only because the beds in the cells were uncomfortable and my parents were unwelcoming but also because the chickens and rabbits needed feeding and caging.

A silver birch had drifted downstream in the night and lodged between Shingle Cove and Brindle Bar, where we lived, and I was worried that rats or a fox might use it as a bridge to get across and create havoc. It took me over an hour to saw it one-handed from the rowing boat and drag the bottom half ashore for firewood. The top half floated away before I could retrieve it. After showering in a cubicle in the garden with river water sun-warmed quite nicely in a tank, and changing, I had no time for breakfast before I set off for work. Nothing dreadful was likely to happen if I was half an hour late, but if I didn't set an example in punctuality – especially after all my nagging at Dodo for her poor timekeeping – who would?

I decided to risk cycling and, despite a few dizzy wobbles, managed to arrive intact with two minutes to spare. At least, I thought, as I put my bicycle around the back and made my way in, I could be sure of a decent mug of tea.

Brigsy stood behind the desk like a landlord with Bantony leaning on the other side like his sole customer, tall and quite muscular with razor-parted black Brylcreemed hair and a slightly spivish air about him, which every woman in Sackwater, other than myself, seemed to find irresistible.

'Marnin', madam,' my sergeant greeted me glumly.

'Morning, ma'am,' my constable greeted me equally glumly, not even running his eyes over my figure as he habitually did to anything not masculine.

'What on earth is the matter?' I enquired. I hadn't seen them so depressed since public sporting events had been banned briefly by Mr Chamberlain – something that created more resentment in many men than the prospect of being required to teach the Germans another lesson.

'Yow tell her,' Bantony said sadly.

'You tell her,' Brigsy pulled rank just as sadly.

'Yes, you tell me,' I commanded Bantony, because he was less likely to turn a simple incident into a rambling saga.

'No gas,' he said, perhaps a little too succinctly.

'We go' no gas,' Brigsy explained.

'There's a leak in Jericho Alley,' Bantony expanded the explanation, 'and we could be cut off all day.'

He delivered that last piece of news with the same gravity a doctor might, to tell me he had found something nasty on my X-ray.

'Or longer,' Brigsy predicted huskily.

'Not to worry,' I said lightly, and they both looked at me, aghast. Had I not grasped the gravity of the situation? No gas meant no tea. 'That shouldn't affect the supply to Dolly's café.'

'No good to me,' Brigsy complained. 'My shift only start an hour ago and if he fetch a cup it goo cold and spilled afore it arrive.'

'Got a blank sheet of paper and a pencil?' I asked, and he

handed them over, watching intently like he expected me to perform a magic trick.

CLOSED, I wrote. IN EVENT OF EMERGENCY CONTACT DOLLY'S CAFÉ, THE PROMENADE.

'My treat,' I said, and pinned the sign on the front door while they went to collect their helmets and gas masks. We were marching up Tenniel Road towards High Road East when Miss Prim, local busybody and powerful irritant, came up behind us.

'Inspector,' she called after me, but the sea breeze must have blown her words away because I never heard them.

'I int sure Old Scrapie is correct,' Brigsy announced as we hurried around the corner.

'About what?' Bantony and I asked simultaneously.

'Sayin' tha' young Humpty' – that would be a much better nickname than Hump, I thought – 'goo rabbitin' round Cain's Pit,' he said.

'You think he is too honest?' I asked in surprise.

'I think he do be too clever,' Brigsy corrected me.

'Good morning, ladies,' Bantony leered at four young ATS girls walking up the hill, but they ignored him. The sight of a man in uniform was no great cause of excitement for them.

It was the ATS girls' duty to operate the searchlights or calculate the range and height of enemy aircraft for the ack-ack guns, but only the men were allowed to press the buttons. That way, the government could pretend that they were not relying on women to fight the war. I wondered how long they could keep up that sham. They may need us to shoulder rifles before the year is out, I thought grimly.

'How do you mean, *too clever*?' I asked Brigsy, whose gaze never lingered on any woman unless he was watching her pulling his pint.

'Waaal,' he began, 'when I'm a nipper – and this stay just between us, madam – my old ma make a good stew.'

'And so you poached,' I concluded quietly.

'I int sayin' I did,' Brigsy fudged, but couldn't bring himself to deny it.

'Shame,' Bantony chipped in, not making a moral judgement on his colleague but regretful that eight stockinged legs had disappeared up the road.

'And?' I urged my sergeant.

Brigsy rubbed the smudge that served as a moustache.

'Well... if I do it... and I int sayin' I do,' he emphasised.

'I sort of understood that,' I assured him.

'I would goo up 'long the path by Packard's Field...'

'To Filcher's Mound,' I realised, 'the old warren.'

'S'pose so,' Brigsy grumped at having his big revelation revealed.

'But that boy told yow he was at the quarry, didn't he?' Bantony asked, capable of watching girls and holding a conversation at the same time – something few other men ever mastered.

'Cain's Pit,' I agreed.

'The little bloyter,' Bantony said.

'I think we need to pay Master Smith a visit,' I decided, and, seeing the alarm on both my men's faces, added hastily, 'after we've had our tea, of course.'

'Your treat, madam,' Brigsy reminded me, as if I could ever forget.

9

THE WITCH OF SACKWATER AND THE CROOKED TRAIL

Sackwater Primary was a small stone building just off Beggar's Lane. When I was little it was run by Miss Morgan, who we were all convinced was a witch. She had a long warty nose hooked down towards a long hairy chin hooked up towards her nose. She had long bony fingers and her eyes bulged so much that I used to imagine them bursting and squirting jelly over her face. Anxious not to spoil her image, Miss Morgan spoke in a cackle, dressed in black and owned a black cat with the ominously satanic name of Enid, which, one of us worked out, was *die* backwards – if you ignore the *n*.

It was there that I met and became firm friends with Etterly, but I was only at the school for three years before I was packed off to boarding school. That was over thirty years ago, but it still came as a surprise to find that she had retired and died, and I wondered cruelly if she had been buried at a crossroads with a stake through her heart.

The current headmistress was Miss Frith, a petite brunette and, in her thirties, quite young for a woman in her position. Miss Morgan must have been at least ninety when she ruled her coven, or so it seemed to me at the time.

'She was a lovely lady,' Miss Frith told me, which came as another surprise. 'She only shouted at everyone to hide her shyness.'

If that was true, Miss Morgan had gone about her job hiding her shyness remarkably well.

'It must be very lonely in your position,' Bantony sympathised, though the way he said *position* sounded like he wasn't just talking about her job. 'A woman on her own.'

'I do sometimes feel the need for a strong man,' she admitted, and Bantony was opening his mouth when she continued, 'to move desks and benches around.'

Smith, she told us, was in her class and break would be finished in a minute.

'He's a lovely boy, and only plays truant because he's shy.'

'I'm quoite shoy,' Bantony told her.

'You probably need a good woman to look after you,' she simpered, and led the way from her office towards her classroom.

'Oyd rather have a bad one,' Bantony whispered to me.

'Behave,' I snapped quietly.

Was Miss Frith wiggling her hips on purpose or did she have a stone in her shoe? Either way, my constable clearly approved.

'I like to see the goodness in everyone,' she told us as we reached the end classroom. 'Children respond to kindness much better than they do to cruelty.'

A little fist clenched my heart as we entered. This was the room where Miss Morgan would beat us with her cane and the hook she kept it on was still on the wall, but all that hung from it now was a picture of the good shepherd carrying a lamb.

The children were already sitting quietly at their desks, but they stood up when we entered.

'Good afternoon, Miss Frith,' they greeted her politely.

'Good afternoon, children. Please retake your seats,' she bade them softly.

I looked on, amazed, as they quietly obeyed. If this was representative of the next generation, I would be out of a job.

'Now, dear children,' Miss Frith cooed, 'I should like you to welcome Inspector Church and Constable Bank-Anthony.'

'Good afternoon, Inspector Church and Constable Bank-Anthony,' they chorused.

'Inspector Church and Constable Bank-Anthony have come to speak to Humphrey Smith,' she announced, and there was the little blighter, hair neatly brushed and tie neatly tied, sitting attentively upright at the front of the class.

'Perhaps we could talk to Humphrey in your office,' I suggested, and Miss Frith smiled.

'No need, Inspector,' she assured me. 'We have no secrets in this school. The Inspector only wishes to know where you found a bone, Humphrey.'

'But I do tell them already, miss,' Humphrey said angelically. 'My dog Gripper find it when I take him for a walk on Priory Lane.'

'Good boy.' Miss Frith beamed.

'But Humphrey...' I began.

'Near Cain's Pit,' he continued.

'Oh, well done.' Miss Frith pressed her hands together. 'Many children accidently join those words together so that the second word sounds most unpleasant.'

'But Humphrey...' I began again.

'And that's the truth,' he assured me.

'Then it must be,' Miss Frith assured me. 'My dear children never tell fibs, do we, class?'

'No, Miss Frith,' they recited. 'Tell the truth and shame the devil.'

'Perhaps Oy could have a word with the little chap,' Bantony suggested.

'By all means,' Miss Frith gushed, and my constable strolled over, his hand on his hip like Johnny Mack Brown in *The Crooked Trail*.

'Hello, Humphrey,' he began. The hand rose, lighting fast, and for a split second I had an image of him gunning Humphrey down, but Bantony had whipped out his truncheon and he slammed it down on the desktop.

Humphrey jumped. I think we all did.

'Goodness,' Miss Frith quavered.

'Now,' Bantony said, 'we can play this the hard way or the harder way.'

Was that a line from a film? I didn't recognise it.

'You can't frighten me,' the boy said.

That was certainly a quote. Edward G. Robinson in *The Racket*?

'No, but Oy can hurt yow,' Bantony snarled.

Same film? I wasn't sure.

'Try it,' Humphrey challenged.

I didn't recognise that line, so I decided to say one of my own.

'Constable Bank-Anthony...' I began warningly, but Miss Frith beat me to the rest of my speech.

She marched over. 'I think that is quite enough of that,' she tremoloed, placing herself courageously between them. 'Please stand back, Constable.'

Bantony, realising he had gone too far, did as he was told.

'Poor Humphrey.' She leaned over to inspect her pupil. 'Why is it always you who has to suffer?'

This must have been a rhetorical question, because she lashed out and caught Humphrey with a stinging slap that made my eyes water just to witness.

'Miss Frith,' I protested, but she wasn't listening to me.

She had Humphrey by the throat and was shaking him so violently that his eyes looked more likely to explode than Miss Morgan's ever did.

'Do you want to die?' Miss Frith said nicely. 'Do you want me to strangle you and dump your odious corpse on the rubbish tip? Do you want to end up like Rudge O'Malley? Or are you going to tell these officers the truth?'

She forced his head back – I hadn't known necks were quite that flexible – and Humphrey made a choking noise, which was about all he could manage.

'Was that a yes?' Miss Frith asked, in the same way she might ask if you took sugar.

Humphrey made a valiant attempt at a nod.

'Good.' Miss Frith let go and stood back.

'Packard's Field,' Humphrey coughed, rubbing his throat tenderly. 'Up near Filcher's Mound. God's truth.'

'Never mind God's truth,' Miss Frith laughed lightly. 'Is it Miss Frith's truth?'

'Yes, Miss Frith,' Humphrey vowed.

'Good boy.' She beamed, and turned to me. 'You see, Inspector? He was just too shy to tell you.'

'Good, then you could show us roughly where tomorrow,' I suggested.

'Oh, Inspector,' Miss Frith tinkled merrily, 'there is no *roughly* about it. Dear Humphrey shall show you *exactly* where or die in the attempt.'

This seemed a little extreme, but it had the desired effect because Humphrey nodded vigorously and said, more than a bit hoarsely, 'Yes, Miss Frith.'

The headmistress opened out her arms as if embracing the whole form. 'And what must we always do, children?'

'Tell the truth,' they chanted, 'work hard, be polite, be punctual, be helpful, be cheerful, sit straight, stand straight, be clean in all our habits and, above all, respect Miss Frith for all our living days.'

To look at their smiling faces you would have thought it was

Christmas Day, but I couldn't help noticing the puddles under two of the other boys' chairs.

'I loike a woman with fire in her belly,' Bantony remarked as we made our escape. 'But she has a blast furnace in hers.'

'Met your match?' I asked.

'More loike moy nemesis,' he reflected ruefully. 'Shame though. She had a lovely pair of—'

'I wonder,' I broke in, 'who was and what happened to Rudge O'Malley.'

10

CAPRICORN, STRINGS AND ASTRONOMY

Gripper led the way with Humphrey Smith trotting after him, me a few yards behind and Constable Box trudging gamely to the rear. It was Bantony's day off, but I thought it unlikely he would spend any of it chasing Miss Frith. The land sloped gently upwards, so gently that I doubt a football would have rolled from top to bottom without a few gentle kicks to help it on its way. In most areas of Britain the rise would hardly have been noticed, but in the great flatness south of the River Angle the incline had been given the gloriously overinflated title of Big Hill.

I was moderately confident we were in Packard's Field, but it was difficult to distinguish which field was which after all the uprooting of hedges and copses.

'How much further?' I called to the boy, hoping I didn't sound like an annoying child at the start of a journey.

'Nearly near,' he called back.

Humphrey seemed to have recovered from his brush with death at the hands of Miss Frith and was his usual cocky self.

'Who was Rudge O'Malley?' I asked when we met up by the milestone on Priory Lane – our starting rather than our finishing point since she had terrified the truth out of him.

Humphrey glanced over his shoulder and lowered his voice.

'You dint ask questions 'bou' tha',' he warned.

'I do,' I assured him. 'I'm a police officer.'

'And she do be' – his voice fell in awe – 'Miss Frith.'

Filcher's Mound was just visible now, a vast pillow of earth rising behind a clump of trees near the top of the so-called hill. To the left I could make out the roof of the old Warrener's Cottage. That must have been unoccupied for decades and was just used as a tool store now. The whole area had been left untouched because it belonged to Sir Hugo Capricorn, who had pulled more strings than a troupe of puppeteers to get it listed as essential woodland, though how it would contribute to the fight against Hitler, without being used for wood, was never clear to me nor, I suspect, to anyone else.

We were close to the edge of the woods now, with a freshly painted sign behind a rusty wire fence reading *Private Property Tresspassers will be prosecuted*, when Humphrey stopped.

'Here.' He pointed down.

Roughly ploughed over but not yet furrowed, it looked pretty much like any other patch of ground to me.

'How can you tell?' I asked, and the boy raised his eyes contemptuously at my stupidity. He would probably be doing that to women for the rest of his life, I reflected, unless somebody showed him that not all women were as buffle-headed as most Suffolk men believed them to be.

'See tha' syc'more,' he said, pointing.

'Yes,' I conceded.

'It cast a shadder.'

'Of course,' I agreed.

'And where tha' shadder cross the shadder of tha' sign is where Gripper dug the bone.'

'But the shadows cross over there,' I pointed, with a nagging suspicion that I was being as dim-witted as he assumed, and the boy curled his lip to show me that I was.

'Know wha' tha' is?' He pointed into the sky.

'The sun,' I mumbled.

'Well, tha' old sun' – he swept his arm around to demonstrate his thesis – 'it move about.'

'Well, actually, the Earth moves,' I said, wondering why I was trying to outdo a grubby truant child with my knowledge of astronomy. Captain Sultana was a patient man – with me at least – but even he was losing hope that I would ever recognise the constellations.

'And at seven this marnin' the sun goo o'er there.' The boy, treating my contribution with the contempt it deserved, swung his arm imperiously to his left.

'How do you know it was seven?' I pounced. Humphrey Smith was not wearing a wristwatch.

'Because,' he explained over-patiently, 'that's when the hooter sound for change of shift at Bentley's.' Bentley's was not the famous car manufacturer but Bentley Vines, a factory near Stovebury, three miles inland. A year ago it was turning out Captain Freeman's Rum, an awful sticky drink made from sugar beet. Now it was rumoured to be involved in producing a new fuel for aircraft. All I knew is that it had a high wire fence and sentries at the gates. 'And when the sun is there, she casts a shadow here,' Humphrey Smith concluded dogmatically. ''Sides,' the boy concluded, 'there's the hole what Gripper do dig.'

'So all that stuff 'bout the sun?' Box queried.

'Load of gander,' the boy confirmed. 'Got your boss goin' though.'

Box scowled. He didn't like a fellow officer being taken for a fool, especially when I was supposed to be somebody he looked up to. He thrust his spade at the boy.

'Dig,' Box commanded.

'Wha'?' Humphrey scowled indignantly.

'I think what Constable Box was trying to say,' I explained sweetly, 'was *dig*.'

11

THE TRADITION OF THE TROWEL AND THE CONDITION OF PATHOLOGISTS

It took a few threats but we soon had Humphrey turning the soil at a fairly steady rate. After five minutes, he stopped.

'Mayhap I get the place wrong,' he pondered, wiping his brow as if he had done a day's hard labour.

'Keep digging,' I said, and he plunged the blade in, turning a sod resentfully. What was that? It was probably just a root. There had been a few already so I nearly ignored it. The soil rolled back over it. 'Stop digging,' I rapped, and he flung the spade down.

'Dig, dint dig. Make your flippin' mind up,' he grumbled.

'Mind your tongue,' Box warned.

'I only say—'

'I know what you say and you dint say it to a-nofficer of the law.'

'But she—'

'*She*?' Box bellowed. 'Dint you refer to the inspector as *she*.'

'He,' Humphrey Smith began again uncertainly, and Box gave him a smart cuff on the side of his head.

I left them to it, going down on my haunches to get a closer look.

'Did you bring the trowel?' I asked Box.

'Oh, yeah,' Humphrey said, with heavy sarcasm, 'I bring a whole pottin' shed.'

'I was talking to my sergeant.'

'You should on looked at him then.'

'I did.'

Humphrey greeted my claim sceptically. 'Can't really tell, the way your eyes go funny.'

'No they—' I began, but the ever-gallant Box came to my defence with, 'Hold your tongue, boy. Int the n'inspector's fault she go' a wonky eye.'

Wonky...? I thought indignantly. Nobody had told me that before.

'Trowel,' I snapped.

'Yes, ma'am.' Box unbuttoned the flap over his right hip jacket pocket and rooted about like he was searching for a lost penny in the bottom of a carelessly packed rucksack. 'I know it's in there somewhere.' He delved in, almost, it seemed, up to his elbow, with much rustling and clanking and the occasional grunt. How cavernous could a pocket be? Poachers hid pheasants in smaller spaces. 'Oh, there you are.'

Box passed the trowel to me, handle first and blade over the back of his left hand, like the king might present you with a ceremonial dagger.

'You find somethin'?' he enquired, leaning over me like he was trying to read my newspaper on the bus.

'I'm not sure.' I scooped some freshly dug earth away and hit a solid object.

Putting the trowel aside, I brushed some light soil away with the side of my hand. There was definitely something there. I pushed in deeper around it and found it was about the diameter of a flattened walking stick. A pathologist would have had a seizure, but I was not in the company of such august men. I took hold of the object and tugged. It stuck. I pulled harder and it slipped out so easily I nearly toppled backwards into my constable. The last time I had done that was in a bomb crater – not one of our happier experiences together.

'What is it?' Box asked.

It was long and shaped a bit like a part of a metal band they put round beer barrels, but it was thicker and less curved and, when I brushed the dirt away, it was white.

'A root,' the boy said.

I had filed my nails with some difficulty two evenings ago but now they looked like I had a career in agriculture – chipped and grubby – with the backs of my fingers grazed.

'A bone,' Box corrected him.

'A rib,' I clarified.

'Well I'll be—' Box declared.

'I tell you it's the spot,' Humphrey crowed as Gripper came racing back to get a closer look.

'Gerroff.' Box pushed the dog away.

'Leave him alo-an,' Humphrey protested as Gripper darted in and out.

'Hold him back or I lay him out,' Box threatened, though I couldn't imagine him deliberately hurting any living creature that wasn't a criminal.

'I goo set him on you,' Humphrey threatened.

'Got a licence for him?' I enquired.

'Course,' Humphrey insisted, but he grabbed Gripper's collar to pull the dog away.

I rooted about some more and found another rib poking up. If this was a whole skeleton, the head should be somewhere to my left. I dug in carefully and hit something almost immediately. It was the top of a skull. I put the trowel aside to work my way down it with my fingers.

'Oh Lor',' Box murmured.

'Gimme a look.' Humphrey pushed forward excitedly. 'Oh Lor',' he breathed as I flicked a small clod away, exposing an eye socket staring blankly back at us.

12

THE TIN MAN AND THE SILENCE OF THE LAMB

Gripper sprang at the rib. I just managed to whip my find away and was about to tap him on the nose with it when I realised what I was doing and tried to push him off, but Gripper knew that this was game. He seized the glove on my left hand with his front teeth and tugged.

'Get him off me,' I demanded, and Humphrey Smith snorted.

His dog wasn't pulling very hard but the playful way he shook his head side to side was making the cup of the false arm grind into my stump.

'He's only frolickin'.' Humphrey ruffled the fur on Gripper's back, though it was difficult to see how it could be ruffled any more than it was already.

'We'll soon see 'bout tha',' Box threatened, pulling his foot back to boot the dog away.

'No...' Humphrey cried.

'Don't,' I completed his sentence because, all at once, I *could* imagine Box deliberately hurting any living creature that wasn't a criminal.

Box lowered his foot.

'Get him off me,' I said firmly to the boy. '*Now.*'

'Only a bit of fun,' he grumbled, taking hold of his pet's nose.

'We are not here to have fun,' I reminded him.

'If the Inspector wanted fun she could have stayed in bed,' Box told him. 'Oh... I dint mean...'

I coughed.

'I should hope not,' I said as sternly as I could manage.

Humphrey Smith forced Gripper's jaws apart and I inspected my glove. It was soggy with saliva but otherwise undamaged.

'Why d'you wear tha' anyway?' Humphrey asked. 'Int cold.' I rolled up my sleeve to show the metal frame. 'Blimey,' the boy exclaimed, deeply impressed. 'A robot like in *The Tin Man*.'

'Exactly,' I said, though I had not bothered to go and see the film when it was on at the Trocadero.

'But why dint they make you a man?' Humphrey picked his nose, probably putting more dirt into it than he dug out.

'Because women are better,' I told him.

Humphrey looked at his finger, disappointed at whatever he had excavated, and then dubiously at me.

'Nuh,' he decided. 'It's 'cause they can't make one good 'nough yet.'

Box raised a hand. 'Inspector Church is near a match for any man,' he maintained loyally. 'So you think we get a whole skeleton, ma'am?' he asked in awe.

He had seen bodies before – we all had – but you never get used to it. At least, you hope not to.

'I don't know yet,' I told him, 'and I don't care.'

'But you do say we coom to look for it,' my constable reminded me in confusion.

'Not for this one,' I said, and brushed some more of the soil away.

'Got a big eye,' Humphrey observed.

'And big teeth.' I showed him, pulling the skull free.

'Sheep,' Box diagnosed.

'A lamb, to judge by the size of it,' I clarified.

Humphrey sniggered. 'Tha's rich,' he chortled. 'Take me from school to dig up an ol' blackface. Wait 'til I tell them all tha'.'

We would be a laughing stock, I knew. Toby, I was fairly confident, wouldn't print it in the *Sackwater and District Gazette* or, if he had to run it, wouldn't make me out to be a buffoon. The *Anglethorpe Times* and the *East Suffolk Courier* were not likely to be so benign. Sharkey would be in eighth heaven with such an opportunity to mock me. I toyed with the idea of trying to bribe the boy but I didn't see why I should let him have any of my very-hard-earned cash, plus it would not look good if he ever came to court as a witness and announced that I had given him hush money.

'If you tell anyone at all about this, I will have you in court for breaking the Official Secrets Act.'

'Int a n'official secret,' the boy objected. 'It's a dead sheep.'

'It is what I say it is,' I assured him firmly.

'Tha'd be least ten year in borstal,' Box predicted. 'And you can't skip school there 'cause you live in it.'

The boy wiped his finger on his shirt.

'Nah,' he decided. 'Int an official secret. You just goo scared they all goo laugh at you.'

Perceptive little brat, I thought.

'Do I really have to tell Miss Frith that you have been uncooperative,' I threatened, and all the bravado drained out of Humphrey like bathwater when you pull the plug out.

'You never goo do tha'.'

'She will too,' Box assured him. 'She's even nastier than she looks.'

I decided to take that in the spirit it was meant. If I took offence at every slight I received from the men, I wouldn't have time to take anything else.

'Shall I come back with you now?' I suggested and Humphrey slumped, his cocksureness shrivelled like a dried raisin.

'Wish I never give you that bone,' he moaned, so miserably

that I felt quite sorry for him – but, as Box had intimated, I am a cruel woman with a hard heart.

'Go.' I pointed dramatically across the field.

Humphrey snorted, obviously not a boy to be deflated for long.

'Take many a year if I goo tha' way,' he told me mockingly, and marched off at a wide angle to my direction, Gripper darting happily around his heels, an entire lamb's rib projecting from either side of his grinning mouth.

13

HELENA RUBENSTEIN AND THE HARD-BOILED HACK

Carol was leaning back in her chair, in the outer office of the *Sackwater and District Gazette*, applying Regimental Red to her lips. We were already being encouraged to use every morsel of our make-up, watering it down where possible, but it would not be long before some women had to substitute beetroot juice for rouge.

'You don't think it's too garish?' she asked, scrutinising herself in her compact mirror.

'Not in the least,' I reassured her, in the happy belief it was.

I did not need to be a detective to realise that Carol had set her sights on her employer and, though I trusted Toby to the ends of the earth, I didn't trust his secretary to the end of her desk.

'He's upstairs,' she told me, clamping the side of her blotting paper between her lips to avoid what she succeeded in doing – smudging.

I made my way up.

Toby was clattering intently at his typewriter, a Craven A drooping from his lips. He looked every inch the hard-boiled hack rather than the jazz violinist he was at heart.

He glanced up.

'Inspector Church,' he greeted me, always correct when he saw me in uniform.

I chuckled.

'What?' he asked, sliding his tortoiseshell reading glasses down his nicely carved nose to see me more clearly.

'You are the only person I know who can make a Remington Noiseless sound like a hailstorm on a caravan roof,' I told him.

'Have to hammer,' he explained. 'The ribbon's getting dry and you try telling the Ministry of Ink you need a new one.'

'Is there such an organisation?' I sat opposite him.

'There will be,' he asserted, proffering a cigarette. I took it gratefully and leaned over for him to light it with a match. Toby gazed at me. 'God, I wish I could kiss you right now,' he whispered, then said, 'I hear you have found a skeleton in Packard's Field.'

'Well, a jawbone,' I conceded. 'But who told you? My men had instructions to keep it quiet.'

'Think they would dare disobey you?' Toby asked.

'Sharkey would.'

Toby perked up. 'Would he?' He picked up a pencil. 'Maybe I should buy him a drink.'

'Put a drop of hemlock in it for me,' I urged, knowing he would never go behind my back. 'Who was it then?'

'Think you can march into Sackwater Primary and interrogate a boy in front of all his classmates and nobody will say anything?' Toby enquired, removing his spectacles to hurr on them.

'I take your point,' I muttered.

'Seems like you let everyone know except me,' Toby observed in hurt tones, polishing the lenses with a white handkerchief.

'It was one of the two reasons I'm here,' I told him. 'But I've been so busy with it I haven't had time and,' I hesitated, 'I wanted to ask you to keep it quiet.'

'The words horse and stable door spring to mind,' Toby commented, placing his specs in a battered leather case.

I tapped my ash into the glass bowl I had given him to replace one he had broken demonstrating its shatterproof qualities.

'I realise a lot of local people must know now,' I conceded, 'but, if you publish the story, the rest of the Suffolk papers will get hold of it and I don't have the manpower to guard the site from every horror-hunter in East Anglia.'

'Horror-hunter,' Toby mused, stubbing his cigarette out, 'is that the official term?'

'I think I just made it up.'

'I might use that.' Toby scribbled a note. 'When you give me the go-ahead,' he added hastily.

One of the many reasons I loved Toby was that he lacked the ruthless streak necessary to be a top journalist. Any other editor would have held the press and had the news on the front page of the very next edition.

'Thank you,' I said.

'Any idea who it is?' he enquired, sniffing something milky-brown in his mug before deciding against drinking it.

'Not yet,' I said. 'But you'll be the first to know.'

'Even before the dreaded Miss Frith?' he checked.

'Well, soon after her,' I assured him. 'I'd like to find if there's anything else out there, but I don't have enough men to conduct a proper search of the field where it was found.'

'You could try Prof Woosters,' Toby suggested. 'He used to write an archaeology column once a week for us – until he got greedy and wanted paying.'

'Thanks, I might contact him.'

'What was the second reason?' Toby asked.

'To invite you to dinner,' I remembered. 'The captain suggested it ages ago but the greatest military defeat in our history got in the way. Dr Gretham and his wife will be there too.'

'Love to,' Toby enthused. 'Tubby's my doctor. Nice chap and probably saved my life. It was him who made me get a chest X-ray when old Dr Griffith said I just had a nasty cough.'

Toby had had TB and half his left lung removed last year but it had not stopped him smoking, though he always rejected my roll-ups. They would only clog him up again, he claimed, whereas his cigarettes fumigated and mopped up any remnants of the bacillus. He could never quite remember which doctor had told him that.

'He's the busiest one of us so I'll get him to confirm a date,' I said, and stood up. 'I must get going.'

'Any chance of that kiss?' Toby asked quietly, and I blew him one. 'Not quite what I had in mind,' he said mournfully.

'Oh, Mr Gregson,' I said, 'if we did half the things you had in mind, I would have to arrest us both.'

14

MR CHAD AND THE DESTRUCTION OF DREAMS

By the time I got back to the station, Dodo was behind the desk, although – even boosted by two thick cushions – she still only just peered over the top like Mr Chad complaining *wot no bananas?*

'Hello, boss,' she greeted me cheerily. 'Brigsy has been called out to deal with an emergency.'

'What kind of an emergency?' I asked, praying she would not tell me something useful like it was an urgent kind.

'Welll,' Dodo began reluctantly. 'Apparently Mrs Briggs found her husband's dirty magazines and threatened to kill him if he did not get rid of them immediately. I did suggest that she probably did not actually mean it, but Brigsy was positive that she did.'

I had met Ida Briggs at a beetle drive in aid of the Lifeboats. She had seemed perfectly pleasant to me, but then one of the most charming women I ever met put two husbands through an industrial mincer and I am not convinced that either of them was dead at the time.

'It doesn't sound like Brigsy,' I pondered. He always came across as a prudish man.

'Indeed not.' Dodo patted her flaming red hair down at either side but it sprang straight up again. 'I did not think he was interested in reading.'

I plonked my helmet and gas mask on the desk. They were a nuisance and I was unconvinced that either would save my life if I was forced to use them. It had been a proud moment for me when I was promoted high enough to wear a cap, and it suited me much better, but war has little regard for millinery fashions.

'How did you get on with the vicar?' I asked, and my constable wiggled her nose.

'Oh, famously,' she replied. 'He gave us two cups of tea and' – she scratched her scalp, her hand disappearing into the red froth of her hair – 'one slice of carrot cake each.'

I exhaled heavily.

'And had he been acting suspiciously?'

'Oh yes, Boss,' Dodo replied. I folded my arms and looked at her. 'Oh,' she realised, 'I ought to tell you why.'

'Yes, you ought,' I agreed as patiently as I could. I had made great efforts to get Dodo to behave in a more mature way and, to be fair to her, she had also made great efforts to comply, but there were still times I had to restrain myself from giving her a good shake.

'He was acting suspiciously because he was suspicious,' she told me.

'Explain,' I commanded, spotting a damp patch on the ceiling and remembering one in Camden that was caused by a body under the floorboards.

'He had been spying on the local defence volunteers with his binoculars and making notes of their activities,' she told me.

'And did he have an explanation for this?' I pressed.

'Yes,' Dodo said simply, but, catching my expression, continued, 'he thought they might be Germans in disguise.'

'So why didn't he report them to us?' I asked.

'He was going to,' Dodo told me. 'But he had a sermon to write on how we should forgive our enemies but it is all right to kill them first.'

The back door flew open.

'If that is you, Sergeant Briggs,' Dodo called over her shoulder, 'do not worry about Inspector Church discovering that you have left your post because she already has.'

Brigsy came in. 'Did she tell you why I had to go, madam?' he asked sheepishly.

'Yes, she did,' I said, 'and I must say I am a little surprised.'

Brigsy ran a finger under his ill-fitting collar. 'Sorry, madam,' he mumbled.

'Your private life is none of my concern,' I said. 'But how dirty were they?'

'Fair disgustin',' Brigsy admitted with a sad shake of his head.

'Dirty enough to be illegal?' I questioned him.

'Oh.' Brigsy fiddled with his tie, making it look even more lopsided than usual. 'I dint know there's a law about it.'

'Oh, come off it,' I said. 'You've booked Charlie Chase in on more than one occasion.'

'Yesss,' the sergeant agreed carefully, 'but tha' is for selling rude magazines.'

Dodo put her hands on her hips like the scolding wife he had no doubt just been confronted by. 'And what is the difference?' she challenged him.

Brigsy coloured. 'Well, his magazines...' He lowered his voice. 'They had' – he paused to give the next word its full impact – '*pictures*.'

'And what did yours have?' Dodo demanded.

'Well, I dint really know.' Brigsy fiddled with his tie. If he had been a Boy Scout, he could have got a badge for the complicated way he had knotted it. 'I dint read them myself – knitting patterns and recipes, I suppose.'

'So these were Mrs Briggs's magazines?' I surmised uncertainly.

'Course they were, madam,' Brigsy replied. 'The only thing I ever cook is a cup of tea.'

'Oh,' Dodo said hopefully. 'Could you show us how?'

'Could but won't,' he assured her, before turning back to me. 'Cat been sick a lot recent so I put the papers down overnight only I forget to clear them up this marnin' and Mrs B ring to say she – the cat – been sick again and the magazines were 'sgustin' and I had to come and clear them straight off. She can't abide sick. Make her sick, it do.'

'How did she cope with the children?' I asked.

'She dint,' he told me.

'But what did she do if they were sick?' Dodo asked.

'She forbid it,' he assured her.

On another day I might have had all the time in the world to chatter over Mrs B's aversion to vomit, but there were other, more pressing matters to deal with.

'Do you know Professor Woosters?' I asked Brigsy.

'No,' Brigsy replied flatly.

'Oh,' I said, slightly taken aback by such a quick and definite response. Normally the sergeant would have ummed and aaahed for at least three minutes before telling me he had a feeling that he might.

'But I know *of* him,' Brigsy said brightly, and I was about to ask if he knew where the professor lived when he said, 'He live in tha' big old house down Calendar Way.'

'Woosters House,' I realised, and Brigsy ran his fingertips over flattened straw tufts seemingly glued to his head.

'Could be,' he conceded. 'Why?'

'It is probably a coincidence,' Dodo speculated.

'Because I want his help,' I said, 'to examine the site—'

'Oh, but you need an optician for that, Boss,' Dodo advised.

I had thought about taking her with me, but something made me change my mind and that something was Dodo.

I rang the exchange and Maggie, the telephonist, answered.

'Does Professor Woosters of Woosters House have a phone?' I asked.

'Who want to know?' she asked guardedly.

'Inspector Church, on police business,' I told her, though it was none of her affair. She was supposed to try to help with all enquiries.

'Little Miss High and Mighty,' she muttered all too audibly, before hardly raising her voice to announce, 'Yes, he has.'

'Then can you put me through, please?' I asked, more nicely than I felt.

'No,' she said. 'He's been cut off.'

'Thank you so much for your unvaluable assistance,' I said sweetly and hung up. I changed my mind about changing my mind. Chivers was not going to lounge about the station drinking tea while I did all the legwork. 'Come on,' I said to Dodo. 'We shall see if the professor is at home.'

'Tell Woosters he's got a sauce,' Brigsy suggested with a not quite suppressed guffaw.

For a moment I thought I might have to explain that to Dodo, but she burst out in a peal of laughter.

'Oh, that is very clever,' she told the sergeant, 'and reminds me of a good joke that Bantony told me once about the sauce of the Nile.'

'Right...' I began.

'S-A-U-C-E not S-O-U-R-C-E,' she spelled out, in case I hadn't got it, which must be the only possible reason I wasn't laughing.

Oh good grief, I thought. We were planning a search for human remains and they were making puns.

'Come on,' I said, and made for the door.

'Wait one moment, please, Boss,' – Dodo slung her gas mask over her shoulder – 'or I shall never ketchup.'

'Wooster dint make ketchup,' Brigsy informed her mournfully.

I will wake up, I thought wistfully, *and find this is all a dream*, but the way my knee jarred when I knocked it on the corner of a bench proved that I would not.

15

THE DIGGER OF BONES AND THE GREEK GOD

Woosters House was, as many buildings in Sackwater were, a High Victorian mansion. Professor Woosters' residence was higher than most, though. Rising five storeys, the frontage consisted mainly of turrets, some crenelated like the towers of a castle, some domed and some topped with spires, so the overall effect was that of a small town squashed together, probably by the Ministry of War, to make it a smaller target for bombers.

'Here we are,' Dodo said, rather obviously, I thought.

'Do not make any jokes about his name,' I warned her.

'Not even the one about—'

'Especially not that one.'

Dodo shuffled her feet like she was trying to roughen the soles of her shoes on the gravelled path.

'But you do not even know what I was going to say,' she objected.

'I don't need to,' I told her. 'People do not like police officers making fun of their names.'

There was a stirrup-shaped bell pull on the wall and, much to Dodo's disappointment, I tugged it. It did occur to me that I was being just as childish as her in making sure I got to it first, but there is no point in being in charge if you have no perks. I could not hear a bell and had just rung again with my ear pressed to the woodwork when the door flew open.

'Clear off, you little blighters,' an old man shouted,

shaking his fist like I thought people only did in *The Magnet* stories. He was a tiny man, his long greying-red beard and manner both reminding me of Grumpy the dwarf. 'Oh, sorry, miss. I thought you were those dratted brats playing pranks again.'

'Professor Woosters?' I enquired, struggling to regain my balance.

'Saucy by name but not by nature,' he assured me, his greying-red eyes magnified like chrysanthemums behind his round steel glasses.

'But he made a joke,' Dodo objected in her stage whisper.

'It's his name and he can do what he wants with it,' I shushed her.

'Quite so,' Woosters agreed. 'I can put it in my soup.'

The professor guffawed at his own attempt at humour and Dodo giggled, but I hate puns almost as much as the people who make them.

'Inspector Church—' I began.

'Inspect your own church,' Professor Woosters flashed back, and Dodo quivered in amusement. I had a horrible feeling she would remember and repeat that one.

'Might I have a word?' I pressed on.

'You can have a whole dictionary of them,' he assured me, but even Dodo did not find that amusing.

'Inspector Church means that she would like to talk to you,' she explained.

'It was a joke,' he said lamely.

'No,' Dodo assured him. 'The Inspector really does want to talk to you.'

'Then she has come to the right place,' Woosters declared.

'I said we had,' Dodo protested, as if I had disputed the fact, even though it was me who had led the way there.

'A human mandible was discovered near here in a field,' I explained, 'and I want to know the best way of investigating the site further.'

'In what era did the bones originate?'

'No more than a hundred years ago,' I told him, remembering my father's remarks about zinc phosphate in the tooth cavity.

'I am an archaeologist,' he informed me.

'That is why I am consulting you,' I tried to explain.

'From the Greek word *arkhaiologia* – *arkhaio* meaning *ancient* and *logia* meaning *lore* spelt l-o-r-e,' he spouted. 'I study artefacts from the ancient world.'

'Yes, but surely the principles are similar,' I pressed, wondering why I was bothering.

'You would think so,' he said dismissively.

'The Inspector would think so because she is correct,' Dodo confronted him, and I waited for the door to be slammed, but Woosters rubbed where his chin probably was inside his shrubby beard.

'A moot point,' he conceded.

'So can you help us?' I pressed him.

'An interesting question,' the professor mulled, 'and my interesting response is *yes*. I shall give you some advice. The best way to go about the job is carefully.'

'That is what I thought,' Dodo chipped in.

'I was hoping for a bit more than that,' I sighed, his eyes seeming to bloom to prize-winning proportions.

''Sss'if,' he hissed.

'As if what?' I asked.

'Sieve,' he repeated more distinctly. 'Sieve the soil.'

'Could we come in for a moment?' I asked, having had enough of chatting on the doorstep like a commercial traveller.

'Why?' The professor whipped off his glasses to peer more

closely at me and I saw they hadn't really enlarged his eyes very much. They could still have got commendations at the village fete.

'Z,' Dodo giggled and, finding her excellent joke unappreciated, spelled it out for us. 'He said *why* so I—'

'I was hoping you might help us find if there are any more bones there,' I battled on.

'Is there any digging involved?' The professor massaged his back like Constable Rivers used to do when he was trying to get off a duty.

'Yes, but—' I was going to explain we could get others to do the spadework when he grinned disconcertingly.

'Then you have come to the right man.' He rubbed his hands together, forgetting he was still holding his glasses. 'Where is it?'

'Packard's Field, near Filcher's Mound.'

'Packard's Field,' the professor repeated, as if it were Tutankhamun's tomb. 'I discovered my first denarius there.'

'And was he still alive?' Dodo enquired.

'It's a Roman penny,' I explained. 'The d in l.s.d.'

'Head of Zeus,' the professor cursed, showing us his glasses, frames bent by his enthusiasm. 'They are always doing that.'

'Tomorrow morning?' I suggested as an opening bid in negotiations, because nobody was ever available when I needed them.

'Ten sharp,' he confirmed, 'and I shall bring my own team.'

16

THE CHARGE OF THE LIGHT BRIGADE AND ERIC THE CLOCKWORK MONKEY

Professor Woosters was already at work when I arrived with Dodo and Box in Packard's Field after our long but not arduous walk up Big Hill. Brigsy would tell Bantony to join us when the constable's shift started. The professor had a team of boys from St Dimlock's Approved School near Thurlmere slouching about boredly.

'Are they volunteers?' I queried, because I had an idea it wasn't legal to force the boys to do manual labour. They were supposed to be being morally improved by their experiences but, even though conditions were much better than in the prison-like borstals, many came out much more hardened and embittered than when they went in.

'Don't you worry your pretty little head about that, dear lady,' a short man in a grey suit told me. He had a swagger stick tucked under his arm, but if he thought it gave him a military air, he was sadly mistaken. There were millions of men and women on our beleaguered island who did not need such affectations.

Several things annoyed me about that sentence. First, it was not up to a member of the public to tell me what I should and should not worry about. Second, my head might have been pretty – and I liked to think it was – but that was not for him to comment upon. Third, I believed that head to be reasonably well-proportioned and certainly not little. Fourth, I was not *dear* to him and he was certainly not *dear* to me. Fifth, I was not a lady – I was a serving police officer. Sixth, he made his remark with such a supercilious smirk that I had to supress an urge to wipe it off his face.

I did think about mentioning a few of those points, but in the end I settled for, 'Inspector Church.'

'These boys are all under my authority and will do as they are told.'

'That was not my concern,' I pointed out. 'Mr...?' This is generally accepted as an invitation to tell someone your name, but the man looked around blankly. 'What is your name?' I prompted.

'Oh,' he realised, 'I thought you were saying *missed her* because one of the boys had thrown something at your young lady.'

He reminded me of Eric, the clockwork, drum-banging monkey I had had when I was five, except that Eric's ears didn't stick out quite as far and my toy had a better haircut.

'She is a woman police constable,' I told him as patiently as I could. 'Who are you?'

'Why, I am Mr Green,' he told me in a way that implied I was rather silly not to have known that.

'And what are you?' I asked, unabashed by my failure to recognise him.

'Just call me *Director*,' he instructed, but I felt sure that I would not.

I went over to where Dodo was talking to the professor. He had a crumpled linen suit on, the colour of sacking, and a pith helmet that would not have been out of place if he was exploring tributaries of the Nile. A bulbous khaki bag hung on a strap on his shoulder.

'Your name gives me Chivers down my back,' he chortled, and Dodo glared.

'It is rather poor form to make jokes about people's names,' she told him stiffly, thereby surrendering her chance to use the pun she told me she had lain awake inventing throughout the night.

'How are you getting on?' I asked him.

'Not very well,' Dodo complained. 'I do not think we shall ever be friends.'

'I was talking to Professor Woosters,' I told her. 'Is that where you intend to concentrate your search, Professor?'

He had pegged out a square around the roughly dug earth where we had found the remains.

'See those markers.' The professor pointed. 'They are what we call *pegs* and I have had them, as you may have observed, pushed into the ground.'

'Yes, I—'

'And those cords between them' – he tucked his thumbs into his waistcoat pocket – 'mark out the area that I intend to excavate.'

'Good,' I said, wondering why I hadn't stayed in at the station with a mug of tea and the copy of *Hercule Poirot's Christmas* I had borrowed from the mobile library.

'I call them *strings*,' the professor informed me with as much satisfaction as if he had coined the word himself.

'Why?' Dodo challenged, and I wandered up the hill.

It was part of my job to listen to answers but, drawing on over twenty years of professional experience, I judged that this was not one worth waiting for. It was then that I made the first find. In fact, I literally tripped over it, sprawling clumsily over a furrow. Luckily for me, the boys hadn't noticed.

'Are you all right, Boss?' Dodo hurried over.

'Of course,' I snapped, more annoyed with myself than her.

There was a loop of wire wrapped around the toe of my shoe and, as I crouched to pull it free, I saw it was attached to a short wooden stake.

'A booby trap?' Dodo guessed.

'A rabbit snare,' I said in disgust. 'I don't mind eating rabbits – in fact, we breed them on Brindle Bar – but when Captain has to kill them, he does it quickly and cleanly. Any poor creatures caught in these are slowly throttled. Some wait days in fear and agony to be dispatched.'

'Oh, how cruel,' she said, as I rammed it into my gas mask box.

The boys were digging in a line from the bottom of the area when I went over. This was greatly preferable to being stuck in a regimented classroom, I assumed, because they worked steadily with an enthusiasm the average local clodhopper would have done well to emulate.

'Oy,' one shouted. 'Watch yerself with tha' spade. Near have my toe off you do.'

'Shouldn't have such big plates,' the other boy told him.

'Plant one in your gob,' the other threatened.

Mr Green scuttled over, bandy-legged, raised his swagger stick and lashed them both across their backs.

'Won't warn you again,' he threatened.

That was a warning?

Dodo hurried over.

'Do not strike those children again,' she told Mr Green fiercely.

On seeing a sympathetic adult, the two boys, who had gone straight back to work with no more than a few grunts, started to writhe their shoulders with loud groans and extravagant grimaces.

'I shall discipline those louts as I see fit,' Mr Green told her.

Dodo drew herself up to her full below-regulation five foot two plus helmet perched on fiery red hair.

'No you shall not,' she insisted, patting the pocket that held her notebook, presumably with the intention of arresting him, and I was just wondering how to defuse the situation when there was a shout.

'Found somethin'.'

Woosters strode over, with me, Dodo and Mr Green close at his heels. Box was lumbering somewhere further up the hill like he was on a country walk.

'Everybody stop digging,' the professor commanded, and all the boys dropped their spades and straightened up with great sighs, stretching and blowing on their hands like they had just finished a hard day's beet-harvesting.

'There.' The boy prodded a lump gently with his muddy boot.

'Don't kick it, you nincompoop,' the professor shrieked. 'It may be a rare artefact like the Viking toothbrush that fat fraudulent freak, Cavenaugh, purloined all the credit for discovering on Thursday 24th April 1902 when he tricked me into excavating the wrong mound.'

Woosters went down on his knees with no sign of concern about the state of his trousers. 'Ah,' he declared triumphantly. 'You have indeed found what you so accurately called *somethin'*.'

The professor dug a hand into his bulging bag, immediately bringing out a long thin trowel, and I wished I could find things in my much smaller handbag half as easily as that. He scooped some soil away, exposing a metal bar.

'Gold,' a stocky little boy declared hopefully. He had a cheery face – he was about twelve or thirteen, I judged – and I wondered what he had been put away for. A lot of *problem* children really had problem parents who probably deserved to be locked up more than their offspring.

'The spoke of a Roman chariot,' Mr Green asserted authoritatively, leaving us in little doubt that he was always stumbling across such artefacts.

'A dagger,' a lanky youth suggested dramatically. He had a bad case of eczema, his face red-raw and scabbed, criss-crossed with scratches.

The professor laid his trowel down, grasped the object and pulled.

'A frying pan,' he cried triumphantly, though I couldn't help thinking that fat freak of an imposter, Cavenaugh, would not be utterly consumed by professional envy.

'Roman?' Dodo asked.

'British.' The professor brandished his pan proudly. 'From the East Suffolk Iron Foundry.'

He laid his trophy on the earth and brought a notebook and pencil out of his bag, with hardly a suggestion of rooting, to make a few notes, then stuck a new peg into the ground with the number one painted on its rounded top.

'Is that a significant find?' I queried as he struggled to his feet.

'All finds are significant,' he pontificated. 'They tell us something that we did not already know.'

'In this case, that there was a rusty frying pan in the field,' I murmured.

Even fully standing, Prof Woosters had to tip his head back to beam up at me.

'Cogently articulated,' he said without a tint of sarcasm, before thrusting the pan into Mr Green's arms, saying, 'Hold that.'

'What?' The recipient looked baffled. 'Why me?'

'Because you are the only one I can trust,' the professor told him, and Mr Green gleamed with pride.

'Dint mind findin' a couple of bangers to goo in tha',' the stocky little boy said wistfully, to general agreement and other suggestions of what would make a good fry-up.

'I prefer my bacon crispy,' Dodo announced, sparking a heated debate.

'Back to work, chaps,' the professor called, but the boys were splitting into two factions over whether eggs should be soft or hard.

Personally, I like a soft yolk to dip my fried bread into, but I was keeping out of what threatened to be a riot.

'Run all off the plate,' one boy maintained furiously.

'Right,' Green said purposefully, and performed a complicated manoeuvre of slipping his swagger stick out and the frying pan under his left arm before raising the stick like that man who led the charge of the light brigade.

Oh, what was his name?

'Do not dare,' Dodo said fiercely.

Something to do with clothes.

'They need discipline,' he told her, and I was starting to agree with him. Spades were being raised in threatening manners.

Not Wellington, of course.

'They need kindness,' she insisted. 'Oh, children,' she cooed. 'Please do return to work.'

And to my astonishment, but not hers, they did.

'Can't argue with loonies,' I heard the lanky boy mutter.

Balaclava? No, that was the same battle but a different garment altogether.

We were hardly back to work when there was another cry. A man's boot this time, roughly made, with no laces and the sole hanging sideways. This was duly written up with great satisfaction, the site marked and handed over to Mr Green.

'Can't somebody else?' he protested, indicating his full hands.

'Oh, give me that.' The professor whipped Green's swagger stick away and, within half an hour, the director was struggling with an empty corned beef tin, the frame of an umbrella and another boot, not matching the first and in better condition.

'Clearly,' the professor told him, 'your boys on the left are not exhibiting the same energy and enthusiasm as those on the right. They have found nothing.'

'You boys,' Green bellowed at them, 'put your backs into it and keep your eyes skimmed.'

'Please,' Dodo prompted him, softly but unheeded.

'Skinned,' I corrected him, also unheeded.

Box ambled back.

'Where have you been?' I asked.

It was not like him to skive.

'Or peeled,' Dodo contributed to our previous conversation.

'Gettin' my bearin's, ma'am,' he told me. 'Use to play hide and seek here I do,' he puffed, though he had had an easy stroll down the slope. 'Or here'bouts.' He surveyed the great expanse of furrowed ground sadly. 'Int nowhere to hide now.'

'I can't imagine you as a little boy,' I commented.

Box was built like a Suffolk Punch and had the same plodding temperament.

'I'm talkin' 'bout when Mrs Box is courtin' me,' he explained. 'I try to hide but she always find me.' He eased his helmet strap where it had risen to dig in under his nose. 'Make a good bloodhound she would.' Box sniffed. 'Wish she is one sometime.' He toed a stone sideways. 'Dog'd be more 'fectionate.' Box paused dreamily. 'And better comp'ny. Find anythin' yet?'

I indicated the heavily laden Mr Green.

'All from this side,' I told him.

'Course it is,' he said.

'Why?' the professor demanded from under our shoulders.

Box exhaled thoughtfully. 'See tha' syc'more at the top?' He raised a hand towards the tree in question. It was the same one that Humphrey Smith had used as a landmark when he brought us to the area. There wasn't much else to fix on.

The professor swapped his gold wire-framed glasses for a silver wire-framed pair, a prolonged procedure involving wrapping the ends over his tiny ears and sliding the unused

17

BOUDICA AND THE TEARDROP MEDALLION

The dig proceeded quite quickly after the professor had directed the boys to work along the line that Box indicated.

'Why would all these things end up here?' Dodo asked as Mr Green staggered by, laden with more corroded household items and rags.

'I suppose anything that's lost gets washed into the drainage system,' I theorised.

'Courtin' couples have picnics here they do,' Box reminisced. 'S'prisin' how many folk goo home forgettin' their kettle or blanket.'

'Especially after they have had a bit of fun in the hedgerow,' Dodo suggested archly, and Box's complexion changed from turnip to beetroot.

'Mrs Box and me never have no fun afore we wed,' he spluttered. 'Precious little a'ter either,' he muttered, probably just to himself but more audibly than intended.

Steady on, Boxy, I thought, *the fresh air must be making you frisky.*

I went to the professor, who was standing near our original site.

'So, if we found the mandible there, would you expect the rest of the skeleton to be up or downhill of the spot?' I asked.

'It is difficult to say,' he told me unhelpfully.

Why do so many people seem to believe that telling me a question is tricky answers my enquiry?

'Have a go,' I urged in the same way I might encourage my daughter – if I ever had one – to try to ride her bicycle.

'I should think – and this is impure speculation based…'

Just get on with it.

'…on years of practical experience…'

I knew I should have brought a book.

The professor droned on with so many provisos and caveats that, if I had been sitting in one of his lectures, I would have dozed off long ago.

'…that, bearing in mind this is one of the lighter bones, the heavier ones, e.g. the femur, would not have been washed as far downstream. But then who am I to judge?' he burst out bitterly. 'I am only the man whose find of Boudica's spear handle was dismissed as a stair rod by jealous pettifogging rivals.'

'The plough will have scattered things as well,' Dodo pointed out sensibly.

'Leg bone,' a giant of a boy roared from ten yards up the slope. 'I find a leg bone.' He plunged his spade into the earth and threw a clod of soil over his shoulder.

'Here,' the boy who had complained about nearly having his toes amputated complained again. 'That goo all in my hair.'

It was difficult to see what difference that would have made. He looked like he had been tunnelling into the earth head first anyway.

'Stop digging,' the prof commanded. 'You will shatter it.'

'And down my neck,' the boy moaned.

We hurried over, every step sending jolting pains through my forehead. I would consult Tubby when he returned, I resolved, forcing myself not to think *if*.

'Looks like a root to me,' I observed.

'That is possibly because it is, Boss,' Dodo concurred.

'Excellent.' The professor rubbed his hands. We had yet to

discover anything that failed to delight him. 'At least that proves my theory that the hedgerow went this way is correct.'

'*Your* theory?' Box huffed indignantly.

'Indeed.' The professor bobbed his head like a sparrow dipping for water. 'You may have told me the ditch was here, but I theorised that there would be a hedgerow alongside it.' He raised his chin proudly. 'Wooster's Hedge, it shall be known as in future.'

'Jepson's Ditch, when it existed,' Box told him, and turned to me. 'Not much point in havin' somethin' that don't exist no more named a'ter you,' he mumbled.

'Leg bone,' the cheerful boy called from a little higher up. 'I find a leg bone.'

'If this is your idea of a joke, boy...' Mr Green warned.

'I do think I goo think on a much better joke than tha',' the boy protested, wounded by a slur on his skills as a humourist.

Nobody needed an anatomist's education to see that the boy was right. We had all seen enough joints hanging in the butcher's to recognise the head of the femur jutting into a hole the boy had just dug.

The professor knelt again and trowelled the earth away. Several boys stopped digging to gather round. To give the man his due, he was patient and careful, not lifting the bone out until he had completely uncovered it.

'Human,' I said, having seen one on the skeleton in Tubby's study often enough and, more shockingly, under a pillow when I searched the home of Megan Priest, the Corkscrew Killer.

'Put tha' back,' a little boy shouted but not, as I thought for a second, at us.

'Shut your cakehole,' the young giant warned, but the little boy was angry.

'Int right, stealin' from the dead,' he insisted.

'Shut your gob or I'll shut it permanent.'

We all hurried over but, being closest and possibly fastest, I got there first.

The giant had his fists clenched but he was not brandishing them threateningly as you might expect from his demeanour. Massive though they were, he had closed them so quickly that I could see something sticking out between the palm of his hand and his curled little finger.

'Show me what's in your hand,' I rapped, and he instantly opened his right fist, but his left flicked back and whatever had been in it flew backwards.

What? Did he seriously think I wouldn't notice?

A thin glitter soared over Box's head and he watched it like a hiker might pause to appreciate a flock of swallows flitting across the sky.

'Oh dear,' Dodo cried, skipping backwards and stumbling over a spade. Why did she always choose the most public places to behave the most eccentrically? 'Howzat?'

She waved her catch triumphantly.

Howzat? Since when had Dodo been a fan of cricket? A picture flickered through my mind – Godfrey Skillern, young and happy, triumphantly holding a caught ball aloft and yelling the same word. I tried to suppress the next image – the last time I had seen him, his poor head smashed by the blow of a hoof.

'What is it?' I asked as she hopped over the furrows towards me.

'Give it here,' the professor demanded. 'All finds are mine.'

'But I do not take orders from you,' Dodo told him nicely, and held out her hand to me, a thin silver chain dangling between her childlike fingers.

The chain held a small flat silver pendant, caked in dirt, and I wiped it with my thumb. It was shaped like a tear.

I licked a grubby finger and cleaned the back, wiping it on my skirt. It was divided horizontally with a wavy engraved line.

a stone bottle rolling a few inches away before deciding that the incline didn't warrant any further effort.

'It appears that you carried it for nothing,' Dodo told him cheerfully.

'What?' he repeated. Had some of the soil got into his ears? 'Where is my swagger stick?'

'Stick?' The professor combed his fingers through his beard. 'Ah yes, I gave it to one of your boys.'

'Which one?'

'Oh, I don't know,' Prof Woosters said airily. 'They all look the same to me.'

You would be hard-pressed to collect such a varied bunch of youths. They came in a wide age range and a good variety of heights, weights and hair colouring.

Mr Green turned on his wards.

'Right. Who has it?'

The boys all shrugged and made a great show of asking each other and demonstrating that their hands were empty.

'I do so hope,' Dodo said, 'that it did not get dropped and accidently buried in all that soil.' But, judging by the smirks from the boys of St Dimlock's, that must have been exactly what happened.

I lifted the skull out and shook it gently, blowing a few times more. The upper central and left incisors had fallen out. The right cheekbone – zygomatic arch, I remembered it was called – was broken and there was a crack in the palate, forcing the upper right incisors apart. The two eye sockets were empty, of course, fissures radiating off the little central holes at the back. Had these cavities once held the sparkling eyes of my friend?

I had had uneasy suspicions when the jaw arrived at the station and they had been confirmed by the discovery of the necklace, but now I had her in both hands. My friend, who I had always told myself I would find alive, was no more now than an empty shell.

'Oh God,' I whispered again. *Etterly*, I mouthed silently. *Oh, my poor dear Etterly.*

The boys went back to digging, spurred on by the spirit of competition.

'I find a rib.'

'So? I find a shoulder blade.'

Bantony joined us.

'Moy new shoes,' he moaned.

'They are filthy,' I raged, completely irrationally, I knew, since the rest of us looked like clodhoppers at the end of a beet harvest. 'And your trousers are an absolute disgrace.'

He had a few taupe specks round the hems.

'Oy—' Bantony began to protest, but Dodo touched his arm warningly.

It was not often she was so sensitive to what was going on.

'Wha' 'bout this?'

'Tha's a turnip, you turnip.'

'I do find a n'arm bone,' the lanky youth crowed, waving it triumphantly.

I knew it was a game to them but, given their miserable lives and the fact they had no idea who they were unearthing, I couldn't really blame them. I doubt they even thought of their discoveries as having been a person. They were just having a day out. But I couldn't watch.

I almost apologised to Bantony, something senior officers aren't supposed to do. It implies that we can make mistakes, which is, of course, unthinkable, but if there was one thing my constable was, it was attentive to women.

'Oym sorry, ma'am,' he said.

'When they have finished, the professor has some boxes...' I said distractedly.

'And sacks,' Dodo contributed.

'Oyl use a box,' Bantony promised. 'A sack isn't dignifoyd.'

'Thank you,' I said, which was the closest I could do to saying sorry.

'You look in shock back there, ma'am,' Box observed as we walked back towards the town.

'I expect Inspector Church is afraid of bones,' Dodo suggested. 'Just like I am frightened of—' I just knew she was going to say *spiders*, after all the talks I had given her about not giving the men ammunition to mock her with. 'Nothing,' she corrected herself unconvincingly.

The sun was setting behind us, the rooftops glowing ahead. Like a much-powdered woman, Sackwater looked prettier from a distance.

'It's when you see tha' necklace, int it, ma'am?' Box probed gently. 'Even 'fore you see the skull.'

'We have found Etterly Utter,' I explained.

'Oh, Boss, I am sorry,' Dodo sympathised, because I had told her all about Etterly when we first went past the King's Oak, 'but, even if Dr Gretham manages to put her back together, I do not think that she will ever work properly again.'

Woman Police Inspector clubs Woman Police Constable to death flashed through my mind. That would sell a few *Gazettes* for Toby and, upset as I was, I couldn't help hoping he would use the portrait photograph he had done of me when he did an article *Sackwater Welcomes First Woman Police Officer* what seemed an age ago, but was still less than a year.

'The girl who goo go' eaten by the Ghost Tree?' Box clarified.

'Except that she didn't,' I told him. 'I have waited twenty-six years for this. She was my childhood friend.'

'Your childhood friend?' Box echoed in sad surprise. 'Oh, I don't know what to say, ma'am,' he said, and then proved it by adding, 'I never even dream you have a friend.'

'But how,' Dodo asked, 'did Etterly Utter get from the tree to the field?'

'That,' I told her, 'is what I intend to find out.'

I suppose I should have said *hope* rather than *intend*, but any confidence I lacked in my ability to do it was brushed aside by Dodo's invincible confidence in me.

'You'll do it, Boss,' she declared proudly as she tightrope-walked along a ridge. 'You always do.'

I couldn't help wondering, as I straddled two furrows, how Constable Chivers would react when she discovered that those earth-caked shoes of mine encased two feet of clay.

19

THE BRASS RING AND THE HAMMER BLOWS OF FATE

I hadn't been back to Eleven Bath Road since the day Etterly disappeared. It had been Sixteen Bath Road in those days, but many Sackwater streets were renumbered over the years, having originally been numbered inconveniently in sequence all the way down one side then down the other.

Occasionally I would catch sight of Mr Utter cycling to work, but he had sold his shop four years ago, generating more business – rumour had it – in the week of his closing sale than he had in the previous year. My parents went there for a bargain and came home with a carriage clock, which fell off the mantelpiece and smashed a month later, either when Pooky was dusting or, if she was to be believed, during a highly localised earth tremor while she was in the garden. Since Mr Utter had retired, I rarely saw anything of him at all and was not looking forward to having to meet him again in such grim circumstances.

Mrs Utter could be seen three or four times a week going to Mason's Grocery Shop and returning with her string bag bulging. But though Etterly's parents must have known who I was, neither of them ever acknowledged me, not with a word or even a nod of the head. Did they blame me for what had happened? I could not imagine why they would.

I took Box with me. He was not the quickest-witted of men but, while Dodo was kind-hearted, she could appear unwittingly frivolous, whereas Box's slowness gave him an air of dignity that would be more fitting in the circumstances.

'If that old Ghost Tree do eat people...' he began slowly as we turned down the road.

'It doesn't,' I interrupted, 'and it is called the King's Oak.'

He pressed his case. 'Folk say it do.'

The street was terraced, with two-storey dark-brick houses opening straight onto the pavement.

'People say all sorts of things,' I pointed out. 'They said there wouldn't be a war and before that they said man would never fly.'

'But if it do...' Box persisted.

'It doesn't,' I insisted, but he was not so easily deflected.

'Why do they never chop it down?' he asked.

'Because some people think Charles II hid in the hollow,' I explained.

Box mulled over this information.

'King Charles?' he pondered. 'Well, he dint be needin' it now.'

I rapped with the hinged ring of tarnished brass and a familiar figure appeared blurrily through the dark green glass cut into squares by pitted lead strips. There was a time when Mrs Utter would be calling for Etterly as she came to let me in and my friend would come cantering down the stairs to greet me, often whisking me away down the street before her mother could remind her what chores remained to be done. But it was an old, slow woman who answered my summons now.

Mrs Utter hinged the door open just enough to peer out.

'Yes?' She looked at me blankly.

'Hello, Mrs Utter,' I said. 'Do you remember me? Betty Church.'

The last time I had called I was shorter than Mrs Utter, but she had to bend her neck back to look up at me now.

I was expecting a cool reception, after Etterly's parents had ignored me for so long, but Mrs Utter rubbed her eyes as if she had just woken from a deep sleep and her expression lit up.

'Betsy.' She beamed, and held out both arms, and I wished later that I had taken it as an invitation to hug her. Lord knew she must have needed all the comfort she could get. 'Coom inside, darlin'.'

With that, Mrs Utter stepped back and swung the door open wide.

20

TREADMILLS AND THE COMFORT OF SWINE

I paused. This was awkward, to say the least. I had rather hoped that my uniform and the presence of Box would indicate that this was not a social call, especially after so many years.

Mrs Utter must have been in her mid-sixties – she had had three miscarriages before Etterly was born – but she had the shuffle of a much older woman, her hair was white, and there was no lustre in those silvery-grey eyes.

'Coom in, my dear,' she urged again, and took my left hand to lead me over the threshold. If she noticed the hardness under my glove, she showed no sign of it. 'And you too, dear.' Mrs Utter flapped her free hand at my constable, who lumbered in after me.

The doorway had yet to be invented that Box could pass through without effort. True, he was a heftily built man, but even the huge double entrance of the town hall seemed to present him with problems. He must have been taught, I often thought, to bowl into a doorpost with his shoulder and then sort of hinge himself in on it, and that was exactly what he did again.

'I'm 'fraid Etterly int here,' her mother told me.

'But she hasn't been here for a long time,' I reminded her hesitantly.

'She dint know you're visitin',' she defended her daughter.

I thought I had wiped my feet properly on the coconut mat sunk into a well that was slightly too big for it, but Box demonstrated that I had done no such thing because apparently it involved shuffling the soles of his boots to and fro like he had been sentenced to work on a treadmill.

'She couldn't know,' I agreed. This was going to be even more difficult than I expected.

Like many houses of that era, there was a long hall leading to the back of the house with the stairs heading straight up on the right. I heard footsteps and Mr Utter came towards us, heavy-browed and rocking on his bow legs as always, but shorter and slighter than I remembered and sparsely haired now.

'Who is it, Mitzie?'

His wife beamed, letting go of my hand at last.

'You remember Betsy, Edwind,' she said gaily. 'But my, how she grow. And this is Constable Box, the nice policeman who help me when I fall in the snow.'

'Oh, that be gooin' back a year or two.' Box tipped the rim of his helmet in a sort of salute cum greeting.

Edwind Utter, I was aware, was watching us carefully.

'You didn't tell me you knew Mrs Utter,' I said.

'Dint know I do,' Box replied. 'I never ask her name when I pull her up.'

'I must put the kettle on,' Mitzie Utter bubbled merrily.

'Let's find out why they coom first,' her husband suggested.

'May we sit somewhere?' I asked, and I saw at once that he understood.

Mr Utter worked his lips against each other.

'Coom through,' he said quietly, turning the white and blue china door handle.

I had never been in the front parlour before. It always surprised me that families with so little space would reserve a room for special occasions – a rare visit from the vicar, a family christening or maybe Christmas Day.

'Oh, but it's a pigsty in there,' Mrs Utter protested.

'And I'm sure the pigs are very comfortable, madam,' Box said gallantly.

It was a pleasant room – net curtains to blur the view for nosy passers-by, four chintzy armchairs with frilled aprons, a grate with the coal built up but, to judge from the highly polished brass surround, rarely lit, an old oak sideboard and a low square table bearing a massive family Bible.

'You must have tea,' Mrs Utter said, a little less certainly.

'Please sit down, Mrs Utter,' I said, and she looked at me askance. It was not the guest's place to give such an instruction to the hostess and she opened her mouth to say something, but Mr Utter said firmly, 'It might be best, dear.'

Mrs Utter sat uneasily. There were too many serious faces for her to ignore them.

'But I int put the kettle on yet,' she protested weakly.

'Inspector Church has something to tell you,' Box said.

'Would—' I began to say to Mr Utter, but he put out his hands like he was trying to catch me in a game.

'I shall stop as I am,' he insisted, and I went down on my haunches to face his wife, looking slightly up into her bemused eyes.

'I'm afraid I have some bad news,' I told her, and she fiddled with a button uncertainly. *Oh God, why does this never get easier?* 'We have found some human remains,' I began. I once made the mistake of telling a couple we had found their child and they were celebrating before I got a chance to say he was dead. 'And I'm afraid the evidence suggests that they belong to Etterly.'

'Belong to?' she asked in understandable confusion at my clumsy choice of words. 'What goo she want with them?'

'They are the remains of Etterly,' I tried again. 'I am so sorry.'

'Etterly?' she said, as if the name was strange to her, and her husband coughed, just once.

'Let me take your arm, sir,' I heard Box say, and glanced back to see my constable guiding a swaying Mr Utter into a chair by the hearth.

'No,' Mrs Utter said mildly, and I rested my hand on hers, folded in her lap. 'She never goo and not say goodbye.'

'I'm sorry, but it is Etterly,' I assured her.

Mr Utter cleared his throat.

'Where do you find her?' he asked.

'Just—' Box checked himself. He knew better than that.

'She is in the mortuary.' I dodged the question. It was not unknown for one or both parents to kill their daughter and report her missing. I could not imagine that they would have harmed Etterly, but since I put on a uniform I have seen a great many things that I could not have imagined.

Mrs Utter gave me a strange smile.

'At least tha's somethin',' Mr Utter said. 'Dint like to think of her lying in tha' cold earth.'

I blew out heavily.

That cold earth? Not even *the* cold earth.

Oh, Edwind Utter, I thought, *what do you know and what in the name of God have you done?*

21

DAHLIAS AND THE COILED LINKS

I thought about Mr Utter's words and decided to let my concerns over them rest for now. Assuming that he was innocent – and, from what I knew of him, that seemed a safe supposition – this was not the time to cross-examine him. He had just been told that his daughter had been found dead, which was enough to muddle any man's thinking.

'We must goo see her,' Mrs Utter said, and put her hands on the arms of her chair, clearly intending to get up and go there now.

'I'm afraid there is not very much to see,' I said, watching her closely. It was difficult to know how much information she could take all at once.

'How much is not very much?' Mr Utter asked sharply, like he was querying a plumber's estimate.

'Perhap we should discuss it without the lady,' Box suggested, just when I had hoped he was being cured of his belief that all women are silly and weak.

'No,' Mrs Utter insisted. 'I've every right to know.'

She was looking at her husband and not at me any more, so I stood up.

'We just have part of her skeleton,' I admitted.

'Her head,' Mr Utter pounced. 'Do you have her head?'

'Some of it,' I said. 'The front and most of the top and part of her lower jaw.'

'Is that it?' Mrs Utter asked.

'That's all we have of Etterly's skull,' I conceded. 'We also have some arm and leg bones and—'

'Arm and leg?' Mr Utter repeated scornfully, getting to his feet.

'What 'bout her clothes?' Mrs Utter asked. 'She's wearin' that nice blue dress. I tell her not to for play but she's stubborn as a donkey, she is.'

I remembered all too well what Etterly was wearing. I remembered seeing it sway as she made her way towards that tree.

'We haven't found any clothes,' I admitted.

'So you can't know,' Mr Utter told me. He came up close, like he was squaring for a fight. 'You can't be sure from a foo' bone. It could be anyone.'

It flashed through my head that, if Sidney had been there, he would have launched into an interminable list of people it could not possibly be, beginning with those who were still alive, but it was obvious what Etterly's father meant.

'The jawbone was of a girl about the same age as Etterly,' I began, and hurried before they could leap on the vagueness of that fact as a source of more hope. 'And she had had a filling where Etterly had one and the same tooth missing.'

'Lots of girls—' Mr Utter broke in, but I had not finished.

'And we found this.' I opened my handbag, took out the envelope, pulled out the flap and emptied the chain into my glove.

'Let me see.' Mrs Utter leaned forwards and I tipped the chain into her cupped hand.

The medallion fell under the coiled links and she rooted through to pick it out, the chain dangling between her fingers.

'Do you recognise it?' Box asked, and Mrs Utter laughed lightly.

'Is it Etterly's?' she asked, like she was trying to remember somebody on an old school photo. 'She goo be glad you found it.'

'Did you ever see Etterly wearing it?' I asked.

'Dint think so,' she said uncertainly as she turned it this way and that.

'Do you?' Mr Utter asked me reasonably. 'I never.'

'Well, no,' I admitted, 'but it's the same design that Etterly drew on a piece of paper in your shop,' I said.

Mr Utter waved my concerns away.

'Always drawin' patterns and the like.' He twisted his face while he considered the matter. 'Mayhap she saw someone else wearin' it,' he suggested.

'And it was carved inside the oak,' I told him.

'The Ghost Tree,' Box clarified unhelpfully.

Mr Utter gave me the sort of look he used to give Etterly when she forgot something or got into a muddle at work. 'Give us quite a turn then,' he told me, 'but dint you worry, young Betsy. There must be a thousand necklaces like tha'.'

'But there's a filled-in U like Etterly carved on the pendant she made for me,' I pointed out.

'Could just be a scratch,' Mr Utter argued.

I had come across this before. People faced with bad news often refuse to accept it. They may not always deny it in such an outright way, but something inside tells them *No, this is wrong.*

'There is a C on the other side,' I showed them. 'Can you think of anyone with that initial that Etterly was close friends with?'

'You,' Mrs Utter pointed out.

'Any boys?' I tried.

'My girl dint goo with no boys,' Mr Utter said fiercely.

'Tea,' Mrs Utter announced, and while she went to make it, Mr Utter told us how his allotment was coming along. He had been obliged to uproot his prized, though never prize, dahlias for potatoes and the last of his flowers were in a vase on the mantelpiece and did not look like they were enjoying their final days there.

'Perhaps you can save the bulbs until after the war,' I suggested uncertainly.

'Dahlias is choobers, ma'am,' Box explained.

Mrs Utter returned with a tray and her best china – willow pattern cups and saucers with matching pot, milk jug and sugar bowl. I had helped wash them once, while Etterly dried.

'Have you kept any of Etterly's things?' I asked, and her mother looked puzzled.

'Why goo we throw any away?' She sat in an armchair to pour.

'She do need them when she coom back,' Mr Utter explained.

Did they both still believe that she would? I would give them time to digest the facts.

'Do you think I could have a look at her old room?' I asked.

'It's like a mess of potage up there,' protested Mrs Utter, and I didn't argue that a mess of potage was a bowl of stew that Jacob sold his birthright for in the Old Testament.

'Why?' Mr Utter demanded.

I thought at first he was challenging his wife about her poor housekeeping, but then I realised he was talking to me.

'I just thought it might help me remember what happened that day,' I said, and there was no need to explain which day I meant.

'But you don't know what happened that day,' Mr Utter pointed out, with better interrogation skills than most of my men had ever displayed.

'I meant up until the moment I last saw Etterly,' I struggled.

If truth be told, I was not sure what I hoped to find after all that time. The police had searched my friend's room for letters and photographs and found nothing of interest.

'Very well.' Mrs Utter sighed – seemingly more upset at the prospect of having her domestic skills called into question than by the discovery of her daughter's remains – and braced her arms to rise.

'Please don't trouble yourself,' I urged. I didn't want her watching me poking about. 'I know the way.'

'It's no trouble,' she assured me.

'Please don't let me spoil your tea,' I insisted, and she instantly relaxed back into her chair. If there is one thing no English man or woman can contemplate with equanimity, it's the ruin of a good cuppa.

'What about yours, ma'am?' Box enquired solicitously.

'Oh, I like it cold,' I assured him, hoping he did not store and repeat that piece of misinformation at the station.

Mrs Utter leaned forwards and began to pour.

'You were always a strange girl,' she told me, quite sternly, and I wondered afterwards if she suspected that I was making it all up.

22

CLARICE MAYNE AND THE CHILDREN OF ISRAEL

The fifth stair used to squeak. Etterly had pointed that out to me when we had sneaked back in on a rainy day so she could avoid Sunday School. Her parents made her go every week in addition to the church services that she hated. The tread still squeaked, I noted, and there was something disconcerting about that. How could it not have changed when nothing would ever be the same again? But I was soon to find much more than that remained unaltered.

Etterly's room was at the top of the stairs. In some similar houses this had been converted into a bathroom, but the Utters rented their house and Sackwater Council would not pay for such frivolous luxuries and so, like many families, they carried a tin bath in from the back yard and filled it with water heated on the cooking range. Usually there was a pecking order to use the bath – father, mother and then children – but Etterly was the adored daughter and always got the clean and warmest water.

I opened the door. The curtains were closed – I remembered Etterly begrudgingly helping her mother to hem those – but enough light seeped in from behind me to find my way across the room and open them.

'Oh, Etterly,' I said, unintentionally aloud.

Her bedroom was still exactly as I had last seen it. I ran a finger over the little oak side table. Clearly Mrs Utter still came in to dust, but she had left everything exactly as it was. Her daughter's jam jar of seashells still stood there, and the Bible her godfather had given her at her christening. Etterly loved to read the Old Testament, not because she was especially devout but she loved the stories. Exodus, with its accounts of the Israelites in the wilderness, fascinated her and she would chatter about it when we went on walks. I was more interested in *Treasure Island* and *King Solomon's Mines*, the nuns at Roedene Abbey having given me a lifelong aversion to the good but not – to me, at least – very interesting book.

The bed still had a rose counterpane with a dark blue stain from when we had tried to make invisible ink that turned out to be all too visible. There was still her second-hand chest of drawers with the wooden handles that didn't quite match each other. I pulled open the top drawer. Etterly didn't have many clothes – few of us did – and some of her stockings had been darned. There was no shame in that. Pooky used to darn my father's and my stockings, albeit grumpily and in big lumps that dug into our heels and toes afterwards.

I'm nosy by nature – you have to be in my job – and I love rooting around people's things, but I was uncomfortable with this one. Etterly would not have liked me to be sorting through her underwear and I could almost imagine her sitting on her bed, watching me indignantly.

What? I asked silently. *Would you prefer I'd sent a stranger?*

There was nothing of any interest. The lavender had almost turned to dust in a little cloth bag that she had made for it. Etterly's best shoes were on the floor in a little alcove. Her coat hung off a hook and her hat was on the shelf above. I could see to the back of the shelf easily now. The last time, I would have had to stand on tiptoes.

There were still two photographs on the single shelf over the head of Etterly's bed – one of Clarice Mayne, the music hall singer, cut out of a magazine and framed. We had never seen Miss Mayne perform because our parents regarded 'I Was a Good Little Girl Till I Met You' as far too racy for young ladies to witness, but we had glimpsed her getting into the back of a black Vauxhall B-Type to be driven all of the fifty yards or so from the Grand Hotel to the Pier Pavilion where she was performing. She wore a tiered cerise dress with a matching bonnet that she had to tilt to get into the car, and was the most elegant woman we had ever seen.

The second photograph was of a little girl who looked very like Etterly but, she had explained to me, was her cousin Effie, who had been taken to live in Cornwall – just a little further than Mars in Sackwater eyes.

Etterly and I kept diaries. I always hid mine under the floorboards. There was nothing really shocking in it, but I didn't want my prying mother to read how I had a crush on Richard McLoughlin or how Etterly and I had provoked two boys from St Joseph's School into chasing us or how I had tried a few cigarettes. Etterly and I didn't tell each other where we kept our journals. It was not that we didn't trust each other; it was more that we didn't trust the adults not to force or trick us into revealing our secrets.

I knew the police had not found any notebooks when they searched Etterly's room, but men are not good at looking for things. How many times has the average wife had to find a sock for her husband when he has hunted everywhere, only for her to spot it immediately in his sock drawer?

There was a faded blue rug with several tassels missing at one end. It had been put alongside the bed so that Etterly could step onto something less cold than the lino floor when she got up. I lifted it but the flooring looked intact underneath. I prodded the pillow. It was flat and hard, but no diary had been slipped inside the case. There was nothing in the bedding either, or under the mattress, when I heaved it up, but wooden slats. I knelt and peered under the bed, then lay on my back and slid beneath. A family of spiders had been hard at work but there was only a blanket of cobwebs secreted there.

Where else? I pulled out the drawers and looked behind and under them to no avail. There was no fireplace and I was pleased about that. I had ruined a good shirt rooting around a sooty chimney once and found exactly what I was finding now – nothing.

The skirting board was well attached to the wall when I tried to prise it away with my fingers. I delved in my handbag for the folding rigging knife Carmelo had given me as a reward for having worked out how to wedge it in my left hand and hinge it open with my right. I was not supposed to carry a weapon and I would never have used it as one, but all the men had penknives for all sorts of purposes – in Brigsy's case, for cleaning tar out of his pipe, Bantony for keeping his fingernails clean. I ran the blade along the top of the skirting and in a few slits between the floorboards, but everything seemed well attached.

There wasn't really anywhere else you could hide a book in that room and Etterly would not have risked concealing it in a room that everyone used. This was the only place she had any privacy. My favourite aunt, Philly, told me that when she was a reporter, she had smuggled a hip flask of sherry into a temperance conference by carving out the middle of a copy of *Foxe's Book of Martyrs*. Could Etterly have done something similar? I opened her Bible near the middle, but it was intact. I shook it but nothing fell out, and I was just going to put it back when a clump of pages flipped over and I glimpsed some handwriting at the top of a page.

Etterly did not strike me as a girl who would write commentaries on sacred text and the first words demonstrated that she had not. *Doggy is such a chop-logger-head*, she had written, in handwriting that made my scrawl look the work of a calligrapher. Sister Bernard had described my efforts as like the scratchings of a hen in the dust and I wondered what she would make of my friend's.

I flicked back and there was more. There was nothing in Genesis, presumably so that anyone opening the Bible at the beginning would not spot my friend's words, but above Exodus 1, where it said *Now these are the names of the children of Israel*, Etterly's journal began.

23

JUSTICE AND THE BLACKBIRD

Etterly had written in the top and bottom margins of each page. The opening entry was *Thursday Janaury 1st. A new year and I do be 16 in September. A wet and windey start.*

My friend would have had her knuckles rapped for spelling like that in class, but she – like most children – had left school at twelve.

'They think I can be a secertary,' Etterly once told me, proving in the same sentence that she probably couldn't.

January 2nd was no more interesting. More miserable weather and cod pie for dinner. The Utters were Methodists but followed the Catholic tradition of fish on Friday.

'Finding inspiration in the word of our Lord?' Mrs Utter asked from behind me.

I struggled to swallow my leaping heart.

'May I borrow it?' I asked, hastily shutting the book, and Mrs Utter tipped her head to one side like a blackbird listening for a worm.

'Haven't you got a Bible at home?' she asked.

'No,' I said. Her head tilted further and I realised that a further explanation was required. *My mother has a fear of Bibles since a family one fell on her head when she was five*, I nearly said, but settled for, 'It was accidently put in the fire.'

'By Pooky?' Mrs Utter asked, and I nodded sadly.

There was a poetic justice in this since our maid had pinned many of her accidents on me, including some that occurred while I was away at school.

'Wellll,' she began, and I saw her hand begin to rise to take it from me.

'Oh please,' I wheedled. 'It would help me feel closer to Etterly,' I said truthfully.

Mrs Utter softened.

'And God,' I added, less honestly.

'Oh, very well,' Mrs Utter conceded, and her hand fell. 'But you must look after it.'

'I will be very careful,' I promised.

'I don't want to have to explain to Etterly that I let her things be spoiled,' Mrs Utter explained.

'But when?' I asked in confusion.

Mrs Utter smiled indulgently at my silliness.

'When she come home, of course,' she told me.

'But she won't—' I began.

'Course she do,' Mrs Utter insisted.

Oh, Mitzie, I thought, ***which bit of 'human remains' didn't you understand?***

24

FALSE HOPE AND A FEW BONES

We were on the pavement before Mr Utter spoke again.

'When can I goo see those remains?'

I hesitated.

'Etterly?' I clarified.

'It's only you say tha',' her father argued.

'You do understand,' I said carefully, but there was no delicate way of putting the question, 'that we have only found a few bones?'

'I int stupid,' he assured me without rancour.

'Now why you want to do tha', Ed?' Box asked gently.

'I thought you people always want families to identify bodies,' Mr Utter countered.

'Well, yes,' I conceded, 'but there isn't very much to go on.'

'You have her head,' he reminded me.

'Not the all on it,' Box said quietly.

'It has teeth,' Mr Utter reasoned.

'Two are missing,' I told him, but he puffed dismissively.

'You think a father dint know his own daughter's smile?'

He had a point there, I supposed, and didn't like to point out that a smile without lips and gums is a very different thing to the one he would have remembered.

'Well, if you are sure you are up to it,' I said doubtfully.

'I have to know,' he insisted. 'We goo been given false hope 'fore now.'

'When was that?' Box asked.

'Week or so a'ter she goo,' Mr Utter told him. 'We ge' a letter sayin' Etterly is held prisoner 'til we goo pay one hundred pound.'

'One hundred.' Box whistled. 'You dint pay it, do you?'

Mr Utter ground the pavement with his toe like he was stubbing out a cigarette.

'I show 'Spector Grove the note,' he answered, 'and he send men to keep watch and catch him. Ge' five year, he do.'

From what little I had heard of Inspector George Grove, it was not like him to catch his man.

'Get off light,' Box commented.

'When do I see them then?' Mr Utter pressed, and I knew he was not going to give up.

'Can you come to the police station?' I asked. The hospital morgue did not have facilities for relatives, and I had not forgotten how one man turned up to view his mother and found her in the process of being dissected. Obviously this could not apply to Etterly, but there were jars with anatomical specimens on the shelf, which the average person would find distressing.

'I can coom now,' he said. 'Just let me get my coat.'

It was a warm day, but men of Mr Utter's generation did not stroll the streets in shirtsleeves unless they were on holiday.

'Come in the morning,' I said, 'about nine o'clock.'

'We do have a cuppa 'round then,' Box promised, as if it mattered, but Mr Utter perked up at that news so, apparently, it did.

25

CHEERFUL MENACE AND THE LONG WAIT

Mr Utter came on the dot of nine. He had put his church suit on, the one he wore for Sunday services, weddings, funerals, christenings. I don't suppose he ever went to anything more formal. It was black with a matching tie and he had a white shirt with bone buttons and an old-fashioned detachable wing collar. His shoes turned up at the toes but were highly polished. I supposed there were few more solemn occasions than identifying your daughter.

Dodo put down her mug. We had been standing in front of the desk, like dedicated drinkers at a bar.

'You do look smart,' she told Mr Utter, though she had never met him before. 'I hope my daddy would make such an effort for me.'

Oh for crying out loud, I cringed, but Mr Utter put a hand on her arm – a strangely unconstrained act for a man of his background, especially with a police officer.

'He would, miss,' he assured her. 'I mean, *Constable*.'

'Would you like to come through?' I asked.

'*Like?*' he puzzled at my choice of words, and all of a sudden I was the one who was putting my foot in it.

'Please come this way,' I tried again, and led Mr Utter along the corridor.

We had two rooms on the left-hand side. The first had been used as a storeroom for junk, which nobody would admit having put there but somebody kept adding to. The last time I checked, there was a stuffed baby crocodile grinning menacingly from an old tea chest.

The second, opposite my office, was used as an interview room. To get there we had to pass Sharkey's lair on the right, where I glimpsed my colleague with his feet on his desk, mouth gaping and eyes closed. I often wished he would shut his door – this was not the professional image of the force we were supposed to portray – but the Shark liked to listen in to whatever was going on in the foyer. I only hoped Mr Utter had not noticed the bottle of The Famous Grouse cradled like an infant in my colleague's arms.

Brigsy had taken it upon himself to follow and closed the door, none too quietly, as he went by.

'What?' I heard the Inspector grunt in surprise as we went on into the room.

Normally I sat across the table from a suspect. Today I had covered it with a cloth from the bottom drawer my mother had accumulated for me when she still lived in hope of palming me onto a preferably wealthy, and even more preferably titled, man. She had given up on that idea. On top of the cloth I had laid the bones in a rough semblance of their anatomical positions – parts of the vault of the skull at the top, jawbone beneath, vertebrae in approximate order of size, ribs to the side of them, left arm, right fingers, pelvis, femur and eight parts of the feet – tarsals or metatarsals, I didn't know which was which. Over these I had folded double a second cloth from the same drawer and laid it over my display.

'There isn't very much to recognise,' I warned, 'and, as I said before, two teeth are missing.'

Mr Utter nodded grimly.

'A man knows his own daughter,' he assured me, and it flicked through my mind that, if my father recognised me, it would only be from the one filling he had found time to inflict upon me.

I lifted the sheet away and hung it over the back of a chair.

'Steady, Ed,' Brigsy said, and took him by the elbow.

Mr Utter seemed steady enough to me. He surveyed the remains with the same interest you might inspect a bad painting.

'Int her,' he said firmly and almost immediately.

'But—' I began.

'Tha's not my Etterly,' he insisted.

'Take a longer look, Edwind,' Brigsy urged.

'Not her,' Mr Utter repeated with hardly a glance.

'I'm sorry, but how can you be sure?' I asked.

Mr Utter pointed, his hand steady. 'Her teeth are smaller than tha' and this do have a breek at the front.'

A *breek* was a gap, but it was more usually applied to things like walls or hedgerows rather than the one between the right central and lateral incisors.

'The trouble is that teeth look a lot bigger when they have no gums,' I reasoned calmly. 'And I know Etterly didn't have a space between her front teeth but there is a crack in the palate forcing them apart. That wouldn't have been there when she was alive.'

Mr Utter looked slightly shaken by that statement. He reached down, took up the thighbone and swivelled it, though I could not see how that would give him a better perspective. Was he looking for signs of an old fracture? I didn't recall Etterly had any.

'Did she ever break any bones? I asked, and he looked at me as if I was mad.

'Did she heck,' he replied scornfully.

'Wha' you thinkin', Edwind?' Brigsy peered over our witness's shoulder.

'She's bigger than tha',' Mr Utter argued, putting the bone back carefully, and I couldn't bring myself to point out that there would have been cartilage on the ends of the femur, and it would have been covered with muscles and fat and skin, and that what he was doing was akin to imagining the size of a chicken from a picked-clean drumstick. 'And she'll be bigger yet now.'

I couldn't argue with that last piece of logic.

'You understand wha' the inspector do say 'bout the teeth?' Brigsy asked quietly, and Mr Utter eyed him scornfully.

'I know you want this settled, Frank.' It wasn't often I heard Sergeant Briggs called by his Christian name and it never sounded right. 'But it int her.' He stepped back, looking at the bits of skeleton with renewed interest. Had he spotted something else?

'What is it?' I urged quietly, but he gave no sign of having heard me.

'I dint know who you are,' Edwind Utter addressed the bones, 'but I pray you are at peace.'

'Amen to tha',' Brigsy said fervently, and I bowed my head.

I hadn't wanted Mr Utter to view the remains because I didn't want to upset him and was sure he would be unable to identify them. What I hadn't expected was him to be so positive in his rejection. It was going to be more difficult than I had anticipated to convince the Utters that their long wait was finally over.

26

RABID DOGS AND THE KALEIDOSCOPE KILLER

It was not very often that I turned to the Bible for inspiration, mainly because I had so rarely found any in there. The morning after Mr Utter's visit, however, I sat in the wheelhouse, the doors wide open to enjoy the warm breeze, a mug of coffee at my side, and turned to Etterly's copy. I had browsed a dozen pages with decreasing interest. There had been a walk with me and Georgie where we had been chased by a ferocious dog and had to shut ourselves in a garden shed while it flung itself against the door repeatedly until the owner came and beat it away with a golf club. It had slavered so much that we feared it had rabies. My father asserted that rabies had been eradicated in Britain for over a decade, but I had heard the false assurances he gave to patients too many times to place much trust in his word.

I found Etterly's reference to our day. *Walk with B and G. Feirce Dog. Liver and bacon, my favrit.* If her journal was merely an aid to her memory, I was unlikely to come across any revelations or insights there.

I leafed through, somewhat discouraged. The police may have failed to find Etterly's journal but it didn't look like they had missed any vital clues.

I searched for the day that Etterly had been attacked by Delilah at Folger's Estate Farm. Surely that must merit a bit of detail and drama. *Farm with B and G and others. Delilas fole. Mutton.* The only thing certain was that Etterly was being well fed.

I don't easily give up in searches. One of my proudest successes as a sergeant in London – and one that aroused considerable resentment in my colleagues – was the capture of Frank Stone, the Kaleidoscope Killer. I had sorted through over eight thousand buttons in a tea chest until I found the one that pointed the finger of suspicion at the murderer. But Etterly's secret journal could have been written on a blackboard left out for all to see without arousing comment.

I rolled myself a cigarette and spun the wheel of my Zippo a dozen times before the almost dried-out wick produced a useable flame. No non-smoker can appreciate the pleasure of your first cigarette of the day. I sucked in deep and held the smoke, letting it flood out of my lungs and through my bloodstream into my brain. Life felt better already.

Saw S, I read. Who was *S*? I could think of a couple of girls – Sally Brown and Susan Thurler – that we came across occasionally. The only boy I could think of was Godfrey Skillern. It was obvious to all that Godfrey liked Etterly, but I rather suspected that he liked Darklis at the farm even more.

Nothing much happened for a few more days. Etterly continued to work in the shop and to be fed a nourishing diet.

Saw S again, I read. *He is even nicer than I thought.*

This was positively Shakespearian by Etterly's standard. She had actually expressed an emotion and not mentioned food. I had not realised the latter played such a big part in her life. But who the hell was S?

The next day she had helped her mother clean out the pantry. The day after that nothing at all happened, apparently.

I miss S, Etterly had written in tiny letters, as if that fact alone was almost too revealing. I wracked my brains. Simon Laflin? Surely not. Simon was a year younger than Etterly – quite a difference given that boys mature much more slowly, if at all – and he was a pleasant enough boy, but he did have a habit of wiping his nose on his sleeve.

Etterly *Wrote note to S* the next day but *couldn't send it.*

Why not? Could she not get away from her parents? Did she not know the address? Was she afraid to send it in case it invited rejection or was intercepted? I had always thought of my friend as an open girl, but now even her secret diary was secretive.

Later that day she *Tore up note* and the day after that she was *miserabel.*

Dad wouldn't let me go out.

Was that the time I had called and seen that symbol on the brown paper bag?

I had destroyed my own journal a long time ago. It was too full of adolescent yearning and embarrassing crushes for me to want to read, and I shuddered to think what somebody else might think of it. For the first time, I regretted that move now. It might have been possible to tie in my rather more detailed accounts of the days with Etterly's abrupt entries.

Managed to meet S again. So happy!!!

Oh, come on, Etterly. Give me a few clues – where did you meet him? Was it by chance or arranged? Didn't either of you say anything?

X'd I saw minutely inscribed in the bottom margin of the left-hand page, just beneath *Unto.*

It didn't take much to work out that Etterly and the mysterious S had kissed.

So happy. Hardly slept was at the top of the right-hand page.

Why had Etterly not confided any of this to me? I thought we always told each other everything, not that I had anything of that nature to disclose.

I turned the page. This was turning into the sort of book my mother read cover to cover to check if it was suitable for me, before announcing it was not.

Met S and X'd, Etterly declared boldly. *BC a bit better Pooky told me.*

That was it. It was when I had chicken pox. Etterly, I vaguely recalled, had come to visit but had been turned away. Of all the times I had been privy to my friend's secrets, I had to choose that one to contract a contagious disease.

Dad has taken bad against S. Say his sort is all croox.

At last, some more information. Who, I wondered, would Mr Utter know and disapprove of so strongly? The Smarts sprung to mind. They were a notorious criminal family and even though Etterly and I knew nothing of their protection rackets and brothels, we knew enough to stay well clear of them. Anyone on Jubilee Road might be regarded as undesirable. Probably a quarter of the men who lived there had some kind of criminal conviction, but we had always shied away from the area.

I stubbed out my cigarette. It had reached the stump and I had hardly smoked it. The grey ash blew onto the floor. The captain wouldn't like that. They don't talk about *shipshape* for no reason, he was fond of telling me. I stood up to get a dustpan and brush, absent-mindedly putting my weight on my left arm but being reminded instantly by the pain jolting up my stump and by my toppling sideways as the elbow hinges gave way. My head hit the table beside me, sending my not-quite-finished mug of coffee flying across the room and depositing the Bible on a, fortunately, dry spot.

'Merda,' I swore as I picked the book up.

A corner of paper jutted out and at first I thought I had damaged Etterly's Bible, but I saw almost immediately that it was a darker shade than the pure white pages. Obviously I hadn't shaken the book vigorously enough when I checked it in my friend's bedroom.

The loose sheet had some drawings on it – swirly Es and Ss intertwined, then a curved E beside an S, then a circle divided in four, rather like the seams of a tennis ball, then a drawing of the circle split along the vertical curved line into two teardrops, one upside down, and I realised that each teardrop was made of an E to the left bounded by an S to the right, with the horizontal curved line being the middle arm of the E.

'Etterly and S,' I explained to myself as I went to get a mop.

There was just time for a shower before I got ready for work – at least, there would have been if the water tank hadn't been empty. Not for the first time, the pump had died.

27

WHITE FLAGS AND THE LOST BOYS

Captain Carmelo and Tubby Gretham returned. They had met up after Tubby was informed he was not allowed into any of the makeshift military wards and Carmelo found that one of the crew members had broken his ribs, falling between boat and harbour wall. Tubby had sailed a bit in the past and would be able to administer medical aid more immediately if he went to the beaches and so they decided to team up.

They were flopped back in their chairs in the wheelhouse when I returned and having a couple of large gins – my gin, I realised, but I had had plenty of their drink in the past.

Both men were exhausted and they stank of diesel, sweat and stale blood.

'Have you eaten?' I asked, and they looked at each other questioningly.

They couldn't remember.

'I've got six rashers of bacon,' I told them. 'and the hens have been laying well. I'll make some brunch.' They listened without enthusiasm. 'How was it?' I asked and they both stared at the deck.

'It was not good,' Carmelo said at last.

'A bloody fiasco,' Tubby burst out. 'We were evacuating an army with pleasure boats.'

'The navy did what it could,' the captain protested wearily.

'I'm sure they tried,' Tubby conceded.

'Did you manage to get many men out?' I asked, disconcerted.

They were normally so exuberant, especially when they got together over a bottle, and I had never seen them like this before.

'We did two trips,' Tubby told me.

'And we were set for a third but they told us it was over,' the captain said bitterly. 'Madonna! *How is it over?* I ask them. *It is not over*, I say. *We have men still there*. So many, Betty, and now they are prisoners of the Germans.'

The captain said that last word with disgust. He had seen enough Germans in the last war not to be fond of them.

'We have known this was coming for years,' Tubby said furiously. 'And what did we do? We sat and watched them build up their army by the millions and a navy second only to ours and the biggest air force in the world.'

He slammed his fist down, forgetting he had his gin in it and splashing it all over himself.

'But you and all the others saved most of our army,' I tried to console them, topping Tubby's glass up for him.

'Army?' Carmelo snorted. 'They have no equipment but for their rifles. Everything was left.'

'They were frightened, defeated boys,' Tubby told me. 'What use will they be when we are invaded?'

'Do you really think we will be?' I asked, though I was convinced of it as well.

'What's to stop them?' Tubby challenged.

'The English Channel,' I said. 'And the Royal Navy.' Carmelo nodded approvingly at that inclusion. 'And the Royal Airforce,' I added, and they both raised their glasses.

Neither of them would hear a word against the RAF since Jimmy had joined up.

'God help them if they do come,' I said. 'Do they really think that men like you will put up their hands and surrender? Do they really think the women will? Can you see me waving a white flag?'

I felt a bit silly after that bit of rhetoric but when I looked at the men, they both had tears in their eyes.

'Did I hear mention of bacon?' Tubby enquired, surveying his glass sadly. It was empty again and I don't think he had spilled it this time.

'Anyway, I'm glad you're both back,' I said. 'The pump for the shower needs fixing, Carmelo.'

'Pity you have not married yet,' he commented. 'You will make a good nag.'

I puffed indignantly but I loved him for the *yet*.

'I need your help with a skeleton,' I told Tubby, and his weary eyes glowed.

'Got it with you?'

'Couldn't get it in my bicycle basket,' I told him. 'It's at the station.'

'I could take a look tomorrow.'

'I'd be glad of your opinion,' I said, and went to the galley.

I should have asked Tubby about my headaches, but I didn't want to worry him or, more truthfully, I didn't want him telling me to take time off work.

28

TWO WORDS AND THE RESISTANCE OF CARTILAGE

Tubby inspected the skeleton with a connoisseur's eye.

'Not bad,' he said. 'We have nearly a third of the bones and you managed to put most of them in the right place.' He sorted out some of the carpal-tarsal-meta-whatevers, then gave his attention to a badly chewed shoulder blade. 'Fox, I should say.' He picked up our original find, the jawbone.

'We never found the other half,' I informed him stupidly because, of course, it would be there if we had.

'Well, your father was right about the probable age and sex,' he commented.

It was not often I felt a glow of pride at any of my father's achievements, so I decided to make the most of it. It was unlikely to be a feeling I would get very often, if ever, again.

'Sixteen, female,' I confirmed.

How matter-of-fact that sounded, just two words to sum up a life.

Tubby poked around what we had found of the skull – the front of the head and the upper face, basically everything except the dome at the back.

I looked hard but could not see Etterly. The girl I knew had skin and muscles and all the other tissues that make a person look like a person. All I was seeing was the scaffolding.

'The trouble is,' Tubby continued, 'most of the more delicate bones are missing. They might give a better idea of trauma – the hyoid to indicate possible strangulation, for example, or more finger bones to tell if they were broken or dislocated. A fractured nasal cartilage indicates brute force, but cartilage doesn't have the same resistance to decay. Pity we don't have all the upper teeth.' Tubby put the skull down. 'But the remaining incisors could be useful for matching to photographs.'

'Could they have been knocked out?' I asked with a shiver.

I am not normally squeamish, but I was talking about my friend and how she died and I did not like to think that she might have been brutally murdered little more than a mile from where I was.

'Quite possibly,' Tubby concurred. 'Teeth don't usually just drop out of a healthy jaw, even after death.'

'Wouldn't the bone have to be broken?' I suggested, hoping he would change his mind.

'Not necessarily.' Tubby strolled around the table, watching the remains like he expected them to do something. 'Alveolar bone is quite flexible, especially in young people. A traumatic blow can expand the sockets, making the teeth pop out, but the bone will spring back again.' He puffed out his cheeks briefly. 'You must have seen as much in your father's surgery. He doesn't break jaws to perform extractions.'

He did sometimes, but I took Tubby's point and really it only gave more support to what I already suspected. A young healthy girl does not just wander off into a field, lay down in a ditch and die. Sometime after she entered that so-called Ghost Tree, in all probability, Etterly Utter was murdered.

29

BEES, WASPS, HORNETS AND TALKING TO MANIACS

Brigsy and Dodo were engaged in their favourite occupation – drinking tea – with one of our least favourite people – Inspector Sharkey – when I went back to the front desk.

'The pot is still hot,' Brigsy declared, and Dodo went to fill my mug.

'Not too much milk,' I reminded her.

'No, it is not too much, is it, Boss?' she called back. 'That is why I can give you plenty of it.'

Brigsy lit up his trusty old pipe.

'Why don't you use the briar that March Middleton bought you?' I asked, and Brigsy looked more shocked than he had when I told him I didn't know who Nevill 'Nuts' Cobbold, the England footballer from Suffolk, was.

'Int right to use tha' pipe 'cept on special occasion,' Brigsy said, 'and I never have none of them.'

'But this is a very special occasion,' Dodo enthused as the Shark came prowling through, 'because most of our army has been saved to fight another day.'

'Surrender another day,' the Shark said scornfully. 'Didn't give the Germans much of a fight in France. Might as well sue for peace while we can.'

'Never,' Brigsy said fiercely. 'We do have a setback, I grant you, but we rally. I know we do.'

'With what?' Sharkey challenged. 'They left all their equipment when they fled in chaos.'

Brigsy's normally corpse-like complexion was turning an alarming shade of mauve. Even his scraggy neck swelled almost enough to fill his collar.

'Retreated,' he insisted gruffly.

'Turned tail and ran,' Sharkey sneered. 'They will never fight again.'

'This is defeatism,' I observed.

'It's realism,' the Shark sneered.

'Oh my goodness,' Dodo cried, and dealt the inspector such a stinging slap that he reeled backwards.

'What the—'

'I am so very sorry, sir.' Dodo crossed her fingers behind her back. 'But I saw a wasp on your cheek and I was trying to kill it like this.'

Dodo's hand went back.

'Constable Chivers,' I said urgently, and put up my arm. She might just get away with her life and career that once but – much as I would relish seeing it – nothing would save her if she did it again.

'Tint no wasp,' Brigsy mocked, and I gaped. It was not like him to betray Dodo in support of the man he called Old Scrapie. 'It's a bee, that viscous sort they said in the paper,' he said, 'a killer bee.'

'I thought it was a hornet,' I chipped in.

'You don't seriously—' Sharkey snarled. 'Where the hell is it now then?'

'Fly out the window,' Brigsy said, and I glanced over. Luckily it was open in a failed attempt to keep us cool.

The Shark clenched his jaw and his fists.

'You, Chivers,' he snarled, 'are dead.'

Dodo gulped and put her hand to her chest.

'Oh, but my heart is still beating, sir.'

'Not for long,' he threatened.

'Anyway,' Dodo said, unabashed, 'you may be a senior officer, sir, but I will not listen to talk of surrender.'

'I didn't say anything about surrender,' Sharkey argued, 'I was talking about negotiation.'

'You cannot negotiate with a maniac,' Dodo insisted.

I could have argued against that point, but this was not the time to do it.

'Hitler is a realist,' Sharkey said.

Was this the time to remind my colleague that his own father had been born in Austria? I would save that one for another day.

'I cannot bear to hear the courage of our boys being called into question,' Dodo flared up. 'My young man is out there and who knows what fate may have befallen him?'

'Oh,' Sharkey mumbled, completed wrong-footed. 'I'm sorry about that.'

The Shark shuffled back to his office and, unusually for him, shut the door.

'Oh, Dodo,' I said, 'you never told us. Was he taken prisoner?'

'I do not know, Boss,' she told me, her eyes glistening, 'for I have not met my young man yet, but I know he must be out there somewhere.'

'Poor chap,' Brigsy muttered, and I was not sure if he hadn't quite grasped that Dodo was talking about the man of her dreams or whether he was sympathising with whoever she might light upon.

'If needs be, I shall wait for him for ever,' she said dreamily, and I was just mulling over a suitable reply when the front door opened and Etterly's father came in.

He had cast off the shuffling gait, his bowed back had straightened, and his face almost shone with excitement.

'Hello, Mr Utter.' I put down the mug of extra-milky tea I had only just picked up again. 'Has something happened?'

'I tell you that pile of bones dint be Etterly,' he reminded me with triumphant glee.

'Yes, I remember,' I agreed, 'but what has happened?'

'I do tell you what happen,' Mr Utter promised, and I rather wished that he would. 'You try to convince me she's dead but let me tell you, Betty Church, I go' proof positive, my Etterly is alive.'

30

POISON AND THE LIFEBOAT

I chewed on Mr Utter's words. He was screwing his cap in both hands like you would wring a dishcloth.

'What kind of proof?' I asked after a brief pause.

'This.' Mr Utter tossed the cap onto the nearest bench and brought out an envelope with a handwritten address and a stamp on it. I took it from him.

Mr E Utter, 16 Bath Rd, Sackwater, Suffolk, I read. It was postmarked Oxford Street 2-15 PM, with a smudged date.

'Goo our old address,' he observed, because they were number eleven now.

'May I?' I asked, probably unnecessarily, but people can be very funny about you opening their post even when they have given it to you. Constable Beer, when I was at Marylebone, nearly lost the sight in his left eye when an indignant elderly lady plunged a hatpin into it for the same offence.

'Goo on,' Mr Utter urged excitedly.

He was almost dancing on the spot as I pulled open the flap and slipped the letter out. It was on plain white paper.

'*Yore daughter is alive, a well-wisher*,' I read aloud.

'Hurrah.' Dodo clapped her hands, then, catching my expression, whispered, 'Sorry, Boss.'

'When did you get this?' I asked.

'In the second post,' Mr Utter told me. 'Not half an hour back. Jem Davis – he live at sixteen now – bring it straight round.'

'Have you shown it to Mrs Utter?'

'Course I have,' he said with a laugh, a sound I hadn't expected to hear from him again.

Brigsy leaned over the counter like a friendly landlord.

'And what goo Mitzie make on it, Ed?' he asked in the same conversational tone he might have used to start a chat about last night's darts match.

'Jump over the moon backward, she do.' Mr Utter grinned.

'It's not much to go on,' I pointed out, reluctant to kill his hopes.

'Not much?' he said incredulously. 'It say she's alive.' He jabbed the paper with a straight finger. 'Int that enough for you?'

I took a breath.

'You told us you had some letters telling you Etterly was being held hostage,' I reminded him.

'What on it?' he demanded. 'They coom from a blackmailer. This dint ask for anythin' 'cept to rest our minds.'

'Wha' the Inspector is sayin', Ed…' Brigsy said steadily, but I did not need my sergeant to explain my words for me.

'It could be a hoax,' I proposed, but Mr Utter threw back his head.

'You think I int thought on tha'?' he asked scornfully. 'It's signed *a well-wisher.* Why goo a hoaxer say tha'?'

'To make you think it isn't a hoax.'

'Most likely is,' Brigsy reasoned.

'People are always playing jokes on me,' Dodo contributed, 'and it is not always easy to tell when or why they do it.'

Mr Utter stared at us all like a lost traveller who had found himself seeking shelter in an asylum for the criminally insane, but then he clapped his hands together, just once.

'I see what you do and you put them all up to it,' he accused me. 'You can't admit you goo wrong over those old bone.'

I groaned inside and, I suspect, slightly outside, because Mr Utter raised his eyebrows at me.

'I would be delighted if that letter was genuine,' I assured him. 'Etterly was my friend. Nothing would make me happier than for it to be true, but' – I tried to sound reasonable – 'there is no evidence to—'

'Can't you read?' Mr Utter demanded.

'I wonder why *Your* is misspelled,' I said.

'I sorry if he int up to your education standards,' Mr Utter said sarcastically. 'But that's more evidence – if you still need it – he int clever enough to do a hoax.'

Well-educated people often have a misconception that those who didn't have their advantages are unintelligent and the less-well educated often resent that, but it was not often I heard a man with little education say it was a mark of stupidity. Mr Utter, I knew, had clutched at straws and was desperate now to prove they were a lifeboat.

'And look at the postmark.' Mr Utter prodded the envelope. 'It's from Laandan. We dint know nobody from there and nobody from there know us. Why do they play a joke when they never see the outcome? I know you mean well, mawther.' He nodded to Dodo. 'But she know she's wrong – never do confess it though, even when she's a little-un.'

I didn't care for one of my officers to be addressed as *mawther* – which, in Suffolk, meant anything from a young girl to an old crone – and I wasn't fond of being referred to as *she* and talked about like I was still a child. Also, I couldn't think what had led Mr Utter to form that opinion of me. I had confessed to chipping the handle of his Toby jug even though it had been Etterly's fault.

As casually as I could, I handed the letter to Brigsy.

'I hope you are right, Mr Utter, and I am wrong,' I told him evenly. 'But we have the remains of a sixteen-year-old girl that match Etterly's in every way.'

'A bone is a bone.' Mr Utter dismissed my words.

'And wearing Etterly's necklace,' I persisted, and he chewed his lips. 'And buried at about the same time that Etterly went missing,' I told him.

'How can you say that?'

'Because Mr Packard, the farmer, cleaned out and deepened the ditch not long before that,' I told him. 'If there had been a body there at that time, it would have been found.'

This, I suspected, is why the killer – if Etterly was murdered, as looked increasingly likely – chose that spot. The earth would have been turned and still soft.

'It could have been put there long after,' Mr Utter reasoned.

'Not much after,' I told him. 'Mr Packard had a dispute with his neighbour, who filled it with rubbish during the Great War, and it wasn't cleaned out until his land was flooded in 1937.'

Brigsy nodded along.

'Tha's true, Ed,' Brigsy told him firmly. 'It's full of rusty machinery up to then.'

'Tha' letter—' Mr Utter began, but Dodo put a hand on his sleeve.

'It is a cruel joke, Mr Utter,' she assured him.

'No,' he insisted. 'Where is it? Give it me.'

'I'm sorry,' I told him, 'but it's evidence now.'

'Evidence of wha'?' he demanded.

It had occurred to me that Etterly's murderer – assuming there was one – learning of the discovery of her body, might have made a clumsy attempt to mislead us.

'Writing a poison pen letter,' I bluffed, because it wasn't a crime to do so, 'causing distress to you and your wife,' I floundered.

'It's you who goo causin' distress,' he pointed out.

'Interfering with a police investigation,' I said more confidently.

'It's my letter.' Mr Utter stuck out his hand. 'You keep my girl's necklace – if it is hers – and her Bible. Int tha' enough for you?'

'When our investigations are over, I hope to be able to return them all to you,' I tried to reassure him.

Mr Utter jutted his jaw. With all his pain raging inside him, I think if I had been a man he would have attacked me, witnesses or not, but Etterly's father was not a man to hit a woman. I never hid behind my sex, but it had protected me on more than one occasion.

'Why dint you goo home, Ed,' Brigsy urged gently. 'The n'inspector is tryin' to help and Mitzie need you.'

Mr Utter shook his head in disbelief. He turned on my sergeant. 'You've go' kids. You think a father dint know if his own flesh and blood live or die?'

'I do believe some things goo too dark to see,' Brigsy told him gloomily.

Mr Utter snatched up his cap.

'My girl is ou' there,' he raged as he stormed to the door, 'and, if you dint find her, by God I will.'

That was the first time I had known Mr Utter to – as he would regard it – take the Lord's name in vain. He had made Etterly's life miserable for less than that.

31

SAD CATS AND WINDFALLS

I went to see Superintendent Vesty. He was still off ill but ironically, his wife had told me when I rang, he had not been better in years. He still had a stomach problem but the confusion he had suffered from increasingly since the Great War seemed to be lifting and, yes, he would love a visit and, yes he would love to discuss work. He had been feeling useless she told me and, she added confidentially, he was.

The superintendent lived three or four miles out of town on the Titchfold Road. It was a pleasant day, so rather than cadge a lift from Sharkey – the only one who could drive – I cycled.

A hulking farm boy was leading a huge carthorse towards me and I could not help but think of Delilah and the day she could have killed Etterly. *At least your parents would have known for certain*, I thought grimly, and braced myself for the usual ribald comments that locals loved to toss at any woman, especially one pumping her legs on a bicycle.

'Marnin',' he called and tipped his cap in greeting as I pedalled past.

Not even a leering look, I noticed.

Bloody cheek, I fumed as I went around the corner. *I may be old enough to be your mother but I bet I don't look like her.*

Most Sackwater farming women were fairly close to frazzled by the time they arrived at forty, whereas I was still – according to Toby, at any rate – in my prime. The trouble was, I thought ruefully, Toby was a kind and polite man with whom I had an amorous relationship so he would say that anyway.

I stopped to check my rear tyre.

'Fancy a quick roll in the bushes?' the boy yelled.

'Fancy a quick spell in the cells?' I called back at him, and was mortified to find that his invitation was aimed at another woman trudging along behind me.

'Rather have a long-un,' she wheezed in hilarity.

'Dint you worry, darlin',' he guffawed, 'I've go' a very long-un.'

They both cackled.

Oh good grief. She looks old enough to be your gran.

I pushed my bike around the corner because – just to improve matters – I had, as I had suspected, a flat tyre and there was still well over a mile to go.

Greenbank Hall was a good-sized Victorian house standing well back in wooded grounds and hardly visible from the lane. The tall iron gates were open and, from the way they sagged on their hinges, I doubted they could be shut. A blackbird hopped along the edge of the weed-infested gravel drive, keeping an eye on me as I crunched along.

Mrs Vesty opened the door herself. Servants, who would once have filled her residence, were hard to come by now with the war taking young people away and businesses able to pay much higher wages for shorter hours and longer holidays.

She was an athletically slim woman, almost as tall as her husband, who had a few inches over my five foot nine, and strikingly good-looking, her grey hair pulled back in the same sort of Alice band she had probably worn since childhood.

'Good afternoon, Inspector,' she greeted me warmly. 'I saw you from my studio in the tower. Having some trouble with your

school cup, I felt considerably perkier.' He dwelt fondly on the memory and I was about to say he looked healthier than when I had visited him in hospital when he continued, 'But then I have felt worse. When the Hun put some of Herr Krupp's products into my head and chest, I felt a great deal worse. Take a seat, Inspector. Ginger beer.'

He said the last two words so abruptly that it took me a moment to realise he was offering me some.

'That would be nice,' I said.

'Cordelia made it,' he told me, reaching down to a bucket at his side, the dent in his brow ballooning outwards.

I had yet to find the courage to use Mrs Vesty's first name.

'I will leave you both to it,' she said. 'If you need anything, just ring.'

Mrs Vesty pointed to a black field telephone screwed onto the wall beside her husband.

'Commandeered that from a Jerry dugout,' he told me with some pride. 'Handsome woman,' he said to himself as he watched his wife stride back towards the house.

Vesty handed me a bottle – stone with a hinged bung, just like Etterly's lemonade, I recalled.

'Pour me one too,' he said. 'Hand still a bit shaky.'

It looked quite steady to me, but I did as I was bidden.

'It's cold,' I commented in surprise.

'Got an ice-house down beyond the spinney,' he told me. 'Grandfather had it dug.'

'Well, there was no shortage of supplies last winter,' I remembered. The whole of Suffolk had been deep frozen in January.

I filled two glasses with cloudy white liquid and took a sip.

'This is very good,' I said sincerely. It had a strong bite to it.

The superintendent seemed lost in his thoughts for a moment.

'Cordelia tells me you wish to discuss a case,' he said.

'If you are not too tired, sir.'

'Work never made a man tired,' my senior asserted. 'It's idleness that's exhausting.'

I could have argued with the first point – after a long shift, I was often ready to collapse – but I knew what he meant by his second remark. Lack of work makes us all lethargic and where I was stationed now was the best place I knew for doing nothing.

'I don't know if you remember hearing anything about Etterly Utter,' I began.

'Remember the case well,' he said. 'I was a sergeant in those days.' It seemed to fly against the natural order of things for the Superintendent ever to have held such a lowly rank, but he must have had to work his way up, as we all did. 'Stationed in Ipswich, but they drafted a dozen of us in. A sad case.'

'Yes indeed, I—'

'Went into the Ghost Tree.'

'I actually—'

'They never found her, you know.'

'I do, sir. In fact—'

'Let me tell you about it.' Luckily, Vesty paused to take a sip of his drink, because his accounts of anything could be interminable.

'Actually, I know quite a lot about it, sir,' I put in quickly. 'Etterly was my friend and I was there when she disappeared. I believe we have found part of her skeleton.'

'That chap in Baker Street had a few things to say about bones,' Vesty said, and my heart sank. Sidney Grice claimed to like nobody, but he saved his deadliest venom for two people – Charlemagne Cochran, a rival and probably fraudulent private detective, and Sir Arthur Conan Doyle, who Mr G accused of stealing details of his cases and techniques for his fictional detective. Aunty M told me that Sir Arthur had paid Mr G a considerable sum of money to keep one case out of court, known to Gower Street scholars as The Mountain of Terror.

'You do know...' I began tentatively.

'I refer, of course, to Professor Ford Gable.' The superintendent sploshed his drink, unnoticed, down his shirt.

'Of course,' I floundered, though I had never heard of the academic gentleman in question.

'A bone means many things to many people,' Vesty quoted. 'Have a care that what it means to you is what it means to it.'

'Thank you, sir.' I stored that snippet of knowledge in the rubbish bin of my mind, beginning to wonder if I was wasting my time going there. 'We have other evidence that strongly suggests these are the remains of Etterly Utter.'

'And do you know how she died?' Vesty leaned back again, seemingly prepared for a long account.

'Not yet, sir,' I replied, glad to get back to the reason for my visit. 'Though it seems likely that she died violently. Her body was buried in a ditch and she had lost two upper incisors.'

'How do you know they didn't just fall out of the skull?'

'Because the rest of the teeth were rock solid and there was no sign of damage to the sockets.'

'So not extracted by your father?' Vesty observed, quite vitriolically for him, but then he had beef with my father for extracting an upper tooth when it was the lower one that was hurting and then trying to pursue my superior officer for payment.

'Probably lost shortly before she died,' I confirmed. 'There was no sign of healing starting to take place.' I reached into my handbag.

'Have one of mine.' Vesty lifted a pack from the table next to him and I took a cigarette. They were a special brand, encircled with a blue band printed with the name Cuthbert's of Regent Street, and very mild. Personally, I shared March Middleton's taste for stronger flavours, and it occurred to me that Sherlock Holmes would have been delighted to discover the dog-end of such an easily traceable brand.

I hadn't actually been looking for my cigarettes, but I accepted a light and puffed for a decent interval before delving in again.

'Looking for a handkerchief?' Vesty twisted to get his hand into his trouser pocket, spilling some more of his drink in the process.

'No, thank you, sir. I've found what I wanted.'

I produced the cardboard pouch I was using to protect my evidence and slid the contents out.

'A letter,' Vesty said, in much the same way that Dodo might say *a spider*. 'If this is your resignation, I shall refuse to accept it. If that cad Sharkey is being a nuisance, I shall get him transferred.' The last time Vesty had considered moving the Shark on, it was a promotion in Felixstowe, and I certainly didn't want him in authority over me – the irony being that, if he had read the regulations as closely as Vesty and I had, Sharkey would realise female officers were already subordinate to their marvellous male colleagues.

'It isn't, sir,' I hastened, rather touched by his concern.

'Oh, thank goodness,' he said in relief. 'I have got used to having a couple of pretty faces around the place and Chivers is a bit young for my taste.'

I took a breath, resisting the urge to tell my superintendent that he was more than a bit old for me to bother leering at.

'Hot?' Vesty asked. 'Have another ginger beer.'

'No, thank you, sir.' I fought to control my reaction. Women in my mother's generation, though not, unfortunately, my mother, had died to get the vote. What did we have to do to get a modicum of respect? 'Etterly's father received this yesterday.'

I opened the envelope to show him and Vesty wired a pair of half-rim glasses onto his splendidly hewn nose.

'Allow me, sir.' I took his tumbler away before he drenched the paper.

'Actually, it wasn't a bone he was talking about. It was a sonata. Gable is a professor of music,' he told me, and I chucked that fact away as well. 'Oxford Street postmark,' he observed, and held the letter itself up. I had already tried that myself. 'No watermark or embossing.'

'Not very helpful to us,' I commented wryly.

'Oh, I don't know,' Vesty disagreed. 'It tells us it didn't come from a royal palace or a gentleman's club, for example.'

The lack of a letterhead would also have told us that, but I left him to his scrutiny.

Vesty sniffed the paper – something I hadn't done, I was forced to admit to myself. 'Smells like Briggs's pipe tobacco,' Vesty said, like he had discovered a rare and beautiful perfume. Tens of thousands of men probably smoked the Whisky Flake my sergeant had been using lately. 'You don't suppose he—'

'No, I don't, sir.'

'Your daughter is alive, a well-wisher,' he declaimed loudly. 'Not exactly garrulous, is he?'

'No, sir,' I said. 'I was wondering why he would misspell your as y-o-r-e.'

Vesty put a hand to his skull.

'Damn, it hurts,' he said.

'Can I get you anything?'

I half rose, but he waved me down. 'It will pass,' he predicted with a groan and closed his eyes, and I was just getting up again to ring Mrs Vesty when he waved again. 'All tickety-boo now,' he said, though his face was drained and he was trembling all over, reminding me of a case of malaria I had seen once. 'No need to disturb the old girl.'

Vesty blew out heavily and opened his eyes.

'It is odd...' he said, and fell silent, and I was trying to work out what he meant when he explained, 'that he should misspell *your* but get *daughter* right. A man who struggled with orthography would be more likely to put something like d-o-r-t-e-r.'

'Exactly, sir,' I agreed. 'I suspect it is a clumsy attempt to appear uneducated.'

Vesty lifted his glasses, peered under the lenses, then let them fall again.

'The hand is interesting,' he commented. 'How would you describe it?'

'A bit like bad copperplate,' I suggested.

'Why do you say that?' Vesty enquired, handing me the letter back.

'Well...' I took a closer look. 'The lines go thick and thin.' I could imagine March Middleton patiently trying to coax sense from my stupidity and Mr G pouring scorn upon it.

'The vertical lines are the thinnest, the horizontal the thickest and diagonals somewhere between,' I realised.

'And what does that tell us?' Vesty prompted, and suddenly I was back at school being expected to prove a mathematical theorem after I had been daydreaming about being Irene Forsyte, forsaking cold fish Soames for passion with Philip Bosinney.

'I'm not sure,' I admitted.

'Neither am I,' Vesty agreed, and his face spasmed. 'But find a man who writes like that and you have found the writer.'

Or somebody else who writes like that, I thought hopelessly, and watched him lightly dab beside the old wound with his fingertips. He made an odd gurgling noise through his clenched teeth.

'Look out!' he yelled, and ducked. My superintendent exhaled heavily. 'Thought that one had my number on it.'

'I think I had better call Mrs Vesty, sir.'

'No need,' he gasped, but I decided to defy him. This was a personal, not a police, matter. I was still hovering over the telephone when I saw her coming towards us with a brown paper bag.

I met her halfway up the path.

'He is getting bad head pains and he had a brief flashback,' I told Mrs Vesty, and she blinked slowly and despairingly.

'It will pass.' She repeated her husband's words like a family motto.

'I hope I haven't overtired him.'

'It's idleness that is exhausting,' she quoted, and I imagined them sitting around the fire on a winter's evening concocting all these mantras.

Mrs Vesty had black smudges on her chin and nose. I was a bit wary of telling her, but decided she was not the sort of woman who wouldn't want to be told.

I found my mirror. Women police officers aren't allowed to wear make-up on duty but we still like to check our appearance.

'I don't suppose you realise...' I held it up for her to see.

'Oh my goodness.' She laughed and touched her cheek, leaving a black mark on that too. Her hands, I noticed, were filthy. 'I got that repairing your tyre. You know how dirty an oily chain can get.'

'You...?'

'Well, you would have a long walk home, if I hadn't,' she said. 'I only wish I could fix my husband as easily as that.'

'Do you think he—' I began.

Mrs Vesty shooed a wasp away.

'He insists he'll go back,' she replied to my half-formed question, 'but I cannot imagine Ian will ever be well enough to work.'

'I shall miss him. We all will.'

Mrs Vesty thrust the paper parcel at me.

'I hope you like rhubarb,' she said. 'We have had a bumper crop this year.'

I took it gratefully and saw myself out. A hundred yards away, Superintendent Vesty, aka Major Ian Vesty DSO, hero of the Somme, was howling like a child.

32

BATS, RATS AND THE CURLICUE

Dodo and Brigsy were standing in the middle of the room, heads down, when I arrived back at the station.

'It's a pig,' Brigsy asserted. 'Look, there's its ear.'

'It cannot be a swine,' Dodo argued. 'Where is its curlicue tail?'

'Never mind its curly-whatsit,' Brigsy said scornfully. 'Where goo your cat's long furry tail?'

'Tucked up under it,' she insisted. 'She's asleep because that scuffed bit is a cosy fire.'

'Morning,' I greeted them, knowing they would snap smartly to attention.

'Marnin', madam, good morning, boss,' they mumbled without looking up, and I realised they were arguing about the hole in the lino.

'It's a map of Australia,' I announced authoritatively.

'But—' Dodo began.

'With the tip of Queensland missing,' I said firmly.

'But—' Brigsy began.

'What you think of as an ear is the Northern Territory,' I insisted. 'Anyway' – I came to an important decision – 'it is time for tea.'

Normally the most junior officer would brew up, but after we had all experienced Dodo's attempts – too cold, too weak, too strong or too milky to be drinkable – Brigsy took over the duty and making tea was something our desk sergeant did exceedingly well.

'Did I hear the kettle being filled?' Sharkey asked, coming up the corridor.

I hadn't realised he was in, but the Shark often basked in the background rather than go to a lonely home. Old Scrapie had been engaged once, and there were times I felt sorry for him, but they were rare moments and usually fleeting. Some people deserve to be alone and, from what I had heard about the way he had treated his fiancée, he was one of those people.

'Goodness, sir,' Dodo gasped. 'You have ears like a rat.'

'Like a bat,' he corrected her.

'Oh no, sir,' she objected. 'Bats' ears are pointy but rats have round, sticky-out ears.'

I coughed and Brigsy harrumphed to mask our laughter. Sharkey, always simmering, almost came to the boil.

'Did you hear about the letter Mr Utter brought in?' I asked hastily, not because I valued or even wanted my colleague's opinion but as an attempt to save Dodo from at least a verbal lashing.

'Briggs told me,' Sharkey said shortly.

'Why don't you take a look at it?' I suggested, and the Shark tsked.

'From what I hear it's just a crank.'

'Almost certainly,' I conceded, 'but whether it is or not, I would quite like a word with the writer.'

I handed it over and Sharkey glanced at the envelope. Just as Vesty had done and I omitted to, he smelled it.

'Pipe smoke,' he commented.

'Prob'ly mine, sir,' Brigsy admitted. 'Have it behind the desk for a bit.'

'And glue,' the Shark muttered, and shot a glance at me. 'Checked for dabs?' he challenged.

'I didn't see much point,' I said. 'It was well mauled by

Mr and Mrs Utter before we saw it.' And by me when it arrived, I could have added, but didn't.

'Always worth a go,' the Shark instructed with justification. He slid the letter out. 'Same paper,' he said, unfolding it. He held the letter up towards the dim light from the green coolie-shaded bulb hanging from the ceiling over Brigsy's chair. 'Cut from a larger sheet with a sharp blade – knife or guillotine.'

'How can you tell, sir?' Dodo enquired, and I was glad she had because I didn't want to, but I was just as curious to know.

The Shark laid the paper on the upper desktop, reaching down behind for one of the stones Dodo had found on the seashore and thought, rightly, would be useful as paperweights. The trouble was, she never knew when to stop, and there was a miniature beach next to the telephone now.

'Give me a ruler,' he demanded.

At one time, I reflected with a cringe, Dodo would have said George III, but she had grown up a lot since then.

'George III,' she giggled, and I shrivelled inside.

'Shut up,' Sharkey snapped as Brigsy produced an ink-stained length of flat wood. 'Is this the best you've got?'

'It's the only one,' Brigsy told him.

I had a good one in my office, but I was not going to let Old Scrapie use it.

'Have to do, I suppose.' Sharkey placed the ruler along the top edge. It was almost impossible to see the measurements. 'Give me a pencil.' He marked the width on the ruler. 'Pay attention.' He put the ruler along the lower edge. 'A good sixteenth of an inch wider.' He did it again to prove his point. 'It's been cut from a bigger sheet. You couldn't cut that straight with scissors.'

'I could,' Dodo protested. She took great pride in her dressmaking skills and, to be fair, she had reason to. She had made some well-tailored, if lurid, dresses for herself as a break from knitting enough socks to kit out the crew of a minesweeper.

'The envelope is home-made from the same paper,' Sharkey said. 'It's fractionally asymmetric too, and you can smell the gum.'

'Goodness.' Dodo clapped her hands. 'You *are* clever, sir.'

Sharkey glanced to see if she was being sarcastic and decided she wasn't.

'Basic police work,' he said, not out of modesty but to make me look incompetent, which I was beginning to think I must be.

'What about the writing?' I asked – reluctantly, because I didn't want him to show me up, but it would be foolish pride not to seek a second opinion. He picked the letter up again.

'Well, it's obvious,' he sneered. 'A pathetic attempt to look ignorant.'

'But if you were trying to seem uneducated, wouldn't you misspell *Daughter* as well?' I objected. 'Also, you'd write in clumsy block capitals, not in an elegant flow.'

'As I said, pathetic.' Sharkey tossed the letter down again. 'Wouldn't fool a man for ten seconds.'

'Or a woman for five,' I countered.

'Why's it so important anyway?'

I didn't want to tell him that I had nothing else to go on because this was looking increasingly like a dead end.

'It probably isn't,' I mumbled.

'Bring my tea to my office,' Sharkey told Dodo, and slithered off.

'With a little soap in it,' she whispered.

'I'll make you drink every drop if you do,' he threatened without breaking his stride.

'I would not enjoy that,' Dodo decided, and went behind the counter.

'Refill our mugs then brew a fresh pot,' I called into the back room after her.

Brigsy had made a good cuppa as always, and I saw no reason why Inspector Sharkey should enjoy it.

33

WEIGHTS, MEASURES AND CYANIDE

I went to meet Toby at The Compasses. It wasn't our favourite haunt. No women were allowed inside, and few ladies would want to go in there. It was a long, thin pub with solemn customers lined up on pine stools and no space for anything much other than drinking, but it had a bowling lawn – dug up for vegetables – with a shelter where we could sit undisturbed, and so The Compasses had become *our* pub. It was where we had first met socially and, walking through sand dunes across the road, we had first kissed.

As usual, Toby bought us two pints.

'I'm sure they are watering this down,' he said, as was now traditional.

'You could always take a jar of it to weights and measures,' I suggested.

'What, and waste a good pint of beer?'

I laughed.

'What?' Toby asked, then, realising what he had said, he chuckled.

I tried my bitter and was half convinced that he was right. Either that or they were stinting on the hops.

'It's always a bit flat,' I said.

'That's Suffolk for you,' he replied, and I was not sure if he was joking or had misunderstood me.

Toby flipped open his silver cigarette case – a twenty-first birthday present from his father – and gave me a Craven A, cork-tipped to extract all the flavour.

'Any more luck with those bones?' he asked.

I had told Toby about our find but not about my suspicions. It wasn't that I didn't trust him – I did – but, at the end of the day, he was not a member of the force.

'We're still following a few leads,' I replied.

'Which is police-talk for *No*,' he observed mildly.

I hesitated. I don't like to ask members of the public for advice unless I am seeking an expert opinion.

'What do you make of this?' I got out the cardboard pouch and showed him the letter. 'It was sent to Mr Utter,' I explained – unnecessarily, since his name was on the envelope, but Toby kept a tactful silence.

'Haven't seen that for a while,' he said.

'What?'

'Yove.' He touched the first word.

'It says *your* spelled *y-o-r-e*,' I corrected him.

Toby stood his ground. 'Looks like *yove* to me.'

'And what's that supposed to mean?'

'Good old local mawther like you?' he teased. 'I know you went away to school but I'm surprised you never heard it when you played with the locals. *Yove* is just Sackwater for *your*.'

I stared and decided Toby was right. What I had taken for an *r* was really a *v*.

'Sergeant Briggs must be familiar with the word,' I objected. 'Oh.'

'What?' Toby asked.

'I read it out to him first, so he probably assumed that is what it said.'

'We all tend to see or hear what we expect to,' Toby said.

'But why?' I wondered.

'Perhaps the writer wanted to let Mr Utter know he is a local man,' Toby suggested.

'But Mr Utter read it as Y-o-r-e,' I remembered.

'That's handwriting for you,' Toby said. 'Fred Grange, the chemist, told me old Dr Griffith's writing was so bad Fred had to ring up and check that a prescription for Chiver's Tonic didn't say *cyanide capsule*.'

'Is that true?' I chuckled.

'The press never lie,' Toby protested in mock indignation. 'Well, hardly ever... Well, it made you laugh, anyway.' He finished his pint. 'Fancy another?'

'I certainly do,' I said, and Toby reached for my glass. 'Another walk in the dunes,' I clarified.

Toby grinned. 'You'll do anything to get out of your round.'

'Well, almost anything,' I agreed with a hint of a wink.

34

BLOOD AND THE MAGICIAN

Police Inspectors don't pound the beat. I don't think it's actually against regulations, but they are no more supposed to do it than generals are expected to fix bayonets and go over the top. I often think it might make them consider their plans a little more cautiously if they did. In the same way it does anyone above the rank of sergeant good to mingle with the public and see what his or her constables are up against.

My companion this morning was Bantony and we had planned our route to end at Dolly's café.

'Stop it,' I snapped as he turned his head to watch a couple of Waafs sashay past, up Highroad East.

'Oy was only lookink,' he told me. Bantony may have left a lot of things behind when he was transferred from Dudley, but he had never lost his accent. 'Oy can look, can't Oy?'

'Not while you're in uniform,' I told him. 'You are here to protect the public, not seduce them.'

Besides which, I thought, the Women's Auxiliary Air Force was Jimmy's territory.

Bantony smirked. 'They usually troy to seduce moy,' he said, with some justification. 'Anywoy,' he continued, tearing his eyes off another Waaf walking towards us, 'Oy do think of other thinks than girls.'

'Like what?' I asked warily.

'Women,' he told me with a happy grin, and grabbed hold of me. This was outrageous behaviour even by Bantony's standards, and I was just about to give him the biggest reprimand of his life when he said, 'Look where yow treadink, ma'am.' And let go of my arm.

I groaned inwardly. Was this going to be the third time in a week I had stepped in dog mess? Something crunched as I stopped to look down.

'Broken glass,' Bantony explained, just in case I couldn't recognise it.

'From that door,' I said, just to prove he was not the only one who could state the obvious.

A tall, stout man stood staring into the pool of shards. His once-smart grey suit was now so small for him that I doubted he could have buttoned up the jacket, and the waistband of his trousers nestled somewhere under a roll of stomach.

'Where were you when this happened?' he demanded.

'When did it happen?' I asked, and the man threw up his hands.

'This is exactly what I mean. You don't know the first thing about it.'

'All I know,' I told him, 'is that you have a broken window.'

'Oh, hark.' The man cupped his hand to his ear. 'Aren't you a proper Miss Marple?'

'Marbles,' Bantony corrected him incorrectly.

'What happened?' I asked.

'What do you think happened?' He pointed to the pavement.

I blinked slowly.

'Were you here at the time?' I asked with as much patience as I could muster.

'No, I was not,' he shouted, 'and neither were you.'

'Please don't raise yow voice to the Inspector,' Bantony managed to say nicely, but with such underlying menace that the man stepped back.

'Don't you th-threaten me,' he stammered.

'It might help if you told us what you know,' I suggested calmly.

'It was like this when I arrived five minutes ago,' he said, and I took a closer look.

Glass is a bit like sugar or blood – a little goes a long way, and any glazier could repair the damage in half an hour, I would have thought. The lower panel of the door was wooden but the upper had been shattered, leaving nasty jagged edges.

'We don't have enough manpower to keep a regular full-time beat any more,' I told him. The police were exempt from being called up when Chamberlain reintroduced conscription last year, but many had volunteered anyway – so many that the National Service Act had to be amended, forbidding police officers from joining up, by which time the East Suffolk force had lost a great many able-bodied men. 'So we are reliant on members of the public to report crimes.'

'And do your job for you,' he said disdainfully, 'while you sit on your… chair,' the man ended lamely as Bantony coughed warningly.

'What is your name, sir?'

'When I locked up last night it was etched – at great expense – on my front door,' the man ranted.

Bantony shuffled his feet over the shards.

'Take a while to put it back together,' he observed, 'so woy don't yow just tell us?'

'What language are you speaking?' the man demanded, but my constable had had enough.

'Name?' he demanded.

'Waters and Son,' the man replied, almost snapping to attention.

'And which one are you?' I asked.

'Son,' he said, 'Arthur. There's only me left since Father ran off with his secretary and most of the company's cash assets.'

'Good looker, was she?' Bantony asked with interest.

'It seems Father thought so,' the man said sorrowfully, 'only *she* is a *he*.'

Bantony mulled that one over. 'Oy see,' he said in puzzlement.

I had heard about that, but thought it was just local gossip.

'The architect?' I clarified.

'The architect,' he confirmed. 'So now there's just me.'

'And a broken window,' Bantony reminded him helpfully.

A young housewife came along, pushing a pram with empty string bags dangling from the handles.

'Two coppers for one windah,' she commented as she went by. 'No wonder we goo losin' the war.'

'Have you been inside yet?' I asked Mr Waters.

'Today,' Bantony clarified, probably unnecessarily.

'Of course I haven't,' Mr Waters replied with contempt, because nobody could possibly have asked a more stupid question.

'Perhaps we could go in now then,' I suggested, and he got out a bunch of keys that would be the envy of a medieval dungeon keeper to insert a normal-sized Yale into the lock.

'I collect them,' he explained, though nobody had asked. 'It's called cagophily.'

'It's called a waste of toyme,' Bantony commented as Waters opened the door.

'If you could stand clear, please, sir,' I said, and he looked at me quizzically.

'In case there is somebody still in there,' I explained, and Waters scooted backwards like Joe Louis was coming for him, fists flying.

'How could anyone get through that hole?' he demanded when he was at a safe distance. 'They'd be shredded.'

'I have known people to pass small children through to unlock the door,' I explained.

'Gypsies,' the man said.

'Sometimes,' I conceded. 'In you go,' I told Bantony, who looked at me in as much astonishment as if I had told him he was booked as the magician at a children's party.

'Moy?' he said, because, of course, there were a dozen other people I could have been giving that instruction to.

'Yes,' I said firmly, and he swallowed.

Bantony was no coward. If a man had appeared with a shotgun, I had no doubt my constable would have tackled him, but Bantony was terrified of blood and, if somebody was lying bleeding in there, there was no guarantee that Bantony wouldn't end up on the floor beside him. Having said that, I don't think of myself as a coward either, but why risk having to grapple with some hulking brute when I had a constable who was an amateur boxing champion before he started worrying about spoiling his pretty looks?

'Royt away, ma'am.' Bantony stepped inside with a Douglas Fairbanks swashbuckling swagger. 'Police,' he called manfully.

'Go into the back room,' Waters called, suddenly the senior officer, and Bantony flung open the door with a flourish, went through and disappeared.

'Oh!' he cried out almost immediately. 'Oh, please, no.'

35

THE DEAD DON'T TALK AND OFFICERS DON'T SCREAM

Mr Waters grasped my left arm.

'Oh my goodness,' he blurted, finding his fingers sinking in between the struts.

'Let go, please, sir,' I said, and he gave it a squeeze.

'You can't be eating properly,' he scolded, turning into my nanny.

'Let go,' I commanded, eyes starting to water.

'Is he dead?' Waters asked anxiously.

'No,' I said. 'Let go.'

And – third time lucky – he released me.

Much like living men, dead men can't do very much. They can't cook or clean or darn a sock and they certainly can't groan, *Oh, my good God,* as Bantony was doing in anguished tones.

I went inside, down a short hall and right into a small waiting room – a brown leather chair behind a brown leather-topped desk, four chairs, backs to the walls, a red Turkish rug that would go quite nicely in my cabin in winter when I had to step onto a draughty plank floor – and a rear doorway.

'Why don't you call for back-up?' Mr Waters advised from the safety of the street.

'How?' I demanded over my shoulder, eyes fixed on that open doorway.

'Use my phone,' he explained, like I was even more stupid than him. 'It will only cost you fourpence.'

You are seriously going to charge me for assisting you?

'There's nobody at the station.'

'Blow your whistle.'

'I don't have one.'

'Scream.'

'Police officers do *not* scream,' I told him indignantly. 'Constable Bank-Anthony,' I called, 'are you all right?'

Somewhere from the back room came a low moan.

I went towards it.

'Look out, ma'am,' Bantony yelled, and I drew back, raising my handbag. It wouldn't make much of a weapon but it might help fend off a blow.

'It ripped moy best jacket.' Bantony tugged at his sleeve to show me a tear at the elbow.

'What did?'

'That scobbink knife.' My constable waved towards a blade that was sticking out from underneath a wooden box.

I wasn't sure what *scobbink* meant but I guessed it wasn't complimentary.

'What on earth is going on?' Mr Waters' curiosity finally overcame his caution and he came in.

'Why is that knife here?' I asked.

'It's a scalpel,' Waters said.

'Oy thought you were an architect, not a scobbink surgeon,' Bantony said bitterly.

'I *am* an architect.' Waters held out his hands to demonstrate the large drawing board on a desk and, beyond that, a long trestle table bearing lots of little houses arranged into streets.

'Been commissioned to replace the model village?' I asked,

though few of the buildings looked familiar except the spire of St Hilda's Church, still pointing heavenward.

'It is New Sackwater,' Mr Waters declared.

'Do we need a new one?' I asked.

Bantony was busily employed poking his finger through the hole.

'We will after the Luftwaffe have flattened the old one,' Mr Waters declared. 'Look at the damage they did with one bomb.' I didn't need to look. I had been damaged by it myself. 'Just think what a hundred bombers can do.'

There was a visionary zeal in the architect's voice and eyes that I didn't care for.

'Fortunately, we have an aerodrome crammed with Hurricanes at Hadling Heath to stop that happening,' I told him proudly.

Jimmy and his comrades, I felt certain, would not stand by and let us burn.

'Where were they when the last one got through?' Waters demanded, with some justification. Nobody had even seen the stray bomber except Box and I, who both thought it was one of ours.

'What's that building there?' I pointed across the room to an enormous structure that seemed to take up several streets.

'That's the new... town hall,' Waters said shiftily.

'Looks a funny shape to moy,' Bantony said, giving up his exploration of the rip to stroll over. 'Put the loight on please, sir.'

'Woy, I mean why?' Waters asked edgily.

'Just do it,' I ordered.

'Oh, very well.' Waters flicked the switch.

A light came on above his desk and two more over the table, and I went to take a closer look.

'Why,' I asked icily, 'is the town hall shaped like a swastika?'

'To celebrate our victory over the Nazi hordes,' Waters said uneasily and unconvincingly.

'Let me try again,' I said frostily – or whatever is colder than icily – 'and I would prefer a truthful answer this time. Why... is... the... town... hall... shaped... like... a... swastika?'

Waters' forehead was glistening.

'Are yow a German spoy, Mr Waters, or should Oy say *Vorters*?' Bantony asked, and I hoped he was right. Not only would we have aided the war effort and saved lives but the glory it would bring could mean promotions, maybe even medals and, most important of all, another posting for me – back to London, I dreamed briefly.

'How dare you?' Waters shrieked.

'Sounds a bit loike Hitler, don't yow think, ma'am?' Bantony fingered the handle of his truncheon longingly. He would, I was sure, happily beat the ideology out of any fifth columnist he came across.

The glistening turned to droplets on the architect's brow.

'My family have been in this area for countless generations.' Waters brought his voice down an octave or so and a couple of decibels. 'Some even say the town was named after us.'

I rather thought our proximity to the sea and the River Angle might have something to do with it.

'Explain,' I demanded.

'Well,' the architect began, 'some say William Sack came to Suffolk in the fourteenth—'

'*Explain*,' I said in a voice even I found quite menacing.

'Well, if Germany wins – and I for one will resist them to my last breath – they will want to rebuild in a more – how shall I put it? – Teutonic way and, as the only architect in the town—'

'Who will have died resisting them,' I broke in.

'Well, if they captured me, they might be grateful for a pre-existing plan for reconstruction.'

'So you would collaborate with the enemy?' I clarified.

'Only after we had surren… signed a peace treaty.' There was quite a good map of the Nile Delta on Waters' forehead. 'It's taken me months to build that,' he said.

'That is not a point in your favour,' I told him severely. 'It proves premeditation.'

'Of what?' Waters asked nervously, and I was going to say something about defeatism but Bantony upped the stake by hissing, 'Treason.'

My eye was caught by a pencil. I picked it up.

'Do you always sharpen them like that?' I asked.

The lead was trimmed – probably with one of his scalpel blades – to a wedge shape rather than the usual point.

'All draughtsmen do,' Waters told me. 'The edge stays sharper longer.'

'Sharper or longer?' Bantony leaped on his words. 'Make your moind up.'

'Both,' Waters replied in confusion.

I thrust the pencil at him and ordered, 'Write *daughter*.'

'What?'

'Yow heard the Inspector,' Bantony told him. 'Or yow want us to add simulatink deafness to the charges?'

I wasn't sure that was an offence but Bantony had started studying the rule book lately in hope of being made a sergeant, so I decided not to comment in case I had missed something. Since war had broken out, hardly a week passed without a new set of regulations arriving in the post. If Hitler could be defeated by red tape, the war was as good as won, for we had an unlimited supply of it.

Waters opened a drawer.

'If yow have a gun in there, don't even think of reaching for it,' Bantony rapped, truncheon drawn like a sabre. He had been watching a lot of gangster movies since he had come to Sackwater. Apart from fending off women, he had told me, there was nothing else to do on the eastern edge of Britain. Only last week I had caught him practising Bogart's lip spasms in the mirror, though he had told me he was only checking if his teeth were clean.

'I don't have a revolver,' Waters protested.

'Why would yow want one?' Bantony challenged.

'Just do it,' I said wearily. 'Write *daughter* and do it now,' I commanded as he clutched his hair, perplexed, poking himself with his pencil in the ear, saying *ouch* and rubbing the flap gingerly.

'How do you want it?' he asked anxiously. 'I mean, printed or joined-up?'

'In your normal handwriting.'

'*Daughter and do it now*?' he checked.

'Just do it,' I snapped.

I had been looking forward to coffee in Dolly's café on the prom. With a bit of luck, I could have sneaked a smoke.

'Daughter,' he said, stretching the word in his mouth and on the paper.

'Hopeless,' I told him. 'Just write it quickly.'

Waters licked the lead.

'Yow could get poisoning from that,' Bantony warned.

'Actually, that is a common misconception,' Waters told him. 'What we call the *lead* is actually a mixture of graphite, which is carbon, and clay.'

'Oy never knew—' Bantony began.

'Write it,' I snarled.

Daughter, he wrote wordlessly, and stepped back like he thought he could get out of range of my wrath. Many a constable had tried and not found it quite that easy.

'Is that your normal handwriting?'

'Probably a bit shakier than usual,' he told me, sucking his non-toxic pencil like a lollipop.

'Give me that.' I snatched it off him.

'Would you like to keep it?' he asked.

I intended to, but now it looked like I was accepting a bribe.

'I am confiscating it as evidence,' I told him. 'Has anything been stolen?'

Waters twisted his head side to side. 'I don't think so. I don't know.'

'Let me know if there is, sir,' I said as nicely as I could manage. 'That is actually a very impressive feat of model-making,' I conceded. 'How long did you say it took to make?'

'About six months,' Waters admitted, eyes flickering up to mine. 'But my assistant started to build a model of the town about ten years ago.'

There was a bad taste in my mouth. This pig of a man had been anticipating our destruction, invasion and defeat before we had hardly got going. If he had only started recently I would still have loathed him, but I could almost have understood.

'And how long do you think it will take my constable to demolish it?' I asked, but 'Ah—' was all Mr Waters managed before his words were drowned out by the shattering of wood beneath the hammer blows of Bantony's truncheon.

'Oh, spare the church at least,' Mr Waters implored. 'It took Carpenter months to make it.'

'Stop,' I commanded Bantony, and St Hilda's was spared – just as, apparently, Mr Waters thought it would be by the Luftwaffe.

36

MRS GRUNDY AND THE THRILL OF DESTRUCTION

I turned to face Mr Waters.

'Carpenter,' I recalled. 'What was his first name?'

'Douglas,' Mr Waters said. 'Why?'

'Inspector Church asks the questions,' Bantony told him.

My constable was still breathing hard – not so much from the effort, I would think, but from the excitement men get when they destroy things. When we are children, girls build sandcastles and boys trample them down. To be fair, some men change and some were never like that in the first place, but I often wonder how many wars would have started if women were in control.

'Douglas Carpenter?' *Doggy*, as Etterly used to call him. I remembered the lonely little boy, who followed Godfrey Skillern everywhere, telling us, *I'm going to be an architect like my foster-father.*

'Well done,' Waters said mockingly.

Could he really have forgotten so quickly that his life and freedom were in my hands? But you can't take offence at every jibe when you're a police officer. *A good copper doesn't just need thick skin, he needs a suit of armour*, my first sergeant had told me when I was training.

'When did he leave?' I asked patiently.

'About nine years ago,' Waters said. 'I trained him up at

enormous personal expense and he deserted me. Thought he would have more success in London.'

'And did he go there?'

'I expect so.'

'Have you heard from him or anything about him since he left?' I asked.

Waters remembered that he had stabbed his ear and patted it consolingly.

'Yes,' he said. 'I got a letter about a month after he left.'

'And what did it say? Did he give you his address?'

Waters flopped his non-patting hand like he was trying to shake it dry.

'I wouldn't know,' he said grandly. 'I threw it in the fire.'

'So he left on bad terms?' Bantony clarified what was already clear but Waters nodded in agreement.

'I fear so,' he replied gravely because, apparently, one had to treat a male constable's remarks with respect but an inspector's could be derided, providing that senior officer was a woman.

'Any reason?' I asked. 'Apart from your having trained him?'

'We had a disagreement,' Waters replied, sensibly for once. 'Carpenter did a large number of drawings on his own initiative – plans for buildings that nobody had commissioned—'

'Like Nazi headquarters?' I suggested.

'Houses with ridiculous things like bathrooms attached to every bedroom,' Waters puffed, in sure and certain knowledge that we would agree that was a ludicrous idea. 'Or…' His voice trembled with hilarity at the next idea. *What could it possibly be?* I wondered. *Upside down sinks?* '…heating installed in every room from hot-water pipes.'

'And because of that you rejected his letter?' I asked.

'Not in the least,' Waters objected, and I wondered what we

had actually been talking about. 'We fell out when he tried to take his drawings with him.'

'Did he do them in your time?' I asked.

'Oh no,' he assured me. 'I would never have permitted that.'

'On your premises after hours?'

'Oh no. He did them at home.'

'With your materials?' I suggested, running out of ideas.

'Oh no. He was scrupulous in purchasing his own.'

'What then?' I asked in exasperation.

'Well, obviously.' Mr Waters put his fingertips together like a vicar at prayer. 'He did them with my training, *and*,' he put in quickly before I could raise any objections, 'he brought them in for me to peruse, thereby making them part of his training and, therefore, mine.'

'Oy have made somethink of a study of the laws of property recently,' Bantony announced, holding up a notebook as if that were the actual statute he was referring to, 'and Oy think that any court would take the view that yow, sir, are a bit of a git.'

'That's as may be,' Waters agreed cheerfully, 'but I have nothing to fear from either of you since you have destroyed all the evidence.'

I hated to admit it, even to myself, but Waters was right. I had let childish spite cloud my judgement.

'Apart from this.' Bantony held up the book again. 'It is full of sketches, all initialled.'

'Give it here.' Waters darted forwards and Bantony held it up like an annoying adult taunting a child.

'I must advise you that, if you touch my constable, you are liable to be charged with battery, interfering with the police in the undertaking of their duty and perverting the course of justice,' I warned. 'Where was Carpenter's letter posted from?'

'How the hell would I know?'

'Watch yow language,' Bantony warned. He was not so prissy in the privacy of Sackwater Central.

'From the postmark,' I replied. 'And don't tell me you didn't notice. Everyone looks to see where a letter is from before they open – or return – it.'

'London, of course,' Mr Waters said sulkily. 'Oxford Street, I think.'

'Isn't that—' Bantony began.

'It is,' I confirmed quickly.

'What are you going to do about my window?' Mr Waters asked.

Oh, how embarrassing, I thought. *I must have put on my glazier's outfit this morning.*

'If anything was taken, let us know,' I advised. 'Otherwise, Mr Waters, sir,' – I lowered my voice – 'you can take a running jump.'

'Oh, and Oyl tell yow what yow can do with that model,' Bantony said. 'Yow can take all the pieces and stick them...' I coughed warningly. A well-dressed young woman was approaching. '...back to-geva,' Bantony ended, and he spun on his heel with Fred Astairian grace. 'Good mornink, madam, what a lovely' – he looked her up and down and up again – 'day.'

The lady reddened a little, tossed her head and walked on, but I noticed she stopped to stare into the window of Mrs Grundy's Rock Shop and patted her hair to make sure it was perfect, which hair will be if you can balance a tiny hat on top rather than squash your perm into a heavy metal helmet.

'Come along, Constable,' I urged as we went on our way down towards the promenade. 'We have our patrol to finish.'

Bantony managed to tear his eyes off the woman. 'What about moy tea and cake?'

'That's exactly where it ends,' I assured him, and wondered how long he could keep looking at me before I had to scold him for leering.

37

CONTRAPTIONS AND THE GREAT CLOUD

Brigsy had a fresh pot brewing by the time I got back. I had just had tea and a cake with Bantony at Dolly's, but it would have been churlish to refuse the mug he offered.

'Do you remember Douglas Carpenter?' I asked, because our sergeant knew everyone in Sackwater and most people within a ten-mile radius.

'Carpenter?' He chewed the name like a great delicacy.

'Douglas Carpenter,' I repeated.

'Douglas...' Brigsy lit his pipe thoughtfully. 'Carpenter?'

'That's the one,' I encouraged him.

'Douglas Carpenter,' he said with sudden recognition. 'Course I do, madam. Best goalkeeper Biggleswade ever have until he break his head.'

'I meant Douglas Carpenter from Sackwater,' I said.

'Oh.' Brigsy chewed on his pipe. 'What position do he play?'

'He worked at Waters and Sons, the architects on High Road East,' I told him.

'So not Waters then,' Brigsy ruminated, in a great cloud of smoke.

'Nor Son,' I agreed.

Brigsy brightened. 'I do believe I may know who you mean. Is he the one—'

'His parents died when he was young,' I told him.

The light dimmed in my sergeant's eyes. 'Not who I think of then.'

He puffed again, but his tobacco had burned out. I had seen children less disappointed to think they had been forgotten by Santa.

'He was fostered by a Mrs Hornby,' I prompted.

'Why dint you ask her then?' he suggested.

'I may well have to do that,' I agreed, and escaped with my tea to my office.

I could have tried phoning, but I had a pile of forms that needed filling out so urgently that I decided to take a walk instead.

38

THE MAN IN THE MOON AND CREATURES OF THE NIGHT

The Hornbys lived in Mount Chase Avenue, off Mallard Road. If the latter housed the cream of Sackwater, the former was inhabited by the crème de la crème. There were three titled men in those twelve houses, though I was not convinced that if I took the trouble to consult Debrett's I would find Baron Bunnythorpe, the New Zealand-born wool merchant, listed on its pages.

Mount Chase Mansion stood at the end of the road. I have to say I think there is something vainglorious in naming a house after your road, but as I approached the property I began to suspect it might be the other way round. Mount Chase Mansion made Felicity House, my parents' fairly substantial home, look like the porter's lodge standing to the right of the high white-painted iron gates.

I rang a bell and an aged lackey in a long red coat came scurrying out of the lodge. I hadn't seen a lackey for years, let alone an aged one.

'Good afternoon, madam,' he greeted me, face twisting up and sideways briefly towards mine.

'Inspector,' I corrected him. I was the mistress of neither a household nor a brothel, though the second option might be more lucrative than my present employment.

'I do beg your pardon, Inspector. Is Mrs Hornby expecting you?'

Not unless she has psychic powers, I thought, but replied, 'No, but I am expecting to see her.'

'One moment, please.' The lackey scuttled back and I heard him, presumably on the phone – unless Mrs Hornby lived with him – saying *a police lady, madam.*

I am not a bloody lady, I fumed to myself. Toby, I was certain, could vouch for that.

Out came the lackey again, and I couldn't quite decide if his bent posture was an overly respectful bow or the effects on his spine of doing one for years. Unless he made great efforts, all I could see of his head was five hairs carefully glued across a peeling parchment pate.

'I am so sorry to keep you,' he toadied. 'Mrs Hornby will see you at once.'

The ancient retainer produced a key you could club a man to death with and inserted and twisted it in a lock that was probably the size of the average suitcase, clattering levers back with a noise like a sack of spanners being dropped on a metal platform.

'Please follow me,' he croaked when he had heaved the gate back, and he scampered off up the gravelled driveway. For such a shrivelled remnant, he could get a fair pace up. I had known young lags scarper from the scenes of their crimes with less acceleration than this, and I was so taken by surprise that he had a three yards' advantage on me before I was off the starting line. If this was a race, I was reasonably confident I could overtake him, but I wasn't sure if we were being watched from the house so I contented myself with walking briskly in his wake, trying not to look too in awe of the many-bayed five-storey Victorian monstrosity we were approaching. It must have kept a sizeable brick-making factory in work for many a year, I pondered, a little breathless by the time we arrived.

The front entrance was disappointingly small in proportion

to the house. You would have struggled to squeeze two elephants through it side by side, if that was the sort of thing you wanted to do.

The door was opened by a footman. The first and last time I had seen one of those was at Stovebury Hall when some of the local girls were invited to a hunt ball and even he, I found out later, was only hired for the event. This man looked even older than the gateman, but he bowed much more flexibly and stood erect again while I took off my helmet. I followed him through a cathedral of oak panelling into a cavern of oak panelling – walls, floor and ceiling lined with the stuff, chairs, tables and cabinets made of it. I got the message. They liked oak.

'Inspector Church to see you, madam,' the footman announced in reverential tones, bowing so low I thought he was going to kiss his own knees.

'Thank you, Marmaduke. That will be all.'

Marmaduke seemed a bit of a presumptuous name for a servant, I thought. He should have had a more vulgar name, like Martin or Richard or Colin.

'Thank you, madam.'

They finished thanking each other and he left, bowing deeply again as he shut the door.

This sort of charade was something that never ceased to puzzle me. I could understand why servants were servile – it was their job – but why would you want people fawning over you all day long? I insisted that my men showed respect and rather hoped they felt it, but if they toadied like the presumptuously named footman, I would think they were taking the mickey.

Mrs Hornby looked almost as old as her minions. She sat resplendent in white satin on a loftily backed throne and I wondered if she expected me to curtsy. If so, she was about to be disappointed.

'Excuse me not getting up,' she commanded rather than requested.

'Please don't trouble, madam,' I said, hoping I didn't sound like one of her employees.

'Are you collecting money?'

'No,' I told her, though it did cross my mind that if I held out my helmet, she might toss a few sovereigns into it. 'I have come about Douglas Carpenter.'

'Carpenter?' she asked, and I hoped I was not playing the same game as I had with Brigsy, only for her to tell me that he played for Biggleswade until he broke his head.

'Douglas Carpenter,' I confirmed.

'And who is Douglas Carpenter?' she asked imperiously.

'He used to live here,' I said, confused by her confusion.

'When?' she challenged.

'Well, he certainly lived here in 1914 – I think he had been here a few years by then – and I rather assumed he was here until he left Sackwater about ten years ago and that he probably still visited.'

Mrs Hornby rustled, her dress glistening in the sunlight streaming through the tall, wide windows. A bony finger emerged from her long sleeve and tapped a Morse message on the arm of the chair. Jimmy had taught me the code and I had become fairly proficient at telling him to keep quiet by banging on my cabin wall. HSE HSE I got, before deciding it wasn't a message at all, just her irritation with me.

'Tell me, Inspector Church.' She might as well have said *so-called Inspector*, from the dismissive way she addressed me. 'Is this person invisible?'

'No, he—'

'Does he hide in cracks between the floorboards?'

'No, he—'

'Perhaps he inhabits the cellar and only emerges at night.'

She was quite good at sarcasm and I resolved to adapt some of her lines to use with my constables when the need arose.

A lightning flash split my forehead.

'He would have been born around 1904,' I struggled. 'So he would be about—'

'Thirty-six,' Mrs Hornby broke in, oblivious to or ignoring the involuntary whimper of pain that escaped me. 'I learned a little mathematics at school.'

I was only surprised she hadn't been educated at home by a series of governesses.

'I wasn't trying to imply…' I rubbed my brow but it made no difference.

'Nobody by the name of Douglas or Carpenter or a combination of the two has inhabited this house contemporaneously with me,' Mrs Hornby assured me.

'He went to St Joseph's Grammar School,' I persisted.

'I do not care if he went to the moon.' Mrs Hornby reached sideways and tugged a silken cord that dangled beside her from the ceiling. 'Nobody of that name resides or has, within living memory, resided here.'

'But everybody knew he did,' I said, and the stupidity of my words hit me even as Marmaduke grovelled back into the room.

Obviously, unless Mrs Hornby was telling porkies – and I could check up on that – everybody knew wrongly.

'Inspector Church is leaving,' his mistress told him and so, apparently, I was.

'Thank you for your time, Mrs Hornby,' I said with as much grace as I could muster, but she swatted the air as if I was an irritating fly.

On the way back to the gate, Marmaduke opened his heart and told me all about the month's weather – as if I had not experienced it too.

'Do you happen to know Douglas Carpenter ?' I asked without much hope, but it was better than hearing him drone on about the below-average precipitation.

'Douglas Carpenter?' Marmaduke checked. 'Oh yes, indeed, madam.' He chuckled softly. 'How could I forget Doug?'

'But Mrs Hornby denied even knowing who he was,' I told him in surprise.

'Oh, she would,' Marmaduke assured me in a between-ourselves kind of way.

'But why?' I asked as we neared the gate.

'I am afraid,' Marmaduke began, breaking off to clear his throat, 'that Mrs Hornby has no interest whatsoever in association football. Douglas Carpenter,' he mused, 'the best goalkeeper Biggleswade ever have until he broke his head.'

I felt like somebody had broken mine as the gate crashed shut behind me, and I just made it around the corner before I vomited.

'Disgustin',' an elderly lady scolded as she cycled past, 'and you a postwoman too.'

39

BEARS, RATS AND SPONTANEOUS COMBUSTION

I called in on Toby. I hadn't been able to see much of him lately on a personal basis, but this was mainly for business, plus I wanted to remind him of my invitation.

The desk was unmanned when I entered the building, so I called out *Hello*, waited a moment, and made my way up the steep stairs.

Toby had his feet on his desk, his head back, eyes closed and mouth a little open. I shut the door quietly and he shot up as if I had let off a banger next to his ear.

'I wasn't asleep,' he protested, and looked about to get his bearings. 'Oh, I had a dream that I was on sentry duty and you were the sergeant major.'

'It must be my bristly moustache,' I laughed as he clambered to his feet. 'Has Carol got the day off?'

'Gone to cover a story about a boy whose tortoise turned up after going missing three years ago,' he told me. '*Father says, That tortoise a lesson.*'

I winced.

'And you promised you would never hurt me,' I reminded him.

'Sorry.' Toby came towards me. 'I know we have a rule about not being... intimate when you are in uniform.'

He leaned towards me.

'Yes, we do,' I agreed. 'Got a fag?'

Toby went behind his desk to where his jacket hung on the back of his chair and fished out his cigarette case, his hand almost steady when he struck a match.

'Take a seat.'

We installed ourselves facing each other over a heap of old newspaper cuttings, photos of gurning babies and brides happily unaware that they didn't suit white.

'Have you got a scoop for me?' Toby asked hopefully. 'I'm not allowed to print any invasion scares or Nazi parachutist sightings, so at the moment our banner headline is *Sunshine Set to Last All Month* and I can't see that having people ripping copies off the stands.'

He drew in a cloud of smoke.

'Yes,' I said, and Toby coughed, denting his assertion that smoking was good for him.

'Do you remember Etterly Utter?' I asked, and Toby coughed again.

'The girl in the Ghost Tree,' he said. 'One day I'll write a book about that.'

I was not sure I liked the idea of my friend being the subject of the sort of sensational stories Toby dreamed of turning out.

'She was my friend,' I said.

'Oh yes?'

Was it my imagination or was there a forced casualness in Toby's response?

'I believe we have found her,' I told him.

'Dead or alive?' he asked, resting his cigarette on an almost empty ashtray.

'Those bones in Packard's Field,' I told him.

'And you are sure they are hers?' Toby picked up a pencil.

'As sure as we can be. They are of a female of the right age.

There was a lower right tooth missing and I remember Etterly going to have that extracted by my father.'

I reached into my pocket. 'And also I found this.'

I held out the broken chain, pendant dangling.

'May I?' Toby held out a hand and I lowered the necklace into it.

He put on a pair of round tortoiseshell glasses.

'I haven't seen you in those before.'

'I didn't need them before.'

'They make you look intelligent,' I commented.

'Take more than glasses,' Toby told me. He turned the pendant over and back again. 'Well, that's Etterly's all right,' he said, and handed it back.

'What?' I checked in surprise.

The front door opened.

'It ran away again,' Carol announced from the bottom of the stairs then, getting no response, added, 'The tortoise.'

'Oh,' Toby responded abstractedly.

'Coffee?' Carol called.

'You knew her?' I whispered.

'I'll take that as a *yes, please*,' Carol decided.

'You knew Etterly?' I pressed.

'I certainly did,' Toby told me wryly.

40

PRIMING THE GRENADE

I was just digesting Toby's information when Carol brought our coffees.

'Somebody died?' she smirked, looking from face to face.

'Yes,' I told her flatly. 'That's why I'm here.'

'Oh,' she said. 'I'd better leave you to it.'

'I think you had,' agreed her employer, and her lips began to work, but whatever Carol had intended to say, she thought better of it.

'Close the door, please,' I said, knowing full well she always left it ajar to listen in.

'Right,' she said between clenched teeth.

'What?' Toby began, but I shushed him.

'Go away, Carol,' I said without raising my voice, and waited for the sound of the stair treads creaking.

'What's the matter?' Toby asked.

'Why should anything be the matter?' I countered, annoying even myself with such a pointless question.

Toby picked up a pencil.

'I know men are supposed to be insensitive, but even I know when I've been doused with cold water,' he said.

'And why do you think that might be?' I asked, adding a little more ice.

'Well…' Toby twiddled the pencil round and round. 'I would say it happened the moment I told you that I knew Etterly.'

'Why didn't you tell me you knew her before?' I asked quietly.

'I suppose she never came into our conversations,' he replied. 'You never told me she was your friend. Why should I have told you she was mine?'

'I suppose not,' I conceded, and was about to descend from my high horse when he continued.

'We agreed long ago not to ask each other about old boy- and girlfriends.'

'Girlfriends?' I pounced on the word. 'Etterly was your girlfriend?'

'For a while,' Toby admitted. 'But I didn't know you knew her until two minutes ago.'

'But she was a child,' I told him in mild shock.

He had always seemed such a decent man to me.

'She was coming up to eighteen and I was only twenty-two at the time,' he said defensively, the pencil performing somersaults between his fingers. 'It's not like I would court somebody of that age group now.'

Court was such a nice old-fashioned word from what was basically a nice old-fashioned man, however much Toby protested that he was really a frustrated jazz musician.

'She was fifteen,' I informed him.

'Oh.' Toby looked genuinely put out. 'She told me seventeen and she looked it.'

'She probably did,' I conceded.

'Anyway, it was all quite innocent,' he assured me.

Why is it that when men try to make things better, they have a knack of making them even worse?

'How innocent is *quite*?' I asked, though I hadn't really wanted to know up until then.

'Well...' He tapped his desktop with the blunt end of his pencil. SOS, he messaged, subconsciously, I assumed.

'Just a kiss and a cuddle,' he said. 'You can't be jealous of that.'

I didn't ask who he was to tell me I couldn't be jealous. Half the problem was I couldn't get rid of the image of the middle-aged man I knew with the teenage girl I had known.

'When was this?' I asked. It couldn't have been all that long before Etterly disappeared.

'What is this?' Toby asked shirtily. 'Am I under investigation?'

Was he? Perhaps I should drop the matter, but all my training and experience and every instinct drove me onwards.

'You don't like your first name, do you?' I asked, and Toby stared at me.

'No, I don't like being named after a bit character in Sherlock Holmes,' he agreed disagreeably. 'What the hell has that to do with anything?'

'Ever called yourself by another name?' I persisted.

'Is this an interrogation?' Toby demanded angrily. 'Because it certainly feels like one.'

I swallowed.

'I would just like you to answer my question.'

Toby picked up his pencil very deliberately.

'I used my middle name, Simon.'

'With an S,' I realised, unintentionally aloud.

'And an I and a M and an O and an N,' he said sarcastically. 'Can I help you with anything else, *Inspector*?'

'You could answer my question,' I said, hoping I didn't look or sound as shaky as I felt.

'What damned question?' Toby flung his pencil aside and it shot off the edge of his desk.

'When did you go out with Etterly Utter?'

'Just before she' – Toby hesitated, aware that I was watching him closely and not in the way I normally did – 'disappeared.'

'How long for?'

He ran his fingers through his hair. It was a little longer

than was fashionable in that austere age and I wondered, with a shock, if I was no longer secure in my assumption that I would be with him long enough to see his grey becoming the dominant colour.

'I don't know.' He unbuttoned his jacket. 'A few weeks – two or three at most, I should think. She was a lovely girl, kind and fun and – don't hate me for saying this – very pretty.'

'But?'

'She had no interest in the things that interested me – books, music, art.'

'So you got rid of her? I asked.

I hadn't meant it like that, but once you've thrown a hand grenade it isn't usually advisable to try to retrieve it.

Toby's jaw muscles bunched up.

'Am I a suspect?'

I don't know why that floored me. I had certainly been treating Toby like one.

'No, of course not,' I blustered.

'Would you like me to come to the station and make a statement?'

'No, of course I wouldn't.'

Why on earth had I let it turn into this? I had come wanting support and expecting affection.

'Then kindly get the hell out of my office.'

I sat stunned.

'Toby, I...'

'Mr Gregson, if you please, Inspector Church.'

'It doesn't have to be like this,' I blurted out.

'It didn't have to be,' he agreed, 'but now it is.' Toby stood up. A few minutes ago he had been angling for a kiss. Now he was evicting me from his office and, probably, his life. 'Goodbye, Inspector.'

I stood uncertainly.

'Do I have to get my secretary to show you out?'

'I know the way,' I said, with as much dignity as I could muster.

'That was quick.' Carol glanced up.

Spend much more time filing your nails and you'll have no fingers left, I nearly said, but she had done me no harm.

'Yes, wasn't it,' I agreed with what was meant to be a smile, but probably looked like I had stubbed all my toes.

I went out onto the street.

A youth was pasting a poster on a lamp post. I couldn't see what it was advertising. I could have had him for bill-sticking, but what was the point? He would get a fine he probably couldn't afford to pay and, anyway, we would have no other use for lamp posts until that damned fiasco of a war was over, and I had a horrible suspicion that would not be any day soon.

41

THE FEELINGS OF MACHINES

I didn't exactly feel like it, but I went back to the station.

The only living thing there – apart from me and a fat bluebottle trying to buzz its way out through a windowpane – was Brigsy, and he was asleep in his chair behind the desk, mouth gaping and as cadaverous as the first time I had seen him. Roger, the black cat that lacerated Brigsy's hand, had gone. Nobody knew where, but Box had heard stories about the Italian restaurant serving stringy rabbit.

'Douglas Carpenter,' I said loudly, and Brigsy leaped so violently that I instantly felt guilty. I was getting better at feeling that than I wanted to at present.

'Bwuff,' Brigsy said, and set about defurring his throat.

'Sorry, did I take you by surprise?' I asked.

'Oh no, madam,' he assured me.

'Douglas Carpenter is in London,' I told him, and Brigsy rubbed his grey, sunken face sleepily.

'Yes,' he agreed warily, sensing a trap.

'Well,' I said, 'I would like to speak to him.'

'You want to use the telephone?' Brigsy cradled it protectively.

I didn't actually need my sergeant's permission to make a call, but he regarded himself as keeper of a sacred instrument and deeply resented anybody else taking advantage of it.

'No,' I said. 'I want you to.' And his face lit up until I added, 'In fact, I want you to make a great many calls.'

'How many?' he asked suspiciously.

'I want you to ring every architect you can find on or near Oxford Street and then work your way outwards until you find him.'

'Oxford Street,' Brigsy pondered. 'Int tha' in Oxford?'

I leaned over and picked up the phone to place it on the higher front desktop.

'Oh,' Brigsy wheezed, like I had just punched him in the solar plexus, because nobody, not even Superintendent Vesty, used the revered device without our desk sergeant's permission.

'I just need to make one quick call,' I promised, and dialled 100.

Maggie put me through.

'Yes?' my mother answered in her nicest receptionist's manner. It was not unknown for her to frighten patients off before my father even got a chance.

'Is Dodo there?' I asked.

'Dodipops,' she called, without even covering the mouthpiece. 'That woman wants know if you are here.'

I thought about reminding my mother that actually I was her daughter, but I was no more proud of that than she was.

'Of course I am, Mummikins,' I heard, and a minute later there were skipping footsteps in the hall. 'Hello, Boss,' Dodo said, and I tried hard not to hate her.

She was a nice girl and my parents clearly thought so too. I only wanted them to like me so that I could try to like them in return.

'There is a map of London on the bookshelf in my father's study,' I told her.

'Thank you, Boss,' she said. 'Was that all?'

'I want you to bring it here,' I told her.

'Oh, but—'

'Now,' I said.

'Oh, but—'

'I know you are not on duty yet,' I said, 'but if I add up all the times you have been late, you owe the East Suffolk Constabulary a good few hours' extra duty.'

'A little over one hundred and fifty-seven hours, by my calculation,' she confirmed, 'but—'

'Now,' I insisted. 'And don't worry about putting on your uniform.'

'Oh, but—' I heard a third time before I put down the receiver, heavily, to my sergeant's dismay.

It took half a second to recognise the woman in a long pink dressing gown with a turban on her head and a book under her left arm.

'Off to a fancy dress party?' Brigsy eyed Dodo bemusedly.

'I was washing my hair,' she told him haughtily, thrusting the book at me. 'I think that is what you wanted, Boss.'

'Thank you, Constable Chivers,' I said, fascinated by the sight she presented, from fluffy pink slippers to the towering towel wrapped around her head. 'You may go now.'

'Thank you, Boss,' Dodo said, marching out with great dignity back into the street.

'Oh,' Brigsy said for the umpteenth time that day.

'Oh, indeed,' I said, before we both gave way to laughter.

I dumped my father's atlas on the desktop.

'Happy hunting,' I said and, for some reason, Brigsy stopped laughing.

I would have stayed to help but I had some important work to do. My cigarettes didn't just roll themselves.

I perched on my desk and smoked the first one. My office was quiet, the only sound being the prayer inside my head. *Whatever I did, Lord, I'm sorry. Now give me Toby back or, if you won't do that, be a good sport and get me the hell out of here.* Little did I suspect that God was answering my prayer even as I spoke to him. Even less did I suspect that he would use a human agency to grant my wish or that the one he had chosen to enact his will was his good and loyal servant, Inspector Paul Sharkey.

42

HENRY V AND THE WOODWORM

Sharkey's door was open as usual but, unusually, he seemed to be hard at work, writing with his fountain pen. Until now his desk had always been little better than the council rubbish tip – piled with paperwork, overflowing ashtray, mugs half-filled with cold old tea, crumpled greasy newspapers from Phil's Fish and Chip Shop and anything else that came into Old Scrapie's office – but since I last glanced in, about the same time yesterday, everything had been cleared. All that was left now was a mug of tea, a neat stack of papers and a book of regulations.

My heart sank when I saw the last object.

'Church,' he greeted me unsmilingly, sniffing then sipping his tea suspiciously, but I was disappointed – to judge from his satisfied expression – to find nobody had done anything unpleasant to it today.

'Sharkey,' I replied. 'Don't tell me you have acquired a taste for paperwork? I can give you plenty of mine, if you have.'

'Oh, just for this project,' he told me. 'It's a labour of love.'

Sharkey took a nipped dog-end from behind his ear, reminding me of a magician in the Pier Pavilion who once extracted pennies from Etterly's but wouldn't give her any of them when the show was over.

'Oh, yes?' I said encouragingly but not, I hoped, too encouragingly. I didn't want him to sense he had intrigued me.

'I've been thinking,' Sharkey began, and I resisted the obvious response with some difficulty. He placed the cigarette between his lips, making his next words a little less distinct. 'About our manpower situation. What do you make of it?'

It was not often the Shark asked for my opinion. I sensed a trap and walked warily into it.

'Not enough constables for even routine patrols,' I replied, 'and too many senior officers with too little to do.'

Even with Superintendent Vesty on more or less permanent sick leave, Sharkey and I didn't have much to occupy us most of the time. He had taken Box to investigate a new lead on the theft of a bench from Sackwater Railway Station last year, but it turned out to be a pew from St Luke's Church with woodworm and scheduled to be burned. Mr Trime, the station master, still rang us every Wednesday to check our progress on that case and I was always happy to tell him that my colleague was making none.

'In a nutshell.' Sharkey struck a match against the wall, already decorated with thousands of red lines. 'Too many Inspectors. One too many, to be precise.'

A fresh hope sprang up in my mind. Was my colleague thinking of leaving? I would buy everyone, except him, a drink if he was. I'm not a great one for hymns, but 'Oh Happy Day' resounded through my brain.

'Which is why I am petitioning for one of us to be relocated,' the Shark continued, and the song died as surely as if the needle had been lifted from a record because I knew what his next word would be before it had slithered from his lips. 'You,' he concluded.

'Me?' I huffed, and my colleague smiled unattractively. He had good teeth but had spent a great many years coating them in tar and making insufficient efforts to clean it off.

'As the officer with the most years' experience and the longest tenure in Sackwater,' he began, and I just knew he was quoting from the letter he was composing. His handwriting was poor and difficult to make out at the best of times but, even upside down, I could see he was making notes in block capitals.

REASONS TO REMOVE CHURCH, he had scrawled.

'I have a prior claim to the position of Inspector here. Let's face it, Church, we never needed you in the first place.'

'What else have you written?' I demanded, and Sharkey slapped a hand on top of his papers, obviously anticipating my intention to snatch them up.

'Only the truth,' he replied piously.

'For example?'

'Well,' he smirked, 'I have told them how you fanned rumours that Sackwater was inhabited by a nest of vampires…'

'I did no such thing.'

'And almost got Constable Chivers killed in the process.'

'She shot off half my ear,' I protested, and the Shark sniggered.

'And you almost got Box killed by a bomb.'

'The Luftwaffe dropped that,' I objected. 'Or are you saying I guided the bomber here?'

'Then you encouraged Chivers to risk her life in a drain.'

'I tried to discourage her. *You* egged her on.'

'Then you nearly got us both killed by that loony.'

'I saved us, you stinking louse,' I shouted, and Sharkey picked up his pen again.

'Prone to hysterical and abusive outbursts,' he spoke as he wrote.

'This is just a pack of filthy lies,' I seethed, and he did his little smirk again.

'You will have plenty of opportunity to tell that to the committee,' he told me. 'But you can't deny you have a false arm.'

'It's just a pity it sometimes gets out of control,' I said.

'What d'you mean?' the Shark asked me warily. He had seen that glint in my eyes before and had reason to regret it.

'Only' – I smashed my left hand down, shattering his mug and spraying the contents all over his work and even, I was pleased to see, his white shirt – 'that,' I finished, and marched out.

It hurt my stump like hell but it was worth it just to see my colleague's painstaking notes flow over the paper and onto his not-so-tidy-now desk.

'If you want a fight, Inspector Sharkey,' I shouted over my shoulder, 'by God I shall give you one.'

That sounded almost like Henry V, I told myself as I slammed my door, but in my heart I knew, to the men within earshot, I was just a hysterical female.

Thank you so much, I prayed. *I know I asked you to get me out of here but – really? – is this your idea of a joke?*

43

STRANGE STREET AND THE BUCKET OF SAND

Brigsy was leaning back in his chair puffing contentedly on his pipe and browsing somebody's copy of the *Daily Mirror* when I went back to check on his progress. Usually my entry would be a signal for him to hurriedly pretend to do something, but Brigsy only glanced up and said, 'When I goo to war the 'talians are our friends. Dint sound like ol' Muss'lini want to be pals this time.'

'Mussolini is all bluster,' I assured him. 'He knows he can't take on the British Empire.'

'Wish someone goo tell Adolph tha',' Brigsy mused.

'How many phone calls have you made?' I asked.

'One,' he told me proudly.

'One?' I checked I had heard him right.

Brigsy nodded. 'One,' he repeated with great satisfaction.

'And you felt you needed a rest after that?' I asked incredulously.

This was not the sergeant I knew. For all his faults, Brigsy was not usually one to shirk his duties.

'Not much else to do, madam,' he said complacently.

I took a breath. I did not believe Brigsy had misunderstood my instructions.

'I told you to ring every architects' office in the Oxford Street area.'

'I'm sorry, madam,' Brigsy said.

'So you should be.'

'But,' he continued firmly, 'that int what you tell me. You say to ring every architects' office in the Oxford Street area' – Was he going mad? Was I? Were we both? – ''til I do find Douglas Carpenter,' he concluded.

'Are you telling me you have found him?'

'No, madam.'

'Then what…'

'But I'm gooin' to tell you I have.'

'You found Douglas Carpenter with your first phone call?' I asked incredulously.

'Yes, madam,' Brigsy told me with a stumpy grin.

'How?'

'Waal…' Brigsy placed his pipe in the ashtray. 'I do remember Widow Durney who live down Strange Street – or is it up Strange Street?' he cogitated.

Just get on with it.

'Yes?'

'And I remember she's Widow Carpenter 'fore she marry again and I get to wonderin' if she's Douglas Carpenter's aunt mayhap, orrr' – he tapped his pipe out – 'not,' he concluded. There was a bucket of sand at the side of the desk in case of incendiary bombs and I had a strong urge to tip it over his head, but couldn't think of a convincing way to make out it was an accident. 'Soooo…' Perhaps I could get away with just a scoop of it. 'I send Box to enquire and Widow Durney int Douglas Carpenter's aunt at all.'

Oh Lord, give me strength.

I was just about to reach over and shake my sergeant by his baggy old lapels when he concluded, 'Widow Durney is Douglas Carpenter's mother.'

Oh Lord, give me a stout stick.

'Mrs Carpenter is…' I began patiently.

'Widow Durney,' Brigsy informed me again. 'Young Douglas goo tellin' you fibs.'

'But...' I said usefully, before I realised something a five-year-old would have concluded immediately. I had been blinded by the blindingly obvious. I knew now, of course, that Douglas Carpenter was lying about being taken in by a rich family. So why the hell hadn't I worked out that he had made up those stories about his parents being dead?

Douglas had never been any more smartly dressed than the rest of us or had any pocket money or showed us any expensive presents or invited anybody home. If somebody had told me that tale now, I would have greeted it with the scepticism it deserved, but I was a child when he first told me his story and children are almost as gullible as grown-ups. By the time I was an adult, Douglas's version of events was so securely entrenched in my mind as established fact that I stupidly never thought to question.

Was I letting my upset with Toby and anger with Sharkey cloud my judgement? More likely it was the headaches. They were getting more frequent and I found it difficult to concentrate in the throes of one.

'But why would he do that?' I wondered.

'Ever be on Strange Street?' Brigsy smoothed his faint suggestion of a moustache.

'And up it,' I told him, 'though my parents always told me not to.' I clicked my fingers – something else my parents always told me not to do because it was unladylike, though I never saw why it should be an exclusively masculine activity. 'You wouldn't boast about living there.'

'When I'm a constable...' Brigsy paused while he searched his jacket pockets for something.

'When you were a constable, what?' I prompted.

'Found it,' he declared, holding up his pipe knife. 'When I'm a constable' – he recommenced his account – 'if you see a man from Strange Street a'ter hours, you know if he int carryin' stolen goods, it's only for he's on his way to steal them.'

'No wonder...' I began, but my sergeant hadn't finished. Like an ocean liner, it sometimes took a lot to get him going, and often a lot more to bring him to a stop.

'I arrest men and women from there on more on one occasion,' he told me, inserting his tar-stained thumbnail into a notch to hinge the tar-caked blade out. 'Last time, Mr Joyce, the old magistrate, the one with the' – Brigsy twisted the blade around the bowl of his pipe – 'wooden leg, beggin' your pardon, madam.'

'You don't have to apologise for mentioning missing limbs,' I assured him.

I knew the men called me 'Old Stumpy' behind my back, but I had been called a great deal worse and to my face, especially when I was in London.

'No,' Brigsy agreed, a bit too readily for my liking, 'I dint bu' I jus' flick ash on your...' He hesitated to mention anything so indecent as an item of women's clothing.

'What?' I looked down. 'Oh, for goodness sake.' There was a fine grey powder all over the front of my shirt and I knew that, if I tried to brush it off, it would just rub in. I always kept a spare in my office, but I had accidently spat coffee onto it when I read that Charles Lindbergh, heroic aviator and darling of America, was saying that America should support Germany. 'Blow on it,' I instructed.

'Wha'?' Brigsy could not have looked more shocked if I had said *Like a nice time, darlin'*?

'Blow on it,' I repeated, 'or it will smudge.'

I stepped up to the desk and Brigsy recoiled.

'I'm only asking you to blow,' I tried to reassure him.

'Having some trouble?'

I twisted round to see Sharkey had materialised behind me.

'Inspector Church want me to...' The sergeant couldn't even bring himself to say the words, let alone oblige me.

'I just wanted him to blow his ash off me,' I huffed, and regretted it immediately.

'Allow me,' Sharkey said, and I re-enacted Brigsy's recoil.

'It's all right, thank you,' I said hastily.

'No trouble,' he said and crouched, face two inches from my chest, and blew. It took him a long time to clear that area and even longer for me to stop shuddering at the memory.

44

CROW TIME AND THE HALF WOMAN

It was crow time – early evening – when I got back to *Cressida* and I could see the captain standing on the top deck with Tubby, both leaning on the rail and smoking their briar pipes contentedly. They gave me a friendly wave.

Somebody, Carmelo probably, had pulled *Genevieve* across to Shingle Cove ready for me. Jimmy always *forgot* or didn't bother when he visited, and I wondered if he hadn't come. Normally he would be puffing on his new pipe too – somebody had told him it looked more manly than cigarettes – but then I saw Jimmy emerge from the wheelhouse, with what looked like three glasses cradled in his hands.

'Aunty,' he cried, because he knew it annoyed me when we were not even related.

I was very fond of Jimmy and, though I feared for his life, was hugely proud of how he and his comrades risked their lives for us daily, but I was not in the mood for his jokes and how he would try to kiss me. I hesitated but I could hardly spin on my heel and march back up the hill again, so I climbed into the boat and began to scull across. Even after months of practice, this was still an unnerving experience – the boat tended to swing and roll violently before it straightened up, and it was much harder work than rowing.

'Hang on,' Jimmy called, rattling down the steps of the boat and scattering half a dozen hens who had been peacefully pecking in the dry earth. He reached the rope when I was nearly halfway across, took it in both hands and heaved. I shipped my oar and sat back to watch. Jimmy's brown hair flopped over his suntanned face as he pulled me strongly over, dragging the prow onto dry land with my bench still over the water.

Jimmy held out his hand and I climbed out as decorously as I could, which was not very. You can't scramble out of an unstable rowing boat in a ladylike manner when your skirt is rising halfway up your thigh.

'Thank you.' I pecked him on the cheek.

'Talking to my chum Badger today,' he chattered, 'and I found out his mother lives on your old beat. Don't believe you ever collared her, though.'

'Really?' I forced a smile. 'I arrested most of the population of Bloomsbury in my time there.'

'Toby coming later?' Jimmy enquired.

'No,' I said quietly, and Jimmy's eyebrows rose but, uncharacteristically, he let the matter drop.

I ushered him up the steps first.

'I'm sorry' – I kissed Carmelo hello – 'Toby can't make it tonight. His mother is unwell.'

For somebody who made a career of listening to lies, I was remarkably inept at telling them and realised the flaw in my story even as it left my lips.

'Does she need me?' Tubby asked.

'Um, no.' I shook my head too emphatically.

'But if she is so ill that he...' Tubby began, stopped himself and said, 'You look like you could do with a large gin.'

'When couldn't I?' I asked. 'But I'll go and get changed first.'

I went below to my cabin and took off my uniform, hanging it off a hook on the wall. I would brush it down later, and my shoes needed a good polish. The captain usually did those for me.

I didn't need my false arm. They had all seen me without it more than they had seen me with it and my real arm, which ached most of the time, was starting to throb. I unclipped the leather straps. Many a modern woman will know the joy of kicking high heels off at the end of the day. Removing my scaffolding was a hundred times better – usually – but today I caught the hand on the side of my bunk and jarred my stump.

'Damn-damn-damn,' I cursed, resisting the urge to hurl the contraption onto the floor, and that was when there was a knock on the door.

'What?' I yelled, then a thought struck me. Toby had remembered the invitation, cooled down and decided to let bygones be bygones. He was always an even-tempered and forgiving man.

I pulled open the door and saw Greta, Tubby's wife, standing there holding two glasses, and I wondered briefly – as if it mattered – how she had managed to knock. She was a tiny woman with frizzy hair, which I would have regarded as the bane of my life but she always told me was her greatest asset. She could do nothing with it and so that was what she did and saved herself hundreds of hours a year, she claimed, in grooming.

'I told Jimmy one was for me,' she said. 'But they are both for you.'

'Thank you,' I said. 'Come in.'

'It's very cosy in here,' Greta said, handing me one of the glasses and putting the other on my chest of drawers. 'I envy you in winter when the east wind rushes through my bedroom.'

'It's quite snug,' I agreed automatically. 'Cheers.'

I took a big swig.

'I came down to ask if you were all right,' she told me, 'but it is obvious that you are not. Even the men noticed, and I would have to bawl my eyes out for days before Tubby would say *Something wrong, my dear?*'

I smiled. 'Oh Greta,' I said. 'You always cheer me up.' And promptly burst into tears.

Greta took the glass from me and put it down and grasped my hand.

'Have you broken up?' she asked, and I shook my head, contradicting myself at the same time by saying, 'I think so.'

'Here.' Greta let go of my hand and passed me a huge handkerchief. 'I always carry one because Tubby is always forgetting his.'

I blew my nose and brought my crying under control.

'It's Etterly Utter,' I tried to explain.

'Tubby told me about her.'

'She was my friend and – it sounds stupid now – one of the things that kept me going when I was having difficult times with difficult men was the thought that I would find her one day.'

'But not like that,' Greta said.

'Then I found out that Toby used to know her, and I started to ask him questions and he thought I suspected him of killing her.'

'And do you?'

'Of course not.' I took up my glass and drained it. 'Oh, Greta, why can't I just stop being a policewoman for five minutes?'

'Because you *are* one,' Greta told me. 'It's not just a job. You don't clock off at five and stroll past a crime because you won't be a policewoman again until tomorrow morning. Do you think Tubby comes home and stops being a doctor? Your friend should understand that. If you were out to dinner and he stumbled across a big story, would he just go back to his tomato soup?'

One of the many things Toby and I had in common was that we hated tomato soup – it always smelled of sweat to me – but I took her point.

'You love him, don't you?' Greta said.

I should have said *very much* but I only said, 'Yes.'

'Have you told him?'

'No.' And I didn't suppose I ever would now.

'Tell him,' she urged.

'I'm not sure I'll get the chance now.'

'He obviously loves you,' Greta assured me and, seeing my puzzlement, explained, 'You are far too intelligent to fall in love with somebody who doesn't love you back.'

'If only our heads ruled our hearts,' I mused, not very originally.

'Thank heavens they don't,' she said, 'or Tubby would have married Hermione Fawcett-Brown. She was richer, more beautiful and more intelligent than me and she positively hurled herself at him. You know what men are like. Tubby was hugely flattered. He could have been Lord of the Manor by now.'

'Then why didn't he?' I asked, adding hastily, 'not that you weren't a better catch.'

'Because I was tired of being a wallflower, had a few glasses of champagne for Dutch courage, marched across a ballroom, tripping up an earl in the process, and demanded that Tubby danced with me. It was a painful experience for my feet, but we talked and talked and, before the evening was out, we were practically engaged.'

Greta took the other glass, which clearly wasn't mine after all, and had a large drink.

'Go and speak to him,' she said. 'Tubby would be the first to tell you, the longer you leave a wound, the more likely it is to fester and prove fatal.'

'OK,' I agreed, and we went back onto the deck.

The table, I noticed, had been tactfully reset for five.

Carmelo had killed three rabbits for the feast, but we had plenty more and I was sure the men would happily eat our missing guest's portion between them. The captain said grace.

'Interesting case today,' Tubby announced. 'A woman came to see me with her entire left side missing.'

'But she's all right now,' we all chorused.

'Oh,' Tubby said in surprise. 'Have I told you that one before?'

'Once or twice,' Greta told him, putting her hand on top of his and squeezing it affectionately.

I bet Hermione Fawcett-Brown wouldn't have done that, I thought.

'Have I told you the one about—'

'Yes, darling,' she laughed. 'I think you probably have.'

I don't suppose I was the life and soul of the party but with three drunken men at the table, I had no need to be.

Jimmy left first. He had to be back on base before midnight.

'Will you be all right on your motorbike?' I worried.

'Drives itshelf,' Jimmy assured me airily but slurrily, only making me all the more anxious. He leaned over, to kiss me goodnight, I thought, but really to whisper in my ear, 'Do you want me to shlap some shense into him?'

'I'm sure the offer is well meant,' I said, though I suspected, after several gins and a few whiskies, Jimmy just fancied a fight. 'But no, thank you. Goodnight, Jimmy.'

It was a bright night with a full moon and more stars than could possibly be counted. At one time the lights of Sackwater and Anglethorpe would glow into the sky, but now an invader from Mars might pass over islands thinking them uninhabited. In the years ahead, many people, especially city dwellers, would come to fear a full moon because it made it easier for the Luftwaffe pilots to find their targets, but at that early stage we blessed it for helping us find our way around in the much-hated blackout.

I went back on deck and watched Jimmy cross the short channel between us and the bank. At least he could row in a fairly straight line, I noted, and he actually remembered to pull the boat back for me.

'Take care,' I called.

'Albyorite,' he insisted, lurching sideways into a bush.

The Grethams left soon after and then it was just me and the captain, who had fallen asleep in a deckchair.

Toby should have been beside me, admiring that sky and putting his arm around me. I would go round as soon as I could and put things right.

45

EZEKIEL AND THE GHOST OF THE WORD

If there was one part of the Bible I really didn't like, it was the Book of Job. A God who would slaughter all Job's family and servants just to win a bet with Satan seemed petty and cruel to me. It just so happened that the next time I flicked through Etterly's Bible it opened there, and it didn't really *just* happen because, I discovered, the paper was slightly crumpled below where Job was sitting on a dung heap scraping his sores. Not only that but somebody had set about damaging it. The bottom right-hand corner of page eight hundred and three had been torn off and I felt sure this was deliberate. Accidental rips usually run diagonally, or at least curve. This was a dead straight rectangle about a quarter of an inch high and one long, as if she had used a ruler or, more likely, scissors.

His eyes do shine like the stars, Etterly had written in her tiny lettering. I had no idea she was so poetic. *And so I call him...* And that was it.

Call him what? Don't do this to me, Etterly. You're supposed to be my friend.

I peered closely. Bible paper is strong and therefore not easily ripped, but also very thin. Etterly's writing should have made an imprint on the next page, but when I turned over I realised that had been cut out too in exactly the same way, and I was left with a riveting account of how she had been helping her father in the shop, sorting watch and clock parts into clean jam jars.

Cogs and... she had written. Had she realised that the word showed through and so removed that as well?

I'm not that easily discouraged, my friend.

Like a lot of people who have difficulty writing, Etterly had a heavy hand. I took a look at page eight hundred and seven. Luckily, the very bottom had not been written on, which gave me a better chance. By holding the paper up to the light, I thought I could see something.

I took my pencil from my notepad and rubbed the side of the lead gently over the corner of the page. We used to do that with pennies under paper so we could get a picture of whoever had been on the throne when the coin was minted. The first letter to appear in the lighter shading was an S. Was this the name I was looking for? *Springs*, I read.

Oh great, I thought, *now I know what else you put in the jars.*

It appeared that I was going to be frustrated after all, but then I noticed that the first letter was ghosted. A second S appeared more faintly, just to the right of the first, the top half rising above it. I gingerly rubbed a ribbon of grey along the top of Springs and made out some more letters. *Sparkels*, I read.

Three out of ten for spelling.

Etterly often mangled people's names, usually by mistake but sometimes for fun. I was always *Betsy*. Georgie and Nelly, to their annoyance, were *Porgie* and *Belly*. It didn't take a massive leap of the imagination to work out who *Sparkles* was.

46

DONKEYS, SHEEP AND FERRETS

I went back to Folger's Estate Farm. I had thought about taking Dodo with me – she was getting more experience in knitting than police work lately – but even though she had practised hard in my parents' back garden, she was still unsteady on a bicycle and the track through the estate, always potholed, had broken up badly in our last dreadful winter.

The smithy was still there, and I could hear the clang of iron on iron as I dismounted. The paddock where Limelight had been kept was occupied by two donkeys. A Suffolk Punch mare stood tethered to a post on the far side of the cobbled yard, huge and heavy, white blaze running down her chestnut face. Delilah would probably be dead but her foal, Brandy, could still be alive, though an old lady by now. Brandy had an odd brown ring on her back right stocking, I remembered, and I was just approaching to get a closer look when I heard a voice.

'What you pokin' 'bou' for, copper?'

Morphus was coming out of the forge.

'Hello, Mr Harrison,' I greeted him. 'Do you remember me? Betty Church. I used to come here with Godfrey Skillern and Etterly Utter.'

'I recall.' He stepped out of the shadows, a heavy hammer still in his hand. 'So I ask agin. What you pokin' 'bou' for?'

I walked towards the blacksmith. He must have been well into his seventies. His once-black hair was still thick, but silvery now – what I could see of it from under his cloth cap. His face was craggier and more scarred by the countless sparks that must have flown into it, but he still stood erect and muscular and his eyes were as deep a blue as ever.

'I'm come to see you,' I said, 'and your sons.'

'Why?'

'I want to talk to you all.'

Morphus raised his heavy hammer as easily as a lady might swing her parasol.

'When you're a girl you're welcome.' He wagged the hammer. 'And were you but a woman you do be welcome too, but your kind int nothin' but trouble for me and mine.'

'I haven't come to cause trouble for anyone,' I assured him.

'Your bein' here is trouble 'nough,' he told me.

'Not all the police are against you,' I assured him, but Morphus spat on the ground.

'No?' he asked sharply. 'Tell tha' to my Harkles. Do four month for 'ssault and batt'ry he do, two year back, when three clodhoppers set upon him.'

'I didn't know about that,' I said. 'It was before I came back, but I'll look into it. Is Harkles here?'

'Why?' Morphus prodded the hammer towards me. Another couple of inches and it would have smashed my face.

'No, he int.' A man emerged from the stables.

'Hello, Bosko,' I said.

He looked shorter than I remembered, but I was shorter myself then. He was even more heftily built, with a hogshead chest, his upper arms bulging through the sleeves of his loose brown shirt. Unfortunately, time could do nothing to improve his looks. His upper lip still twisted into a sneer and a blackened tooth jutted from under it now.

'And you a copper,' he said, whistling, as he had always done, through his flattened nose. 'Wha' we s'pose to be up to now? Tha'

Rivers he come accusin' us of stealin' sheep 'til they find tha' ram fallen down an old well.'

I was surprised Constable Rivers had had the energy to go ferreting around the countryside. He had normally whinged about his back if he had to walk the length of the promenade.

'How long ago was that?' I asked.

''Bou' five year gone,' he told me, coming up close to us both.

'Constable Rivers is retired now,' I told him. 'And things have changed since I came back.'

'Nice to think so.' Bosko cracked his knuckles. 'But they int.'

'I just wanted to talk, especially to Harkles,' I said.

'He never start tha' fight,' Bosko flared up.

'I don't suppose he did,' I agreed.

Harkles had always had a sunny nature.

'Wha' then?' Bosko demanded, moving closer.

With his bulk and manner, he made a menacing figure, but I had vowed a long time ago never to be intimidated by the public. I took a small step towards him.

'Etterly Utter,' I said.

'Tha' girl what goo in the Ghost Tree?' Bosko rumbled, though he had no need to question it. He knew very well who she was. 'You goo try to blame tha' on Harkles?'

'Of course not,' I assured him.

'Int no *course not* 'bout it.' Morphus spat again and just missed my shoe. 'They try to blame tha' boy on us.'

'Godfrey?' I queried, and he nodded in confirmation.

'They say we let him ride Limelight.'

'But why would you?' I asked. 'You always told him not to.'

'They say he pay us.'

'Well, that's nonsense,' I protested, and Bosko kicked at a raised cobble with his toe.

'So why you goo want Harkles?' Morphus shouldered his hammer.

'It's just that Harkles and Etterly were friends.'

'They near were,' Bosko agreed. 'But he int good 'nough for her sort.'

'Etterly never thought like that,' I protested. 'Nor did any of us who came here.'

'Perhap not then,' Bosko conceded. 'But you all goo high and mighty when you grow.'

'Best you ge' off our land now,' Morphus said, hammer raised threateningly.

The land actually belonged to the Folger family, but I was not going to quibble over property law.

'Can you tell me where Harkles is?' I tried.

'Goo,' Bosko poked a huge fist towards me.

'Does he still live here?' I asked.

'Goo,' he repeated, moving so close I could feel his breath on my face, and I had smelled fresher from their horses.

I didn't seriously think they would attack me, but it was obvious they were not going to cooperate.

'Tell him I called,' I said, 'and I am not trying to cause trouble for any of you.'

'You dint have to try to cause it,' Morphus told me. 'You *are* trouble.'

'Tell him,' I repeated.

Common sense told me to back away, keeping a close watch on them both, but that would have shown fear. I turned on my heel and walked briskly away.

47

JESSICA LAMBERT, MR JARMAN AND THE GENIE

Carol was downstairs, sitting upright behind her desk and making no pretence to be doing anything other than guarding the offices of the *Sackwater and District Gazette*.

'Good morning, Inspector Church,' she greeted me in that pleasant way I greet members of the public I can't abide.

'Good morning, Carol,' I responded. 'Is Mr Gregson upstairs?'

'Yes,' she replied, with the sort of smile you might reserve for men with machetes.

'Good.' I stepped forward.

'But he's busy,' she told me quickly.

I stopped.

'Has he got somebody with him?'

'No,' she said. 'He just told me to tell you he's busy.'

'Just now, or whenever I call?' I asked.

'Whenever,' Carol told me with great satisfaction.

Did she really think if she had Toby to herself she could have him to herself? This was ridiculous. I was not going to be fobbed off that easily. I moved forward again.

'And,' Carol said loudly, 'he asked me to read you this letter.'

She slipped a sheet of paper out from under her blotting pad and unfolded it.

'Show me.' I held out my hand.

'He asked me to read it to you,' she explained slowly, like I was the local simpleton.

'Then you had better do so,' I said icily.

'Please sit down,' Carol said, but it was more of an order than an invitation.

'No,' I said and stayed where I was, standing over her.

Carol slid her tortoiseshell glasses on. I had not seen those before, and I was happy to see they didn't suit her in the least.

'To Inspector Church,' she read, and paused.

'That was a short letter,' I said.

'I was going to clear my throat,' she said, but then didn't.

'Then kindly do so.'

'If you wish to talk to me, I must inform you that I will only do so in the presence of my solicitor, Mr Jarman.'

Good luck with that one, I thought. Jarman had served the Gregson family for a good few decades. In his time he may have given them good service for all I knew, but a post had better hearing than he did now and his memory was not so much wandering as off on a world cruise.

'And that if you attempt to enter my office without an appointment I shall publish an article in the *Sackwater and District Gazette* about your abuse of the rights of the press.' Carol paused.

'Another amphibian in your throat?' I asked. 'I hope it doesn't choke you.'

'No,' she said. 'I was just letting the words sink in.'

'Why?' I asked sweetly. 'Don't you understand them?'

I understood them all too well. All my life I have built a guard around myself. I could never let my parents or teachers know what I was thinking and, after Jessica Lambert betrayed a confidence to our piano teacher, who then went straight to the headmistress, I learned not to confide in my schoolfriends. But I had let my guard down with Toby. I had told him things about myself and my colleagues that could be acutely embarrassing, to say the least.

'If you persist in harassing me, I shall be forced to make an official complaint to your superior officer,' Carol read with undisguised pleasure.

Superior officer? What superior officer? Toby knew damned well that Superintendent Vesty was out of the picture. The only other officer above sergeant was older than me, but we were the same rank. Was Toby Gregson threatening to report me to Sharkey? She must be making this up.

'Give me that,' I said more calmly than I felt, but Carol was already shutting the note in her desk drawer and taking out the key.

'Goodbye, Inspector,' she said.

I clenched my teeth, turned without another word and walked slowly away.

'Oh, Inspector,' Carol called, and I paused. 'You forgot this.'

I turned and saw her dangling my gas mask by its straps with that condescending air I reserve for my constables at their dimmest. For two pence I would have marched off, but what kind of example would that set the public, if I went out and about without it?

'Thank you.' I returned to retrieve it.

'You are so very welcome,' she told me, and I knew then that, with all our shortages, we would never run out of syrup.

You couldn't do it, could you? I raged at the mischievous genie who, I was coming to believe, ruled my life. *You just couldn't leave me with that vestige of dignity.* And, just in case I didn't quite believe what I was saying, I stumbled over a dangling shoelace. At least I managed to stop myself falling, but if I had any doubts about whether or not I looked ridiculous, the hoots of the people at the bus stop made it quite clear that I did.

48

THE BIG SLEEP AND THE SECRET OF BAWDSEY MANOR

There was a new poster up at Sackwater Railway Station. It showed a wealthy couple, her in furs and him with something I hadn't seen anybody wear for years – white spats. Their terrier sat between them and all three looked questioningly at a notice by a ticket office: *Is your journey really necessary?* In case you didn't get the message, it was emblazoned across the top of the picture in big black letters, and in case you wondered who wanted to know, it told you at the bottom – the *Railway Executive Committee*.

In an odd sort of mirror life, there was a notice by the ticket office: *Is your journey really necessary?*

'Day return to London, please, Mr Tape.'

I showed him my pass.

'Is your journey really necessary?' he asked, pointing to the notice and waving to the poster through the hole in his glass screen.

'Yes,' I said. What did he think – I was off on a pleasure trip in full uniform? 'Official police business.'

That phrase usually impresses people and today was no exception.

'Secret?' he asked.

I looked over my shoulder in both directions and leaned forward.

'Top secret,' I confirmed confidentially.

'Say no more,' Mr Tape said, which was just as well because there was nothing else I wanted to say.

'I shan't,' I promised, and Mr Tape tapped his nose in that knowing way that only the unknowing do.

'Very wise.' He nodded very wisely. 'Walls have ears.'

When I was a child, I used to find that expression hilarious. Now I found it irritating and couldn't bring myself to say, *How true*.

'What time is the train?' I asked, and Mr Tape put a finger to his lips.

'I'm not supposed to give out information like that,' he told me, eyes flicking side to side because there was probably a Nazi in one of his pigeonholes. 'But between you and me, it's s'posed to be quarter past,' he whispered, 'but' – and here came the really confidential bit – 'it's running eight minutes late.'

Good, I thought, *plenty of time to get a cup of tea*.

I bought my ticket and thanked him. Hitler would be cock-a-hoop, I pondered, if he knew how difficult he was making life for us already. I made my way to the canteen.

'Take a seat, dear,' Tilly, the tea lady, told me. She found it difficult to imagine women as officers. *It's just pretending until the men come home*, she had told me once with a friendly wink. 'It do be eight minute late last I heard.'

Good heavens, I thought, *doesn't she realise she may have just lost us the war?*

I sat at a table and brought a copy of *The Big Sleep* out of my handbag. I was reading it on Georgie's recommendation. Georgie was in the WRACS now and doing something mysterious at Bawdsey Manor, she had told me in strict confidence. Being stationed so near meant she could come home on leave, but she had had little of that lately.

'You will love how they fight crime over there,' she had told me, and she was right. I was much taken with Philip Marlowe. Anyone who could drink that much, smoke that much, get knocked out and still come out with quips had to be worth knowing.

Contrary to the secret information I had been privy to, the train was not eight minutes late. It was forty minutes late and packed with baby-faced soldiers being taken to the port of Felixstowe to ward off the invasion that must surely follow our headlong flight from France. Brigsy had pinned a map in the back room in the hope of recording our advances, but instead he found himself shading in terrifyingly large expanses of Europe to mark the Nazi conquests. Could these children stop the enemy's seasoned troops? I prayed we would never have to find out.

After half an hour of standing crushed between them and their kitbags and refusing invitations to sit on their laps, the carriage emptied and I had my choice of seats before it filled again with naval recruits on their way to London and wanting to know if they could sit on my knee. Surprisingly – to them at any rate – they could not. To make matters worse, I had found myself in a non-smoker.

I used to love trains, watching the scenery glide by, but now the windows were blacked out except for a viewing slit and you had to stand up to see out through that. I had lowered the window in the door and sat by it to get a view and some fresh warm air.

'Blimey, it's draughty,' a burly youth whinged and he pulled the strap to reseal our compartment, to everyone's approval except mine. It was a warm day and a dozen young sailors are not quite as fragrant as you might imagine.

I buried myself in my book and Philip was just talking about having a hangover from women when we pulled in at Liverpool Street. There were no announcements and no platform signs, no room in the cafeteria to get anywhere near the counter and, to cap it all, the Ladies was *out of order.*

Is your journey really necessary? the posters nagged.

Bit late now, chum, I thought, while the man and his wife and their dog still looked nonplussed.

I made my way to the Regency Hotel to freshen up and smoke a much-needed cigarette. The bar was open but no bourbon on the rocks for me, unfortunately. Instead, I settled for what Sidney Grice used to describe as *an intoxicatingly strong cup of coffee* in the lounge before I ventured into the bowels of the earth and the horrors of the Metropolitan Underground Railway.

49

TIME AND THE MONGRELS

I emerged from Euston Square tube station on the corner of Gower Street. March Middleton was away, in pursuit of the one-headed Dobermann of Gripley Green. I thought this was a joke when she apologised for not being able to meet me, but five people had died already, she told me in all seriousness.

University College stood, pillared like a Greek temple, to the left, with the red cruciform hospital on my right. The road surface was still made of wooden blocks to muffle the sound of hooves, though ninety per cent of traffic was motorised by those days. Few other than delivery men relied on horse-drawn transport any more.

I paused outside number 125. It looked like any of the other houses, except that there were iron shutters over the windows now. Aunty M was away on business and did not want a repeat of her experience when she had gone home to find the Toulouse Torturer waiting with his equipment in her bathroom. She had refused all offers of a police guard as a waste of manpower. *I would rather you protected the women sleeping on the streets than one old lady comfortable in her bed*, she had told the Chief Constable.

On I went along the straight white row until it was crossed by Store Street. To one end was the Senate House building, its great white-stone and glass centre towering over two hundred feet, and I wondered if it would be obliterated one day. H. G. Wells's portrayal of cities being destroyed when he wrote *The War in the Air* didn't seem like science fiction any more.

I turned right towards Tottenham Court Road and soon found a polished brass plaque on the wall of number forty, announcing that this was the premises of Bullbrook and Carpenter, Architects and Surveyors, though it did not claim membership of any Royal Institutes or Societies.

Through the side window I saw a grey, middle-aged man standing, engrossed, behind a table with acres of paper spread out over it. He had a pencil poised mid-air but didn't appear to be doing anything with it.

There was no bell or knocker on the red-painted door, so I let myself in. It was a reasonable sized office, about fifteen feet square. The man looked up through thick-framed glasses as I came in.

'Good morning, madam.' He screwed up his eyes. 'I mean Officer.'

It took me a while to recognise Douglas Carpenter, even though I was expecting to come across him. Time is rarely kind and she had not wasted much charity on him. Douglas Carpenter had acquired a great deal of fat since I had last seen him. He had stored it under his clean-shaven chin and wrapped it in a bulging brown waistcoat. Grubby red sacks hung under his watery eyes. His hair had thinned and retreated in a disorderly manner halfway up his head. His nose looked longer and chunkier. Tubby always insisted that noses don't grow in adults but here was living proof that he was wrong.

'Hello, Douglas,' I said, and was just wondering if I too had changed so much that I needed to introduce myself when he whipped off his round-rimmed glasses.

'Betty?' He peered towards me like a man lost in the fog.

'Hello,' I said again, almost as taken aback as he was.

'Oh, I see you are a policeman now.' Douglas came towards me.

'I mean woman,' he corrected himself before I did, his eyebrows rising shaggily. 'And a sergeant?' he reckoned.

'Inspector,' I told him.

Douglas looked me up and down in disbelief while he searched for a word. 'Blimey' appeared to be the one he was looking for, and his eyebrows settled down.

'I have come to see you,' I told him and his left cheek twitched like it had been prodded with electrodes.

'How did you find me?' he asked, more guiltily than Terrence Bailey had when I tracked him to his human abattoir.

50

BEAUTY AND THE BEAST

Those shaggy eyebrows cowered behind Douglas's spectacles but there was nowhere for them or their owner to hide.

'My sergeant sent a constable to see your mother,' I told him.

'Mrs Hornby?' he asked, and I sighed despairingly.

Douglas had not been the quickest off the mark as a youth and he had aged badly, but could he really have gone so senile as to imagine I still believed his deceptions?

But you did, until recently, a small voice reminded me. *Shut up, small voice*, I told it fiercely.

'I did speak to Mrs Hornby,' I told him, and his stringy moustache twitched. 'And' – I paused to watch the rest of him start to squirm – 'guess what she said.'

Douglas's moist eyes scrutinised my shoes.

'She had never heard of me,' he mumbled.

'And then,' I continued, 'we contacted your real mother.'

Douglas dragged his eyes up but couldn't actually persuade them to meet mine.

'Oh,' he said, then realising that was not an adequate response, added, 'I see.' Douglas shuffled, reminding me of when he was plucking up courage to ask Etterly to dance in the village hall. 'Can you really blame me? Have you any idea what it was like being brought up in Strange Street? Even people who didn't know it mocked the name, but anyone who did treated me like the criminal they had decided I already was or would soon become.' Douglas swallowed noisily.

'Why Mrs Hornby especially?' I asked, and he waggled his head.

'She had an enormous house. I saw her once when I was doing a paper round, until Mr Volter, the newsagent, found out where I lived and decided I couldn't be trusted to collect the money, even though I had been doing it with no problems for three months by then. She was so pretty and smartly dressed and spoke so beautifully, I thought *I wish you were my mother*, and the more I thought about it, the more I wanted it to be true and so I decided to make it true and so,' he ended simply, 'it was.'

'It never even occurred to me that you weren't especially... well dressed,' I admitted as tactfully as I could. Douglas's appearance had verged upon the ragged at times.

His eyebrows snuggled together.

'It occurred to a few boys at my school, not to mention Mr Hales, the headmaster, but I told them my adoptive mother was anxious that I wouldn't get bullied for being too posh and that she hadn't sent me to a public school because she wanted me to be able to mix with people from all classes.'

'I do find one thing strange,' I confessed, and the mongrels perked up.

'How I got away with it?' he suggested.

'No,' I replied. 'I'm wondering why you haven't asked me the most obvious question, the one everybody asks me.'

'What?' he asked.

'No,' I said, 'not what or who or where or when but...' I opened my arms for him to fill the gap with the missing word.

'Why?' he realised.

'Well done.' I tried to clap sarcastically but my left wrist flicked backwards and jammed so I found myself flapping my right hand as if I was swatting a wasp off my jacket. 'Most people would wonder why I had come before they asked how I had arrived.'

'Well,' Douglas began, and I caught a glimpse of his old, lopsided boyish smile. 'I don't suppose you have come to arrest me for pretending to have been fostered.'

'No,' I agreed, 'I have come to question you about the disappearance of Etterly Utter.'

51

PENCILS, POSTMARKS AND KILLER BLOWS

There was something theatrical in the way Douglas's jaw dropped. In my experience, people don't do that any more than ladies swoon at coarse language or maids cry *Lawks a mussy*.

Douglas cleared his throat.

'Surely,' he said, when he realised I was not going to add to my statement, 'you don't think I had anything to do with that?'

I waited. Sometimes people will come out with all sorts of things to break a silence, but this was not one of those times.

'We all had something to do with it,' I reminded him.

'I was there,' he conceded, 'but that was all. I didn't see her go anywhere near that damned tree. I wasn't even interested in the girl.'

I was starting to believe Douglas until his last sentence.

'Oh, come off it,' I scoffed. 'All the boys were interested in Etterly.'

'At first,' he agreed. 'She was a darned pretty girl, though, personally, I preferred Georgie or you.'

'Let's just stick to the subject of Etterly,' I suggested, and Douglas almost visibly stumbled.

'I'm sorry, that just sort of slipped out.'

'Just tell me why I have come to see you, Douglas,' I said coolly.

'Don't *you* know?' he asked with a Cheddary grin.

'Tell me,' I pressed, but the grin remained like when a film reel sticks just before it snaps or melts.

'You've become very formal, Betty,' he said with manufactured levity.

'Inspector.' I tapped my epaulette, to reinforce the idea that I had become very formal indeed. 'Tell me.'

'I'm sure I don't know,' Douglas blustered, almost as convincingly as a bald barber promoting hair restorer.

'Let me give you a clue,' I said, reaching into my handbag to slip the envelope out of its protective sleeve.

Douglas could not have stared at my exhibit with much more horror if I had produced a human head still dripping blood.

'But how?' he gasped.

'Yove,' I said, and he looked at me blankly.

'I'm sorry?'

This took me aback a bit. It was supposed to be if not my killer blow, at least the one that rocked him, but it had glanced off his chin without so much as making him blink.

'Excuse me.' I pushed past Douglas to the table, slipped the letter out and flattened it on the table over a plan of what looked like a balcony, but not one, I hoped, designed for the Führer to address Londoners from. 'There.' I ran a finger under the word.

'That says *Your*,' he protested, and I tapped the letters one by one.

'Y-O-V-E,' I read out.

'Y-O-R-E,' he corrected me.

'That means *long ago*,' I told him, 'as in *days of yore*. The possessive pronoun is Y-O-U-R.'

Douglas flared.

'Is that why you've come?' he huffed. 'To give me a spelling lesson?'

'No, of course not.'

Those watery eyes looked ready to overflow.

'If I had wanted to be humiliated, I could have stayed in

Sackwater,' he protested. 'You think it wasn't bad enough coming from Strange Street without being mocked by all the boys and teachers because I couldn't spell?'

'I never knew you couldn't,' I said. 'I don't think any of us did.'

If I had, I might have been on his trail much sooner.

'Oh,' Douglas said, and a thought struck me.

'Why,' I asked, 'did nobody ever see you going in and out of your parents' home?'

'They did,' he replied, 'occasionally, but I just told them I was doing charity work for the local church and visiting the poor.' He laughed hollowly. 'That was a joke – the poor visiting the poor.'

I backtracked.

'You spelled daughter correctly,' I pointed out.

'I looked it up because I knew I would get it wrong,' Douglas told me, before admitting shamefacedly, 'didn't think I'd get *your* wrong though.' He opened and closed his hands repeatedly as he collected himself. 'Is that really all you had to go on – thinking it was some obscure local word?'

'I knew the letter was written with a draughtsman's pencil because the vertical lines were thicker than the horizontal,' I told him, feeling very Sherlockian.

'Plenty of people use flat-cut pencils,' Douglas objected. 'Builders and decorators, for a start.'

Oh, I thought.

'The postmark helped,' I struggled on, feeling more Watsonian now.

Douglas clicked his tongue. 'So you haven't done anything clever at all. Waters told you my address, didn't he?'

'He doesn't know it,' I said indignantly. 'He threw your letter unopened into the fire.'

'Oh, for pity's sake.' Douglas threw up his hands. 'If that's true he's a bigger fool than you,' he told me. 'I put ten shillings in that envelope to repay him for the compass and dividers set I took with me.'

'You sent this to the wrong address,' I remembered, showing him the envelope.

'No, I didn't,' he protested indignantly. 'The Utters lived at Number Sixteen Bath Road.'

'Number Eleven,' I told him.

'Then they must have moved,' he asserted. 'I remember Etterly telling me she was soon to be sweet sixteen and live at number sixteen.'

'They are still in the same street, but the numbers were altered,' I told him.

'Because of the stupid system they used to have,' he recollected. 'How was I supposed to know that?'

'You weren't,' I agreed, 'but a local man would. A local man who wasn't local any more would only know the old address.'

'I suppose,' Douglas agreed reluctantly.

'Which brings me to the reason I came here,' I told him and, from the hint of a nod he gave me, I knew that Douglas knew what I was going to ask him next. 'Why,' I said, and he winced in anticipation, 'did you send this letter?'

52

DUTY AND THE RUINS OF THE MAN

Douglas stepped sideways and leaned backwards.

'I wanted Mr Utter to know that his daughter was all right,' he told me.

I would come to the obvious question later, I decided.

'Let me put it this way,' I tried to explain. 'Imagine you had lost a prized possession – your mother's wedding ring that you had intended to give your sweetheart, for example.'

'I have no sweetheart,' he told me, and I just managed not to respond that I was unsurprised. 'And my mother had a brass curtain ring on her finger until she lost it because it was too big.'

'I'm asking you to imagine,' I reminded him.

'All right,' he flapped. 'I'm imagining.'

'And you were very upset,' I ploughed on. 'Then you receive a letter telling you that the ring has been found but with no indication of who found it or whether they intended to return it to you. How do you think you would feel?' He opened his mouth, but I hadn't finished. 'Would you think *Thank heavens my ring has been found* or would you think that you were no better off than before, that the writer might even be joking or taunting you?'

Douglas mulled that over.

'I wanted Mr Utter to know that his daughter was all right,' he repeated, thereby erasing everything I had just said.

'Do I really have to take you through the last two minutes' conversation again?' I sighed.

'I take your point,' he conceded irritably.

'At last.'

'I see now that it was mistaken but I was trying to reassure Mr and Mrs Utter.'

I wasn't going to admit that, bizarrely, Douglas had succeeded and reinforced their conviction that Etterly, whose remains I had uncovered, was still alive. I needed him to come down from whatever higher ground he had thought he occupied.

'What happened to you, Douglas?' I asked.

'I've put on a bit of weight,' he admitted. 'I probably don't eat enough potatoes.'

I hadn't meant his appearance but, while he was in a cooperative mood, I decided to come straight out with it.

'I didn't know you all that well, but you seemed such a sensible boy,' I said, not really wanting to be cruel but knowing I had to be. 'Now, I'm sorry to say, you're behaving like a twit.'

I expected indignation at those remarks, but Douglas only chewed his lower lip and pinched the bridge of his nose.

'I wasn't just me. It was everything,' he said. 'Everything changed when Godfrey died.'

'Godfrey Skillern?' I checked in mild surprise. They didn't go to the same school or play in the same sports teams.

'Who else?' he demanded bitterly.

'But...' I hesitated, remembering how Douglas used to follow Godfrey around, even though he was largely ignored.

'Godfrey was a good friend to me,' Douglas said. 'He found out about where I really lived and never said a word to anybody else. I shan't ever forget that.'

'Even so,' I said carefully, 'a lot of us liked and admired Godfrey and we were very upset by his accident—'

'Oh, for God's sake, Betty,' Douglas croaked hoarsely, 'did it never even occur to you that it wasn't an accident?'

Douglas stepped back and semi-sat on the edge of the table, and I stepped back to get a better look at the ruins of the man.

'It occurred to me, of course,' I admitted, 'but there was no evidence to suggest—'

'Evidence?' Douglas burst out. 'I have plenty of that.'

'If you really have evidence that Godfrey was unlawfully killed—'

'How clinical that sounds,' he broke in.

'—You have a duty to give it to the police,' I continued.

'Oh, I have plenty of evidence,' Douglas insisted, 'but I can never show it to you or anybody. It is the evidence of my own eyes.'

Douglas was trembling.

'What did you see?' I asked, stepping back towards him.

He shook so violently, the table rocked.

'I saw Godfrey Skillern,' he choked. 'I saw him being murdered.'

53

BLOOD AND THE MAN

Douglas buried his face in his hands, sobbing. It seems heartless, and maybe it is, but I went over and pulled his fingers apart. March Middleton had told me it was one of the first lessons Sidney Grice taught her – to check for real tears – and there was no doubt that Douglas was crying.

'Thank you,' he wept, taking hold of my hand, mistaking my cynicism for sympathy.

I waited.

'I'm sorry,' he said, and pulled his hands away to search for a handkerchief.

'Have mine.'

'No, really,' he protested, but he took it and used it anyway, and I was just wondering whether to tell him to keep it when he tucked it into his breast pocket, where it sagged untidily.

'Tell me what you saw, Douglas,' I urged softly.

'I saw him being murdered.'

He had told me that already and it was obvious I was going to have to prise the information out of him morsel by morsel.

'Where?' I asked.

I knew where Godfrey had died, of course, but not where he had received his injuries.

'In Packard's Field,' Douglas said. 'The night before Godfrey actually died. He was attacked with some kind of hammer. He tried to fend the blows off with his arms, but they were too strong for him. He—'

'They?' I queried.

'The blows,' he said, annoyed at my interruption.

'So not more than one attacker?'

'Do you want me to tell you or not?' he griped.

'Go on,' I told him coolly.

'He was hit on the head – two or three times, I think. It was difficult to see. Then he fell to the ground.'

'And where were you?'

'Coming up the hill on the other side of the ditch. I saw him through a gap in the hedge.'

'Did you see his attacker?'

'It was a man,' Douglas said. 'A ruffian, but I couldn't see his face.'

Ruffian? I didn't think anybody said that any more.

'What was he wearing?'

'I don't know – a dark jacket and a flat cap, I think.'

'Then what happened?'

'I heard Godfrey moan and the man was going to hit him again. He had the hammer raised.'

'What kind of hammer?'

'How the hell would I know?' Douglas protested. 'I didn't see a label on it.'

It never ceased to puzzle me – even when they are cooperating – how uncooperative witnesses tend to be.

'Was it the sort of thing you might put a picture up with, or' – I tried to think of another example – 'use to break down a wall?'

'More like a sledgehammer,' Douglas said, 'in size, but not so big.'

'So the same in size but not so big?' I queried.

'Yes,' Douglas confirmed, because that made perfect sense. 'He was wielding it with one hand and I think he had

Godfrey with the other, by the throat or collar. I couldn't see very well.'

In my experience, people usually have a worse view than they make out. Those who claim to have an excellent viewpoint have a reasonable one and those who admit to having a poor one have virtually none.

'So did Godfrey drop, or was he lowered to the ground?'

'It was more like he was thrown down,' Douglas told me, 'but I couldn't—'

'And then what?' I broke in. He was beginning to sound like a theatregoer complaining about his seat.

'I heard a girl shouting *stop, stop, leave him alone*, and then I saw her run up. I don't know where she came from. It was like she had climbed out of the ditch. He threw his hammer down and grabbed her by the throat.'

'And then?' I pressed.

'And then I ran away,' he admitted shamefacedly.

'To get help?' I said, without much confidence.

'I just ran away,' he mumbled. 'I was frightened.'

'So Etterly died trying to protect Godfrey and you ran away,' I observed in scantily concealed contempt.'

'Etterly?' he queried in bewilderment. 'Etterly wasn't there.'

I didn't react to Douglas's statement for some time. I took my gas mask box off my shoulder and put it on the one corner of the table that wasn't covered in blueprints and pencilled plans and balanced my helmet on top. I looked at the ceiling and I looked at the floor and then back at him.

'Who was it, then?' I asked.

'I don't know,' he said.

Please don't tell me you couldn't see very well.

'I couldn't see very well,' he told me. 'But I saw enough to know it wasn't Etterly. I don't think I knew her.'

'Describe her,' I ordered him, and Douglas shrugged.

'She was just a girl.'

'What do you mean, *just* a girl?' I demanded angrily.

Carpenter tugged an earlobe.

'I meant that was all I could make out – that she was a girl,' he explained. 'I only saw the back of her.'

'Blonde? Brunette?'

'Brown hair, I think. It was starting to get dark.'

'So how can you be so sure the boy being attacked was Godfrey?'

'He was turned towards me. I saw his face.' The memory shot through Douglas's face and he staggered back to fall into an upright wooden chair. I pulled out another and sat facing him, four or five feet away.

'Tell me about it,' I pressed.

'It was covered in blood,' he said, shaking his head and left hand like a man might shoo an annoying waiter away. 'I couldn't bear it. I just ran.'

'Why didn't you go for help?' I asked, careful not to sound as condemnatory as I felt.

'I did,' Douglas insisted.

'You just told me you didn't,' I objected.

'Well, I didn't mean to, but I did,' he mumbled.

'Who did you go to?' I demanded.

I had looked through our records and there was no mention of anything like that. There had never been the slightest hint that Godfrey's death was anything other than a riding accident.

Douglas fixed his eyes on me and there was something accusatory in that stare.

'Police,' he said, and though I had heard that word spiced with hatred and fear many times, I had never heard it laced with so much bitterness. 'I ran and told the police.'

54

SECRETS AND BITTERNESS

If this had been a staring contest, I would have lost. I blinked.

'You went to the police?' I asked disbelievingly. 'Which station?'

'No station,' he said. 'I found a policeman.'

Douglas gripped the arms of his chair, rather like I imagined a condemned man would in the gas chamber.

'Who?' I challenged.

'I don't know his name,' Douglas said.

'This is all sounding too convenient,' I told him. 'You see a murder but you can't see the murderer. You see a girl try to help but you can't see what she looked like. You find a handy policeman but you can't remember who it was.

'He was a sergeant,' Douglas said, which narrowed it down considerably. Sackwater Central and Coastal probably had a fair number of constables in 1914, but they were unlikely to have had more than two sergeants in each station. I could look that up easily enough. In the meantime, I couldn't face another protest about how poorly he could see.

'Just tell me what happened,' I snapped.

'I ran down the hill and onto Priory Lane.' Douglas fiddled with his collar. 'At first I just wanted to get away. I kept thinking he must have seen me or heard me and imagining him chasing me. I thought I heard him panting down my neck, until I realised it was my own breath. There was a light on in Brush Cottage so

I rushed up the path and hammered on the door, but there was no reply.'

'Miss Benson lived there,' I recollected. 'She was deaf as a post.'

'That's probably why she didn't hear me,' Douglas speculated in all seriousness.

'Continue,' I sighed.

'I ran back down the path,' Douglas complied. 'There was a man coming up the road. I couldn't see him clearly. I just stood there, paralysed with fear. I thought it was the murderer. It didn't even occur to me that he was coming from the wrong direction. *You there*, he shouted at me. *You there, halt*.'

'But you just told me you couldn't move,' I pointed out.

'I had started to run away.'

'It would be a great help,' I told him wearily, 'if you could tell me the sequence of events in sequence.'

'I'm trying.'

Try harder.

'So what happened then?'

'Well, I halted, of course,' he told me in the same tone a parent might use with an especially irritating child.

'There is no *of course* about it,' I told him in the same tone a parent might use with an especially irritating child. 'If a suspected murderer had been coming for me, I wouldn't have felt obliged to obey.'

'It was the way he shouted it,' Douglas tried to explain, and I was just about to pour scorn on that remark when he succeeded in explaining. 'I think he actually said *You there, halt, Police*, and as he got nearer I saw he was wearing a uniform with a peaked cap.

'*What you up to?* he asked. *Bit of house breaking?* I denied it, of course, and told him what I had seen. *Where was this?* he asked, and so I told him – *Packard's Field, up near the Warrener's Cottage*.'

'Which is more than you have told me so far,' I sniped.

'The sergeant looked at me oddly and got me to repeat everything...'

He must have been a glutton for punishment, I ruminated.

'And at the end of it all he said *Know what goes on in those woods, boy?* I told him I didn't, and he said, *If you know what's good for you, you won't try to find out*. I wouldn't, I promised him. *Sounds like your friend was being nosy*, the sergeant said. *There's things go on up there not even the King knows about – new secret weapons – special bombs and gases and X-rays.*'

I hadn't realised anyone in the East Suffolk Force had such a vivid imagination. None of my men did.

'*Have you ever heard of the Official Secrets Act, boy?* he asked me, and I told him I had, though I hadn't really. *Whatever you think you've seen tonight, you haven't*. I started to protest, but he slapped my face. *You haven't seen anything*, he said. *Know what'll happen to you if you tell a soul about this? The same as happened to your friend. Where do you live*? Mount Chase Mansions, I told him, and he slapped my face – really hard. It made my ears jangle. *Know what that was? That was the last lie you tell me*. I told him my real address. *Well, when you get home, boy*, he said, *you don't tell your mother, your father, your brother, your sister, your uncle...*'

'I get the picture,' I interrupted before he recited the whole family tree.

'*Not even your best friend*, he said. *Open your mouth*. I did as I was told, and he grabbed me by the throat. *See this?* He held something up, but it was too close for me to see.'

You have an unrivalled skill in not seeing, I thought, but only snapped, 'Go on.'

'*It's a secret microphone*, he said. *Know what you're going to do?* I said I didn't. *Swallow it*, he said, and stuck it in my mouth. *Swallow it and don't chew it or I'll ram it down your throat with my truncheon.* So I swallowed it,' Douglas told me. '*Now we'll be able to hear every word you say or anyone says to you*, he said.'

'And you believed him?'

'Of course I did.'

'Let me put it this way,' I tried again. 'How many wires did it have dangling out of your mouth?'

'None, but he said—'

'Did he say it had a radio transmitter?'

'Yes,' Douglas agreed readily. 'Have you come across ones like that?'

'How big was this microphone?' I asked.

'I don't know,' Douglas said helpfully. 'About the size of a sweet, I suppose. In fact, it tasted a bit minty.'

'Do you think it might have been a mint?' I suggested despairingly.

'No.' Douglas stamped on the idea.

'Just think,' I urged, 'how big a microphone is.'

'The RAF have throat ones now.'

'Now,' I agreed, 'but even they need to be plugged into a radio with a battery and then just think how big those things would have been in 1914. You would have had less trouble swallowing a tea chest.'

'Yes, but...' Douglas objected. 'Oh, Lord.'

There were thick white flecks of saliva appearing around his mouth and I found it difficult to take my eyes off them.

'I know you were young and frightened, but did you never think afterwards?' I asked, a bit guiltily, because I had accepted his nonsense about his parents without question until I had met Mrs Hornby.

Wipe your mouth, I willed him, but it is difficult enough

getting men to follow my spoken commands, which doesn't give my unspoken ones much of a chance.

'I did wonder if it might have… passed through,' he admitted.

'Describe the sergeant,' I instructed him.

And don't you dare say you couldn't see him properly.

'I couldn't see him properly,' Douglas dared say, but saved himself from a tongue lashing by quickly adding, 'but…'

'Yes?'

This was like digging out winkles with a blunt pin and I could only hope the effort was more worth it.

'He didn't really look like a policeman,' Douglas began, and paused again, but I left him to it. I was not going to drag every syllable out of him. 'He was short and not very well built and he had a bony face. He was quite weedy.'

'Fynn,' I whispered involuntarily. It was supposed to be him who gave out information.

55

THE DOG AND PEACOCK

Douglas brought out my handkerchief. *Oh thank goodness*, I thought. The saliva was gathering and thickening around his lips, but he only wiped his hands on it.

'Yes, the policeman was thin,' he agreed. 'Even his chest was caved in.'

'I am talking about Sergeant Fynn,' I explained, not at all sure why I should have to. 'You must have seen him patrolling the town before and since then. When we were children, we could hardly get away from him.'

Wipe your mouth, I willed.

'Ah, but that's where you are wrong.' Douglas wagged a finger and I really don't like people doing that to me. I am not – whatever I have been called – a disobedient dog, and I won't be spoken to like one. 'This man looked exactly like Sergeant Fynn and spoke exactly like him, but he couldn't have been because he told me I had never seen him before.'

Douglas mopped the streaks of saliva from his mouth. *Oh thank goodness*, I thought, with good reason this time. I was glad to see the last of them, but he could definitely keep my handkerchief now. He mopped the nape of his neck. Who on earth does that? His forehead looked like he had been out in the rain, but he didn't even give it a dab and I couldn't be bothered to try willing him again.

Douglas's complexion was turning into that sort of grey you see in people who have already died from heart attacks.

'I don't want to talk about it any more,' he bleated.

I considered telling him it wasn't a question of what topics of conversation he enjoyed. Sooner or later he would have to talk about his experiences that night, whether he wanted to or not, but I would leave it for now and give him time, I hoped, to get his memories a bit more organised.

'You said you wanted to reassure Mr and Mrs Utter,' I reminded him. 'Did you have any reason to believe that what you wrote was true?'

'Of course I did,' Douglas insisted, and I corrected my earlier impression – extracting winkles was a much easier job.

'And what was that reason?' I groaned.

'Because I have seen her,' he said.

Coming from the man who kept protesting he couldn't see anything, this should have been a refreshing change, but I had more reliable witnesses when a two-headed hound, spotted prowling Peacock Lane, turned out to be a couple of whippets being taken for a walk.

'Where?' I asked, and Douglas coloured.

'I'm afraid I can't tell you that.'

'Can't as in you don't remember or can't as in won't?' I asked.

'The latter, I fear,' he confessed.

I flicked through my choices. I could bully Douglas and demand the information. I could even threaten to arrest him for withholding evidence, but I decided to try a softer approach first.

'Are you protecting somebody?' I asked. 'A married woman, for instance?'

'I am protecting myself,' Douglas confessed.

'From a jealous husband?' I guessed, but Douglas shook his head.

'From being exposed.'

'Were you engaged in a criminal act?' I probed. 'If so – and you have genuine information – I will do everything I can to make things easier for you.'

'I took to the drink after I left school,' Douglas told me. 'Just as soon as they would serve me in The Compasses. I didn't really like it – it made me sick at first – but I liked the way it had of deadening memories.'

It had certainly done that, I reflected, and refrained from enquiring if he had ever vomited up the marvellous microphone.

'But it deadened my morals, too,' he told me, his face so tragic as to be almost comical. 'I have had terrible thoughts and done terrible things, Betty.'

I did not bother, now that Douglas was in a confiding mood, to insist he used my rank.

'Have you broken the law?' I tried again, and Douglas furrowed his brow.

'I don't think so,' he decided. 'I used a torch once when I got lost in a maze of alleys.'

I suppressed a smile.

'I shall not be pressing charges for that,' I told him, 'but an ARP warden might be less understanding.'

'I am too ashamed,' Douglas said.

'Is it something to do with sex?' I suggested. I liked to think I had a pretty broad mind on that topic. Cruelty could still shock me, and abuse of the innocent always did, but after a couple of decades fighting crime, few things surprised me.

'I have disgusting thoughts,' Douglas began again. 'And not just thoughts. I have been with women,' Douglas burst out, and I was about to respond with a sarcastic *congratulations* when I realised he was confessing rather than boasting.

'Many men have,' I assured him.

'Wicked women,' he whispered.

'Prostitutes?' I asked. I couldn't be bothered with all that *ladies of the night* rubbish.

'I used their bodies to gratify my filthy lusts,' he burst out.

A police*man* would probably have told Douglas that was what whores were there for, but I had spoken to enough of those girls and women to know that most of them were forced into their trade by circumstances or criminals and that many of them were little better than slaves.

'You don't have to tell me this,' I said gently, not at all sure why he was.

'If you want the truth, I do,' Douglas insisted, hugging himself protectively.

'Go on.'

'Because it was in one of those places that I met Etterly,' Douglas told me, his head sagging with his shame.

56

COURAGE AND THE CARDIFF CLAN

I should have seen that coming but I didn't, and for some reason I was more taken aback than when we discovered that skeleton.

'Are you telling me Etterly is a prostitute?' I clarified.

'No.' Douglas uncurled a little. 'I am telling you she's a madam.'

'She runs a brothel?' I asked stupidly, because in all my speculations of what could have happened to my friend, this was not one of the scenarios I had come up with.

Douglas nodded miserably.

'And you are sure it was her?'

'Positive,' said the man who never seemed sure about anything. 'She calls herself Clarice Terry, but I would know her anywhere.'

The name rang true – a combination of Clarice Mayne, whose picture was still in Etterly's bedroom, and Ellen Terry, the actress we had on cigarette cards. People usually combine the names of others when they have to make something up on the spot.

'Did you speak to her?' I asked.

'Only to tell her what kind of girl I liked – tall and blonde, with a good figure – like yours used to be.'

Some women might have been insulted by that, but I ignored it.

'Did she remember you?' I asked, and he grunted.

'I have changed quite a bit since that rounders game,' he told me, as if I might not have noticed. 'Etterly didn't recognise me but I recognised her the moment I set eyes on her.'

'What makes you so sure?' I pressed. 'Everybody changes in twenty-six years. We were little more than children then.'

'I knew who you were straight away,' he pointed out reasonably. 'She was older, of course, but she still looks much the same. I didn't quite believe it until we spoke. She still has the same voice, though she speaks posher now.'

'And you didn't tell her who you were?'

'What could I say?' Douglas reasoned. 'Hello, I'm the innocent boy you knew and now I wish to—'

'I take your point,' I broke in. 'Where is this place?'

Douglas hesitated.

'You are going to tell me,' I informed him flatly, and he fiddled with the top button of his waistcoat.

'Huntley Street,' he muttered at last. 'The Pink House.'

'Not Green?' I double-checked.

The Green House had an undeservedly racy reputation, but was really just a club where ladies could go to socialise without male interference. March Middleton had joined it when she first went to London back in 1882.

'Pink,' he insisted. 'The doors, window frames and all the decor are—'

'Huntley Street,' I broke in. 'How convenient.'

Douglas caught my disapproval.

'Men have urges,' he excused himself.

'Women have them too,' I informed Douglas, and his mouth curdled.

'Don't be disgusting,' he scolded, suddenly a paragon of propriety.

'A sentiment you might do well to remember,' I snapped.

'I pay them,' he asserted.

'But not enough,' I told him firmly. 'How many times have you been there?'

'About a dozen,' he said. 'I wrote that letter after the first time but I didn't post it for a while. Wish I hadn't now.'

'And you have never said anything to make her suspect you know her?'

'Of course not,' he declared. 'Because then she could make trouble for me. It's not unknown for these places to blackmail people, you know.'

'Yes, I do,' I told him. Barri Driscoll, head of the so-called Cardiff Clan, had a good many policemen dancing to his tune by enticing them into his establishments and taking secret photographs. I like to think that my arrest of the ringleaders of the Paper Chain Gang at least weakened his control a little. 'Are there any bodyguards there?'

'Two, at least,' he told me. 'One on the door and one upstairs.'

'Then I can hardly stroll in wearing my uniform,' I mused.

'You can't go in there at all,' Douglas told me in horror. 'They would kill me if they found out I had told you.'

'Your concern for my safety is touching,' I told him.

'It's your job to tackle criminals,' he retorted.

'And you have made it yours to give them money,' I replied tartly, but didn't give him time to respond. 'There are two options. I can organise a raid with the Marylebone Police Station and risk bringing the wrath of the underworld upon your head, or you can entice this woman out.'

I could not bring myself to say *Etterly* because I was still not convinced that Douglas was not mistaken, though I thought it unlikely he was lying. What would he have to gain by such an act?

'I wish I had never written that letter,' he moaned, and I wished he was not quite so addicted to repeating himself.

I glanced at my watch with its specially lengthened strap fastened around my mechanical wrist. 'I will give you thirty seconds.'

Douglas jumped to his feet.

'Think you can frighten me?'

'Yes,' I confirmed, and it was obvious that I had. His face glistened with as much sweat as it might after playing a vigorous game of tennis in the full sun.

'Well, you can just think again.' Douglas darted around me with an agility I hadn't thought him capable of.

'What the hell?' I demanded, jumping back to place the flat of my hand on the door.

I had no intention of chasing and rugby-tackling him on a Tottenham Court Road bustling with shoppers.

Douglas ducked under my arm.

'Don't make me do it,' I warned.

'What?' he scoffed, and reached for the handle.

'This.'

My left fist connected with his jaw. Apart from the fact that my hand was encased in regulation black leather, this was almost literally a case of the iron fist in the velvet glove. I hadn't meant to hit him quite that hard and the impact sent a shock of pain up to my shoulder, jolting Douglas's head back. He slumped, stunned, onto the floor.

'Bloody hell.' Douglas felt his jaw dazedly. 'What was that for?'

'That cannot be a serious question,' I replied, but, looking into his aggrieved eyes, I saw that it was.

Douglas rubbed his head groggily.

'What the hell did you think you were up to?' I challenged.

'I just wanted to get away,' Douglas told me.

My arm was throbbing, but I had no intention of letting him see that – he might have been tempted to make another escape bid if he knew what pain I was in – but I could not help it making my eyes water.

Douglas peered at me.

'Are you crying?' he asked.

'No,' I assured him. 'I have hay fever.'

‘Oh, how horrid for you,’ Douglas sympathised, and for a second he was the young lad watching us play rounders all those years ago. ‘Have you tried liquorice? Mr Waters swears by it.’

But I had lost interest in that topic.

‘We are going to Huntley Street now,’ I told him. ‘And if you attempt to run away again or warn them in the brothel, I will see you in the dock for treason.’

‘Treason?’ Douglas scoffed. ‘Visiting a brothel?’

‘Conspiracy to assist the enemy,’ I bluffed, ‘by attacking an agent of the Crown.’

‘What – who?’ Douglas protested.

‘Me,’ I told him.

This was guff, of course, but I was dealing with a man who continued to believe into adulthood that he had swallowed a transmitter and that Sergeant Fynn wasn’t Sergeant Fynn purely because he said he wasn’t.

Douglas looked doubtful, then thoughtful, then teetered on the verge of panic.

‘Oh my Lord,’ he gasped. ‘You can be hanged for treason in war, can’t you?’

I turned the door handle.

‘Just take me there, Douglas,’ I said, ‘and don’t try anything clever.’

Not much danger of that, I cogitated as I stepped onto the pavement.

57

THE KNOCK AND THE FERRET

Our destination was only a few minutes' walk from Store Street and so, as I had sarcastically observed, very convenient for Douglas's place of work. It was also far enough away for Douglas not to be recognised. In a city where people hardly know what their neighbours look like, a distance of a couple of streets is enough to grant anyone but the most famous almost complete anonymity.

'She's probably out,' Douglas suggested nervously. 'I bet she *is* out. You should come back later – next week, perhaps. I think she said she was going on holiday – visiting an aunt on the south coast – yes, I'm sure she said that now.'

'Stop babbling,' I commanded as we crossed Chenies Street.

Huntley Street ran parallel to Gower Street, but was much shorter and narrower and the properties were less imposing.

We stopped outside a terraced house, shuttered against prying eyes, the woodwork all painted a lurid shade of pink and, for the genuinely dim, there was a sign on the wall: *The Pink House*.

'This is it,' Douglas told me.

'Why do you think I stopped?' I asked grumpily.

'I was only trying to help the police with their enquiries,' he sulked.

'How do you get in normally?' I asked.

'I knock – three times, pause, two times, pause and three again.'

'Then do it,' I said. 'And if that is some kind of warning code, you had better enjoy your last moments of freedom while you can.'

Douglas mopped his brow with his sleeve.

'If you are not back here with this woman in three minutes, I will have this place swarming with police officers,' I threatened, not at all sure how I could organise that in under twenty-four hours, if at all.

'But how?' he asked helplessly.

'Oh, I don't know,' I snapped. 'Just tell her that her hair's on fire.'

'I'll do my best,' Douglas promised.

'Just bring her to me,' I said, holding my watch up ostentatiously, my jacket and shirtsleeves slipping upwards.

'Oh my Lord,' Douglas exclaimed. 'What happened to your arm?'

'It's having an operation and I don't have time to go with it,' I explained, irritably and ludicrously. 'Three minutes starting… *now.*'

'But…' Douglas began.

'Five seconds gone.'

Douglas scurried up the two steps and rapped on the knocker. Three, pause, two, pause, three – just as he had described.

I hurried to stand a little back up the road, out of line of sight. A panel hinged open.

'Gingernut,' Douglas said.

He hadn't told me that one. The door opened.

'Rather early for you,' a man's voice commented – it was light and well-spoken, the sort of voice that might welcome you to a cocktail party.

'Couldn't wait any longer,' Douglas said, and I heard the man laugh before the door shut.

That was thirty seconds gone, but I knew I could not possibly hold him to such a tight schedule. I drew back a little further. From an open window across the street a light orchestra was playing

'By the Sleepy Lagoon'. It was a pleasant enough tune, but about halfway through it clicked and jumped back, to replay a few bars until it hit the same spot, clicked again and re-repeated itself.

'Turn that bloody thing off,' a man shouted.

'I told you you'd scratched it, you great steamin' cowpat,' a woman yelled.

'Shut your cakehole, you scrawny cat-faced vixen.'

The music went off and she was just comparing him to a ferret-featured pole-skunk – whatever that might have been – when the pink door opened and Douglas came staggering down the steps looking injured but, as far as I could judge at first sight, uninjured.

'She told me to leave,' he gasped in disbelief. 'And they had a new girl starting today, untouched and very nervous.'

'I haven't got time to tell you how much that disgusts me,' I said, 'but you do have time to tell me exactly what happened.'

'I rushed up to Etterly and told her that she must get out at once because her hair was on fire, just like you told me to, and she told me to get out and her gorilla pushed me out of the door.'

'You utter twit,' I said.

'Is that a joke about her surname?' Douglas asked.

'No, it is not,' I told him. 'You are the joke and not in the least bit amusing.'

'What was I supposed to do?' he whinged.

'Oh, for goodness' sake... hold that.'

I thrust my helmet into his arms, marched up to the door and did the secret knock. Almost immediately the panel opened and a well-groomed young man appeared, black hair immaculately razored and black moustache immaculately trimmed, the image of a perfect gentleman except for the scar going from the left corner of his mouth to his ear.

'Who gave you the code?' he demanded.

'Douglas Carpenter,' I replied, and heard a whimpered *No* behind me. 'Your last visitor.' The whimper turned into an incoherent yelp.

'I'll deal with him later,' the young man promised pleasantly. He scrutinised my face, which was all he could see of me. 'If you want a job, you're too old. If you want a girl, you can have one for free if you let the other customers watch.'

'Say yes,' Douglas urged quietly.

'I wish to speak to your madam,' I told him, never pleased to be told I was past it but not overly disappointed that I wasn't eligible to work there.

'What about?'

'A great many things,' I said.

'You will have to be more specific,' he said smoothly, and my right hand shot out, fingers gripping his moustache.

'Yowshitow,' he said, and foolishly tried to pull away. 'Kinghell,' he shrieked.

'Is that specific enough,' I asked, 'for you to let me in?'

'Can't reach the lock,' he said, eyes streaming as I gave the clump of hairs a twist. 'Cheezuzcries. You'll have to let go.'

'Oh dear,' I said. 'We seem to have reached an impasse, the difference being that the experience is a great deal more painful for you than it is for me.'

'I'll frinkillyou,' he writhed.

'If I interpret your mangled sounds correctly, you give me little incentive to release you,' I told him, hoping I sounded at least a little like Aunty M.

'What's going on, Bill?' a woman called.

Bill? That sounded much too common and chummy a name for the would-be suave thug who I had in my grasp, and I wondered fleetingly if he had done a swap with Marmaduke. More importantly, though, I knew that voice. It was a little deeper and slightly hoarser than when I had last heard it, but it was unmistakeably hers.

'Clarice,' I called, because I was not about to reveal her identity. 'It's me.' Then, realising how useless that piece of information was, added, 'Betty, Betsy Church.'

We all do it – repeat what we have just been told.

'Betsy? Is that really you?'

'It's me,' I confirmed.

'Oh, for pig's sake, stop shitting about, you muttonhead,' she commanded. 'Just open the door.'

Bill's left shoulder dropped and I heard a bolt sliding.

'Step slowly away,' I commanded and, not loosening my grip, pushed open the door as he drew back.

I stepped over the threshold and let him go. There was saliva on my fingers and I regretted letting Douglas have my handkerchief now.

A tall, slender, striking woman in a long red dress with gold threads in a leafy pattern stood facing me about ten feet away. Her face was paler than I remembered, but perhaps the effect was heightened by her strong red lipstick and heavily mascaraed eyes and her dark hair, cut shorter and clipped back, blacker than I recalled. She was older, of course, but I had not the slightest doubt that Douglas had been right. After twenty-six years of anxiety, doubts, nightmares and imaginings, and within a matter of days of being certain I had unearthed her remains, my friend stood before me. At last I had found Etterly Utter.

58
VELVET AND THE SCENTED PALACE

I swallowed.

'Hello, Clarice,' I said, only to find my childhood friend looking at me aghast.

'Oh shit,' she breathed. 'You're a shitting copper.'

Her parents, I thought idly, would have sent Etterly to her room with no supper for such foul language.

Bill had been inspecting his upper lip in a full-length mirror, but he spun round, eyes streaming.

'What the…?' he managed.

'Shut the door, Bill,' Etterly ordered, and he moved slowly towards it. 'Today,' she told him sarcastically.

It was a long rectangular hall – all pink, of course – hung with candlelit chandeliers, much needed since all the windows were heavily curtained. Three single doors came off either side and double at the far end. There was a throne-like chair, presumably the madam's, and half a dozen unoccupied velvet chaises longues around the sides.

I stepped further inside to let him get around me and heard two bolts slide across. The air was sickly with a flowery scent.

'Stand in front of me,' I said, but nothing happened.

'Do it,' Etterly told him, and the doorman edged around in a wide arc, watching me malevolently the whole time, to stand behind her left shoulder.

'Who else is with you?' she asked sharply.

'Just the customer who came in before me,' I replied.

'Ex-customer,' she corrected. 'Now get the shit out of here.'

Etterly's language may have coarsened since I knew her, but she didn't seem to have increased her vocabulary much.

'I haven't come to cause trouble,' I assured her.

'You're a shitting copper,' she hissed. 'How good do you think that is for business?'

'I—'

Bill pumped up his chest. 'Madam won't tell you again.'

'Want another sore lip?' I challenged unwisely.

He could have done me a great deal more harm than I could him and, if Etterly had decided to give him a hand, I would come out very much the worse.

'That was your last warning.' Etterly's tone had a steeliness that I had never known in her. 'Unlock the door, Bill.'

Bill edged around me, clearly taking my warning more seriously than I had, and pulled back the bolts.

'Now, get the shit out of here,' Etterly snarled. 'And you tell that lump of lard out there if I see him hanging around Cartwright Gardens again, he'll be fish food.'

I looked in Etterly's face. It had been kind and animated with a love of life once. It was sour and cruel now.

'Tell him yourself,' I said.

'And don't think of coming back with reinforcements,' she warned. 'There's not a copper in London wants to get on the wrong side of my boss.' She jerked her head towards Bill and stumbled half a step sideways. 'Open the door and see the bitch out,' she commanded.

'Oh, Clarice,' I sighed sadly, 'I could never be a fraction of the bitch you have become.'

'Shit off.' She waved her hand, her thumb briefly sliding down her palm to give me a glimpse of four fingers.

I tossed my head.

'It took me a long time to find you,' I said, 'and I wish to hell I hadn't bothered.'

'Get out,' Bill said.

'She gives the orders here,' I told him. 'You're just a useless flunkey with a swollen lip.'

And, quite pleased with that parting shot, I brushed past him out into the sunny London air. It stank of petrol and horse dung, but somehow it seemed cleaner than the scented palace of pleasure I had just exited.

59

VICTORIA SPONGE AND THE SEEKER

Douglas Carpenter was still outside, as instructed, but he had sidled along the pavement ten yards away to the junction with Chenies Street and was twitching nervously when I approached.

'Ever go to Cartwright Gardens?' I asked, and he would have looked at me in much the same way if I had asked how often he visited Outer Mongolia.

'What on earth would I want to go there for?' he asked, which was as good a denial as I had hoped to get.

'You can go back to work now,' I told him.

'That's it?'

'What else were you expecting?' I asked.

'I don't know.' He wiped his hands on my handkerchief. 'Did they say anything about me being banned?'

'Oh, yes,' I assured him airily, 'but I sorted it all out for you. You won't have to worry about going there again.'

'But—'

'Because you can't,' I told him, 'and if the madam sees you again, she intends to have you thrown in the Thames.' Douglas was pale already, but he drained a sort of fresh putty colour. 'But you needn't fret,' I continued. 'In fact, you won't be able to. You'll be dead.'

Douglas let out a most satisfactory squeak.

'What can I do?' he asked desperately.

'I'll tell you what you can't do,' I promised. 'You can't run away. They will find you and then, if you are lucky, we will find what's left of you. Go back to work and wait there until I return.'

'How long will that be?' he asked. 'Only, going there has made me a bit… restless.'

'Let me explain what *banned* means,' I said patiently. 'It means *banned*, and while we are running through a few definitions, *wait* means *wait*.'

Douglas put a hand to his throat.

'Perhaps I should try to talk to Etterly,' he suggested. 'Remind her of the old days when we were all chums.'

'Goodbye,' I said firmly, and shooed him away.

Douglas made a pathetic figure as he shambled off. His shoulders were hunched and he shuffled his feet and I might have felt some pity for him if I hadn't known that the main reason for his dejection was that he might not be able to use a girl for his own gratification and I had more important things to worry about, the most urgent being where I could freshen up and get a half-decent beverage.

The Great Russell Hotel supplied me with an excellent pot of coffee and a not-too-bad slice of Victoria sponge, and after consuming them with three cigarettes, I took an easy walk to Cartwright Gardens. The houses there were arranged in a D shape around a private garden. At one time Gaslight Lane had branched off the crescent, but it had been demolished before the Great War and you would not know from the regular arc of houses that it had ever existed. Gaslight Lane was notorious for the Garstang Massacres in 1872 and ten years later Sidney Grice and March Middleton had investigated another gruesome murder there.

The railings that once enclosed the garden had been sawn off, as had many throughout the country to use in shipbuilding, though I sometimes wondered how useful they really were or whether Mr Churchill just wanted to make it clear that this war was going to affect us all.

The lawns had been dug up and planted with carrots and a scarecrow stood wonkily on guard with four sparrows perched on its arms, beside a small memorial stone that Mr G had had erected many years ago. I strolled over to take a closer look. CHARITY 'CHERRY' MORTLOCK. 1859–1917, A SEEKER OF TRUTH, I read. It was not like him to be sentimental or to spend money when he didn't have to. *I think she reminded him that he was almost human*, Aunty M told me once. *I only wish that he had remembered it*.

There were still benches set inside the low wall with its iron stumps, but I paced the paved perimeter path restlessly. I had been ten minutes early, but I waited half an hour. Somebody was putting up their blackout screens on the first floor of number ten. There were a good few hours of daylight left but people who were old or infirm often had to get somebody else to do the job for them and this was not always at a convenient time. Mr Hall in Hambleton Road, Sackwater, was bedridden and left his windows permanently sealed.

A young couple strolled to number four, pausing for a kiss on the doorstep, and I wondered if they knew what Aunty M had told me – that Rachel Samuels, an elderly widow, had been battered to death on the ground floor of that house in the 1870s.

It was only a twig snapping, but I was so engrossed in my thoughts that I nearly jumped out of my skin.

60

HANRATTY AND THE CHUFFY DUNT

I spun around.

'Hello, Betsy.'

'Etterly.' I pulled myself together. 'I was in another world.'

Etterly Utter pulled a wry face. 'Wish *I* was.'

'How did you get into this one?' I asked, but she gave no sign of having heard me.

'I knew you'd understand,' she told me. 'Bill mightn't even have got it if I said, *Meet me in Cartwright Gardens at four o'clock*.'

'How's his lip?'

Etterly rolled her eyes. 'Not so wounded as his pride.'

'Shall we sit down?' I suggested, but Etterly shook her head.

'Safer to keep moving. Then we can see anyone approach.'

'Are you in danger?'

'Consorting with a copper?' she piffed. 'What do you think?'

'So it's not your… establishment?' I enquired, and she snorted.

'Mr H owns the Pink House and everyone in it, including me.'

'Hanratty?' I asked quietly, and even though there was nobody in sight, she only gave the slightest hint of a nod in response.

I had come across Arushad Hanratty when I was a sergeant. Grandson of Hagop Hanratty, one of the most notorious of criminal overlords of the late Victorian era, Arushad had lost the family's iron grip on Limehouse to the Chinese gangs but had tightened it in Bloomsbury, and I had heard it said he also collected 'rent' from much of Regent Street. He was one of the few people I found genuinely frightening and it was probably his ability to inspire such fear that made him so successful.

'How did you find me?' she asked.

'Your last customer,' I told her. 'He came from Sackwater, too.'

Etterly wrinkled her brow, just as she used to when she worked in her father's shop.

'Sackwater.' She weighed the word carefully. 'That seems a very very long time ago.'

'You've lost the accent,' I commented.

'That's not all I lost.' She sighed. 'What's his name?'

'Douglas Carpenter.'

'Don't remember that.'

'You called him Doggy,' I told her, 'because he was always following people around.'

'Doggy?' she repeated incredulously. 'That useless lump? I'd never have recognised him in a month of Sundays.'

'You haven't changed much,' I said, and her face set.

'On the outside, I like to think,' she agreed, 'but there's a very different person in this head now, Betsy.' She grimaced. 'And you an inspector? You always said you wanted to be policeman.'

'And you an actress,' I recalled.

'So we both got our wishes,' she meditated. 'I'm on stage all the time there.'

'What happened, Etterly?' I asked, and she exhaled through her mouth.

'Nothing good, Betsy,' she whispered. 'Once, you would have been the first person I confided in. Now you're the last.'

'Because of my job?' I checked, but Etterly didn't respond. 'I won't arrest you for working in a brothel.'

My friend greeted my statement humourlessly. 'I almost wish you would. If nothing else, it would get me out of there, but that's the least of my sins.' Etterly's gaze drifted away. 'I have done bad things, Betsy.'

'To customers?' I asked.

'Before I even came here.'

'Tell me,' I urged, and Etterly stopped in her tracks.

'I've said too much already.'

'Maybe I can help you,' I suggested, but Etterly shook her head violently.

'If our friendship meant anything...' she said.

'Of course it did, and it still does.'

'Go home, Betsy. Say you never found me. Say you heard I died that day.' She grimaced. 'Not so far off the truth as you might think.' Her gaze hardened.

'But what will happen to you?' I asked. 'Can you trust Bill not to betray you?'

Etterly snorted. 'Bill will keep his trap shut. I've caught him sampling our wares a good few times. You expect that, but if Mr H finds out that Bill has been spoiling our unspoilt girls and lowering their market value, Bill will be cat food before he can piss himself.' While Etterly searched through her handbag, I opened my gas mask box, and while I took hold of a short wooden stake, she brought out a lipstick. 'I have to go now, Betsy.'

'I'm sorry, Etterly,' I said, 'but I can't let you do that.'

'What the shit?' she demanded, as I looped the rabbit snare over her wrist.

61

TWISTER MAGHULL AND THE SPARROW

Etterly yanked away but I had a tight grip on the stake as a handle.

'What the shit?' she cursed. 'You nearly sliced my fricking arm off.'

How awful that would be, I thought.

'Stop pulling,' I advised, and she did.

'What the shit?' she demanded again, though to be fair to her, I hadn't answered her the first time. 'It fricking hurts.'

'You can loosen it a bit,' I told her, 'but try any more than that and you'll be picking your hand off the ground.'

I watched carefully as she eased the wire from where it dug in.

'You have a very limited range of curses,' I complained.

'Dint you believe it.' Etterly grinned, and for a second I was walking along the promenade with the girl I had once known.

'I'll take your word for it,' I assured her.

'You can't arrest me,' she stated matter-of-factly.

'Why not?'

Etterly rubbed her wrist.

'Because you'll never get anyone to testify against me,' she said.

'Is that a threat?' I glanced over.

'It's not me who makes threats,' she said. 'Nor will my master. He'll just do it.'

It disturbed me to hear Etterly refer to him as her *master*, but if anyone could demand such a term of respect, Hanratty was that man.

'You think I can be intimidated?' I asked, and Etterly snorted.

'No,' she replied. 'I think you can be killed.'

'I'll risk it,' I said. 'Anyway, I have no intention of arresting you.'

'What then?' Etterly swung round to stand at right angles to me.

'Fancy visiting Douglas Carpenter?' I asked, and she sniffed.

'No I f-pigging don't.'

I was quite touched at the way she modified her language for my benefit. Not many people would bother in the same circumstances.

'That is exactly why I snared you,' I told her. 'If I had suggested it, you'd have run a mile.'

Etterly pressed her left shoulder against my right and leaned on me.

'Think I can't anyway?' she asked with more than a hint of menace, pushing against me now.

I wasn't sure what she was up to, but I stood my ground.

'I have twenty years' experience detaining people against their will,' I told her, 'many of them bigger than you and some of them armed, and I have never lost one yet.'

This was not quite true, but it wasn't entirely my fault 'Twister' Maghull got away. A sparrow landed on my epaulette.

'Always a first time,' she said, quite merrily, and it was only then that I saw a glint and a blur of steel as Etterly plunged a knife into my arm.

The blade ripped through my jacket. I felt it jar and saw it emerge from the other side.

'My uniform,' I cried, and the sparrow flitted away.

'What the—' Etterly stared at the knife, the handle still in her hand, the point sticking out on the other side.

'That's why you did all that turning and pushing,' I realised. 'It was to distract me.'

I rolled up my sleeve and Etterly let go of her weapon and put a hand to her mouth.

'Oh, Betsy,' she cried, suddenly my friend again. 'What have they done to you?'

'Took it off just below the elbow,' I told her.

'But how?'

'Painfully,' I told her. 'If I let you pull the knife out, will you promise not to use it again?'

Etterly huffed in amusement.

'You think people keep their promises in my world?'

'In our private world they do,' I assured her, and raised my false limb.

'Perhaps.' Etterly retrieved the dagger.

'Why didn't you stab me in my right arm?' I asked.

'I was going to,' she assured me with her old Etterly twinkle, as if it was one of those pranks we used to get up to, like tying string from people's door handles to their neighbour's so neither could open their doors. I occasionally scolded children for doing that now, though I found it difficult to be as stern as I was supposed to be. Sharkey would cuff them, which is probably why they played the trick on him occasionally.

'So why didn't you do it first?'

'You might have tightened your grip in pain and used your left hand to fight me off,' she reasoned. 'If I did your left and you tried to defend yourself with your right you'd have had to let go.'

'You've used that knife before,' I surmised.

'Only in self-defence,' Etterly insisted, dropping it back in her handbag.

The sparrow came back, pecking at one of my pips. I brushed it away.

'Have you ever killed anyone?' I asked, and my friend sighed.

'Oh, Betsy,' she said wearily. 'If only you knew.'

'Tell me,' I urged, but she tightened her lips.

'No.' Etterly scanned our surroundings. 'The longer we stand here, the more danger we are in,' she said.

'All right,' I said. 'Let's walk.'

'Just a minute.' Etterly pulled her coat off her right shoulder and draped it over our wrists. 'OK,' she said, and off we set.

62

THE BEAUTIFUL AND THE DAMNED

Tavistock Square was busy. It hadn't been dug up yet and the railings were still there.

Mothers with prams were starting to take over responsibility for their own babies, but judging by the number of white aprons, nannies were by no means extinct. A group of officers lounged, smoking, near the statue of Louisa Aldrich-Blake, one of the first of my sex allowed to be a surgeon in that still very masculine world. BMA House stood on the east side and I doubted that there were many women in there, unless they were taking shorthand or cleaning. Most movingly, I felt, was the Tavistock Clinic, an all-too-rare establishment that specialised in treating shell shock. Thirty-odd years ago, men and even boys were shot for suffering from it. I could only hope we would be more understanding of the illness in this conflict.

Etterly was shifting about under her coat and I readied myself to rein her in if she tried to loosen the loop.

'If I ran off now,' she whispered in my ear, 'you could never catch me in the crowd.'

'And how would Mr H react if I turned up at your place of work with a few colleagues?' I asked. 'Ones from Sackwater, who haven't been bribed or blackmailed and can't be intimidated because they don't even know who he is.'

'Point taken,' Etterly conceded, and to my surprise her fingers closed around my fist and squeezed it affectionately. 'You and me,' she said, 'just like the old days.'

I didn't see any reason to point out that our relationship had changed somewhat since I joined the force and she entered the underworld.

The front door of number forty Store Street was locked. I raised the knocker, let it fall and counted to ten. Nothing. I banged twice and waited again. More of nothing.

'Allow me.' Etterly grasped the knocker and crashed it down repeatedly, hard and fast.

Douglas opened the door a crack with a look of sheer terror.

'What the—' he began on seeing me, but I pushed past without a word into his office, my friend in tow but letting go of my hand.

'Etterly,' Douglas cried excitedly. 'Have you come to let me back into the club?'

'Keep dreaming,' she advised as he bolted the door.

'I used to feel sorry for you,' I told him. 'Now I feel sorry for your victims.'

'Victims?' he echoed incredulously. 'Nobody makes them do it.' He pointed at Etterly. 'Ask her.'

'Don't,' she advised.

'You think they let you do those things because they enjoy it?' I demanded.

Douglas pinched the bag under his right eye. I have seen it many times, the peculiar acts people perform when they feel under pressure – fiddling with ears and noses, rearranging things on their desks or tables.

'Well, some of them probably do,' he speculated, without much conviction.

'Ha,' Etterly said scornfully, and flipped open her cigarette case. Douglas leaped forwards to give her a light, his hand trembling so much in his excitement, and the flame so high, that her hair nearly caught fire after all. 'Stupid man,' she muttered, and he beamed, just as he used to when the other boys were mean to him, and I supposed – now as then – it was his way of not letting people see he was hurt.

Etterly glanced around the room at the blueprints spread over his desk and rolled into racks on the walls.

'Admiring my work?' he asked.

'No,' she said. 'Just thinking *what a mess*.'

'I've been very busy,' he announced proudly. 'All I need now is a few more customers to buy my designs. I have some revolutionary ideas. Have you never wondered, for example, why lifts have to go inside buildings? Why not put them on the outside and save valuable floor space? Or lofts – we waste so much space when—'

'Are you going to take this off now?' Etterly talked over him, holding out her left arm.

'Crikey,' he exclaimed. 'You've arrested her.' He took a closer look. 'Is that a new kind of handcuff or can't you afford—'

'Shut up and go behind your desk,' I broke in, and Douglas bristled but did as he was told.

I released Etterly and she leaned against a green metal filing cabinet. Her father would have told her off, if not for the smoking, then certainly for the slouching, I contemplated. *You'll end up like Mrs Barrow*, he used to warn, if ever his daughter relaxed her spine. Mrs Barrow was an elderly hunchbacked woman who walked through the town almost touching her ankles, but the only time Etterly was likely to resemble her was when we children used to imitate the old woman cruelly behind her back. Etterly always had a good posture. I had known people comment on how gracefully she moved.

'Why don't you scarper?' Douglas asked. 'I could give you a hand.'

'Do you have amnesia?' I asked. 'I told you to be quiet.'

'Amnesia?' He scratched his head. 'I can't remember.'

Etterly and I rolled our eyes. We had heard that joke in Mother Goose – ironically, one of its few memorable gags, but not funny even then.

'Are all your customers like him?' I wondered, more interested in getting her on my side than in her reply.

'Dough-face?' Etterly mocked. 'The girls laugh at him.'

'I'm still here,' he reminded us. 'Anyway, you're just saying that.'

'He likes them to beat him,' she told me, spitefully, I thought, and Douglas hung his head.

'I need to be punished,' he confessed.

'For what you do to them?' I queried.

'That,' he admitted, 'and for deserting him.'

And for the first time the pity I had felt for Douglas when he was a boy stirred in me again.

'Who?' Etterly asked, and he raised his face miserably to her.

'Nobody,' he mumbled.

'Got another fag?' she asked. 'That was my last one.'

'Only roll-ups.' I got out my tin box, wedged it into my left hand and opened the lid.

'Does it hurt?' Etterly took one gingerly, as if she thought a prosthetic arm might be contagious.

'All the time,' I told her, 'but it's better than it used to be. I had an operation and they gave me a lighter limb.'

'I was just wondering why you wore a glove,' Douglas said.

'Took you a long time to notice,' I commented, and flicked the wheel on my Zippo to light both our cigarettes.

'Didn't know coppers could have fake arms,' Etterly said.

'They aren't supposed to,' I agreed, 'but then, when we were girls, they weren't supposed to be women either.'

I looked at this oddly familiar stranger. We had been through so much together, but then we had been through much more apart. She was pretty once. Now she was beautiful, but there was an ugliness in that beauty. It had been painted on her face by the corruption she must have seen and engaged in.

'What happened, Etterly?' I asked, turning my back on Douglas. 'Why did you disappear?'

'I can't tell you that.' Etterly exhaled through her mouth.

'Can't or won't?'

'I thought I could save myself,' she said softly. 'But, my God, Betsy, from the moment I left, I was damned.'

63

THE LONG ARDUOUS JOURNEY OF GONE WITH THE WIND

Etterly coloured like she was going to cry, but drew on her cigarette and composed herself. Women in both our professions have to learn not to show weakness.

'That's not a fancy dress costume you're wearing, Betsy,' she reminded me, 'and it's not a nunnery I'm running.'

She waved a hand, the smoke billowing around her.

'Have you done something you think I might have to arrest you for?' I pressed.

'You could say that.'

'Can you tell me what it was without going into details?' I tried.

Etterly eyed her cigarette.

'Not much tobacco in these,' she commented.

'Wartime,' I said.

'I can get you plenty.'

'On the black market?' I asked, but didn't wait for an answer. 'Whatever trouble you are in, you know you can trust me to do what is right.'

My friend laughed acidly. 'That's exactly what I'm afraid of.'

She tossed the cigarette down and stubbed it out with the toe of her red high-heeled shoe.

'Hey, that's my carpet,' Douglas objected, rising out of his seat to peer over at the damage.

'The Inspector told you to shut up,' Etterly reminded him, 'so do it.'

'Sorry,' he mumbled, and sank back.

'Can you tell me when?' I asked.

Etterly toyed with a big black-stoned ring on her little finger.

'Take a guess,' she challenged.

'Just before you went away,' I suggested.

'The night before,' she agreed.

I mulled that over. It couldn't be anything to do with Godfrey. She was gone well before he died.

'I thought you seemed a bit distracted in the rounders game,' I said, 'but not that badly.'

'Funny how we can hide things when we have to,' she remarked, which was true enough. Nobody really knows what goes on in other people's minds.

Etterly got out her compact to freshen up her make-up.

'You can go now,' I said.

'But you don't have to,' Douglas suggested wistfully.

'I was talking to you,' I told him.

'Excuse me—' he began.

'She already has,' Etterly pointed out.

'Come back in an hour,' I said. 'We should be finished by then.'

'This is *my* premises.' Douglas jumped out of his chair indignantly. 'I worked long and hard for Mr Bullbrook to put my name on that plate.'

'And how long do you think he will keep it there after you've appeared in Marylebone Magistrates' Court?' I asked.

'What for?' he asked nervously.

I jogged his memory. 'I gave you a list before we set off. Do you really want me to add to it?'

'No, of course not,' he assured me. This was just as well,

because I couldn't think of anything other than the treason charge, which would never even get to court.

'And' – I wagged a finger at him in an extremely annoying way – 'if you *ever* mention this to anyone, I shall let Mr Hanratty know that you took a police officer to one of his establishments.'

Douglas pinched the bags under his eyes so hard I thought they might burst.

'Hanratty,' he breathed. 'I've heard bad things of him.'

'They are all under-exaggerated,' Etterly assured him.

'But she made me,' Douglas whinged, the skin blanching in his grip.

'And I'm sure Mr Hanratty will take that into account,' I assured him, cringing as I watched.

'Ouch,' Douglas said, realising that he was hurting himself.

'Goodbye,' Etterly said sweetly. 'Oh, and should you forget that you are banned from the Pink House, Bill will be only too happy to remind you.'

'Ohhhh,' he whinged, like a child being told he couldn't go out to play.

'Just go,' I snapped, and Douglas scurried away.

64

OLD ABINGDON AND THE SPANNER

I shut the door and rebolted it.

'I won't tell you what I did just because he's gone,' Etterly warned, checking the still-red ring on her wrist.

'Tell me something else then,' I suggested. 'The man hanging about under the trees the day you disappeared – was he anything to do with it?'

'You could say that,' she conceded.

'Did you know him?'

'Perhaps.'

'Who was he?'

Etterly put her handbag on a chair, flipped open the box on Douglas's desk, took out a cigarette and lit it.

'Want one?'

'I'd rather have an answer,' I said.

'You'll have to settle for that.' She handed me hers and helped herself to another.

'You introduced me to smoking,' I reminded her.

'Did I?' She fumbled with her lighter.

'In my parents' summer house.'

Etterly inhaled thoughtfully. 'Oh yes, I remember.' She toyed with a pearl earring – a present from an appreciative customer? 'I suppose I was a bad influence on you, really.'

'I suppose you were,' I agreed, though I had never thought of her like that. 'What happened when you left?'

'I ran,' Etterly said simply. 'I didn't have a clue where I

was going or what I was going to do. I only knew I couldn't go home.'

'I'm surprised nobody saw you,' I commented.

'After the first fifty yards or so I had the sense to stop running. I kept my head down and walked. I didn't go far – just to your parents' home.'

'Felicity House?' I double-checked in surprise.

'I saw your father in the driveway.'

'Did he see you?'

Etterly shook her head.

'He was half under the bonnet of his car, banging away at something with a wrench,' she told me. 'I said *Good morning Mr Church* and he muttered something about you being out, so I went into the back garden.'

'You must have gone straight past him,' I realised incredulously.

'He asked me to hand him a spanner,' she recalled with a little laugh.

My father had an old Abingdon at the time and spent longer fiddling with the chain drive and cursing under his breath than he ever did behind the wheel.

'And he never thought about it afterwards,' I commented in despair. 'Stupid man.'

'I hid in your summer house,' Etterly said. 'I didn't know where else to go and I thought you might help me run away or even come with me.'

'We often planned to do it,' I recalled, and Etterly half-smiled.

'I waited until it was dark,' she continued. 'Then I threw gravel at your window, but I couldn't attract your attention.'

'I went to my grandmother's room that night,' I remembered, 'on the other side of the house, but I couldn't sleep.' An image flicked through my mind. 'When I went back, I heard something and looked out. I thought I was imagining it, but I might have seen you. It was just after midnight.'

'The church clock was chiming,' she confirmed.

'Oh, Etterly,' I said, 'and I thought my father was the stupid one.'

I fiddled with my hair at the back. It had felt like it was coming undone but, as I discovered, it was one of the few things at the time that wasn't.

'I didn't know what to do,' Etterly continued. 'I'd had a drink from the outside pump but I was starving and, most of all, I was frightened.'

'So what *did* you do?'

Etterly fiddled with her own hair, but I didn't think she was consciously imitating me.

'I decided to go home,' she said, 'where I should have gone in the first place. My mother would give me some supper and my father would know what to do. He would explain that I wasn't really a bad girl and the judge might take pity and not have me hanged.'

Etterly put her right hand to her throat.

'Did you kill somebody?' I asked.

'I've said too much.' Etterly rattled her nails on the wall.

'They couldn't have executed you anyway, under the age of sixteen,' I informed her. 'The Children Act put a stop to that.'

In 1908, if I recalled correctly from my training.

Etterly puffed out her cheeks.

'I know that now,' she conceded, 'but I didn't then.'

'What did your parents do?'

'Nothing,' she said simply. 'I never got there.'

65

THE STONEY WAY

Etterly blew a chain of smoke rings, one of the many useful things she had taught me.

'I didn't get far,' she said. 'I was just on the corner of Everton Road when a police car pulled up. I thought that was it. I'd been tracked down and was going to be arrested, so when the driver said *Get in*, I did.'

'Did you recognise him?'

'It was dark,' she told me, 'so I couldn't see his face and he had a peaked cap pulled low.'

The streetlights used to go off at ten thirty, I remembered. Now they were never on.

'I panicked,' Etterly said, and took another drag. 'He didn't even ask but I confessed everything.'

'Did he take you to the police station?' I asked.

'I wish he had,' Etterly said. 'I was so scared and confused and tired I didn't even notice he was heading out of town until we were on the Felixstowe Road.' Etterly exhaled. 'I asked him where we were going but he just said *Where would you like to go* and I said *Home please* and he said *Try again* so I said *London*. I hadn't planned anything and it was just the first place that came into my head.'

'We often talked about running away there,' I recalled, and Etterly turned away.

'The copper said, *Well, this is your lucky day*. Then he said, *You've been a naughty girl. I like naughty girls*. We could go all the way, if I liked, he said. I thought he meant to London, but he pulled into some woods a couple of miles past Stovebury. I knew something was wrong, but I didn't really know what, or maybe I didn't want to. He dragged me out of the car. *Ever done it with a man?* he asked, and I knew what that meant. *No*, I said, *never. Good girl*, he said. *Take your shoes and stockings off.* I did and he pushed me back against a tree and pulled my skirt up. He was panting already and I was terrified but then suddenly he pulled away. *I've changed my mind*, he said. *We won't go all the way after all.* I thought he meant he would leave me where I was, but then he made me put my hand down his trousers and after he said, *That's all I ever want them to do but they always make such a fuss.*'

'Oh, for God's sake,' I sighed.

My friend fell silent, but I didn't try to chivvy her along. She would speak, I was sure, when she was ready.

'So, I thought that was it,' she said. 'I had done what he wanted and he would leave me alone. With a bit of luck he would take me home.'

Etterly laughed ironically. I wished I could see her expression but I knew that, whatever she was going to tell me, she didn't want to do it face to face.

'But then,' she continued, 'he said, *I have a business acquaintance who'll pay good money for a lovely unspoiled girl like you.*'

'I ran for it,' Etterly continued, 'but I soon realised why he had made me go barefoot. The ground was rough and covered in sharp stones and thorns and he caught me easily. He dragged me back by my hair and threw me into the car. The door handle was jammed so I couldn't jump out. He made me wear a blindfold out of my stockings and drove on. I didn't have a clue where I was – I'd never been out of East Anglia before – but I knew from all the noise we must be in the city. He stopped the car and dragged me out and into a house.' Etterly's voice dropped. 'That was where I met a man who scared the shit out of me then and ever since.'

Etterly exhaled slowly and grabbed hold of the edge of the desk as if she was drunk.

'Hanratty,' I said.

'Got it in one,' she confirmed, 'though I didn't see him or anything at first.' Her head came up again. 'They didn't give a shit if I heard them or not. *There's your money*, Mr H said. *Have a good trip back to Bristol.* The copper must have said we came from there and Londoners can't tell the difference.'

'Suffolk folk all sound like yokels to them,' I agreed, 'and he wouldn't have wanted them to know where he was from.'

They would have been able to tell from his uniform, I realised, and was just about to say it when my friend turned back to me. '*Lovely Somerset filly*' – she mimicked Hanratty's voice – 'just waiting to be broken in.'

'Oh, Etterly,' I said worthlessly, and she twirled a lock of her black hair round a finger, just as she would do when we were children and she was upset.

'I didn't want anyone to tell my parents what had happened to me. They would never let me over their threshold again.' Etterly let go of her hair. 'So I let him believe it.'

'I know it was dark but would you recognise the policeman if you saw him or heard him talking again?' I asked.

'Oh, yes.' Etterly tossed her head. 'I almost forgot to tell you that bit.'

'What?' I asked, and she coughed lightly.

'I *did* see him,' she declared. 'The blindfold had risen up a bit and when I tipped my head back, I saw him clear as I see you.'

'So would you recognise him again?'

Etterly's eyes widened.

'I recognised him there and then,' she said, almost spitting out her next word. 'Thin.'

It took a second to register with me.

'Fynn?' I checked.

Etterly flicked ash on the floor.

'Who else?' she asked.

In Lady Olga Sayer mysteries, the criminal, when she unmasks him, is always the least suspicious character – the vicar, the vapid debutante or the little old lady. In real life, the criminal is almost always the person you first suspect. The burglar is the man who has just come out of prison for burglary. The man who smashes a window at Stovebury Hall is the under-gardener who the marquess has just sacked.

'Who indeed?' I agreed, because I couldn't think of a policeman more likely to behave in such a vile way than the retired ex-Sergeant Fynn.

'Fynn realised,' Etterly continued. 'He had taken his jacket and cap off in the car. Oh, Betsy, you should have seen his face. *Hell, she's seen me*, he said. *Don't worry*, Mr H said. That was my first glimpse of him too. *She won't be going anywhere*. And Fynn said, *I was hoping you'd say that* and laughed.'

I will have you, you bastard, I vowed.

'I wet myself,' Etterly admitted shamefacedly, and I reached out for her hand, but she didn't take mine.

'He won't get away with it,' I promised, and Etterly raised her eyebrows.

'You won't get me to give evidence,' she assured me, 'so I think he probably will.'

66

IF

I thought about Etterly's words and decided I would worry about them later.

'Was this in the Pink House?' I enquired.

'We were in Cable Street then,' she told me. 'Smaller and much dingier. My first client was a nice little man. He chatted about some book he had just read while he undressed and carefully folded his clothes and told me not to worry, then he knocked me to the floor and took me, all the time reciting poems from the book, something about treating two imposters.'

'If,' I said.

'If what?'

'It's the name of a poem by Kipling. *If you can meet with Triumph and Disaster and treat those two impostors just the same*,' I quoted. 'I had to learn it at school.'

'That's the one,' Etterly declared, and took a long last drag on her cigarette. 'Then afterwards he dressed very carefully, tipped his hat and wished me a good day. *I shan't be using you again*, he told me, *I only like them unsullied*. The madam came in and told me to get cleaned up and brush my hair. *Tell the next one you're a virgin*, she said. *He's one himself so he'll never know*. I had four that night. The last one showed me pictures of his wife and children.'

She closed her eyes briefly.

'How did you get to be a madam?' I asked, and Etterly ground her cigarette out in Douglas's ashtray.

'Slowly,' she said. 'We worked in shifts so our *entertaining* rooms were in use all the time. We slept in the attic, two or even three to a bed. After a year or so I was a seasoned worker and started to help look after the new girls. If they lasted long enough, they did the same, but they still looked up to me so I more or less took charge of the top floor. There was a lot less trouble with me running things because the girls liked me, but they knew I wouldn't stand for any shit. Then I got ill.'

'How ill?' I asked.

'Bad enough,' she told me. 'Normally I'd have been thrown out. They don't house and feed girls who can't work, but Violet, the madam, liked me. She told Mr H that I was worth hanging on to – customers asked for me – and so he kept me.' Etterly swayed sideways. 'While I was off, I got chatting to Vi. I told her how I used to work with my father. Probably laid it on a bit thick, because next thing I knew I was helping with her accounts – Mr H likes to run things like a proper business. Then, one night when she was too sloshed to work, I took over the front – welcoming customers and seeing they got what they wanted. Mr H turned up and he was impressed. I told him about doing the books as well – not to get Vi into trouble, but to convince him not to get rid of me before I was well enough to go back to work.'

'You *wanted* to get back to it?' I asked incredulously, and Etterly pulled a sour face. 'Have you forgotten what he promised Thin?' she challenged. 'I remember it every waking hour. When Mr H lets a girl go, he doesn't give her flowers. He damages her so nobody else will want her – ever. I heard of more than one girl, who he thought might cause trouble, ended up chained and dropped in the sewer. There's a manhole in the cellar.'

'Were there any witnesses?' I asked.

'None that would talk to you,' Etterly assured me, and hung her head. 'I didn't know he was unhappy with Vi already. She was short-changing him, slipping cash under her garter when she thought no one was looking, and she'd been drunk before – abused a couple of important customers, one a senior copper. *Want the job?* he asked, and I knew better than to turn an offer down from Mr H. He was getting rid of her anyway, he told me, but I was sorry to see the last of Vi. She was good to me and I liked her – when she was sober. She was not a happy drunk.'

'Do you know what happened to her?' I asked and Etterly chewed her lip.

'Last I saw she was being dragged down the stairs, begging Mr H and screaming obscenities at me.'

'And so you became the madam.'

'I had no choice,' Etterly insisted, though I was not condemning her. 'Things had been slack, Mr H told me, and he wanted them tightening up. Turnover wasn't half what it should have been. *Double it*, he told me, just like that. *You've got six months*.'

'And did you?'

Etterly ground her cigarette out on the wall.

'More than,' she said, with undisguised pride. 'The first thing I did was give all the girls a night off. I told them they could have one night a week each in future, if I had no complaints, and an extra night a month if they got special praise. I started a comment book and the clients loved filling it in – anonymously, of course. Most of the comments were childish and obscene, but overall they were useful. I got girls to go with each other and men to pay extra to watch. For an even bigger fee, they could join in. I got girls to dress up as French maids or schoolgirls, nuns or nurses, whatever the man's fantasy was. They'd always done a bit of that, but I bought them proper costumes and coached them in their roles – just like the acting I always wanted to do.' Etterly sucked in. 'Within a fortnight we were so busy we had to make more rooms in the attic and sleep the girls in another house. I doubled turnover in four months. We had to move to bigger premises in Huntley Street within the year.'

She paused to get a silver hip flask from her handbag.

'You must be very proud,' I said drily as she took a drink, 'going from shop girl to madam of a thriving brothel.'

'I was,' Etterly said defiantly, 'until one of the girls, who had her customer tied up, cut off his equipment and hanged herself while he bled to death. I was devastated. She was such a lovely, sunny girl. Everybody liked her. But when I got the others together to break the news, one of them said *What did you expect?* And they all agreed with her. I'd been so preoccupied with running things I'd forgotten what it was like to be in one of those rooms, a toy for somebody's animal lusts. I'd forgotten how we always acted happy because we were punished if we didn't, and from then on I felt sick with revulsion at every penny I took from every man who came through that door.'

'How long ago was that?' I asked.

'Nearly three years now.'

Etterly looked drained. I lit us both a cigarette and she brought out her hip flask.

'Can't you leave?'

'Course I can,' she assured me, 'by the sewer. I know far too much for Mr H to put me out to grass.'

Etterly offered me her flask. I took it and sniffed. It wasn't gin or whisky. It was too sickly sweet, but not sherry.

'Laudanum,' Etterly told me. 'Alcohol and opium.'

'Do you take it regularly?' I asked.

'How do you think I sleep at night?' she sneered.

I was wondering about that, I thought, but I stubbed out my cigarette too and said nothing.

67

HEARTS AND ASHES

I handed Etterly her flask back.

'You haven't asked about your parents,' I reminded her, and she jolted like I had prodded her with an electric cable.

'I don't want to know,' she insisted, grabbing her handbag off the chair.

'They are alive and…'

'I do *not* want to know,' Etterly yelled hoarsely.

'Have you any idea what they have been through?' I demanded. 'Their lives have been hell for twenty-six years.'

'Think I've been having a party?' Etterly steadied herself on the desk. 'For Christ's sake, Betsy.' She swept the ashtray off to smash against the wall and shower in fragments between us. 'What do you want from me?'

'It's not for me,' I said, and Etterly looked away.

'They probably think I'm dead by now.'

'We found human bones in Packard's Field,' I told her, 'and we thought they were yours. I went to tell your parents, but they refused to believe it. They've kept your room the same.'

Etterly worked her lips against each other. 'Really?'

'Come home, Etterly.'

She tried to get past me, but I stood firm.

'I'm a whore, Betsy,' she said huskily. 'They would not even look at me if they knew.'

'They needn't know.'

Etterly looked me in the eye and I then realised why she had stumbled in the Pink House, and swayed and had to steady herself every now and again, and the real reason she had leaned against me in Cartwright Gardens. She was losing her sense of balance.

'When you say you got ill...' I asked tentatively.

'I got a dose,' she admitted.

'Syphilis?' I checked.

'The pox,' she confirmed.

'Did you get treatment?'

'For all the good that did.'

I hesitated. 'And has it recurred?'

'Course it has,' Etterly replied bitterly, 'two years later when I'd forgotten all about it. I got the rash and a sore throat and fever. God, I felt rough. Vi told everyone I had the flu. I bet she wished she'd never bothered.'

'And now?' I asked quietly.

'Another rash,' she said, 'All over, with headaches – terrible ones like my brain is on fire – and stabbing pains in my back and my legs are going numb. People go mad with this, Betsy. They turn into drooling idiots.'

'Not all of them,' I told her. 'With some people it goes away again.'

Etterly stepped back, the glass crunching beneath her feet. It was broken glass on the pavement that led me to my friend, I reflected. 'Sooner or later it will get me,' she prophesied. 'And they will wish they had never known me then.'

'They love you,' I protested, but I had a terrible feeling that Etterly was right.

I was just hoping, if they saw her, her parents would change their minds.

'They love the little girl who still played games and went to church,' she assured me and took another step forward, but I stood firm. 'Let me past,' she said wearily.

'We haven't finished.'

'I will get out of here, Betsy,' Etterly vowed, 'even if I have to crawl over your body.'

She still had the knife, I remembered.

'I haven't come here to fight you,' I said quietly, and stepped aside.

'What then?'

'I want to help.'

Etterly laughed mirthlessly. 'Then go back to Sackwater.'

'At least let them know you're alive,' I begged.

'No,' she insisted as she went past me, 'and neither will you or you will break their hearts.' She yanked the door open. 'If you are seen with me by the wrong people, you might or might not get hurt, but I will be tortured and killed.' She went out. 'Don't try to follow me, Betsy, and *never* come back.' Etterly's voice cracked. 'Not if I ever meant anything to you,' she finished huskily, and something like a wave of pain flitted through her before she set off.

I hurried out onto the pavement.

'Etterly,' I called uselessly, and her shoulders slumped, but she didn't hesitate or even glance back. 'Etterly,' I whispered, and watched my old friend turn the corner into Huntley Street. 'Goddammit,' I cursed, and slammed the door to march off towards Gower Street.

Was this what I had waited twenty-six years for – to find my friend a prostitute and that she wanted nothing to do with the parents who had kept their despair at bay with irrational hopes? And just when it turned out that Mr and Mrs Utter were not delusional after all, I was supposed to leave them unknowing for the rest of their lives?

Where was the divine justice in all that?

A woman police constable came towards me.

'Are you part of it?' she said, and I saw that her uniform was all wrong. Her jacket didn't even match her skirt.

'Of what?'

'The striptease,' she explained. 'We're supposed to be there in ten minutes.'

I suppose I could have arrested her for impersonating a police officer, but I only said, 'Sorry. I have another appointment elsewhere.'

'Ooooh,' she said, waggling her head, and stuck out her tongue. 'You have appointments, do you? Well, aren't we high and mighty?'

'Excuse me.' I walked on.

'Your costume is rubbish,' she called after me. 'Stuck-up cow.'

68

KNEES, ELBOWS AND THE UNEXPLODED BOMB

Half an hour later I was at Liverpool Street Station and remembering – apart from a slice of cake which hardly counted – I hadn't eaten since a rushed breakfast. I toyed with the idea of delaying my departure and getting something back at the Regency, but Carmelo had promised me a rabbit stew so I decided to hang on until I got home.

I had to run but just managed to catch the train, flinging myself, I was pleased to find, into a smoker, but having sipped from the cup of good fortune, I appeared to have drained it dry and thrown it away. The compartment was packed, and I found myself squashed between several fat businessmen puffing foul pipes. Just as I was resigning myself to a couple of hours of that, we pulled into a siding for the rest of the night.

'Unexploded bomb on a bridge,' Mr Trime, the station master, explained when I struggled, crumpled, frowsy, tired and depressed onto Sackwater Railway Station in the morning. 'Fancy a cuppa?'

I could almost have committed homicide for a good brew right then, but I just had time, if I hurried, to be ten minutes late for duty.

It had taken me twenty-six years, but – I wondered, as I spotted that damned poster again – had my journey really been necessary?

'She is never tardy,' I heard Dodo saying as I pushed open the door. 'She must be dead. There can be no other possible explanation.'

Dodo had her back to me, I saw as I came in, and Brigsy, glancing over, gave me a wink.

'Fancy a bet?' he said. 'Sixpence says Inspector Church will arrive before you can say *steak-and-kidney pie*.'

'Oh, but I dislike kidneys,' Dodo told him. 'I cannot forget what comes out of them.'

'Wha'?' Brigsy asked, and Dodo, even though she thought they were alone, leaned over the desk to whisper her reply. 'Never!' our sergeant gaped in disgust.

'I fear so,' Dodo confirmed wisely.

'Well, I never, did you, Inspector?' Brigsy marvelled, and Dodo leaped round.

'Oh, but you are not dead,' she exclaimed.

'Only half-dead,' I told her. 'I've been on a train all night. Tea please, Brigsy.'

'I can...' Dodo moved sideways.

'No, you can't,' I said firmly.

Dodo pouted and Brigsy went into the back room.

'You must have gone a long way, Boss,' Dodo speculated.

'Just from London.'

'Oh, but you could have come directly here,' she informed me.

'No! Why didn't I think of that?' I asked wearily.

'I am surprised you did not, Boss,' she told me, and I bit my tongue.

It would not be fair to take it out on her.

'Any soyn of Old Stumpy yet?' Bantony called, coming in, probably from a night in the cells. 'Oh, mornink, madam.' His eyes flicked side to side, seeking an escape route. 'It's a koynd of local cider.'

I knew that was one of their nicknames for me and I had called my inspector worse when I was in London, but I just wasn't in the mood.

'Where is it sold?' I asked. 'You can buy me a pint of it.'

But Bantony was saved from coming up with an answer to that by Brigsy emerging from the back demanding, 'Who used all the tea?'

'I might have spilled some down the sink,' Dodo confessed, intertwining her fingers, and I might have just about forgiven her even that had she not added, 'but only a teensy-weensy bit.'

Teensy-bloody-weensy? That did it. How many times had I nagged Dodo about using baby language in front of the men?

'Well, you can go out and get some,' I ordered.

'Mason's int open 'til nine, madam,' Brigsy pointed out, taken aback by my sharpness.

'Right,' I said. 'To work.'

'Oyve just finished my shift,' Bantony informed me, and made for the exit.

'You've just finished your sleep,' I corrected him. 'Stay.'

'Oh, but Oy ain't had moy breakfast,' he objected, but I was in no mood to listen to excuses, real or imaginary.

'Well, that's a shame,' I snarled. 'I haven't eaten since this time yesterday.'

'Is that a new diet, Boss?' Dodo asked. 'Because I do not think it has made you very happy.'

'No, it isn't. Be quiet and pay attention,' I said abruptly. 'I want a list of every crime, solved or unsolved, committed within a ten-mile radius of here on the day before Etterly Utter disappeared.'

'And when was that, Boss?' Dodo enquired, reasonably enough.

My mind went blank. What the hell was wrong with me? It was a date I remembered every day of my life.

'Oh, for goodness' sake, just look it up,' I ordered. 'And, if there's nothing in our records, check with Anglethorpe and the local papers.'

'But...' Bantony began.

I had no idea what objection he was about to raise, but I immediately un-raised it.

'Just do it,' I snapped, and strode off towards my office to the accompaniment of muttering from Bantony. 'No, I didn't get out of the wrong side of my bed this morning,' I yelled back. 'I haven't been in it yet.'

'So whose bed *was* she in?' Dodo stage-whispered.

'Not moyne,' Bantony murmured, 'unfor-tune-ately.'

I nearly about-turned and charged back, but I was fairly certain there was a clause somewhere in the East Suffolk Constabulary Revised Rules and Regulations 1940 that said inspectors shall not swear at constables and slap their silly faces.

Sharkey was slumped over his desk. Why the hell should he get any sleep? I took the handle and slammed the door as hard as I could.

'Oh, my Aunty Mabel's bedsocks!' Dodo cried. 'She has shot herself.'

'No such luck,' Bantony assured her.

'Watch it,' Brigsy scolded. At least he still had respect for me. 'You nearly tripped over the fire bucket.'

'No such luck,' I scowled, and slunk into my lair.

Somebody was attacking my forehead with an axe.

69

MUSSOLINI AND THE MAGNIFYING GLASS

I settled behind my desk with a cigarette and browsed updated directions from the Ministry of Labour and National Service. Strikes had been declared illegal a few weeks ago and apparently we were supposed to arrest anyone downing tools or encouraging others to do so. I wasn't very happy about this. In my experience, most working men and women needed every penny they could earn and only refused to work if they had genuine grievances. Mine, however, was not to reason why. I just hoped never to be called upon in such a situation.

I heard voices in the corridor.

'No, sir. It must have been a breeze wha' shut it, ' Brigsy was saying and, moments later, he was in my office, a big brown mug steaming and one hand behind his back.

'Emergency tea from Mrs B,' he told me with a grin, 'and…' He produced a small parcel wrapped in greaseproof paper and I could smell what it was before he had even handed it over. 'She think you might like this, madam.'

'A bacon sandwich,' I cried, then instantly realised, 'but this comes from your ration.'

'We got plen'y more,' he assured me.

'You are a poor liar, Sergeant Briggs,' I said.

'I try my best,' he sniffed, wounded at my slight on his dishonesty.

'Thank you,' I said. 'I will replace it.'

'No need for tha',' he told me, even less convincingly.

'I goo look through the old charge books for 1914,' he continued.

'We still have them?'

'Oh yes, madam, and ones from the old station gooin' back near a hundred year.'

'Blimey,' I exclaimed, and Brigsy blushed at my coarse language.

'We keep them on the top floor,' he said, and it suddenly occurred to me that I had never been up the stairs of Sackwater Central Police Station. There was a door at the bottom between cells two and three, but it was always kept locked in case a prisoner tried to escape through it. When Constable Rivers was with us, he had told me it was derelict.

'Anything else up there?' I asked.

'More things,' Brigsy said brightly, 'int in there than are.'

I sipped my tea and inhaled the aroma of the sandwich.

'What did you find?' I asked.

'Cobwebs, mainly,' Brigsy replied, 'and mouse droppin's.'

'In the charge books,' I clarified.

'Oh, them,' Brigsy realised. 'Lot of drunk and disorderlies, a couple of drunk in charge of a minor, a foo breaches of the peace. The day in question, though' – he paused for dramatic effect – 'a caution.'

'Who and why?' I had intended to wait for Brigsy to go before I made a pig of myself, but my stomach was digesting its own lining. I opened the paper with the same care that Howard Carter must have peeled back the wrappings of Tutankhamun's mummy.

'Threatening behaviour,' Brigsy said. 'Sergeant Fynn gave the caution.'

I took a bite.

'Awm vey roe va...' I began.

'Sorry, madam?' Brigsy queried, unfamiliar with Baconese.

I chewed, swallowed, and washed it down with a glug of tea.

'And they wrote that in the charge book?' I tried again.

'Things int as hectic then as now,' Brigsy assured me, but they could hardly have been quieter unless a fascist saboteur put a sleeping draught in our water supply, as we had been warned might happen by the Ministry of Misinformation, as Toby had started to call it. 'Prob'ly bring him in to charge then change their mind and caution instead.'

'Who was cautioned?' I asked dispiritedly.

Quite honestly, I had more interest in my breakfast than some ancient bit of rowdiness.

'Difficult to read the writin',' Brigsy warned.

'Desk sergeants weren't half as good as they are now,' I said magnanimously, and Brigsy preened the smudge on his lip. 'If you get the book, maybe I can decipher it,' I suggested, and stuffed more sandwich into my mouth.

My sergeant trudged off in his odd, stiff-legged stride and I tucked in greedily, melted butter squirting out and oozing down my chin.

'Dint look like she like bacon,' I heard him tell Dodo. 'She int hardly touched it.'

What? Was I supposed to ingest it whole?

Back he came and placed the book open in front of me but, in my gluttony, I had literally bitten off more than I could chew, and my cheeks bulged like a child blowing up a balloon.

The book was damp and dusty. It smelt like the back of Teddy Moulton's shop and the writing was small and smudged. I was impressed that Brigsy had managed to glean as much information as he had, but I had spent much of my youth translating my father's scrawl when even he had trouble deciphering it.

'Tha's the one.' Brigsy prodded an entry as I munched doggedly at my food and I rifled through my handbag for my magnifying glass.

March Middleton had sent it to me after I had been forced to admit we did not have one in the station when she came to help in my search for the Suffolk Vampire. I swallowed and had a hasty drink before I choked.

'Well, it's definitely Sergeant Fynn,' I agreed, taking another swig of tea. 'But the ink has run a bit on the suspect's name.' I bent low over my glass. 'Looks like *Murphys... Harrison*. Morphus!' I exclaimed.

'That gypo,' Brigsy said contemptuously. 'I never do let him off with a caution if it's me.'

Doesn't sound like anything that would make Etterly flee and be afraid to return for, I cogitated.

'I speak to the editor of the *Gazette*,' Brigsy informed me. 'He say he'll have a look through their record but it goo be nice to ask him yourself – begging your pardon, madam – his words, not mine.'

Nice? Did Toby really mean that? Would he really like to speak to me, or would I find myself on the front page as Sackwater's answer to Mussolini for harassing the press?

'Thank you, Brigsy,' I said, 'and please thank Mrs Briggs for the tea and sandwich. I can't remember when I enjoyed my food so much. It's absolutely delicious.'

Brigsy slapped the book shut, sending clouds of mould into the air, coughed and walked off, leaving the door open, while I gorged myself on the rest of my breakfast.

'Gettin' very sarcastic,' I heard him say sadly. 'And tha' goo be my lunch.'

Hunger assuaged, tiredness took over. I went to the lobby.

'I have some important letters to write,' I told Brigsy, 'so I am not to be disturbed under any circumstances.'

'Righto, madam,' he replied, and I was nearly back in my office before I heard him murmur, 'sweet dreams.'

What a cheek. I would have words with my sergeant about that – after I had caught up on my sleep. By the time I had finished doing that, Brigsy had gone home and I was almost due to do the same.

70

HACKLES AND HOMICIDAL MANIACS

Dodo was in charge of the desk when I returned to Sackwater Central the next morning. Whatever she was knitting, the wearer would have to like bright pink.

'There is a letter for you here, Boss.' She put her needles and wool down and waved a scruffy sheet of paper over her head, like a stockbroker trying to offload shares.

'Who from?' I asked.

'From whom?' she corrected me, and my hackles rose. 'Oh, sorry, Boss. That just came out.'

'Just tell me,' I huffed.

'It doesn't say,' Dodo said, and I held out my hand.

'It doesn't smell of pipe tobacco or perfume,' she told me, standing up to pass the note over the desktop.

At least she was trying, I thought as I unfolded it.

INSPECTER CHURCH MEAT ME AT THE TREE TEN SHARP COME LONE was pencilled in ill-formed capital letters.

Miss Frith would have rapped the writer's knuckles for that handwriting, spelling and lack of punctuation, I thought.

'The Tree,' Dodo wondered. 'Is that a public house?'

'The King's Oak,' I assumed.

It was the only tree of any significance in Sackwater that I could think of.

'The Ghost Tree?' she whispered, as if it could hear her.

'The King's Oak,' I repeated firmly, because it couldn't.

'Oh, but everybody else calls it the Ghost Tree,' Dodo objected.

'We don't, because we don't believe in ghosts,' I assured her.

'I do,' she assured me back.

'How did the letter get here?' I asked.

'It was on the doormat when I arrived twenty-two minutes ago.

She should have been on duty thirty minutes ago, but I would worry about that another time. Also, the station should have been manned and I would worry about that then and there.

'Who was on desk duty when you arrived?'

I knew who should have been, but I wanted Dodo to tell me.

'Well, Brigsy should have been here,' she admitted, reluctant to split on her sergeant, 'but he had a sort of emergency. She was choking and coughing up sort-of hairballs.'

'What?' I asked incredulously. 'He can't keep disappearing every time that dratted cat is sick.'

'I am not sure that Brigsy would like you to refer to her like that,' Dodo told me, and I was about to call it worse than that when she continued. 'He has a lot of respect for Mrs Briggs.'

'I wasn't talking about her,' I sighed.

'Well, I was,' Dodo told me. 'Apparently Mrs B has been feeling very hungry with rationing.'

'It's not that bad,' I objected, feeling even more guilty about accepting the bacon, 'yet.'

'It is if you have a husband with Brigsy's appetite.'

I assumed she was still talking about food.

'Please just explain what happened.' I sniffed the letter and found Dodo was correct. It didn't smell of tobacco or perfume but of something she hadn't been told to identify and therefore didn't. At some stage, that piece of paper had been almost as near as me to some bacon. That narrowed it down to almost every house and café in the country.

'I have been given to understand,' Dodo began, sounding like she was giving evidence in court, 'that Mrs Briggs was given to believe, by one Doris, that she could stave off her hunger by eating wool, unravelling one of her son's old pullovers and boiling the strands. Unfortunately—'

'I get the gist,' I broke in, and Dodo pursed her lower lip.

For a police officer, or even for a woman, she was remarkably easily wounded.

'Are you going to go?' Dodo asked.

'To see Mrs Briggs? Certainly not.'

'To the tree?' Dodo explained in the same annoyingly long-suffering way I often spoke to her.

Strewth, you are making me as stupid as you.

'Yes,' I said.

'It might be a trick,' she warned, picking up her knitting.

'That has occurred to me.'

I had not forgotten the time I was locked inside it.

'Have you forgotten the time you were locked inside it, Boss?' she enquired, slipping on a pair of wire half-moon spectacles to inspect her work.

'No.'

'By the Suffolk Vampire,' she reminded me, in case I was confusing the incident with all the other times I had been trapped in trees by homicidal maniacs.

'I do not have amnesia yet,' I snapped as she looped her wool dexterously over the tip of a needle and did some complicated manoeuvre with it.

'When shall you have it, Boss?' she enquired, peering at me over the rims of her spectacles like a disgruntled judge.

'Never, I hope.'

'That's the spirit,' Dodo said approvingly. 'And shall you defy the final injunction in the message and take a large number of officers with you?'

'No,' I said.

'Just one?' she asked, like a child badgering for a treat.

'No one.'

'Not even me?' Dodo pouted.

I was tempted to say *Especially not you* but I satisfied myself with, 'Not even you.'

'Oh,' Dodo cried, partly in disappointment and partly because she had dropped a stitch.

I changed my mind about being completely unaccompanied. The message was probably a practical joke and I would pace around in the dark until I got bored, but it could also be from a crank and somehow the word *dangerous* went nicely with that type of person.

I went to see Mrs Cooksey. I had bumped into her occasionally in Sackwater over the years and she would usually stop for a chat, but I had not been to her house in The Soundings since I had called on her the day she had umpired our rounders game and Etterly went missing. Today she was out, but her husband was at home and only too happy to cooperate. He could probably have done the job very well himself, but a police inspector can't ask a member of the public to look after her.

'Is this Mrs Cooksey good-looking?' Bantony enquired.

'Very,' I told him, 'if you like women in their early fifties.'

My constable did the smile I had caught him practising on more than one occasion.

'I loike a woman with experience,' he told me, though I suspected he also liked women with no experience whatsoever.

'Captain Cooksey teaches unarmed combat in the marines,' I warned.

It was a lie, but I would let Bantony find that out for himself.

Mr Cooksey had volunteered the day war was declared and was most aggrieved to be rejected because he had had rheumatic fever.

'It wasn't patriotism or any drivel like that,' he had assured me. 'I just wanted to get out of that bloody office. It's so unfair.' He had scratched his forehead. 'I can swear like a trooper but they won't let me be one.'

71

THE HEAD OF KARL MARX AND THE WORDS OF WINSTON CHURCHILL

'The lights are going out,' Winston Churchill had warned us in his Defence of Freedom and Peace speech a year before war was declared, and his prophesy had certainly come true. The lights had gone out all over Sackwater. There was not a chink of illumination in The Soundings that didn't come from the sky and that was overcast with just the edge of the moon glowing behind a cloud shaped uncannily like the head of Karl Marx.

Bantony should be at his post in one of Mrs Cooksey's first-floor front windows but I couldn't see him, which at least meant whoever had sent the message wouldn't be able to either – assuming he, she or they turned up.

I had both of my torches with me – one painted over so that only a thin beam could escape through the glass, the other unpainted in defiance of every warden this side of Felixstowe. It shouldn't have surprised me because I saw it all the time in my own profession, but it was remarkable how a little power intoxicated some people. *You'll be the first to swap that armband for a swastika*, I had heard an indignant woman tell Warden Harlock when he shrieked in her face that a pinhole in her blackout curtain was a guiding beam for the looft-wafer, as he termed it.

Not wanting to break an ankle, as Gordon Skillern had done when he was racing to help his brother, I turned on my

ARP-approved torch. The moles were labouring at a rate that would have delighted the new Ministry of Works. We were all being exhorted to abandon leisure and toil longer and harder and I wondered how many senior civil servants had given up their golf since they guided us so triumphantly into war.

I gave the tree a wide berth as always when I made my way around it. The luminous dial on my watch, which would probably have given Harlock a seizure, said nine fifty-two. I had wanted time to scout around a bit first. *Always have a recce before you go into action*, Vesty had advised me, and he should know. He had led hundreds of men into battle.

I scanned the square with the thin beam and spotted three rabbits unconcernedly bobbing about by the bench where Major Burgandy used to sit. An owl hooted unseen from one of the trees but they paid no attention.

The ground hadn't been ploughed yet, though the council was already planting vegetables in flower beds on the promenade.

'You coom then,' a man said from nowhere, and I jumped.

A dark shape emerged from between the doors of the tree.

'Stay where you are,' I rapped.

'It's only me, Betty.'

'Inspector,' I corrected automatically. 'Who are you?'

I shone my unpainted torch and he shaded his eyes from the glare.

'You int forgot me?'

'Put your hand down.'

The man did as I had instructed and I turned my torch off. I had seen enough. It was as if an old photograph had been crumpled up then smoothed down again. The eyes were still intense blue and the backswept hair still thick and black.

'Hello, Harkles,' I greeted him. 'Why the secrecy?'

He came forward.

'My father goo kill me if he know I talk to you.'

'And Bosko,' I said. 'I thought he might attack me when I visited the forge.'

Harkles snorted.

'Bosko dint hurt a fly,' he assured me. 'It's him tell me abou' you callin'. The old man never say a word. *Goo see her*, Bosko say. *She's still a good sort, not like the rest of her kind.*'

'My kind?' I queried, unsure if he meant town people, women or members of the police.

'Coppers,' he confirmed, 'and Gadje.'

That last word I knew meant non-Romanies, which was almost every resident in the area except for the Harrisons.

'I can't help being a Gadjo,' I told him, 'and I'm proud of this uniform.'

I put the torch back in my bag.

'Dint seem right,' he said wryly, 'you a n'nspector and me still tendin' horses. You know I do a stretch?'

'Bosko said it wasn't your fault,' I said.

'Clodhoppers call me a stinkin' gyppo,' he told me resentfully, 'and worse. My dad always say stay clear of trouble for you do always be in the wrong when you're Romany. I try to walk off but they coom at me so I fight back. Then the shanglo coom and break us up.'

'Shanglo?'

'Police,' he explained. 'All the farm boys say I start it. The judge say he could give me a fine but he goo sick on my kind coomin' causin' trouble.' I could see Harkles more clearly now that my eyes had adapted to the dark. His eyes were wide with anger and his full lips tensed against each other. 'My kind,' he repeated in disgust.

'I wish I had been here,' I said. 'I would have spoken up for you.'

Harkles leaned his head back to look at the stars.

'And say what?'

'I could tell them you are honest,' I pointed out. 'When Etterly lost her purse in Brooks Meadow, you found it and gave it back to her.' It all sounded a bit feeble when I said it, but I was trying to bring up the subject of my friend as casually as I could.

Harkles puffed the warm night air through his open mouth like he was blowing a smoke ring.

'Etterly,' he mused.

'You were sweet on each other,' I said, and he tipped his head sharply sideways.

'She tell you tha'?'

'I found her diary,' I said. 'And she wrote both your initials intertwined and carved them inside the tree. E and S, because she called you Sparkles.'

Harkles huffed. 'Dint glitter much now,' he said wryly, and dragged the toe of his boot in a line through the dusty grass. 'We court for while,' he admitted, 'but we dint dare tell. She say her dad goo lock her up if he see her with tha' filthy gyppo again and my dad say he take his belt to both on us.' Harkles' shoulders juddered. 'He never goo hard on me but I see him knock Bosko cold on the ground with it more than one time.'

I remembered Morphus's belt, heavy with iron studs and hoops, and having seen another, less attractive side to him when I visited the other day, I could well believe he would use it.

'What happened to Etterly, Harkles?' I asked, and his head slumped as if what was in there had become too heavy for him. 'What happened?' I pressed.

Harkles stepped backwards, and for a second I thought he was going to run, but he was only getting a better look at me. Was he having second thoughts?

'I have not come to cause trouble for you,' I vowed. 'You have my word on it.'

Harkles mulled things over.

'All right,' he decided. 'I goo tell you wha' I know.'

72

MRS GUNN'S LETTER BOX AND THE COMMUNIST MANIFESTO

The Karl Marx cloud had shifted and overlapped another so that it now looked more like Mrs Perkins, Carmelo's hen, than the author of the Communist Manifesto. More importantly, it had uncovered the half-moon, which gave us a semi-decent light.

I'm not sure who started it, but we found ourselves walking towards the bench. The rabbits, fearless in the face of a taloned predator, panicked at the sight of me and almost knocked each other over in their chaotic efforts to escape. We sat down, me in Major Burgandy's place and Harkles on my left, so close we were almost touching.

'Tell me,' I urged.

'You say Etterly and me are sweet on each other,' he began.

'Weren't you?'

Harkles looked straight ahead.

'She's sweet on me,' he said, 'very, and I like her. She's a fine pretty girl, near 'nough a woman.' He glanced across at me. 'Your mother ever tell you men are only a'ter one thing?' He blew out of the corner of his mouth. 'She's right.'

That makes a change, I thought, but asked, 'And did you get it?'

Poor as the light was, I felt sure Harkles blushed at my question.

'Int used to talk to women this way,' he confessed.

'Believe me, I've had far more embarrassing conversations than this,' I assured him.

It had taken two hours to get out of Stephen Carson how he had got his member trapped in Mrs Gunn's letter box.

'We kiss and cuddle,' Harkles said, looking into the distance, 'and I try more but she say wait 'til we are married.'

'And were you going to get married?' I asked.

Harkles tensed, as most men do when the subject of matrimony arises.

'Etterly think so but I never say it,' he told me. 'I'm more thinkin' what a trim figure she go' and how I like to ge' my hands on it.' He clicked his tongue. 'That shock you?'

'You'll have to try harder than that,' I assured him.

'Truth be told, I have 'nough on Etterly,' Harkles told me. 'She give me a necklace with the shape of a tear and our initials on it and show me how it fit with her half to make a circle and say it mean we stay together alway.'

He pulled a face.

There was something else that had been puzzling me.

'Why is there a C carved on one side?' I asked, and Harkles looked briefly nonplussed.

'Int a C,' he said. 'It's a horseshoe.'

'What happened to it?'

'I tell Darklis give it her back.'

'And did she?'

'Dunno.' Harkles scratched his nose. 'Know who was proper sweet on Etterly?' he asked, but didn't wait for a reply. 'Bosko – worship the ground she tread, he do.'

'You'd never guess it,' I remarked.

'He never show it, for he know he's ugly and repel her,' Harkles said.

'Actually, Etterly rather liked Bosko, even before he saved her life,' I recalled. 'She always stood up for him and said he was nicer than we knew, and it wasn't his fault a horse damaged his face.'

Harkles worked his hands around each other as if he was washing them.

'Int no horse,' he announced. 'Dad do tha' when Bosko's hardly walkin' and I'm a babe in arms. He tell me himself once when he's fired with rum. Dya give Bosko too much attention and keep sayin' how pretty he is and not givin' Dad his way.'

'Who's Dya?' I asked.

'Dya mean mother.' He locked his fingers. 'He slap her too and she run off with us when I'm 'bout ten but Dad find her and beat her bad and take Bosko and Darklis and me home.'

'Why did he want you?'

'We're good workers even when we're little and he'd dint need pay us.' Harkles shrugged. 'And he dint want Dya to have us.'

'Have you heard from your mother since then?' I asked.

'Not a word,' Harkles said bitterly. 'Bosko goo see her three year ago and Dad beat him so hard when he come back he dint walk for a week. He never speak on her to this day a'ter tha'.'

When I got a chance, I would ask Bosko about this. The Morphus I had known, until my last visit to Folger's Estate Farm, seemed a placid man, good-humoured and patient with us children, who must have often got in his way. In the meantime, I couldn't see where this conversation was leading, unless Harkles was going to claim his father had a hand in my friend's disappearance.

'What had this to do with Etterly?' I asked, and Harkles rubbed his face with both hands, his day's stubble rasping.

'You need to know how Dad is,' he said, 'then you understand why Etterly goo do what she do.' Harkles dug his fingers hard into his cheeks. I saw the skin blanch around them. 'She never mean to kill anyone.'

73

OLD MAN PECKHAM AND THE RAGE

Harkles' nails were black and thick but, luckily for him, they were broken short or he would have gouged his face, so tightly was he clutching at it. I twisted to use my right hand and touched his.

'You'll hurt yourself,' I warned.

'Think I care?' he asked, but slid his hands down and away like a man waking from a deep sleep. 'Darklis had a boy,' he announced. I thought at first he meant his sister had had a baby, but then he added, 'from Sackwater.'

'Who?'

'Dint know,' he told me. 'But Dad do and he goo wild. He hate us getting' close with outsiders. Think they will split the family and turn us into Gadje.'

'But he always welcomed us,' I objected.

'He want to show the world we int all vagabonds,' Harkles explained. That wasn't a word I had heard used recently. 'So he want to be on good terms but he hate all on you. *Stuck up townies*, he say, *comin' here when they want, like they own the place, 'spectin' us to entertain them. We're just as much pets to them as the horses*.'

I digested that news in mild shock. It was like finding you are the least favourite niece of a favourite uncle.

'He always seemed so nice,' I mumbled.

'Can be,' Harkles agreed, 'but he change when the drink is on him and the drink is on him most times he int workin'.'

'So what happened?'

'I'm on the land, cuttin' up a tree fallen 'cross Creaky Lane,' Harkles said. 'When I goo home, Shadrach is back from drivin' the tractor. He tell me dad say he find a boy been givin' Darklis jewlury and he lay into her – shoutin' – and he give her a slap and she run off and he goo look for her.'

'Had he hit her before?'

Harkles lowered his hands slowly onto his thighs.

'Never touch her, not even when she talk back at him.'

'Did he find her?' I asked.

'Drag her back by her hair and throw her in an old horse box behind the stables.' Harkles rubbed his knees. 'Keep her in there best part of a fortnight, he do. Say it teach her a lesson. Shadrach take her provisions secret but even he daren't let her out.'

'No wonder she went to live with your mother,' I commented, and Harkles plucked at his cheek.

'Must be near midnight when Dad coom back.' He clapped his hands together. 'And then I'm with Etterly so I dint know nothin' 'bout it 'til later. He—'

'Hang on,' I broke in. 'How does Etterly come into this?'

'We dint see much on each other,' he told me, 'with the row our dads make, and, truth be told, I'm not too bad on it.' Harkles tapped his knees with his fists. 'Etterly is gettin' too serious and not givin'...'

Harkles flopped his arms.

'You what you wanted?' I prompted, and he nodded.

'But she turn up tha' night,' he continued. 'Her parents goo see her aunt who goo sick in Ipswich so they stop the night and send Etterly to sleep with another aunt but she come to me instead.'

'Go on,' I urged.

'Nothin' much happen 'til Dad show up. Shadrach is workin'

on straightnin' an axle in the forge and we can't get up to anythin' with him 'round,' Harkles told me with a sigh.

Was I supposed to sympathise that he hadn't been able to gratify his lust with my friend that he wasn't really *sweet on* when she loved him?

'What did he say or do to Etterly?' I asked.

'Nothin',' Harkles said, and I was beginning to think he was having a joke at my expense.

'What do you mean, *nothing*?' I demanded.

'Wha' I say,' Harkles sniffed. 'He dint do nothin' to Etterly 'cause he never see her. We're in the forge, talkin' to Shadrach and me helpin' with the bellows, when we hear Dad shoutin' for us. Etterly is stepped out the back for she feel hot with the fire on a warm night and she stay there – for the time anyways. Dad coom in. He's been on the rum – I can smell it – and in a fight 'cause his lip's split and he's in a rage like I never do see afore. Why int Shadrach done fixin' the tractor? He's a lazy good-for-nothin'. He raise his fist. Shadrach is bigger than Dad but he's 'fraid on him so he goo out and Dad turn on me. He say I put Darklis 'gainst him. I tell him she dint need help from me to see what a khul he is.'

I didn't need Harkles to translate *khul* for me. He had warned me once not to step into a pile of it.

'Why weren't you frightened of him?' I asked.

Harkles legs were joggling up and down.

'He never raise a hand to me afore but he goo for me now,' he replied. 'I mean really goo. He punch me, six, perhap seven time. He kick me and knee me in the belly. He slap me so my head ring.'

Harkles scratched his chest distractedly.

'Where was Bosko?' I wondered.

'He's called to help the calvin' at Peckham's Farm.'

'And?' I asked, and Harkles pinched his right cheek hard.

'Dad say, *You int nothin' but a pretty girl. Well, I soon put an end to tha'*. And he take me by the throat and I think he goo throttle me but he start draggin' me to the fire and sayin', *Think I made Bosko ugly? Tha' int nothin'. I'll roast your face 'til it's pork cracklin'*. And I'm choking and tryin' to pull his hands off my neck and kickin' his legs, but he's got a rage strength on him. We've just stoke the flames and they come out the coal hole lickin' my hair and skin. I dint see Etterly nor hear her 'til she yell, *Let him goo*. But Dad just say, *I goo deal with you in a minute, bitch*. And he step right to the furnace and lift me off the ground and make to throw me in, but I hear Etterly yellin', *I say let him goo*. And I hear a thump and all at once Dad let goo and fall down and I fall part under him but Etterly pull me out, sayin', *Sparkles, darlin', are you all right?* And she help me up to my knees and I see Dad lyin' on his back. His eyes are open and his mouth and I put my ear to it and there's not a breath. *Wha' you do?* I ask, and Etterly hold up a lump hammer and say, *I hit him with this*. And I say, *Christ, Etterly. You goo kill him*. And she keep sayin', *I just mean to get him off you*.'

Harkles shuddered.

'But your father is still alive,' I objected.

'Take him a good while to come round,' Harkles told me, before adding, with some satisfaction, 'and he still got a dent in the back on his head big 'nuff to hold a duck egg. But he dint stir and his eyes roll up when I pull the lids back. Etterly just stand there sayin' over and over how she dint mean it and then she start to cry – so I say, *Goo home, Etterly. I goo sort this out. You never coom tonight. Shadrach won't say nothin'*.'

'So did you intend to take the blame?' I asked, and Harkles snorted.

'Not likely. I was goo get rid on him – throw him in the river or bury him some place and say he never coom home tha' night.'

'So did she go?' I asked and Harkles bobbed his head.

'She dint want to but I told her, *Goo. Dint say a word. Just behave like nothin' happen.* And she back out of the forge into the yard but Bosko's home from calvin' and he coom see what the noise is and she walk straight into him. Bosko grab Etterly to steady her and she scream. I see her face in the light from the forge and it look like she see her own ghost. He say, *I see wha' happen* and she pull away and run off down the lane. Bosko make to follow but I say, *Let her be. You'll fright her more* and Etterly disappear into the night and tha's the last I ever see on her.'

'She—' I began, but that was all because the peace of The Soundings was broken by a rush and a shriek that nearly made me leap out my skin.

74

DIZZY AND THE DUTCHMAN

Harkles sat impassively.

'Screecher,' he explained. 'Caught a coney.'

'I know,' I said, annoyed with myself for jumping. I may have been a townie but I knew an owl when I saw one. 'It just took me by surprise.'

One moment the rabbit had been chomping contentedly on the uncut grass round the base of a horse chestnut, the next it was carried off, squealing helplessly, to be ripped apart. I could only hope it would die quickly.

'So that's it?' I asked. 'Etterly ran off and you never saw or heard from her again.'

Harkles shook his head.

'I only say I never see her,' he said, which was true enough.

'Have you heard from her?' I asked a bit too eagerly, and was rewarded with a snort.

'Not from her,' he conceded. 'Of her.'

'When?' I demanded, my mind going through the possibilities. Had she written to Harkles? Had somebody else seen her?

'Next marnin',' he said. 'Bosko worry all night. He mean to help Etterly when he get hold on her but she take it wrong.'

There was another, fainter squeal. *Please just die.*

'He came to The Soundings,' I surmised.

'Not Bosko,' Harkles said. 'He worry he frighten her 'gin. So Shadrach goo in his stead. He's on his way to Bath Road when he see Etterly playin' rounders, so he wait…'

'Under a tree,' I said. 'I saw him, but I didn't recognise him because he was in the shadows.'

Also, Shadrach was a much less familiar figure to me than his brothers.

'Then he see girls step in and out the Ghost Tree and wait there 'til Etterly goo in.' Harkles gestured towards it with his thumb. 'He ge' close by and whisper. *Etterly, it's me, Shadrach. Bosko see wha' you do last night.* He mean to set her mind at rest, but she take it like a threat and the next he know she's off out tha' hole.' Harkles jerked a thumb towards the King's Oak. 'And runnin' faster than tha' old coney ever do. Shadrach dint want to chase her through the streets so he decide to wait for her to calm and explain next day tha' Dad int dead and int her fault.'

'And where were you when this was going on?' I asked, and saw him tense.

'In the cellar,' he mumbled. 'When Dad do come round, he say *Wha' hit me?* And I say *I do* and he beat the khul out of me and throw me down the steps.' Harkles blew out noisily through his nose. 'If he dint be weak'ed by the knock Etterly give him, he'd have killed me. He try to follow down but he's taken dizzy and fall over. Still gets spells now. He lock me in.' Harkles cracked his knuckles. 'Three day 'fore he let me out and only then 'cause he need me to work the farm.'

'Did you, Bosko or Shadrach hear or see anything of Etterly again?' I asked.

'Nor sight nor sound,' he replied.

The rabbits were emerging again, apparently unconcerned by the loss of their relative. The once-Marxist-once-henlike-now-more-similar-to-a-teapot cloud passed back over the moon, leaving us back in near darkness.

I stood up. 'Is that it?'

I looked down on Harkles. He was slumped forwards, hands back on his knees.

'Tha's all I know,' he assured me, and raised his head.

'Thank you,' I said, and squeezed his shoulder, 'and your brothers for trying to help her. I would thank them myself, but…'

'He only see you off 'cause of Dad,' he assured me.

'I know that now.' I straightened my jacket. It had risen at the back.

Harkles stood and surveyed the sky.

'Bosko still pine for Etterly,' he said. 'She's the one and only love on his life.' He clicked his tongue. 'Dint know she like him too. Feel bad now for I take her off him.'

'You've done the right thing tonight,' I assured him.

Harkles pinched the bridge of his nose like people do when they take their spectacles off at the end of the day.

'Mayhap,' he conceded, without conviction, 'but a long time too late. It dint do nobody no good now.'

'On the contrary,' I told him, 'you have been very helpful.'

And for once I meant it.

I waited until Harkles had joined the night before I waved to Bantony as a signal he could come outside.

'They're a funny pair,' he told me. 'She asked if Oy loike gin rummy and when Oy say Oy don't drink on duty, he just smile and say it's a game.' Bantony put on his helmet. 'But I told them it's a serious matter, troyink to get an officer of the law intoxicated and then they do what yow're doink now – laughink at me.'

'I'm sorry,' I managed to gasp, but I wasn't really.

75

THE FALLING AND THE FALLEN WOMEN

Brigsy was puffing contentedly on his pipe when I turned up at the station the next morning. Everyone who wasn't off duty was out on patrol.

'Don't you get fed up of being stuck behind a desk all day?' I asked, and he couldn't have looked more shocked if I had asked who he wanted to win the war.

'Fed up?' he wheezed bemusedly. 'No, never, madam. I count each minute wasted when I int in here doing my duties.'

'What about when you are having dinner?' I asked.

'Well, tha' int wasted,' he conceded.

'Or having a pint and playing darts in the Unicorn?' I added.

'Well, not tha',' he granted me.

'Good,' I said. 'Then you won't think it time wasted if we go for a walk.'

Brigsy blushed. 'Well, I...'

'To see Mr and Mrs Utter,' I added hastily.

Did he really think I was inviting him to go skipping hand in hand down, or up, Lovers' Lane?

'Oh,' he breathed in relief, 'that do be quite in order, madam.' And five minutes later I had hustled my sergeant outside, pausing only to put an annoyingly uninformative BACK IN ONE HOUR sign on the door.

Brigsy was one of the few people I knew who actually looked at home in his tin hat. He had worn it in the trenches of Flanders. Admittedly, it was rusty in patches – from having adorned a scarecrow in those halcyon days when we deluded ourselves that we had been through the war to end all wars – but if it had saved him from the Kaiser, Brigsy reasoned, it would do perfectly well against a Charley Chaplinesque corporal.

'Dodo tell me you have a secret assignation last night,' he chattered as we went down Tenniel Road.

'I met an informant,' I agreed, before he got the wrong impression. Promiscuous men are generally admired and envied, but any woman who has had more than one boyfriend in her life is a nymphomaniac and one step away from prison and/or an insane asylum.

'Just like the real police do.' Brigsy nodded approvingly.

'I *am* the real police,' I told him firmly.

'I know that, madam,' he hastened to assure me. 'I mean the real police in stories.'

I didn't have anything useful to say to that, or anything at all really, so I concentrated on trying not to hum 'Little Brown Jug'. Much as I enjoyed Glenn Miller, it was an annoying tune and, like many annoying tunes, I couldn't get it out of my head.

We paused to watch a shopkeeper refilling one of the sacks piled outside his window.

'Dratted kids keep taking the sand to play with,' he complained.

'Well, they can't get on the beach, can they?' I reasoned indulgently, pushing to the back of my mind the time I had harangued two boys for doing exactly the same outside the station.

'Goo you forget when—' Brigsy began to remind me.

'That was altogether different,' I assured him over the words swirling around in my head – *Ha ha ha, you and me, little brown ... shut up!* – until we turned down Bath Road.

A minute later, we stopped at number eleven.

Please don't tell me we're here.

'Here we are, madam,' Brigsy announced, springing forwards with never-before-demonstrated agility to beat me to the knocker.

He had an unusual technique, raising the brass ring perhaps half an inch and lowering it carefully to produce the volume of tap you might make putting your book down on a table.

'You'll have to knock harder than that,' I told him as a blurred form enlarged and solidified through the leaded green glass into Mrs Utter.

'Hello, Sergeant Briggs.' She beamed, but her face fell instantly. 'Oh, you do bring Betsy with you.'

'Hello, Mrs Utter,' I greeted her. 'I didn't know you two knew each other.'

'Nor me,' Brigsy puzzled, scratching under the rim of his ancient helmet. 'Oh, now I remember. You goo fall in the gutter...'

'And you help me gather my shoppin'.' She nodded.

What? I thought. *Does this woman spend her life falling over in front of officers?*

'Then the next day,' she recalled happily, 'I trip on a pavin' stone.'

Apparently she does.

'And that nice Inspector Sharkey do come help me up,' Mrs Utter burbled on. 'A perfect gent.'

I could have spent the rest of the day explaining why my unesteemed colleague was not nice, far from perfect and anything but a gentleman, but we had not come to discuss him.

'Is Mr Utter in?' I asked, and she scowled at me for interrupting a grown-up conversation. 'I would like to talk to you both.'

Mrs Utter grimaced.

'S'pose you better come in.'

No front parlour for us today. We went into the back room.

When I was a child I had seen Etterly splashing about in a tin bath in front of the fire there. Today, Mr Utter sat at the table, apparently doing nothing. He had no food or newspaper in front of him but was staring into space.

'Hello, Mr Utter,' I greeted him.

'Dig up another bone?' he asked, without removing his gaze from the middle of nowhere.

I had thought hard about what to say to the Utters. I hadn't promised Etterly not to tell her parents the truth but, as she herself had insisted, it would be heartless to announce that she was alive and wanted nothing to do with them, and I had not told the men yet, either.

There was no tea in the offing and we were not offered a seat, though Mr Utter remained on his.

'I wanted your opinion,' I announced.

Brigsy shot me a look of surprise – it was not something he had heard me say before – but Etterly's parents nodded understandingly. What could be more natural than me asking their advice? I may have grown taller than them and donned a uniform, but I was still young Betsy in their eyes.

'Dint be shy, dear,' Mrs Utter encouraged me, and Brigsy cleared his throat at the very thought.

'It's just that I've come across a couple in a very similar position to you,' I began. 'Their daughter ran away from home over twenty years ago, but—'

'My Etterly never goo run away,' Mr Utter told me firmly.

'It's just that your situation is closest to theirs that I know of,' I struggled.

'Go on, dear,' Mrs Utter urged.

'And now she wants to go home.'

'Why dint she then?' Mr Utter demanded.

'Because she's afraid her parents will not want her back,' I said, and they looked at me blankly. I waded in. 'Her parents are regular churchgoers.'

'So are we, dear,' Mrs Utter told me, as if I wouldn't remember the times they had lectured me in my childhood about my absence from services. My parents rarely went unless there was a good funeral.

'She thinks they will condemn her because she has given herself to men.'

Brigsy shifted uncomfortably at the way the conversation was going, but the Utters seemed to take it in their stride.

'As a harlot?' Mr Utter clarified.

'Yes,' I said simply.

'So how do she think they want her in their house?' Mrs Utter asked contemptuously.

'She has repented her ways,' I assured her.

'As we make our beds…' Mr Utter recited piously.

'But would her parents want to push her back into that life?' I pressed.

'As we make our beds…' Mrs Utter re-recited, even more piously.

'I am minded of a number of things in the Bible,' Brigsy said, and my heart sank. 'The parable of the Prodigal Son, for example.'

Good for you, Brigsy.

'He just take his inheritance early,' Mr Utter reminded him.

'He rejoiceth more of that sheep, than of the ninety and nine which went not astray,' Brigsy quoted.

'Tha' sheep is lost,' Mr Utter responded. 'It dint goo fornicatin'.'

'Mary Magdalene was a prostitute,' I pointed out.

'The Bible dint say that, Betsy,' Mrs Utter told me. 'It say she's a sinner.'

'Tha's true,' Brigsy agreed reluctantly.

I knew I should have paid more attention at school.

'Surely it is Christian to forgive.'

'But it say nothin' in the Bible 'bout forgettin',' Mr Utter chipped in.

'What parent would turn their own child away?' I pressed.

'Dint you raise your voice to us, Betsy,' Mrs Utter scolded.

I wasn't aware that I had, and I could have insisted on being addressed by my rank, but I knew it would not assist my friend.

'I'm sorry,' I said, and I was, not for getting emotional but because I knew there was nothing else I could do. 'I am sorry to have troubled you,' I mumbled, and was just about to go when Brigsy said, 'Wha' if your Etterly—'

'She int tha' kind of girl,' Mr Utter broke in sharply.

'But jus' imagine she is,' Brigsy said, calmly but firmly. 'Goo you take her back?'

Etterly's parents looked at him and then at each other.

'If our Etterly walk in that door now...' Mrs Utter waved a hand. She was actually indicating the pantry door, but I wasn't going to quibble. 'Steeped in vile sin with wicked men' – she swallowed – 'I spit in her face, I do.'

'Thank you,' I said as politely as I could. 'That is all I wanted to know.'

'I hope that poor girl's parents dint feel the same as Mr and Mrs Utter,' Brigsy mused as we strolled back to the police station.

'They probably will,' I replied glumly, and shooed a pigeon out of my path.

'Where you come 'cross her, madam?' Brigsy asked.

'In London,' I told him, and Brigsy nodded wisely. 'A second Babylon,' he pronounced. 'A Sodom and Gomorrah.'

But with good shops, I thought.

'What did they get up to in Gomorrah?' I asked, and Brigsy blushed.

'The good book dint say, madam,' he told me. 'For it must be too shockin'.'

'Like Anglethorpe on a Saturday night,' I postulated, and Brigsy pondered.

'Not quite,' he decided, 'tha' bad.'

76

BADGER AND THE WIRE

Jimmy was already there when I got back to *Cressida*.

'He is in the bad way,' Captain had warned me before I went down to the sitting room. 'But I shall let him tell you.'

Jimmy was slumped over a half-empty bottle of Johnnie Walker.

'One in there for me?' I asked, and he held out the bottle without looking up.

I went down on my haunches, put the bottle to one side and took his hand.

'Badger's bought it,' he told me flatly.

Badger was his best friend, Bobby Badgero.

'Oh, Jimmy,' I said. 'I'm so sorry.'

'After all the shoot-ups he had, we thought he was indestructible,' Jimmy continued in a monotone. 'His cockpit caught fire and the canopy jammed. Went down in the drink.' Jimmy curled up, spilling his drink over both of us. 'I heard him... on the radio.' He shook his head violently, trying to throw the sounds away. 'Screaming,' he whispered. 'Screaming for his mother.' Jimmy gave way to sobs before demanding, 'How the hell will she cope? His father caught it in the last one. Badger was all...'

Jimmy broke down again.

'Has she been told?' I asked when he had stopped shaking.

'She'll have got a wire,' Jimmy said bitterly, 'and the Wingco has written, but he doesn't know her. Badger took me there on a couple of leaves and she's been up to the Heath. Daphne, her name is – game old girl – drank us all under the table.' Jimmy ran a hand through his hair. 'Oh, for Christ's sake, Betty, Ronny was going to motor Badger and me down there to stay this weekend.'

She lived, I remembered him telling me, in Bloomsbury.

Jimmy reached for the bottle.

'Don't,' I said. 'It's too savage to numb.'

'Oh, Christ,' Jimmy said, and I got to my feet.

'Stand up,' I urged, and he looked at me, his face blotchy red, suddenly a small lost boy.

'Why?'

'So I can hold you,' I said, and took him in my arms.

Any other time he would have tried to take advantage of such intimacy, but that evening Jimmy held on like I was a pillar in a stormy sea.

After a while, Carmelo joined us.

'I have lost friends,' he said. 'I watched them drown in burning oil.'

He had never talked about it before.

'And how did you get over it?' Jimmy asked.

'I have not,' the captain said, crossing himself, 'and I never shall.' He patted his pockets for something that wasn't there, probably his pipe. 'I saw them again at Dunkirk.'

We went on deck and leaned over the rail with Jimmy in the middle. The breeze from the estuary blew his fringe over his eyes and he brushed it aside automatically. In either of the other two forces he would have been sent to the barbers well before then.

'Look at her.' Jimmy pointed to Mrs Perkins, pecking at the earth. 'Not a care in the world.'

'Maybe you can still go and see your friend's mother – for one day only,' Captain suggested. 'It will be helpful for her to see how you loved him.'

'I don't know.' Jimmy exhaled heavily.

'If you don't visit bereaved people, they don't think you're being tactful,' I told him. 'They think you don't care.'

Jimmy started trembling and I put my arm around his waist.

'I went to see Etterly Utter's parents today,' I said. 'They still think their daughter is dead, but if I tell them she is alive and how she has lived, she will still be dead in their eyes.'

'The Ghost Tree girl?' Captain asked. 'Tell us about it.'

'Over a Scotch?' Jimmy asked hopefully.

'Just one,' I conceded, and we went back inside to fill our glasses.

77

FYNN AND THE HARDENED HEART

I went alone to Sergeant Fynn's house. It was an end terrace on Pencil Street, twenty yards from where Tubby Gretham had his consulting rooms. An elderly woman in a faded floral pinafore answered my knock. She was tiny, with sparse white hair.

'Mrs Fynn?'

'Yes, dear?' She peered out. 'Oh, you do be a policewoman.'

'My name is Inspector Church,' I told her.

''N'inspector,' she repeated, clearly impressed. 'Do you come to see Dereck? He *will* be pleased. Our daughter come when she can but she live abroad in Devon, she do, and we dint get over many callers.'

'Yes, I have,' I said dejectedly.

Mrs Fynn looked so pleased I didn't have the heart to tell her this was not a social call.

'Come in, Inspector.' Mrs Fynn swung the door open wide in welcome and I stepped into a gloomy hallway. 'He's up the stair,' she told me. 'Do you mind if I dint come? They play havoc with my knees. First door on the right.'

'I'm sure I'll find him,' I assured her with slight relief.

At least I wouldn't have to ask her to leave us alone.

'Then after we goo have a cuppa, we do.' She winked like this was some great conspiracy we were hatching between us, and I found myself saying, 'That would be nice, thank you.' And wishing I had thought of an excuse.

I made my way up.

'Watch the banister,' she called. 'It's a bit rickety.'

'Thank you.'

Upstairs was so dark I could hardly make out the outline of the door frame as I felt my way along the wall. I found it and knocked.

There was no reply, so I went in. This room was better lit because the curtains were open and, being at the back of the house, there were no nets. Sergeant Fynn lay on his back, arms crossed, eyes closed and mouth agape, and if I hadn't been told he would welcome me, I might have thought he had been laid out. He was pretty much as I remembered him – sallower and skinnier, if that was possible, his skin pulled tight on his face like he had been mummified, and there was something wrong with his lip. He had lost his Kitchener moustache. Perhaps he had handed it in with his truncheon when he retired. His teeth snarled at me from underwater in a glass on his bedside table.

'Hello, sergeant,' I said, loudly enough for him to hear, I hoped, but not to shock him, and the eyes sprang open.

'Who are you?' Fynn's voice was husky.

He rose a fraction from his pillow.

'I'm sorry if I alarmed you.'

'That dint answer my question,' he snapped, having lost none of his old charm.

'I'm Police Inspector Church,' I told him, and he squinted into the light. 'You knew me as Betty.'

To be fair, I was probably a silhouette against the sunshine, but this was not a man I felt like being very fair to, especially when he curled his lip.

'We never even have female in the force when I'm in it,' he told me, though I was all too aware of that, 'let alowun promote one. No man take order from a woman.'

'My men do,' I assured him, and he sniffed loudly.

'Can't be real men then,' he commented.

'They are, and I am proud of them,' I replied with more feeling than truth, and the ex-sergeant snorted.

'So why do you come?' he asked, sinking back into the hollow of his pillow.

His hair was sparse, greasy and uncombed, and his striped pyjama top looked like it would benefit from laundering, but Mrs Fynn was frail and probably struggled to look after him at all.

'Do you remember Etterly Utter?' I asked.

Had he flinched at my question or in pain? It was impossible to tell.

'Utterly Etter?' he mis-repeated as stupidly as he had the day he came to Felicity House. 'Girl in the Ghost Tree?'

I really couldn't be bothered correcting him on either of those names.

'That's the one,' I agreed. 'You interviewed me at home.'

Fynn wiped his mouth with the back of his hand.

'What was your name?'

'The same as it was a moment ago,' I told him, and he patted the bed like he was inviting me to sit on it. If so, I had no intention of accepting the invitation. I put my helmet and gas mask on a pine chest of drawers and leaned against it.

'Your father was the dentist,' he remembered.

'Still is,' I said, and glanced outside.

A scrawny tabby limped across the back yard.

'You were a sturdy girl then,' he recollected.

I recoiled and was about to respond when I realised this was not a comment on the way I was constructed, but in our part of Suffolk *sturdy* meant *awkward*. My memory was stirred when he said it, though.

'We'll come back to Etterly in a minute,' I promised. 'But shortly after she went missing, a boy died.' Before I had even mentioned the name, I saw the middle finger of Fynn's left hand twitch like he was playing a double bass. 'His name was Godfrey Skillern.'

There went the finger again.

'What abou' him?'

No *The boy in The Soundings?* or anything like that.

'Do you remember him?'

'S'pose.' The finger dug into his grey top blanket.

'I saw Douglas Carpenter the other day,' I continued chattily, and the blanket bunched up.

'Who?' He rasped his heavily stubbled chin with the knuckles of his right hand.

'I'm surprised you've forgotten him,' I said. 'You made him swallow a microphone.'

His feet shifted under the bedding.

'A micro—' he began in mock puzzlement.

'Phone,' I confirmed.

'What the hell you goo on 'bout, girl?'

'Inspector Church,' I corrected him, '*Sergeant* Fynn,' I added, just to rub it in. 'He bumped into you the night before Godfrey died.'

The knees bent up, dragging his feet with them.

'Dint know when tha' is,' Fynn rasped.

'I find your defensive attitude interesting,' I remarked.

The feet slid back down, one at a time.

'And I do find you question me in my own bedroom a bloody nerve,' he responded hoarsely.

'Would you rather I took you to the station?' I suggested.

Fynn's laugh turned into a coughing fit and he had to raise himself on one elbow and turn away from me to clear his chest.

'Good luck with tha',' he told me convulsively.

'You think I haven't got the authority?' I challenged.

'I think you int go' the medical skill.' Fynn flopped back onto his pillow. 'Last time I try ge' downstair I cough up so much blood I near die. Take two men ge' me back up here.'

Fynn held out his right hand and I saw it shimmering wet with dark red.

'What's wrong with you?' I asked, but his eyes drifted away. 'Cancer?' I persisted, and Fynn winced.

'Tha's the size of it,' he agreed, and I was discomforted to find that I couldn't bring myself to say I was sorry.

'How long have you got?' I asked, shocked at my own callousness. This was a fellow human being after all but, if I was right, he had hardly behaved like one.

Fynn pulled a bloodied cloth out from under his sheets and coughed into it.

'Shouldn't be here now,' he told me dully.

'Then you have nothing to lose by telling me the truth,' I pointed out while he examined the glutinous matter he had just brought up. 'Let me start you off,' I suggested. 'You were on your way up to Filcher's Mound.'

'Was I?' Fynn challenged, and then I knew I was right. No innocent man would have responded like that. He would have flatly denied it or demanded to know what this was all about.

'To meet Morphus Harrison,' I continued.

'Who?'

'Oh, come on,' I objected. 'You can do better than that. You cautioned him earlier that evening for a breach of the peace.'

Fynn swallowed noisily.

'Think I remember tha' from near thirty year on?'

'It was unusual in two ways,' I said. 'First, a caution wouldn't normally be entered in the charge book. In fact, I looked through that year and couldn't find another example.'

'You sayin' we dint keep a record of cautions?' Fynn wheezed.

'Oh, you kept records,' I agreed. 'The old filing cabinets are full of them, but they didn't go in the charge book. That, not surprisingly, was reserved for charges.' I didn't bother giving him time to think of a lie about that. 'Secondly, Morphus is a gypsy and since when have they been let off for something like that with a warning? Two weeks before that you personally arrested a gypsy woman who was selling pegs for swearing at a housewife who sent her away.'

'Wha' then?' Fynn wriggled a few inches up his pillow.

'Morphus had at least one previous conviction,' I said. 'He did six weeks for threatening behaviour at the beginning of the year. Think a magistrate would have been sympathetic the second time around? Six months at least, I would say, and how gently do you imagine gypsies were treated in prison?'

'Mayhap tha's why I let him off,' Fynn suggested, eyes narrowing.

'Sergeant *Big-hearted* Fynn?' I mocked. 'I remember you when I was a child. You were Hitler before we'd even heard of the man. You took Morphus in, intending to arrest him. You wrote as much in the book, but then you let him go. At first I wondered if he had bribed you, but that wouldn't explain why you just happened to be heading up towards Big Hill as Douglas Carpenter was running terrified away from it.'

'It was on my beat,' Fynn muttered.

'Did sergeants have a beat in those days?' I wondered. 'They don't now.'

'Wha' then?'

'I felt uncomfortable when you came to my parents' house,' I told him, and he shifted uneasily but didn't ask why, so I answered his unspoken question myself. 'It wasn't because you were a policeman or because of my friend—'

'Utterly Etter,' he contributed helpfully.

'But because of the way you eyed me up and down. That wasn't a look I got used to until I was a few years older.'

'You imagine it,' he told me wearily.

'You liked young girls,' I said. He opened his mouth to respond but had to struggle to suppress a cough instead. 'And Morphus Harrison had one, a real beauty of a daughter called Darklis.'

Fynn went into a fit of coughing.

'I int well enough for this,' he managed.

You never will be, I thought. Normally I would never have dreamed of harassing a dying man, but since he was almost certainly one of two people who knew the whole truth and this could well be my last chance, I hardened my heart.

'Do you want to spend your last days in a cell awaiting trial?' I threatened, but Fynn curled his lip again.

'You never get a warrant with me in this way,' he sneered, ''specially an old copper.'

This was almost certainly true, and I was not that cruel anyway, but I was interested to note he didn't claim that I had nothing to hold him on.

'Does your wife know what you have done?'

Fynn shifted, whether in physical or mental discomfort I couldn't judge.

'Dint you bring her into it.'

'Or your daughter?' I asked, and Fynn tried to sit, arm swinging weakly in my direction.

'You leave my Annie out of it,' he raged before flopping back, exhausted.

'I will make you a deal,' I said. 'I will keep quiet if you tell me the truth.'

'I int sayin' nothin'.'

'Very well,' I picked up my gas mask.

'Wait.' Fynn wheezed, and seeing the man lying there

suffering I couldn't help feeling sorry for him, but I was even more sorry about the harm he had done. 'I can't—' He stopped and I knew it was expecting too much of him to put his guilt into words.

'All right,' I compromised. 'I will tell you what I know and you will tell me if I'm wrong.' Fynn's head dipped an inch towards his spasming chest, which I took as consent. I put my mask down again. 'Morphus Harrison got into a fight. His lip was split. I don't know what the argument was about or who was in the wrong and, in all probability, you didn't either, but he was a gypsy and so you arrested him and took him to the station. He had been in trouble with the law before and knew that he would get a longer stretch this time. He was lucky to have kept his job and home after the first time, but a good blacksmith who can also work as a farrier can be hard to replace, plus he had three strapping sons. A second conviction would only confirm what everyone was probably telling Squire Folger already – that you can't trust these people – they are all thieves, liars and drunks.'

'They are too,' Fynn agreed.

'Morphus was desperate to make a deal. I expect he offered you money, but he didn't have enough for you to go through the bother of explaining his release.'

'Ten shillin',' Fynn confirmed contemptuously.

'He must have noticed the way you looked at his daughter, Darklis. I certainly noticed the way you looked at me.'

'She was shinier,' Fynn told me meanly. Did he seriously think I would be wounded?

'And so he offered to let you have some time with her. I don't suppose you were allowed to...' I paused to think of a way to phrase it, but I needn't have bothered.

'Didn't want to take her,' Fynn told me. 'I just liked them to—'

'I don't need the details,' I told him in disgust. I had had enough of those from Etterly. 'For some reason, you waited three weeks.'

'I'm sent to help out at Angleford,' he confirmed.

'Then Morphus took Darklis up Big Hill. They were probably heading for the Warrener's Cottage by Filcher's Mound, where you were to meet them. You wouldn't be disturbed there and if there were any poachers about, they would soon scarper at the sight of a uniform. What nobody anticipated was that Godfrey Skillern would turn up. He was in love with Darklis and had sneaked out to see her. He must have seen Morphus take her off the estate and followed. Darklis might have had no idea what was expected of her, but she would have known something was wrong and she struggled. Maybe her father slapped her. Whatever happened, Godfrey intervened. He was a strong, athletic boy but he was no match for a blacksmith used to fighting real men and carrying one of his hammers.'

'Why?' Fynn whispered, choking into that bloodied rag again.

'Perhaps he was going to threaten you if you tried to go too far,' I speculated. 'Or he might have intended to lure you there with his daughter and finish you off so you couldn't revive the charges later. He could have told Darklis he was protecting her and she would have kept quiet rather than let him hang. Douglas put up more of a fight than you'd expect – I believe he boxed at school – but he was no match for her father. Beneath his amiable surface, Morphus was a hot-blooded and cruel man. Enraged by Godfrey's attempt to interfere, he struck him with the hammer. Darklis tried to intervene but he had gone too far to be stopped now. He might have meant to quieten his daughter down or he may have decided on the spur of the moment to silence her permanently. Either way, he killed them both.'

Fynn's chest rattled. 'How can you know that?'

'Godfrey, the follower, had a follower of his own,' I replied.

'The boy you caught running away and terrified into keeping quiet – Douglas—'

'Carpenter,' Fynn interrupted, and closed his eyes.

'He saw it all.'

'I dint have nothin' to do with their deaths,' the old man told me, his legs twisting up again.

'Yes, you did,' I insisted angrily. 'You blackmailed Morphus Harrison into taking his daughter there.'

'He dint take much persuadin'.'

'And then you silenced a witness. You let the murderer of two young people go free.'

'He dint mean to kill them,' Fynn protested weakly.

'And you believe that?' I scoffed. 'Godfrey must have managed to get away. Maybe he lost his attacker in the woods. Morphus probably expected to find his body in the morning. Meanwhile, he got a spade – the cottage was used as a tool store – and buried his daughter in a ditch. If Godfrey hadn't lived long enough to stagger into town, Morphus would have buried him too and said they eloped together. The three sons went looking for Godfrey, believing he had had an accident.'

'Is tha' it?' Fynn sighed.

'Far from it,' I assured him. 'We have hardly begun on Etterly Utter yet.'

Fynn exhaled so long and loudly that I thought it might be his death rattle, but his eyes were still open and alert.

'You betrayed the trust she put in your uniform,' I accused him. 'You made her... *service* you. You sold her to a brothel, you stinking—' I almost gagged on a torrent of invective, but none of it could match the obscenity that lay before me.

'All speculation,' Fynn said, and closed his eyes.

'I have spoken to Etterly,' I told him, and the lids sprang open. 'She has told me everything.'

Fynn chewed his lips between his gums.

'Still gooin'?' he said, with as much interest as if we were discussing a stray cat. 'Thought she be weer out 'fore now.'

'Or murdered,' I added, and he didn't bother denying it.

'You can't prove any of tha',' Fynn wheezed. 'Ge' her in the box,' he challenged. 'And see who the jury believe – a police sergeant who retire after forty year unblemished service or a raddled old whore from the streets of London.'

'We both know you won't face a trial,' I said wearily, and suddenly I couldn't bear to be in that room with that man a minute longer. 'You were a copper, God damn you,' I spat. 'You were supposed to be the man Etterly could turn to and trust. You were supposed to protect her. How many other girls...'

What was the point? I snatched up my things and charged out onto the corridor. Another moment and I might have throttled the life out of him, but nothing I could do would match the death that lay in store for Sergeant Fynn. Was this God's judgement?

Where were you, I prayed, *when all this was going on?*

But if anybody answered, I couldn't have been listening.

'Just in time for tea,' Mrs Fynn told me cheerily as I rushed down the stairs, stumbling in my hurry and grabbing the banister, remembering just in time that it was rickety.

That would have suited you just perfectly, I thought bitterly, *if I had come a cropper.*

'I have to go,' I told Mrs Fynn, and her face fell tragically. I was probably the only company she had had for months. Who else would visit her vile husband? Tears sprang up in her eyes. 'I'm so sorry,' I said, and meant it – for her, for Darklis and for Godfrey, but Sergeant Fynn, I told myself, could rot in the hell he had created for them and Douglas Carpenter. He may be suffering now but that was nothing compared to the nightmare worlds he had plunged Etterly and her parents into for over a quarter of a century.

78

RATIONS AND THE TRICK

Jimmy looked very smart when he turned up in his uniform at Sackwater Central Police Station.

'Special delivery,' he said. 'Can't stop. Just wanted to thank you and Captain for making me go to see Badger's mater.'

We hadn't exactly forced him, but I appreciated the sentiment.

'How did it go?' I asked.

'Much better than I expected,' he said. 'Four of us went in the end. They had an impromptu memorial in the local church. She's a remarkable old girl – ended up with *her* consoling *us*.'

'Did you mention about the possibility of her coming to Sackwater when she feels up to it?'

'Arriving on Thursday,' he told me.

'Really?' I said. 'So soon? That's very brave of her.'

'She wants to help,' Jimmy said.

'I just hope they'll agree to see her,' I worried.

'If they won't listen to her, they won't listen to anyone,' he assured me.

'That,' I said, 'is exactly what I'm worried about.'

Box was just emerging from the back with a steaming mug.

'Can I get you a tea, sir?'

'Thanks, but I can't stop,' Jimmy said.

At least you haven't done your flying gag, I thought gratefully.

'Must fly,' Jimmy said, and I cancelled my gratitude. 'Literally,' he added, and they roared with laughter.

I expect it worked better on people who hadn't heard it a hundred times before.

Jimmy bustled out.

'He say he—' Box began, but I really couldn't bear to have Jimmy's little joke explained to me.

'Have you been to the farm?' I butted in, and Box huffed indignantly.

They would discuss it later, I knew, how women, especially me, lacked a sense of humour.

'Folger's Estate Farm?' he asked, because I had definitely asked him to visit one in the Outer Hebrides.

'Yes,' I replied.

'Today, ma'am?' he clarified, for I was sure to be interested in a trip he had taken there five years ago.

'Yes,' I replied again.

'Yes,' he told me, and before I got out my penknife, the one with a special attachment for removing information from constables' mouths, he continued, 'They dint look pleased to see me.'

'I did warn you they wouldn't be,' I reminded him.

'And Mr Harrison dint take kindly when I tell him if he cheek you again I would match the dent on the back of his head with one at the front,' Box assured me with some satisfaction.

That was commendably loyal of my constable, but I hadn't sent him there to avenge a slight on my dignity.

'And did you deliver the message?' I asked.

'In private and in person,' Box assured him.

'Well done,' I said. 'Is that my tea?'

'Is now,' he told me.

'You haven't been drinking from it?' I asked warily as I took the mug.

'Not today,' he assured me.

'Thank you, I needed that,' I said, drinking gratefully.

'Mind you, I dint recall when I last washed it,' he said.

'Very funny.' I smiled, just to prove that, even though it wasn't, I did have a sense of humour.

I dumped my parcel on the desk, much to Brigsy's barely suppressed indignation. This was his territory and he guarded it jealously.

'I want you to make a phone call,' I told him, and my sergeant perked up.

'To Miss Middleton?' he asked hopefully, though I had never asked him to ring her yet.

'To Great Yarmouth Police Station,' I told him, and – if it is possible to do such a thing – Brigsy perked down. 'And another one,' I continued, but he was not going to have his hopes raised again, 'to the Ministry of Food.'

'For extra rations?' He raised his hopes after all.

'No,' I said, and he lowered them. 'I want you to check on the whereabouts of these people.' I passed my sergeant a slip of paper. 'And I shall see you tomorrow.'

'Probably,' Brigsy agreed gloomily.

'Oh,' I remembered, 'and that's for you.' I tapped the box.

'What is it?' he asked suspiciously, because I was always having live hand grenades brought into the lobby for him to defuse.

'Two rabbits and half a dozen eggs,' I replied, 'as a thank you to you and your wife for my bacon sandwich.'

Brigsy clasped his hands like a love-struck girl.

'A present,' he gushed. 'From Captain Carmiallello.'

Close enough, I thought.

'And me,' I added.

After all, I helped feed and house those animals and had sat up half the night when we had a fox prowling the opposite bank.

'Well, I do thank you very much,' Brigsy said, 'Captain Carmiallello.'

'And me,' I tried again, to blank looks.

'Dint know why she think it funny I int washed my mug,' I heard Box saying as I exited the building.

79

THE RADIOGRAM MURDERS AND WHODIDIT

I had thought about taking Bantony with me, but letting him loose in a brothel would have been like asking a child to look after the stock in Sammy's Sweet Shop, before Mr and Mrs Sterne had been interned as enemy aliens. Box was too obviously a policeman. Even in civvies he walked and talked so much like a copper, he might as well have had *Constable* tattooed on his forehead. I couldn't order Dodo to accompany me, but then I didn't have to.

'What about the dress I wore on my first day here, Boss?' she suggested. It was a summer frock, red paisley with blue trim on the collar and short sleeves – the neckline too low and the hemline much too high. A few people had mistaken her for a prostitute that morning.

'That would be perfect,' I said, but I did wonder, when I collected Dodo from Felicity House, whether she had grown a bit since she came to Sackwater. The dress looked closer-fitting than I remembered and from the looks she got, from barely disguised lust to undisguised disgust, it had not lost its powers over men.

'You only goo 'titled to free travel in uniform,' Mr Tape told me, and he may well have been right.

I was in the dress I had worn the last time – though I was still hoping it wasn't going to be the very last time – I had been for a drink with Toby.

'We are on official business,' Dodo told him, and he looked

at her dubiously at first, but then in a way Mrs Tape might well have had something to say about.

'The concession' – that was probably the biggest word Mr Tape knew and could pronounce – 'is for officers in uniform,' he insisted.

'Chapter nine, section four, paragraph three of the Emergency Powers Act defines a uniformed officer as one who is in or is normally attired in uniform but is wearing other clothes in pursuance of his or her duty,' I bluffed, and the next thing he was pushing two little cardboard tickets into his stamping machine before I had a chance to invent a penalty for impeding us.

'Remember the first time we came here, Boss?' Dodo chatted as we queued at the ticket barrier.

'I'm hardly likely to forget.'

A man had bled to death before our eyes on the platform, the first person to be dubbed a victim of the Suffolk Vampire by the local and national press.

'Let us hope that does not happen today.' Dodo crossed her fingers.

'Not very likely,' I reassured her, and we were just on time to climb aboard the train and claim the last two seats in our compartment, me by the window next to a silver-haired old lady who was either in a deep sleep or dead, but I was not going to check her pulse.

I had finished the excellent Raymond Chandler and was quite enjoying *The Radiogram Murders*, a recent whodunnit by Lady Olga Slayer.

'Oh, I have read that,' Dodo declared, catching sight of the title.

'Don't spoil the ending,' I warned as we pulled out of the station.

'Of course I won't, Boss,' Dodo assured me merrily, bringing out her needles and wool. 'You'll never guess she did it.'

Seeing as the story was set in a monastery, with the gardener's daughter being the only female, this was something of a giveaway. I dropped the book in my handbag and caught up on my sleep instead, and I was happily sharing a cigarette by a campfire with Gary Cooper when we pulled into Liverpool Street Station.

'Were you dreaming about chickens, Boss?' Dodo asked over a considerably grown length of knitting.

'Why?' I wondered.

'It is just that you kept saying coop,' she told me. 'But I don't understand why you told it to kiss you.'

'I was talking about kismet,' I assured her, 'the fate that awaits all hens.'

'And men,' a stuffy-looking lady in the corner said, reaching for her carpet bag on the luggage rack.

I shifted my false arm uncomfortably.

'And women,' Dodo chipped in.

'I said men to include women,' the lady told her.

'They rarely do,' I observed, to blank looks all round.

'It is probably a joke,' Dodo whispered. 'The men at work are trying to teach her how to make them.'

Who? I wondered indignantly. *Brigsy with his rapier wit? Box with his lightning repartee?*

'And what work do you do?' asked a middle-aged woman.

Funny how we could all strike up a conversation when we were about to say goodbye.

'Oh, I am a prostitute,' Dodo assured her, getting into the role she had to play later.

'I say,' spluttered a stout woman in tweeds. 'I always wanted to be one of those.'

'That's disgusting,' the possible vicar's wife protested. 'If you wanted to be one, you should have just gone ahead and done it.'

'Must be super fun,' giggled a flapper who was at least ten years too late and twenty too old to be a flapper.

'Well, really,' the silver-haired lady protested. 'I have never heard anything like it. I'm a prostitute and, let me tell you, it's jolly hard work.'

I'm? What, still?

'And what do you do?' the tweed lady asked me, lowering the window by its leather strap.

'She is a police inspector,' Dodo said gaily.

'Has she arrested you?' the aging flapper flapped anxiously.

'Oh no,' Dodo laughed, 'she is taking me to a brothel.'

'Jolly good.' The silver-haired lady patted me on my scaffolding. 'About time we got some protection.'

'Just don't ply your trade on the Underground,' I warned Dodo.

'Of course I will not, Boss,' Dodo told me, fluttering her eyelashes at a middle-aged porter standing by with his trolley.

We went straight to Huntley Street.

'Are you sure you want to do this?' I enquired anxiously.

'Just try to stop me,' Dodo replied. 'But do not try really because you would probably succeed, being more sturdily built than me and superior in rank and intelligence.'

'Very well,' I said. 'Good luck.'

I waited several houses back and watched her knock busily at the door.

'Oh, you poor man,' I heard her say. 'What on earth happened to your lip?'

A coal lorry crawled by, blocking my view and deadening Dodo's voice, and by the time it had gone, so had she.

I stood at the bus stop and tried to look like I was waiting for a bus, succeeding all too well, it appeared, because a double-decker pulled up in under a minute.

'Well 'op on, darlin',' the conductor called out to me.

'Thank you,' I told him, 'but I'm waiting for a ninety-seven.'

'Aint no such bus,' he told me.

'Look like I'll have a long wait then,' I remarked, and ignored his comment about my resemblance to an unintelligent domesticated bovine.

I lit a cigarette and paced up and down, but I was hardly a quarter way through it when Dodo came out and across the road to me. She did not look at all happy.

'Are you all right?' I worried.

'Obviously not,' she fumed. 'Apparently I am too old. Too *old*?' she raged. 'I told them about the white-haired woman on the train and they just sniggered and said I should go and work with her. I was so cross that I whipped out my warrant card to arrest them all on the spot.'

'You didn't?' I gasped. How on earth had she escaped alive?

'Only it turned out to be my ration card and before I could say the words, the man with the sore lip chortled and told me there was a butcher's shop on Goodge Street because I needed a bit more rump. I told him I preferred lamb but he only laughed even more, so I told him he was halfway to being a halfwit – that was rather quick of me, I think – and he stopped laughing and showed me the door.'

'Oh, for goodness' sake,' I groaned.

'That is exactly what I said,' Dodo assured me.

'Did you even get a glimpse of Etterly?' I sighed.

'Oh, I got more than a glimpse,' Dodo assured me. 'She is very pretty and elegant, is she not, Boss?'

'Did you get to speak to her?'

'No, of course not,' Dodo said crossly. 'That stupid man was there all the time.'

'Right,' I huffed.

'But I did manage to pass her the note,' Dodo continued.

'Did anybody see you?' I asked.

'Well, Etterly did, of course,' Dodo replied as another bus went by.

'Time for a quickie?' a corporal, hanging onto the pole, yelled out.

'Oh, what a shame,' Dodo moaned, 'he has gone before I could think of a retort.'

'*No* would have sufficed,' I told her. 'Did anybody else see you?'

'On the bus?' she wondered, then realised, 'Oh, you mean in the Pink Palace, as Mr H likes to call it. Well, the man with the lip did, and another rather menacing-looking fellow who came in near the end. Etterly called him Mr H.'

'They all saw you pass the note?' I asked in horror.

'No, Boss,' Dodo explained patiently. 'They all saw me, of course, but only Etterly noticed the note and she slipped it into her décolletage without even a glance.'

'I think you've earned a drink, Constable Chivers,' I said, wondering if the café on Capper Street would still be open. 'My treat.'

'Thank you very much, Boss,' Dodo set off down the street. 'They do a good pint of bitter at the Rising Sun.'

80

STONE STEPS AND THE LAST DROP

Etterly was already there when we arrived at Cartwright Gardens, but as we approached she started walking.

'I am surprised that she did not observe us,' Dodo remarked.

'Oh, she saw us all right,' I assured her as we followed about ten yards behind, along the straight line of the crescent, down Mabledon Place and left down Flaxman Terrace, a long street made to feel even narrower than it was by five-storey terraces to either side until they gave way to lower, older buildings, the brickwork blackened by the best part of a century of soot from the countless chimneys of our capital city.

Etterly walked steadily on, never glancing back or pausing until she turned abruptly through a gate on her right. We quickened our pace.

'Do you think we have been followed?' Dodo whispered – quietly for a change.

'I hope so,' I murmured, and peered back up the way we had come.

Once through the gate we found ourselves going into the back yard of the Queen's Head, a three-storey pub, which appeared to be closed for the afternoon. We were just time to see Etterly disappear and we followed her down a flight of stone steps into a low-ceilinged cellar.

There was a billiards table down there and Etterly stood behind it, cue in one hand like she was preparing to play, but more, I suspected, as a potential weapon.

'Who's your crackpot friend?' she asked.

'This is Constable Chivers,' I said, and Etterly flipped the cue to hold it thick end up, like a club.

'If this is a trap—'

'It isn't,' I assured her. 'I didn't want to endanger you by approaching you in the street and I couldn't think of any other way to get a note to you. I assume they would open your post.'

Etterly lowered the cue, but only a fraction.

'So what do you want?'

'You to come home,' I said simply.

Etterly stared.

'Don't you think I've dreamed night and day of leaving here?' She raised her face as if she was interested in the ceiling. 'But it isn't that simple.'

'They think you come from Somerset,' I reminded her. 'So they would never look for you in Suffolk.'

'Think it's easy to disappear?'

'Yes,' I said. 'The local press won't give you away.'

'People talk.'

'You have a cousin a year older than you who went to live in Cornwall when she was four.'

'Effie,' she agreed. 'What of it?'

'You've changed enough over the years for people to believe she's come back.'

Etterly looked me in the eye.

'And there's the small matter—'

'Of Morphus Harrison?' I butted in, and Etterly screwed up her face just like she used to when her father scolded her.

'I thought you would find out about that.'

'I found out much more than that,' I told her. 'First, Morphus isn't dead.'

'He looked pretty dead to me,' she scoffed.

'He was concussed,' I said, 'but he came round. Bosko was trying to calm you down that night.'

'Shit,' Etterly breathed. 'It was just how he grabbed me when I was in a panic,' she explained. 'I always had a soft spot for Bosko. Wish I'd told him when I had the chance.'

She pulled a rueful face.

'Bosko asked Shadrach to go and explain the next morning, so his brother waited when he came across us playing rounders in The Soundings to reassure you that he had seen what happened and his father was sore and enraged but alive.'

'Shit,' Etterly said. 'So all that – all this shit – everything – was for nothing.'

'There's still time to put some things right,' I said, 'and you can start by coming back to Sackwater.'

'Think my parents would have a whore under their roof?' Etterly objected. 'For shit's sake, Betsy. They nearly threw me out when I said *bloody* once.'

'We goo learn better since then,' a man's voice said, and I turned to see Mr Utter coming down the stairs.

'Dad?' Etterly gasped so softly that even I, who was nearest, hardly heard her.

'Judge not lest ye be judged,' he quoted as he reached the bottom step. 'Betsy try to tell us tha' but we dint listen. A young airman called Jimmy,' he continued, 'bring a mother what lose her son. Mrs Badgero, call her *Daphne*, she say. *I would take my Bobby back no matter what he do*, she tell us. *Just to be able to hug him once again. Dint goo lose your child while she have breath in her body*, she tell us.'

Transcribed into Suffolk, I thought.

Etterly shivered.

'I do come to ask you three things, Etterly. Forgive us for not finding you.' Mr Utter stood beside me now, tiny and old and trembling.

'How could you?' Etterly asked quietly. 'I live in another world.'

She placed the cue, shakily, on the table.

'To forgive us for our hearts were hard with wha' we thought was goodness,' Mr Utter continued, walking around the table towards his daughter.

'What the—?' Etterly looked up sharply at the sound of more footsteps on the stairs.

'Hello, Etterly,' Bosko said shyly.

'Bosky.' She took a step towards him.

'I coom to help if there goo be trouble,' he said. 'And your dad int been to London 'fore now.'

'But why...' Etterly touched her face.

'Your mother collapse when she hear you do live,' Mr Utter said. 'She never doubt it but she never believe it neither. She's well 'nough now but I dint think her up to it if you say *no*.'

'Say no to what?' Etterly asked.

'Come home, darlin',' Mr Utter said.

'I...' Etterly hesitated to explain. 'I have a disease.'

'Let us look after you,' Mr Utter said.

'You aren't young any more,' Etterly said tactfully.

'I can help,' Bosko assured her. 'Harkles has been called up and I try to join but I'm unfit with my blind eye.'

'There are men who might come for me and you could get hurt.'

'Think I'm 'fraid of a city boy?' Bosko scoffed.

'And I will gladly give my last drop to protect you,' Mr Utter said, and he didn't seem quite so small now. 'So will your mother, if needs be. Come home, darlin'.'

'I'll only bring you trouble,' Etterly warned shakily.

'And we only give you love,' Mr Utter vowed. 'You do be in hell, Etterly, but trust me and I will lead you out of it here and now.'

He held out his hand, beseechingly, but Etterly didn't take it. She stepped forwards and wrapped her arms around him.

'Oh, my darling Daddy,' she sobbed, and he tried to reply but his words were too broken.

I swallowed.

'We will be outside,' I said, almost dragging a spellbound Dodo back up the stairs.

81

RULES, FOOLS AND DOUGLAS BADER

We all took the train back but had to take seats in three different carriages, with me in a non-smoker – no fug, but no cigarette for me either.

Jimmy stood on the platform, waiting.

'How did it go?'

'Even better than I hoped,' I told him. 'Thank you, Jimmy.'

I kissed his cheek.

'No, thank *you*, Aunty,' Jimmy said. 'You brought light into Badger's mother's despair. I wish you could have seen her when I took her to meet the Utters. She was marvellous.'

Jimmy ran his eyes up and down Dodo in her little dress. 'What time do you get off duty?' he asked, and she looked up at me.

'This very minute,' I said.

'Fancy a drink?' Jimmy asked. 'They do a good pint at the Unicorn.'

'Really?' Dodo asked with calculated innocence. 'I am not sure if I like beer.'

'Well, now's your chance to find out.'

'Care to join us?' Jimmy asked me, with a little shake of his head.

'Another day,' I replied.

'Looks like it's just you and me then,' he told Dodo.

'Do you think I ought to change first, Boss?' she asked me, and I was about to reply that I most certainly did when Jimmy assured her hastily, 'You look fine as you are.'

'I'll see you tomorrow,' I said.

Etterly appeared, arm in arm with her father.

'Liver and bacon tonight,' he was telling her.

'My favourite,' she laughed.

'You coom for supper?' Mr Utter invited me.

'Yes, do,' Etterly urged.

'Thank you,' I said, 'I would love to, another day, but I have to be back on duty.'

In truth, I thought it best to give the Utters time with each other.

Bosko was standing back awkwardly when Mr Utter held out his hand.

'I say bad things 'bout you and your kind,' Etterly's father said, 'and 'specially when you court my girl.'

'That was Harkles, Dad.' Etterly nudged him with the same embarrassment he might have caused her twenty-six years ago.

'Do it?' Mr Utter exclaimed. 'They all look the same to me.'

'Bosko is better looking,' Etterly told her father, and Bosko rubbed the back of his neck bashfully.

'Int pretty like Harkles,' he protested.

'The world is full of pretty men,' she told him. 'But a good man is hard to find.'

'You goo lose your accent,' Mr Utter said, like he had only just noticed.

'I soon goo ge' it back,' she assured him.

'I must be going,' I told them all.

Alone, I thought, and wondered if it really had to stay that way.

The station was deserted when I went back to change – nobody to greet me with a welcoming mug of tea, but also no one to annoy me. There was such a pile of letters on my desk you might have thought I had been away all week. I pushed them to one side and smoked a cigarette to steady my nerve, but it didn't help. It was now or never, I decided. I checked myself in my compact mirror and set off down the road.

The sign on the door said *Sackwater and District Gazette* and the little one below it still said *Open*.

'Won't be a moment,' Carol said, without looking up.

She was concentrating on typing a letter, having recently graduated to using three fingers, with mixed results.

'It's all right,' I said, 'I know the way.'

'You can't—'

'Oh, Miss Danbury,' I said, 'you have a great deal to learn about what I can and cannot do. The former list is ever increasing while the latter dwindles by the minute.'

That was actually a modified quote from Sidney Grice, but as far as Carol – mouth agape to say nothing – was concerned, it was one of my very own.

The door was open as I got to it and Toby was seated, working behind his desk.

'You can't—' he began.

'Oh, Mr Gregson,' I said, 'you have a great deal to learn about—'

'Never mind that sub-Gricean claptrap,' Toby said coolly. 'Come in and shut the door.'

I don't take kindly to being bossed about as a rule, but today I never-minded the sub-Gricean claptrap and did as I was told.

'I shouldn't have—' I began again.

'No, you shouldn't,' Toby agreed, putting down his pen.

'I'm—'

He stood up.

'I'm sure you are.' Toby strode around his desk, eyes glittering. 'And so am I. It's a pity you have that rule.'

'Which one?' I asked as he drew near.

'The one about not kissing when you're in uniform.'

'March Middleton—'

'An admirable lady, but why are you bringing her into this?'

'She told me Douglas Bader—'

'A man of great courage and determination, but why are you bringing him into this?'

'He has a mantra—'

'As well as two tin legs?'

'Rules,' I quoted, 'are for the obedience of fools and the guidance of wise men… and women.'

'I bet he never said that last bit.'

'Just shut up,' I said, 'and kiss me.'

'Did he say that too?'

I started to laugh, but Toby put a stop to that by doing just as I had instructed.

82

BONE, BLOOD AND VAPORISATION

The station was still empty when I returned. I put the kettle on. Sifting through the pile of letters on my desk – mostly of little interest – one in particular caught my eye. The address was written in Superintendent Vesty's hand. I knew it from his old memos. He had sent me a personal note, thanking me for visiting him and hoping I had enjoyed the rhubarb.

My superior had been notified of Sharkey's attempt to have me posted elsewhere.

'Please inform your colleague that if he is genuinely concerned that there is a dearth of Constables and a superabundance of Inspectors at Sackwater Central Police Station, he is at liberty to request demotion to redress the balance,' I read.

Sergeant Sharkey had a delicious ring to it, I decided, and *Constable* sounded even better, but I knew all too well that it would only induce him to withdraw his suggestion. It seemed that Old Scrapie and I were destined to work together for a long while yet.

I rang March Middleton. She always took a keen interest in my cases and, apart from giving me advice when Humphrey Smith brought the jawbone into the station, it was my godmother who had brought Sidney Grice to Sackwater all those years ago.

'It is a pity that we could not devote more time to tracing Etterly,' she told me, 'but at least Mr G was correct about that poor Godfrey Skillern being killed, probably by a blacksmith.'

Was I mishearing things? Had I misunderstood at the time?

'I'm sorry?' I queried. 'Did he tell me that?'

'No, darling,' Aunty M said, 'but I wrote to you about it – four letters, as I recall – a hasty one just before we boarded the ferry to Palma and three more over the next few months. I cannot remember the exact details, but Mr G had the metal fragments he found near that oak tree analysed and calculated that they came from a blacksmith's hammer – something to do with the way the steel is heated and repeatedly annealed in use. From the way they were intermingled with bone fragments and blood clots, he thought they must have been washed out of the head wound as Godfrey lay dying.'

'Oh,' I said. 'I never received any letters about it.'

'I did wonder why you hadn't replied,' she told me, 'so I sent the last one by special messenger and your mother signed for it.'

'Really?'

'Then I received a letter from your father asking me to desist from that line of correspondence as it was distressing you,' she continued. 'I felt I had no option other than to comply with his wishes.'

'Oh,' I said again.

'I also sent a report to Sackwater Central Police Station and got a very polite reply from a Sergeant—'

'Fynn,' I broke in.

'The very man,' she agreed. 'I assume you know him.'

'All too well,' I agreed. 'I'll tell you about him in a minute.'

'When I saw no reports of an arrest being made,' Aunty M continued, 'I think I assumed that the local police could not gather enough evidence to convict anybody, but I was very ill around that time and on the trail of the Devil Dog of Dartmouth… Are you quite well, dear?'

'Yes, thank you, Aunty,' I lied.

'I only ask because your speech is a little fuzzy.'

'It's probably a poor line.'

'Are you still suffering from tinnitus?'

'Yes… and headaches,' I admitted.

'And what does Tubby think?' she enquired, but my hesitation was all the answer she needed. 'Consult him,' she told me. 'Today.'

83

THE HOLIDAY AND THE HAUNTING

'I suppose you might as well have them now,' my father said the next morning, grumpily handing over a bundle of letters tied in grubby brown string.

I glanced at the envelopes. There were four of them, all in March Middleton's hand and postmarked in the summer of 1914.

'Why did you not give them to me?' I demanded.

They had all been opened.

'We saw how disturbed you were after she came here with Mr Grice.' My father inclined his head as a sign of respect for the great man. 'And we didn't want to upset you again.'

'I see,' I said, prepared to forgive my parents' stupidity as at least being well intentioned.

'The trouble is,' he continued, 'when you get into these states you go all purple and blotchy and your nose runs. It's really too much to expect your mother to witness.'

'I see,' I said again, with an iciness that would have frozen the River Angle in midsummer.

'I knew you'd understand.' My father reached to pat my shoulder. 'I don't know why your mother has such a poor opinion of you.'

Something made my father pull his hand back. Perhaps it was the unintended snarl that escaped my lips or the glare that would have turned the Angle into steam.

It could have been my anger that brought it on, but I had

never known the lightning to flash so dazzlingly and without any warning and somehow I had ended up sprawled on the floor with my father kneeling at my side.

'Not a simple faint,' he said. 'Your pulse is strong. Follow my finger with your eyes.' For once I obeyed him and he clicked his tongue. 'We need to get you to hospital, darling.'

Darling? He had never called me that before. *Dear God, I must be dying.*

I struggled to get up on my elbows.

'Later,' I said, fighting his attempts to restrain me.

'Now,' he ordered.

'Later,' I insisted. 'There is something I must do first.'

I got shakily onto all threes.

'Oh, for goodness' sake stop acting the goat,' my mother scolded, entering the surgery.

Brigsy was behind the desk, with Box and Bantony propping it up on the other side, supping from big mugs of tea.

'Still one in the pot, madam,' Brigsy told me with a disapproving look. 'Might help with your hangover,' he muttered, and went into the back room.

I let him think that. It was easier than admitting to the men that I needed my head examining.

'How was your holiday?' Bantony asked me.

'Ma'am dint have a holiday,' Box corrected him before I could. 'Only a day trip.'

'A day's work,' I insisted to sceptical glances, 'and it went very well.'

'Did you make those phone calls?' I asked Brigsy when he returned.

'No sign of them with either,' he told me.

'Right then. I have a job for both of you,' I told the two constables, and they tensed up. 'After you've finished your tea.'

Both men relaxed.

'Then you can come with me to Folger's Estate Farm,' I told them. 'I am going to make an arrest.'

I still felt weak and shaky, but I was determined to see this through.

'Who, madam?' Brigsy queried.

'Morphus Harrison,' I replied.

'The gyppo?' he clarified.

'The blacksmith,' I confirmed, and Bantony looked at me quizzically.

'For what, ma'am?'

'For murders,' I replied. 'Godfrey Skillern and Darklis Harrison.'

And probably Morphus's wife, I pondered. As Brigsy had just informed me, the police at Great Yarmouth had no record of her or Darklis and, being a port, they kept strict tags on all residents. Nor did the Ministry of Food, who they would have to have registered with to get a ration card.

'Darklis?' Box checked in surprise.

'That was her bones we found in Packard's Field,' I told him.

'His own daughter,' Bantony mused. 'Let's hope he resists arrest.'

'I think that's a fair assumption,' I assured him.

It was why I wanted them both with me.

'But tha' necklace,' Box remembered. 'You say it belong to Etterly Utter.'

'It was the half she gave to Harkles Harrison,' I explained. 'He was going to break up with Etterly and asked Darklis to return it to her.'

'Etterly Utter,' Bantony mused. 'Oy wonder what happened to her?'

'That,' Brigsy told him, 'is something we may never know, int it, madam?'

'Probably,' I agreed.

I hope so, I thought.

Mr Utter planned to introduce his daughter as Effie, his niece from Cornwall, to the neighbours that very morning, but as far as Sackwater was concerned, her disappearance would remain a mystery and Etterly Utter was the girl condemned to haunt the Ghost Tree for ever more.